A kilt is still a kilt . . . unless it's the legendary wedding kilt. Any man who kidnaps his bride by throwing the tartan over her head will be blessed with a happy marriage—but it will take a dusty attic, a locked door, and a night alone before this couple discovers their happy ending in Christina Dodd's "Under the Kilt."

Every rose has its thorn . . . especially Rose Mackenzie-Craddock. When they were children, the willful girl was the thorn in the earl of Strathyre's side. Now, she is a beautiful woman driving him wild. But even grown-ups can play some interesting games in Stephanie Laurens' "Rose in Bloom."

Tomorrow is another day . . . unless you're Margaret Pennypacker, who must find her brother *tonight* to prevent him from making a disastrous Gretna Green marriage. Instead, she lands in the arms of a handsome, vexing Scotsman determined to teach her one very important lesson in Julia Quinn's "Gretna Greene."

A bride by any other name . . . is still a bride. Or is she? Lachlan Sinclair thinks the woman he's met is perfect. Hasn't Fate itself decreed that she'll save the Sinclair clan? Until there's a wee problem—she's not his bride after all in Karen Ranney's "The Glenlyon Bride."

More Dazzling Romance From

Christina Dodd
MOVE HEAVEN AND EARTH

Stephanie Laurens
TEMPTATION AND SURRENDER

Julia Quinn
WHAT HAPPENS IN LONDON

Karen Ranney
A SCOTSMAN IN LOVE

Christina
DODD

Stephanie
LAURENS

Julia
QUINN

Karen
RANNEY

Scottish Brides

AVON

An Imprint of HarperCollinsPublishers

This is a work of fiction. Names, characters, places, and incidents are products of the author's imagination or are used fictitiously and are not to be construed as real. Any resemblance to actual events, locales, organizations, or persons, living or dead, is entirely coincidental.

AVON BOOKS
An Imprint of HarperCollins*Publishers*
10 East 53rd Street
New York, New York 10022-5299

Under the Kilt copyright © 1999 by Christina Dodd; *Rose in Bloom* copyright © 1999 by Savdek Management Proprietory Ltd; *Gretna Greene* copyright © 1999 by Julie Cotler Pottinger; *The Glenlyon Bride* copyright © 1999 by Karen Ranney

ISBN 978-0-380-80451-1
www.avonromance.com

First Avon Books paperback printing: June 1999

Avon Trademark Reg. U.S. Pat. Off. and in Other Countries,
Marca Registrada, Hecho en U.S.A.
HarperCollins® is a registered trademark of HarperCollins Publishers.

Printed in the U.S.A.

20 19 18 17 16 15 14 13 12

Contents

Christina Dodd
Under the Kilt
1

Stephanie Laurens
Rose in Bloom
67

Julia Quinn
Gretna Greene
169

Karen Ranney
The Glenlyon Bride
261

Scottish Brides

Under the Kilt

Christina Dodd

One

Scotland, 1805

"Andra didn't tell you about the marriage kilt?" Lady Valéry sipped the wickedly strong whiskey and relished the warmth it spread through her aged veins. "My heavens, what did you do to offend? The MacNachtans *always* drag out that marriage kilt to show everyone, whether they wish it or not."

The fire warmed the study, the candles lit the darkened corners, the clock ticked on the mantel, and Hadden sat, long legs stretched out before him, the very portrait of masculine power and grace.

The very image of offended virility.

Lady Valéry hid a grin in her goblet. The boy—he was thirty-one, but she considered him a boy—did not take rejection well.

"Andra MacNachtan is unreasonable." He scowled into his goblet. "A black-headed, noodle-brained woman without a care for anyone but herself."

Lady Valéry waited, but he said nothing more. He only gulped at his whiskey, his fourth since dinner and three more than the usually temperate drinker ever consumed.

3

"Yes. Well." She returned to her scheme. "The marriage kilt is exactly your kind of tradition. There's a ragged old plaid cloth that's reputed to bring good luck to the newly-weds if it's wrapped around their shoulders . . ." She paused artfully for effect. "No, wait, let me think . . . if they kiss the sporran . . . no, perhaps it was something about wifely obedience. If I could remember the tale, I would tell you, and you could copy it into your treatise. But I'm an old lady; my memory's not what it used to be—"

Hadden lifted his bloodshot blue eyes to glare at her.

Perhaps that was laying it on a little too thick. Hastily, she abandoned that tack and, in a brisk, no-nonsense tone, said, "And I was never interested in that old-fashioned balderdash. I remember the 'good old days'—smoking fires, galloping clap, gin slums. No, give me my modern conveniences. You young folks can go poking around and call those days romantic and worthy of note, but I don't."

"It's not just *your* youth I'm recording, Your Grace, much though you would like to believe that."

Surly and sarcastic, she noted, his usual state since his return from Castle MacNachtan almost two months ago.

"It's a whole way of life. Since Culloden, Scotland has changed. The old ways that have existed since William Wallace and Robert the Bruce are disappearing without a trace." He straightened his shoulders, leaned forward intently. "I want to record those fragile fragments of culture before they are gone forever. If I don't record them, no one will."

Lady Valéry watched him with satisfaction. He'd been this emphatic and enthusiastic almost from the first moment he'd arrived at her Scottish estate, a skinny, frightened nine-year-old. He'd taken to the open spaces and gray mists of the Highlands. He'd grown tall and hearty as he roamed the glens and braes, and he'd discovered in the clans and the ancient ways of life a continuity his own existence lacked.

Not that his sister hadn't made a home for him—she had—but nothing could substitute for two parents and a place to call his own.

Lady Valéry had hoped, when she sent him to Castle Mac-Nachtan, he would find his place there.

Instead, he'd come back silent and grumpy, brooding in a manner quite unlike his normal personable self.

Once Lady Valéry had diagnosed the malady that vexed him, she had resolved to set all to rights, and her plan, as always, was working perfectly.

"I understand now. You're tactfully telling me you're not interested in the MacNachtans' wedding kilt because it's not important." She set her goblet down with a thump. "I don't blame you a bit. It is an obscure legend, and rather absurd, and the MacNachtans are a dying clan. That girl, that Andra, is the last of them as far as I know. Yes, you're right." She acted as if he had spoken. "If you don't record *their* history before that clan fades away, it will be of no consequence."

Hadden's drink halted halfway to his mouth, and his fingers tightened on the cut-glass sides of his goblet. "Castle Mac-Nachtan is two hard days of riding from here," he muttered.

"That's true," Lady Valéry acknowledged. It had taken her courier two days to get there, one day to search out Andra's housekeeper and get an answer to her letter, and two days to get back.

"The roads are mud. The crofters are poor, the castle's disintegrating, and it was none too fine a castle to begin with. And Andra MacNachtan is destitute and proud as the devil in spite of it, and so vain of her honored Scottish ancestry that she can't see what's right before her nose."

Lady Valéry smiled at Hadden, knowing she had well and truly set the hook. "So, dear boy, a noodle-brained woman like Andra MacNachtan *is* of no consequence?"

He stood, over six feet tall, a blond giant, handsome, irresistible, and so bristling with irritation at Lady Valéry that he almost forgot his displeasure with Andra. "She damned well shouldn't be."

"When will you leave?"

"Tomorrow morning." Standing, he tossed his whiskey into the fire and watched the flames blaze up. "And the tale of this marriage kilt had better be true, Your Grace, for if I go all that way to make a fool of myself, I'll hop a ship to India and make another fortune, and you'll not see me for many a long day."

"You'd break an old lady's heart?"

"Not if she's a truthful old lady. Now if you will excuse me, Your Grace, I will go pack."

She watched him stride out, dynamic, overbearing, and so virile he made her long to be fifty years younger. "Oh, I am truthful," she murmured to herself. "About the marriage kilt, at least."

"Busted clean in half, it is, and I dinna know how I will fix it without more pipe." Andra's steward sounded dimly satisfied as he declared their catastrophe. "A'course, my great-great-great-great-grandfather put it in, and 'tis a miracle it hasn't busted sooner."

Andra stared at the still-dripping end of the pipe that carried water from the well to the kitchen. It *was* a miracle it hadn't broken before, and she'd run out of miracles about two months ago.

"It's created a dreadful flood," Douglas added unnecessarily.

Andra lifted her foot out of the three inches of water submerging the floor of the subterranean dungeon she euphemistically called the wine cellar. "I noticed." She noticed more than that. When the pipe had broken, it had sprayed the barrels of salted meat and soaked the bins of barley and rye. An almost-empty barrel containing the last of their wine listed drunkenly from side to side.

The Clan MacNachtan had reached its lowest ebb, and she had no idea how to raise it from this depth of poverty and despair—or, rather, how to raise herself, for she was the last of the family. She wanted to give up—she would have already given up—except for Douglas, sixty years old and really quite good at repairing misfortune after he'd finished bellyaching; and her housekeeper, Sima, the only mother she'd had since her own had died when she was eleven; and the cook and Kenzie, the half-blind ostler; and the crofters and all the folk who depended on her to keep them safe from madmen and Englishmen.

And when she'd done just that, refused to agree to a crazy Englishman's contemptible demand, they'd acted disappointed or troubled or irritated according to their natures. As if she, the last of the MacNachtans, should actually marry a lowlander. Bad enough that she had—

"Mistress, how are we goin' t' pump all this water out o' here?"

She took a quivering breath but couldn't answer. She didn't know how they were going to pump the water out.

"An' how do ye want me t' fix the pipe?"

She didn't know that, either. She just knew that life, always lonely, always hard, had recently grown so difficult that she didn't know how she could bear to continue to lift her head off the pillow in the mornings.

Plucking the sweaty kerchief off her head, she used it to wipe her neck. She'd been helping boil the laundry in the kitchen when the water suddenly stopped; she looked like the lowest, poorest crofter who inhabited the ancient Mac-Nachtan lands, and she ached in every bone. She would hate to have anyone see her like this, certainly not—

"That guid young man Mr. Fairchild would know what to do," Douglas said. "Seemed t' me he knew a lot about plumbin'."

Andra turned on Douglas so quickly, she made waves. "What do you mean by that?"

Her steward looked surprised and exorbitantly, suspiciously innocent. "Why, nothing, but that he seemed knowledgeable about every little thing. Even pipes."

She closed her eyes to shut out the sight of the wizened old man's amusement. She shouldn't have reacted to the sound of Hadden's name, but Douglas had been nagging at her ever since . . .

"He's not here, is he? So we'll have to do without him." She kept her tone level and her voice soft, two things she had had trouble doing these last weeks.

Douglas nodded approvingly. "At least fer a change ye're not shriekin' like a kelpie."

And Andra felt her ready irritation rise. She turned her back, ostensibly to study the pipe, and found her attention caught by the true scope of this disaster. An entire section had burst, ancient copper worn thin by a hundred and fifty years of water flowing through it.

Burst. Broken. Worn out. Like everything else in Castle MacNachtan. She and everyone under her care were living in a crumbling relic, and day by day matters were getting worse. Everyone looked to Andra for salvation, but what could a twenty-six-year-old spinster do to repair stone or to grow crops?

Behind her, she heard the patter of Sima's footsteps down the stairs and the swish of Douglas's stride through the water. She heard the whisper of their voices, and she swallowed hard to clear the lump from her throat. A lump she experienced far too often these days.

"Mistress," Sima called, and her voice sounded softer and kinder than it had for many a day. "Dinna fash yerself about this now. Ye've had a hard day. Come on up t' yer chamber. I've fixed ye a nice, warm bath."

"A bath?" To Andra's shame, her voice wobbled. Resting her hand on her throat, she steadied herself before she spoke again. "It isn't even time for supper."

"It will be by the time ye've bathed, and it's a guid supper we're plannin', too. Some o' Mary's potato scones, hot off the grill, and a wee chicken in the pot. Maybe I'll make yer favorite."

Later, Andra realized the chicken should have offered her the clue. The only time Sima usually allowed a chicken to be killed was if someone were sick, or if the chicken was.

But at that moment, all Andra wanted was warm water and the illusion of comfort. "Cock-a-leekie soup?" Turning, she stared at the spare, iron-faced woman who had been her nurse.

"Aye, the very same," Sima assured her.

So Andra allowed herself to be herded upstairs to her bedchamber, bathed with the single, hoarded bar of French, rose-scented soap. Her sole pair of white silk stockings was offered and donned, as were her garters with the lacy flower by the bow. Her fresh white petticoats rustled as Sima tied them around her waist, and she raised her arms as Sima slipped her best gown of rose dimity over her head. Her length of straight black hair was coiled atop her head in the most elegant style Sima knew, and, as the finishing touch, Sima wrapped a Belgian lace shawl around Andra's shoulders.

Andra permitted all this without protest, imagining that she was being cosseted like a child.

In truth, she was being trussed like a sacrificial lamb.

And she realized it when she walked into the flame-lit dining chamber with its intimate, linen-draped table set with two places, and saw him.

Hadden Fairchild, scholar, Englishman—and her first, her only, her lover.

Two

Andra didn't quite hiss when she saw Hadden's broad shoulders propped against the mantle, but she allowed herself a little puff of exasperation mixed with defensiveness. He stood there, showing no signs of the hard journey, impeccably dressed in a jacket, trousers, cravat and waistcoat bearing the stamp of London sophistication. The man himself, big, braw and hearty, gathered the fire's glow and magnified the light in the gleam of his blond hair, the warmth of his golden skin, and the luminescence of his heather-blue eyes.

Damn him. Did he have to challenge her with his stance, his vigor, and his obvious ability to make himself at home in *her* castle?

Sima put her hand in the middle of Andra's back and gave her a push, and Andra stumbled into the room and almost fell to her knees.

"Please," he said, his tone frightfully superior and his accent very English, "you don't have to kneel. A simple curtsy will serve."

Automatically she dropped into the common Highland intonation she hoped would annoy him. "Ye're insufferable."

"Aye." He could do a Scottish accent even broader than hers. "As bad as a lassie wi' no more guid sense than Fairie Puck."

He looked as if he should be more ornamental than useful, but he could do everything better than she could. Change a wheel, deliver a babe, dig a well, soothe a child's fears, write a letter, love a woman past any qualm . . . no doubt he could also repair a pipe. But she, Andra MacNachtan of the Highland MacNachtans, didn't have to stand here and have her face rubbed in his endless, exasperating competence.

With a flourish, she tossed the shawl around her neck and turned away, prepared to stomp back to her bedchamber or the wine cellar, or anywhere Hadden Fairchild was not.

She found herself facing Sima. Sima, who had taught her everything about hospitality and manners and now shook such a stern finger that Andra found herself cowed. Reluctantly obeying that mute and powerful mandate, Andra turned back to her company, expecting to see Hadden grinning at Sima, wordlessly thanking her for making Andra submit to courtesy's demand. But he was not grinning, and he certainly was not looking at Sima. His attention remained fixed on Andra, like a man-wolf who scented his mate.

But just because her body recognized and welcomed him on a primal level, that did not mean she was his mate. This softness, this trembling, this desire to run to his arms and seek shelter there—these were nothing more than a wee bit of weakness at the sight of the man who had taught her passion. Never mind that he wordlessly commanded her; Andra MacNachtan was no one's fool, and she would not obey.

Shaking off her lassitude, she spoke, her voice weighted with insincerity. "Mr. Fairchild, how pleasant to have you visit us again. What brings you back to my corner of the Highlands, and so soon after your last visit?"

He straightened up, away from the mantel, and took a step toward her. "You lied to me."

His blunt accusation shook her. Of course she had; it had been a matter of self-preservation. But how had he discovered it? "What are you talking about?"

"I'm talking about the marriage kilt."

Hidden in the folds of her skirt, her hands clenched, then relaxed. "The marriage kilt. The MacNachtans' marriage kilt?"

"Do you know of another?"

"No," she said reluctantly.

"And there is one?"

With even greater reluctance, she admitted, "Aye."

"Would you tell me why, when you knew I came on Lady Valéry's behest to gather the traditions of Scotland and record them, you failed to tell me about the marriage kilt?" He walked toward her on silent feet, his shadow falling on her, the smoke of the fire chasing after him as if it wished to caress him. "You told me about the stone on the hill, reputed to be placed by giants, and about the wishing well from whence the ghosts rise on All Hallows' Eve—things so common to Scotland, they were not worth writing down. But the marriage kilt—you said nothing of that."

Of course she had said nothing. The four days he'd spent with her had been a time set aside from reality and duty. For four brief, enchanted days, she had cared little about shouldering her duties as a true leader of her people should. She had cared only about Hadden and the way he made her feel.

Not love; she knew about love. That was what she had felt for her uncle before he'd been put to the horn, and her father and her brother before they'd fled to America, and her mother before she'd died of grief.

This had been a different kind of emotion—carefree, full of laughter and unexpected passion. She hadn't cared that he would inevitably walk away; she had only cared about grasping one perfect moment before it was too late and she died an old maid worn down by her burdens.

"The marriage kilt?" he prompted.

She lifted her chin and looked at him. He stood too closely. She could see each strand of his hair, trimmed and combed and damp, smell the scent of heather and leather and soap, sense his outrage fed by the need for her that smoldered in him. Every hair on her skin lifted, but she wouldn't step away, and she dared not look away. She didn't remember him being so tall, and she had never thought she would be afraid of him.

But she was.

"I didn't remember it." A lie.

Which he recognized. "You didn't remember it," he repeated. "You didn't remember the pride of the MacNachtans."

"No." Another lie, but better to tell a lie than to acknowledge her own skittish decision to never think about marriage, mention marriage, and, most especially, not to dream about marriage and how it would be to share her life with one man who would be there for her forever . . . or until another vista beckoned. "Why would I remember that old thing? It's hidden in a trunk somewhere, and I never think of it."

"Lady Valéry said the MacNachtans drag it out to show all their guests."

"I don't." It would have been better if she could have held his gaze. But the blue flame in his eyes scorched her, and her nerve broke. She looked off to the side.

"Coward." He only breathed the word.

Yet she heard. She heard everything he said, but she could not hear everything he thought. They were not so attuned as that. She would not allow it to be so.

The silence mounted as she watched his hand rise from his side toward her. Toward her face, there to stroke her cheek as he had loved to do. His outstretched fingers quivered as if he fought the need to touch her. Fought it as much as she fought the need to be touched.

A footstep outside the doorway made them spring apart,

and Sima bustled into the chamber followed by two beaming maids. One carried a steaming tureen of soup, the other a basket with the promised potato scones. The maids placed the food in the center of the small, round table while Sima took in the scene at a glance. Andra thought she heard a small huff of exasperation before the housekeeper burst into speech. "Sit ye both down and eat yer fill o' me fine cock-a-leekie soup. 'Tis a long time until mornin', and a fair climb t' the top o' the tower."

Startled, Andra asked, "The tower? Why the tower?"

"Why, that's where th' marriage kilt is."

"Been listening at the door again?" Andra asked.

"Not at all," Sima said in lofty disdain. "Mr. Hadden talks t' me, and he told me why he had come. Shocked, pure shocked I was that ye hadn't shown him before."

Shocked. Nothing had shocked Sima for years. But on his first visit, she'd made her allegiance to Hadden clear. That could have been because he deliberately set out to enchant her, and every other female on the estate.

"I like women," he said. "Especially strong, capable women. My sister is like that. Lady Valéry is like that. And you, Lady Andra . . . you're like that."

"Sturdy, that's me," she answered with all the cheer she'd taught herself.

"Sturdy? Not at all." His gaze ran over her with the care of a connoisseur. "You look almost fragile."

Sima interrupted with all the presumption of which she was capable. "She works too hard. She needs a man."

Andra could scarcely contain her horror. "Sima!"

Hadden had only grinned at her. "A man to take care of her and do the heavy work. I couldn't agree more."

After that, Sima had cared not that he was a foreigner. She, and every other foolish maid, had been vocal in their adoration.

So when Andra had sent him away, Sima had been equally vocal with her opinion of Andra's poor sense and unfeeling heart, and she dared insinuate that Andra used her indifference to hide a weakness.

Foolishness, of course. Andra was strong. Self-sufficient. In need of no one. No one.

"I also told him that ye had no bairn on the way. He seemed more than a wee bit concerned about that." Smirking, Sima watched as color scorched Andra inside and out. "Although why he should be when ye're not wed is beyond this auld woman's understandin'."

Beyond her understanding, indeed. Sima understood human nature and needs with an almost fey comprehension, and Andra had no doubt the old woman was mixing a witch's brew with her crooked finger. Only Andra couldn't quite comprehend the plot. Thinking of the rickety stairway that circled around and around; the trapdoor in the floor; the big, dusty room with its windows so dirty they almost didn't allow any light in, she asked suspiciously, "Why the tower?"

"I've been worried about the effect of dampness on the old things." Sima pulled the high-backed, armed, and cushioned chair away from the table.

Andra took a step toward it.

"Mr. Hadden, you sit here," Sima instructed.

Andra stopped and watched, tense with resentment. Before, he had always insisted she take the master's chair. He'd held it for her, seating her first with charm and courtesy. Now he accepted Sima's homage with all the presumption of a noble, long-lost divinity, and seated himself with only a terse word of thanks to the manipulative old beldam.

And Sima beamed as she pulled out the other, less formal, and quite armless chair. "Sit ye here, dearie, and rest yer tired feet. She's been workin', Mr. Hadden, way too hard since ye left. If I didn't know better, I'd say she missed ye."

Without missing a beat, she continued, "Mistress, the tower's dry, ye must admit; ye can see for miles, and there's a good cross-breeze when the windows are open."

Torn between chagrin and gratitude, Andra seated herself. "Do you think the kilt is admiring the view?"

As Sima patted her arm, she also plucked Andra's shawl from her shoulders. "Ah, a witty tongue she has, isn't it, Mr. Hadden?"

"I have cherished her—" his gaze ran over her bosom, now exposed by the low neckline, "—wit."

Andra leaned forward, a hot retort on her lips.

Sima's fingers grew suddenly tight. She shoved Andra against the chair back and burst into speech. "Me and the lasses have been doing spring cleanin' these last few days. 'Tis spring, ye ken, and a guid time to be cleanin'. So we aired the linens and dusted the mementos and rearranged everything in the trunks, and we put the kilt up there, too." She nodded at one of the maids, who filled the bowls and placed one in front of Hadden and one in front of Andra. "Ye'll want t' have a full stomach fer yer adventure."

Andra touched her forehead. She didn't remember a time when Sima had chattered so. It must be Hadden's influence; another catastrophe she could put on his doorstep.

"She's lost weight." Hadden spoke to Sima, but there could be no doubt he spoke of Andra; his gaze battered her across the stifling intimacy of the shrinking table.

"Aye; with one eye closed, she looks like a needle," Sima answered, showing her treasonous willingness to speak of Andra as if she weren't even present. "She hasn't been eating as she should."

"Why do you suppose that is?" he wondered.

"I've been busy," Andra said.

"She's been pining," Sima answered at the same time.

Fed up to the gills with Sima and her stupid notion that a

woman needed a man to make her whole, Andra snapped, "Leave us to eat in peace."

"O' course, mistress."

Sima curtsied, the maids curtsied, and they whisked themselves out so quickly Andra had the definite feeling she'd lost that round. But how could she win, she wondered morosely, when everyone in the castle clearly thought their mistress was daft?

"Eat your soup," Hadden commanded, as much at home playing imperious master as he had been playing captivating guest.

She wanted to answer that she wasn't hungry, but for the first time in two months, she was. Ravenously, voraciously hungry, her body demanding sustenance after a famine. As she picked up her spoon, she skidded a glance at Hadden. Having him back had released one appetite—God help her if it released another.

Wisely he kept his gaze on his own bowl and refrained from commenting on her avid consumption of the flavorful soup. Yet somehow he watched her, for he passed the scones whenever she finished one until she could eat no more. Then he put down his spoon.

"You'll take me to the tower now."

She leaned back in her chair. "What makes you think you can command me in such a tone?"

"The food put new spirit in you," he said. "Something you needed no more of. Yes, I do command you to take me to the tower. You owe me that, at least, Andra."

"I owe you nothing!"

His hand came down over hers where it rested on the table, and when she tried to jerk back, he tightened his grip. "Yes, you do. Remember what you said to me when you sent me away? That I'd forget you as soon as you were out of my sight? Well, I haven't. I think of you, I dream of you, I thirst for you—and if all I can get from you is a chapter in my treatise, then I will take that and live off of it until I die."

His palm was rough over the top of hers and blisteringly warm . . . just like the rest of him. She remembered his warmth, moving beneath her, thrusting above her, and the memory made her capitulate.

She would do anything to make him let her go. As she rose, his hand again tightened on hers. Until she said, "Come, then. I'll take you to the tower."

Three

Hadden could scarcely contain his rage as he followed Andra up the dim and winding staircase to the tower. The woman had had him in turmoil for two bloody months, and now she had the nerve to walk ahead of him up the narrow, rickety steps, tormenting him with the sway of her hips. How much of this mindless teasing was a man expected to bear?

If only it weren't mindless. If only she were teasing him on purpose, enticing him into her arms. But she wasn't. She wanted him to go away.

She'd *sent* him away.

The first time he'd seen her, she'd been standing in the stream, skirts tied up, laughing at the antics of the sheep that struggled to escape their yearly dunking. She had been handsome and carefree, the symbol of springtime in Scotland and everything he'd ever wanted.

He had just come from London, where he'd been hunted for his fortune, noble background and blond good looks, and there he'd grown to despise those jaded souls who would do anything, however dishonorable, for their own pleasure. Despite the tightening in his groin and the craving that coursed through his veins, he resolved he would not debauch a Scottish peasant maiden who might not dare to reject a wealthy English nobleman. That would be the act of a cad.

But when he'd discovered she was the woman Lady Valéry had sent him to meet, principle went out the window.

However, Hadden had never seen a woman work so doggedly, without stopping, as if the perpetuity of her people depended on her and her alone.

Which, apparently, it did. She supervised the washing of the sheep, consulted with the shepherds, encouraged the women who baled the wool, spoke with the men who would transport it to market, discussed with her weavers how much was needed for their own purposes. All this while caring for her household and servants and treating him with grace and hospitality.

She liked him; he knew she did. Indeed, when a Fairchild went out of his way to make himself attractive, there were few women who could resist him. And Hadden had the added advantage of being able to help with Andra's burdens, for, unlike most Fairchilds, he was competent and not afraid of hard work. But of what purpose were charm, good looks, and ability if the lady he desired could not find the time to be enticed?

Thus, on his third day at Castle MacNachtan, he arranged with her people to take Lady Andra away from the drudgery that was her life. As she stood in the stableyard, and with the assistance of every able-bodied man at MacNachtan, he lifted her before him on the saddle and kidnapped her for just one day while she laughed and protested that she had work to do.

But she didn't protest too hard. Once away from the duties that had bound her, she had helped him devour the food and drink Sima had packed for them. She'd held his hand as they wandered the hills, picking flowers. She listened with gladness as he sang the old Scottish tunes. She'd been silent and listened to the wind as it whistled through the crags.

When the afternoon had waned and they had started back, she turned in the saddle and kissed him. Mashed his lips, actually, until he stopped his horse and taught her better. Taught her to slow down, taught the pleasures of taste, taught her how to open her mouth and slide her tongue alongside his.

Hadden halted on the stairway behind Andra and put his hand to the wall to steady himself. The memory of that kissing sent his blood surging. The horse had moved restively between his legs, she had lain across his lap, pressed to his loins, and he'd been in a fever to take her. At once. Everything in him had clamored to claim this woman.

Even now, here on the uncomfortable and perilous tower stairs, he knew that if she gave him one smidgen of encouragement, he would throw her skirts up and bury himself inside her. Yet she gave him no encouragement. She didn't even realize Hadden had stopped. She continued to climb the stairs, and Hadden continued to watch her with rapacious intent, brooding about that afternoon and the hot, vibrant excitement of their first kiss.

He hadn't seized the chance to take her then. Painstakingly, he had righted her, and they had ridden back to Castle MacNachtan. The memory of his own restraint infuriated him now, although later, when she had crept into his bed and shyly, daintily debauched him as only a virgin could do, he had thought he'd won all. He'd been triumphant, silly in love, convinced he had just waged the most successful campaign he had ever waged for a woman's heart, for it was the only *important* campaign he had waged for a woman's heart.

And in the end, she'd rejected him.

"I never meant . . . you can't . . . I can't marry you." She *snatched up the corner of the wool blanket, covered herself,*

and crawled across the mattress away from him as if he'd threatened to harm her. "Why would you ask such a thing?"

He was as stunned as if she'd brought out an axe and tried to put it through his skull. "I've been courting you. You've been responding. Last night, you came to me." He gestured around at the archaic, curtained bed that had witnessed the sweetest, most gentle and tremulous loving he'd ever experienced. "My God, you were a virgin. Of course I want to marry you!"

She stopped sliding away and leaned toward him, a vision of tumbled hair and swollen lips. "Because I was a virgin. Well, let me tell you—"

"No. I don't want to marry you because you were a virgin! I wanted to marry you regardless of your state of chastity. But when a woman has reached your age and not tumbled into bed with a man sooner, the man she tumbles with assumes she loves him!"

A certain expression crossed her face.

And he knew right away he'd stated his case badly. He could almost hear Lady Valéry quoting, "A woman of your age?"

So he hastily added, "And I love you. I wanted to marry you yesterday. The day before. The first time I saw you!"

"Infatuation," she said flatly. "You're a nice man in the throes of infatuation."

That was when he lost his temper. "I am not a nice man," he roared.

He might not have even spoken. She said, "Now . . . you've got to go away."

A nice man. He'd brooded about that one phrase. *A nice man.* He still brooded about it. Apparently she thought he treated every woman the way he'd treated her, and fell in and out of love with obnoxious regularity. In fact, looking back, he realized she had a decidedly odd opinion of men, and he still didn't know why.

But he would find out. Oh, yes, he would.

Andra poked her head around the curve of the stairs where she'd disappeared. "Are you out of breath from the climb? Shall I help you with my arm around your waist, old man?"

She didn't even realize the danger she courted. He smiled, depending on the shadows to hide the menace of his intent. "Yes," he invited. "Come down and assist me."

Something—the tone of his voice, the flash of his teeth, or perhaps that knowledge of him that she had gleaned through the mingling of their bodies—must have warned her, for she stared down at him for one still moment, then said briskly, "I think not," and her head bobbed out of sight.

He heard the clatter of her soles on the stairs as she hurried upward, and his smile widened to a savage grin. *Run away, little girl; you'll not outrun me.*

Her own valiance stood his stead as a weapon, for it would never occur to her to admit to alarm. Even now, as her footsteps slowed, he knew that she was telling herself to stop being such a ninny, that he was a civilized man who could be depended upon to be a gentleman.

She didn't realize that the veneer of civilization wore thin when a man was deprived of his mate.

It grew warmer as he climbed upward, and he caught her at the place where the stairs slanted sharply upward, becoming more of a ladder. Andra stood, head bent against the tight constraint of steps and wall and ceiling, her fingers tucked into the handle of the trapdoor, a sconce on the wall barely lighting the stygian darkness. "Can you lift the hatch?" she asked. "Or shall I?"

That stupid valiance of hers must be blinding her to the instincts of primitive woman. She should be fleeing him, but instead she taunted him, inquiring without actually asking if his manners had evaporated when she'd banned him from her bed. They had, but he saw no reason to tell her so now.

They were not yet completely away from the inhabited part of the castle and the restraints enforced by the presence of other, more civilized people.

Taking care to touch no more than the tip of her elbow, he guided her toward the wall, away from the drop that descended to the base of the tower, and passed her. He pushed back the shiny steel latches and lifted the sturdy wooden panel. With the screech of metal and wood, he shoved the trapdoor up and across the floor of the chamber above.

A sudden brightness descended from the tower, and a draft of fresh air relieved the stuffiness of the stairway. "The servants must have left the windows open. I'll speak to Sima when we are done here." Her tone made it clear she wished that would occur soon.

The spring of his anger wound tighter. "Indeed, you should. Your servants take too much on themselves."

The irritation that infected him spread to her. He could tell by the color that bloomed in her cheeks and the flash of her dark eyes. She bit her resentment back, and he rejoiced. She didn't want to give in to his passion, not any kind of passion, and that meant she feared the results.

She had loved him; he knew it, and he would discover what megrim had made her withdraw from him. That was his mission this evening—not getting her alone, which he badly wished to do, or even viewing the MacNachtan marriage kilt, which he now used as a pretext.

"Are there mice?" he asked.

"Probably."

"I don't like mice."

"What a craven."

She ridiculed him, and he did no more than bow his head. If she were fool enough to believe him craven, she deserved what she got, and more.

She moved forward, and he stepped down and gestured her upward. He saw the flash of wariness when she realized how smoothly he had maneuvered her, but she hesitated only a moment before brushing past him.

She thought him a gentleman, or at the very least that she could manage him as she managed everything else in her barren life. She didn't realize that the layers of civility had been peeling away from him: on the ride here, during that interminable dinner, on the long ascent up the stairs. He watched her climb the ladder, watched as her slender ankles rose to eye level, and watched as she glanced down at him. She couldn't retreat, but she did snap, "Stop leering at my legs and follow me."

"Was I leering?" He skipped every other rung until he stood directly behind her. "Imagine that, a man appreciating his woman's attributes."

Placing her hands flat on the floor, she boosted herself up. "I am not—"

His hand cupped her bottom, lifting her, turning her. Then his arm swept down and knocked her knees out from under her. The boards thumped as she landed, and he sprang up and over her. Trapping her between his outstretched arms, his weight supported on his hands, he said, "Yes, you are my woman. Let me remind you how much my woman you are."

"Mr. Fairchild . . ." Her brown eyes observed him cautiously, her fingers hovered close to his chest, but she kept her tone brisk and impersonal. "What was between us before is no longer a matter of importance."

"At one time not too long ago, I thought you a shrewd woman." He lowered his body onto hers, inch by heated inch. "I have changed my mind."

Four

Hadden kept his legs between Andra's, using his knees to press against her skirts, pinning her in place. The scent of soap mixed with the scent of him, and his breath huffed from beneath his parted lips. Her fingers hovered so close to his chest that she could feel the heat of him, but she shrank before his forward motion. Something in her insisted she not touch him. Not if she wanted to cleave to her resolution to remain alone and not risk—

She could see, through the blackness of his pupils, the determination that steered him. His breath caressed her cheek. "Andra."

A like determination blazed through her; he would not intimidate her. She shoved at him hard. "Get off me, you big oaf. Who do you think you are? Some kind of English reiver?"

He rolled off her and flopped flat on his back, covering his eyes with his arm. She experienced a measure of satisfaction—and unacknowledged relief. She wasn't so wrong about her reading of Hadden's disposition, then. He wouldn't kick a dog, or slap a servant, or kiss a lass against her will. He was a nice man, a malleable man.

In time, he would do as she'd predicted all those months ago. He would forget about her.

Sitting up, she looked at his outstretched figure. Yet she had imagined he would forget before Castle MacNachtan disappeared at his back. And she never thought he would have been so irate. Cautiously, she slid away from him and farther into the attic. Could there be other facets of his character that she had evaluated incorrectly?

"Is that it?" He sounded carefully bland, like a gambler determined not to show his hand, and still he hid beneath the cover of his arm.

"Was that what?" she asked cautiously.

"Was that the reason you wouldn't accept my suit? That I am English?"

"No, of course not."

"Then it's my family."

"Your family?"

"Perhaps the infamy of the Fairchilds has spread even into the Highlands of Scotland. You've heard the tales, and you're reluctant to graft such a shrub to your illustrious family tree."

Startled, she considered him; he was handsome, honorable, and kind, she could scarcely believe his protestations—and she'd be damned if she'd tell him the real reason. "I've never heard of your family."

"Then you're worried that my sister raised me, and she did not, perhaps, do as well as parents would. Yet let me assure you, she loved me dearly and taught me well. I have the manners and morals of a man raised by the sternest father."

"I know that, for in the Highlands," she said loftily, "we judge a man by his character, not by his background."

He took his arm away from his face and stared at the ceiling. "Really? And how do you judge my character?"

She swallowed. "You said you wanted to marry me, but I knew you didn't . . . you were just infatuated."

Turning his head, he examined her thoroughly. "Really."

She scooted a little farther away and wished she could scoot down the stairs and out the door, and run and hide from that enigmatic, knowing gaze. She didn't like the combination of restraint and recklessness he displayed. It made her unsure of herself—and of her control over him. She wasn't used to feeling like this: nervy, like a horse to be broken and ridden at will. She was the lady, and always in command.

Why, then, was her heart beating a little too fast? Why did her breath catch, and the faintest dew cover her forehead? Was it because she feared he would force her to tell him the truth? A truth that even she pretended did not exist?

Deliberately, as she had done so many times these months, she turned her mind away to tasks and duties. She couldn't think about it now, so she looked around the chamber. After all, a mistress must oversee the labor of her people.

And the condition of the tower proved that her people could be depended upon, regardless of the task. All traces of dust had been swept away. The floorboards, although old and splintered, had been scrubbed. The glass windows sparkled, and two of them were barely open to let in fresh air. Spiderwebs no longer festooned the corners. Unneeded or worn furniture stood about the chamber: a chair stripped of its cushions; a bench; a tall, aged lamp table.

Trunks had been gathered from all over the castle and transported up the stairs, and Andra grimaced as she imagined how the men must have complained. But she, more than anyone, knew the futility of arguing with the housekeeper when she was set upon a scheme, and this chamber was, after all, truly spacious and bright. Perhaps Sima was right. Perhaps it would be good to store the family valuables up here.

Although Andra wasn't looking at him, she was aware

when Hadden sat up. Even though he was across the open trapdoor from her, he seemed too tall, too muscled and too intent on her for comfort.

Not that she knew anything too much about men and their desires, but she suspected that primal glare meant she'd best hurry with the kilt, or she'd be fighting him off.

That hadn't been what happened before. No, last time he'd been here, she had done the seducing, and a good job she'd done of it, too, for he'd proposed marriage before morning.

She woke to find him looking at her with a wondrous glow in his eyes, as if she didn't have the mark of the pillow on her cheek and her mouth didn't taste like the bottom of the well and her hair wasn't a witch's black tangle.

"Andra." He smoothed the hair away from her face with a tender brush of his fingers. "You're the woman I love. Please marry me."

Damn him for dragging reality into her fantasy. And damn her for wanting to squall like a frightened infant when he'd asked.

She swallowed several times, fighting much the same reaction now. "The kilt. Sima said it was in the trunk. So go look before it gets dark."

"In the trunk?" He looked over at the line of five chests, some so ancient the seams were splitting; others, although old, still in good repair. "Which trunk?"

Did he have to be difficult? And couldn't Sima have been a little more specific? "You can explore."

"Will I know the MacNachtan marriage kilt when I see it?"

He had a point, much though she disliked admitting it. And she knew she had to help him find the MacNachtan wedding kilt so she could send him away with a clear conscience. "I'll assist you in completing your purpose."

He made a noise deep in his chest, not a laugh, not a rumble; more of a growl. "No one else can."

Standing, she discovered that her knees wobbled, but the goal of showing him the wretched kilt and getting away from this unwanted intimacy steadied her. "In fact, you don't have to do anything, you big, lazy lummox. I'll search for you." She started toward the trunk farthest to the left, and he began to follow. "No." She held out her hand to halt him, then lowered it hastily before he noticed the trembling. "I'll do better if you're not looking over my shoulder."

Stopping, he said, "Gracious as always, Lady Andra."

Gracious? She didn't care about gracious. She cared only about speed. As she stood in front of the first trunk, she glanced out the window. It was July, high summer in Scotland. They had two hours of sunlight left until nine o' the clock.

But the trunks were deep and wide, five trunks filled with the history of the MacNachtans, and she knew as she knelt before the first one that the hope she cherished, of finding the kilt in there, was a crazy hope.

Nevertheless, she held her breath as she lifted the lid and cleared away the first layer—plain paper laid over the contents to protect them from dust. Beneath were tartans, lots and lots of tartans, and for one moment Andra allowed herself to revel in the smell of ancient cloth and old memories.

Then, as Hadden paced, she pulled out the carefully folded plaids. The MacAllister tartan, the MacNeill tartan, the Ross tartan. All tartans of the families that had, at one time or another, married into the MacNachtans.

But no MacNachtan tartan, and certainly no marriage kilt.

She shook her head at the hovering Hadden, and he strode away from her.

Carefully, she replaced them and covered them with the paper.

Then, from a distance, she heard the hollow, eerie sound of . . . voices? Swinging around, she demanded, "What was that?"

"Your mice." He stood frowning at a tall end table as if its location annoyed him.

Though she strained, she could hear no more. An errant breeze ruffled her hair, and she relaxed. Of course. She could hear the servants speaking from down in the courtyard.

She moved to the next trunk while, behind her, Hadden dragged something along the floor, entertaining himself in some manly furniture rearrangement. She didn't care, as long as he didn't hover.

The scraping noise stopped, and the back of her neck prickled. Glancing behind, she saw him, lingering too closely for comfort, and she glared.

He glared back, then swung away, and as she lifted the trunk lid, she heard another something being towed across the floor.

Men. How well she knew they had to have something to keep them out of mischief.

Inside the trunk, she found a cured sheepskin laid face down so its fleece could buffer the contents from impact. Plucking that free, she laid it out on the floor, then peered inside at the paper-wrapped, odd-shaped objects that filled the trunk. Removing an item, she weighed it in her hand. Light, oblong, knobby. Uncovering it, she jumped, dropped it—and chuckled.

Five

*The sound of her laughter softened his ire and irre-*sistibly drew him to her side. He hovered above her, wanting to brush the tendrils of hair off the delicate skin of her neck and press his lips there. He wanted to sweep her into his arms and love her until she had no energy to tell him no. He wanted to . . . he wanted to talk to her, damn her. Just talk, explore the byways of her mind, get to know her. And that seemed to be what frightened her most. In a soft voice, the one he used to calm a fractious horse, he asked, "What's so funny?"

"My great-uncle."

He didn't even know she'd had an uncle. "What about your great-uncle?"

"The man was a wanderer. He left Scotland as a youth— that was after Culloden; he'd been much involved in fighting against the English, and it seemed a wise thing to do—and he traveled the wide world. When he came back years later, he brought some unusual mementos."

She spoke freely, something she had not done since he'd uttered those fateful words—*marry me*—and Hadden bent closer. "What is it?"

She picked up a wooden mask, dark, painted with extravagant designs, and staring from empty eye sockets, and waved it at him. "From Africa. Uncle Clarence said the native women hung them in their huts for protection from the evil spirits." Smiling, she passed the grotesque thing up to him.

"It would certainly frighten me." He turned it from side to side.

"And this." She unwrapped a painted clock, carved with intricate swirls and sporting hidden doors. "From Germany."

Hadden squatted on his haunches, laid down the mask, and took the clock. "Quaint."

"Ugly," she corrected.

"Well . . . yes." His breath caught when she shared a smile with him.

"When wound up, it keeps perfect time, and on the hour, a bird pops out and sings."

Gingerly, he tried a little humor. "I can't believe you don't keep this downstairs in the great hall."

"We did until my uncle . . . until he left." Her smile vanished; she bit her lower lip. "Then we put it away, for it made my mother cry."

A puzzle piece, Hadden realized; she missed her uncle and ached for her mother's pain. "Why did he leave?"

"Memories are long here in the Highlands. There were those English who took over estates abandoned by the outlawed Scots, and one remembered Uncle Clarence and threatened to turn him over as a rebel. Uncle knew the family could ill afford that." She shrugged as if it didn't matter when it so obviously did. "So he left."

Moving slowly, Hadden seated himself on the cushioning sheepskin, stretched out his long legs, and kneaded his thighs as if they ached. "But he must have been an elder! What did this Englishman think he could do?"

Her gaze slid sideways toward him. She watched his

hands move up and down along his muscles, and unconsciously she mimicked him, rubbing her legs with long, pensive strokes. "He could seduce his old sweetheart away from her miserable English husband and take her with him, that's what."

She injected humor into her tone, but she wasn't truly amused. Sorrow lurked behind the brave smile, the lifted brows.

"He was the black sheep, then," Hadden pronounced.

"Not in the MacNachtan family. In the MacNachtan family, *all* the men are black sheep." Sitting forward, she delved into the trunk as if she could hide behind the contents.

But she couldn't hide from Hadden. Not when he was getting the answers he'd sought. "Who else?"

"Hmm?" She raised her ingenuous gaze to his.

He didn't believe the innocence for a moment. "I never heard this before. Who else was a black sheep?"

"Oh . . . my father, for one." The paper rustled as she unwrapped the knobby bundle, and a five-inch-tall stone statue of a naked woman with bulbous breasts emerged. She chuckled again, but this time her mirth seemed forced. "Look. From Greece. Uncle thought she was a fertility goddess."

"Really?" He barely glanced at the ugly little figurine. "What did your father do?"

"After Uncle was exiled, Papa decided to make his stand for Scottish freedom, and in an excess of patriotism—and whiskey—he rode to Edinburgh to blow up Parliament House."

Hadden had seen the noble pile of stone last time he'd visited Edinburgh, and said acerbically, "He didn't succeed."

"No. He and my brother drank their way through every pub in the city, telling everyone of their plan."

Hadden's astonishment grew. "Your brother, too?"

"My mother said they did it on purpose, telling everyone

of their scheme, because they were both too kindhearted to think of actually hurting anyone, English or no." Andra unwrapped another package and showed him a statue of much the same size as the other one, but made of bronze.

As she held it up to him, the miniature woman dressed in a cord skirt saluted Hadden, her golden eyes ablaze.

"From Scandinavia," Andra told him. "My uncle said she was a fertility goddess as well. The natives put quite a store in her."

Hadden plucked the female deity from her fingers. "Are they in prison in Edinburgh?"

"Who? Oh, my father and brother." Andra's elaborate casualness didn't cozen him. "No. They were put to the horn, outlawed—a matter of great pride to them—and they fled to America. My father died there, but my brother writes occasionally. He's married quite a hearty woman, born in that country, and he's doing well."

"How old were you when all this occurred?"

"Eleven."

"I see." Hadden saw more than she wished. Her men, the ones who should have defended her against all hardship, had abandoned her for ineffectual glory. She had been posed on the cusp of womanhood, ready to dance, to flirt, to be courted by the local lords, and instead she'd had to become the sole pillar of stability in the MacNachtan clan. "Your poor mother," he said experimentally.

Her fingers shook a little as she unwrapped another package. "Yes. Well, Mother was frail to start with, and when the soldiers came, they upset her, and she took to her bed . . . look!" She cradled a delicate clay statue of a woman in a full skirt, naked from the waist up, clutching a snake in each hand. "From Crete. We think . . ." Her voice trailed off. She frowned at the bare-breasted creature, rubbing the feminine curves slowly with her fingertips. Then she looked up at Hadden. "You don't want to know about this."

"About the fertility goddesses in all their bare glory?" Then, with obviously unwelcome shrewdness, "—Or about your family?"

It told him volumes when she gulped and jerked back. "Don't be daft. About the goddesses, of course." She tried to shove the goddess back into the trunk, but he rescued the painted figurine and placed her on the floor with the others. Andra scurried to the next trunk, if one could be said to scurry on her knees.

"Andra." Hadden laid his hand on her arm. "Tell me the truth."

Andra flung open the lid with such vigor, the aging wood cracked. "I'll find it in here," she said feverishly. "I'm sure I will."

"Find? . . ."

"The marriage kilt." The paper crackled as she peeled it away. "That is why you came, isn't it?"

It wasn't. He knew it. She knew it. But the lass vibrated with unfettered emotion, frightened by what she knew and what he guessed. She couldn't face him, couldn't face the truth, and he supposed he understood that.

Yet he didn't like it, and his anger rose again.

How dare she compare him to those other men? To the worthless milquetoasts in her family?

And how dare she compare herself to her mother, a frail creature crushed by the loss of her husband and son? Andra was not frail; she was strong, facing life and all its trials without flinching. He had his suspicions, and if they were right, it was life's dividends that she feared.

"Would you like to hear the tale of it?" she asked.

Recalled to the conversation, he asked, "Of what?"

She huffed like a steam engine. "Of the marriage tartan!"

She stilled when he approached, and waited until he picked up the sheepskin. "Tell me." He gathered the goddesses and strategically distributed them throughout the room. Returning to the trunk he brought out more well-wrapped treasures. He smiled at the lusty treasures he found, and distributed them, too.

A man could not be too thorough.

"The marriage kilt is the kilt worn by the first MacNachtan when he married." She was dropping tartans in a pile beside her, searching with more vigor than grace. "He was an older man, a fierce warrior, and one reluctant to take a woman to wife, for he believed exposure to such softness would weaken him."

"So he was wise." He didn't wait for her to respond to his provocation, but wandered away again, to drape the sheepskin across an aged bench of solid oak.

"Wise as are all men," she said tartly. "But one day he was forced to pay a visit to the MacDougalls, for they were stealing his cattle, and there, in their stronghold, he met a girl."

"I already foresee his downfall." The evening sun had reached that point on the horizon when its beams shone directly into the chamber, burnishing it with the glory of light.

"She was a beauty, and he loved her at once, but she was proud and wanted nothing of him, not even when he washed and trimmed his hair and beard and came a-courtin' like a youth smitten with his first sweetheart." He heard her voice sweeten with the Scottish brogue as the rhythm of the tale swept her. "She would have none of him, so he did what any full-blooded MacNachtan would do."

"Kidnapped her?" he ventured, because right now kidnapping seemed a right and clever course to take.

And her reply delighted him. "Aye, kidnapped her as she wandered the hills. But she was no frail flower. She fought so much, he stripped away his kilt and flung it over her head to blind her, and wrapped her up so she couldn't strike him, and thus carried her away."

She sat, holding a folded, tattered tartan in her hands and smiling at it.

Walking up behind her, he asked, "What is the ending of the story?"

"They were verra happy all their lives together." She craned her neck to look up at him. "And this is it. The Mac-Nachtan marriage kilt. In our family, it's a tradition that the groom throw it over the bride's head and sweep her away. It's said that every union thus blessed will be a happy union."

Leaning over, he took the kilt and spread it wide over his hands. It was old, so old that the black and red and blue of the plaid had faded to an almost indistinguishable blend. The stitching had given way, and the hem was more fringe than cloth. But along the middle, the wool was well woven.

He smiled at it, then at her.

She saw his intention in his stance, in his amusement, and because she knew him better than any other living person knew him. Standing, she eased away.

"I already kidnapped you once. It was one prime day that lives in my memory—but apparently not in yours, and now I know why. I was too pleasant, too kind." He lifted the tartan. "I failed to follow tradition. I didn't cover you in the marriage kilt."

She bolted for the now-closed trapdoor.

"No use, my lady," he said. "You're mine."

Six

Grasping the handle on the trapdoor, Andra tugged.

Nothing budged.

She tugged harder.

It was solid, unmoving. She glanced behind her, and still Hadden stalked onward, coming relentlessly for her. She gave one last desperate yank—and the handle came off. She tumbled backward, and the marriage kilt floated over her head.

Hadden wrapped her in it and in his arms, and his deep voice crooned, "Surrender, darling. Your loyal servants have locked us in."

The musty old cloth leaked light like a sieve, and she could have grabbed it and ripped it off her head, but reverence for the MacNachtan past restrained her, and Hadden had no compunction about taking advantage. He lifted her from behind, and she bucked like an unbroken filly, twisting, trying to escape from an embrace that felt too right.

He placed her on a hard, flat surface, high enough above the floor that her feet dangled. He swept the kilt away, and her face was level with his. She sat on the narrow square of the lamp table, her back against the wall, Hadden pressed between her legs.

"Kidnapped. Kidnapped as surely as the first MacNachtan kidnapped his bride. I have fulfilled the conditions. I am your groom." His blue eyes sparked as he spoke.

If she could have, she would have shot flames from her eyes. "You are not my groom. I'm not living my life guided by some wretched old superstition—"

"Why not? You're living it guided by some wretched old fears."

Her breath caught in her throat. Did he know? Had he guessed? Or had someone told him something they should not? The thought of such a betrayal grated at that private part of herself, the part even she never dared to face, and she accused, "You planned this."

He matched his nose to hers and in a low, intense tone, said, "Not I, lady. If I wanted to take you where you could not escape, I know of lonely places on the moor better suited to our kind of loving. No, for this, blame your own trusted servants."

Relief mixed with indignation. He didn't know. But— "What do you mean, 'our kind of loving'?"

Bold as you please, Hadden placed his palm over the warmth between her legs. "The kind without affection or kindness or love."

She grabbed for that hand. "It was never like that."

"You used me."

A just accusation, and she wanted to think of some clever answer. But how could she think when he ignored her attempts to break his grip and instead lightly and rhythmically pressed his fingers against her. His touch initiated a longing low in her belly, sweeping all other sentiment aside. "This won't solve anything," she said weakly.

"It will solve everything."

"How like a man to be so simple."

"How like a woman to complicate a simple situation." In a lightning-swift move, he slid his other hand up under her skirt.

"Please, will you—"

"I will," he pledged, crowding her even more. "I am."

She let go of his one hand and lunged for the other as it made its leisurely way up her leg, which was encased in pantalettes and stockings. The loose hand now moved to circle her breast. She grabbed for that. He nipped at her lips, then swept them with his tongue. She caught his ear between the pinchers of her fingers and pulled his head away. The hand beneath the skirt skimmed over the sensitive skin at the top of her thighs.

He swarmed over her, stinging her senses with unsubstantial nibbles and soothing kisses. As she took action on one front, he moved to another. She was always one step behind. She'd never confronted such resourceful tactics before, and she objected with silly squeaks of dismay. "Don't! Blast you. No! Not there! Not—"

Opening the slit in her drawers, he lightly touched her sensitive feminine bud, then abruptly, without finesse, buried his fingers inside her.

Her eyes opened wide. She flattened her spine against the wall. Lust—ah, it had to be lust—swept her away, tumbling her along like a pebble in a spring flood.

She'd been in a rage of disappointment and embarrassment for so long, she hadn't consciously thought about her body or his body or how they'd mingled so magnificently for one night two months ago. Yet her erotic dreams had come frequently, bringing her to lonely completion, and they must have kept her body in readiness, for his fingers slid in dampness.

Dampness. Just because the sight of him had excited her, and the scent of him fed her perceptions. But if her body was weak, her mind was not.

"I can't respond. Too many disturbing memories stand between us." After she spoke, it occurred to her he could have laughed. After all, she was obviously responding, regardless of any distress in her mind.

But he didn't laugh. Instead, he stroked her slowly, heating her more. "We have all kinds of memories between us. The days we worked together. The evenings spent playing chess and laughing. The night . . . darling, do you remember the night?"

His voice sounded smooth, warm, sincere, and intent on her and her only. With that voice alone, he could seduce her, and she flexed her thighs to shut him out.

That didn't work. Instead, the resultant pressure heightened her response.

And he noticed, for he was smiling. That warm, audacious, masculine smile that raised her ire and melted her bones.

"For a woman who not so long ago was a novice, you do this very well." He might have been petting a cat, taking pleasure in her sensual stretching.

"I don't respond on purpose." She hacked at his left arm where it lay on her legs, but he replied by wrapping his free arm around her and nuzzling below her ear. She jumped when his breath raised the little hairs, and jumped again when his tongue licked the sensitive skin. "Unfair," she snapped.

He didn't draw back, but only paused. "Why unfair?"

"Because you learned what I like, and you're using it against me."

He chuckled, his amusement wisps of cool air on her heated flesh. "I'm not using it against you." Between her legs, his fingers slid back and forth in a sweet friction. "I'm using it for you. And for me, too. You're going to give me what I want."

"What's that?" she snapped. "Satisfaction?"

"Yes." His thumb rubbed her until heat radiated along nerve ways already sizzling with fury. "*Your* satisfaction."

She wanted to give a crushing retort, she really did, but she was afraid that if she opened her mouth she would moan. He made her feel good. He made her feel *more*. More than last time, more than ever before, more and fabulous.

Shocking, to be so angry yet so aroused.

He wasn't shocked. He was aroused, too. She could tell by the rocking motion he used when he moved. The table rocked, his fingers rocked, he rocked, and something inside her responded to the rhythm she felt inside and out. Her muscles within rippled without her volition, and Hadden touched her ear with his tongue.

She convulsed.

She didn't give herself up to the soul-searing pleasure. No, she fought it, but neither Hadden nor her body gave her a choice. She shuddered, maintaining silence, clutching at the edge of the table. She wanted his relentless fingers to stop, but when they did, and pressed against her hard, she convulsed again.

"Beautiful," he whispered. "Just what I wanted."

She breathed in short gasps. "Just what . . . *you* wanted?"

He hadn't kissed her mouth or touched her breasts or massaged her skin. He hadn't taken time or done any of the things he'd done that first time when she'd crept into his bed. He'd just grabbed her between the legs, a crude, overgrown lout of a man, and in a few minutes brought her to ecstasy.

Not even the light of the setting sun softened the thrust of his chin or the impudence of his gaze. Such a deceptive thaw would have reassured her, and she wanted to make a statement, to refuse him in some definitive manner.

But this blatant assault had robbed her of wit, and the

sight of him irritated her more than she could bear. Incited her more than she could wish. So she shut her eyes against him.

Slowly he withdrew his fingers. He fumbled at her waist with that hand. The other hand moved along her back.

Her eyes popped open, and she grasped his wrists. "What are you doing?"

"I'm unhooking your gown."

"Why?"

"So I can do this." He slid her bodice down.

"No!" She clutched at the neckline, but he was opening her chemise, and she dropped the gown and tried to save her frail modesty.

Too late. He had her undone, and, cupping her breasts in his palms, he lifted them until they pressed together, then buried his head in the seam. His tongue flicked back and forth, wetting one breast, then the other, raising goose bumps on her flesh and bringing her nipples to hard, aching awareness—awareness that he hadn't yet given them the attention they thought they deserved.

Even her nipples rebelled against her control, and she clenched her fists and tried to smack him away before he realized how he aroused her.

That didn't help. Her gown dropped into her lap. He caught the stool with his foot and dragged it close, then knelt before her like a mortal before a goddess. He gave her belly the attention she wouldn't allow him to give her rigid nipples. A day's growth of whiskers rasped the tender skin.

Earlier, he hadn't touched her in any affectionate manner at all; he had simply crammed his fingers inside her and demanded a response. This time, he hadn't touched her most intimate place, and still she went under.

His mouth captured one nipple and he suckled, drawing her helplessly into orgasm. Grasping a handful of blond hair, she held him there and closed her eyes, muffling little whim-

pers against the back of her hand, riding passion as if she'd
been born to do so—or as if he'd been born to teach her.

Gradually, the spasm retreated. Laying his head against
her chest, he murmured, "You're glorious, lass." He stared
up at her as if he exulted in the spectacle of her flushed face
and trembling lips. "I want to be inside you; I want to see
you look like that every day."

She didn't know much right now, but she knew enough to
deny him. "No," she whispered.

"I could make you feel like that whenever you wanted. All
the time."

All the time? How did he think she would live through
that? "No," she said a little more strongly.

His lips, soft, wide, and generous, eased into the smile
that told her he knew what she was thinking. "We might die
of it, lass, but what a way to go." Standing, he smoothed a
kiss across her forehead. "And next time you perch on a
table, my love, you'll remember me. Won't you?"

Seven

With both hands on her waist, Hadden lifted Andra down. With one hand, he steadied her as she tried to hold her gown up, keep her balance, and channel strength into her shaky knees.

And her drawers and petticoats dropped around her ankles. She stared at them stupidly. How had that happened?

"That gown'll do you little good, all unfastened as it is." He pried the neckline out from between her fingers and let it fall. Holding her hands away, he spread them wide. "You look like a martyr in one of the old paintings. Are you prepared to be a martyr, darling?" His gaze dropped to her figure, barely concealed by a drooping chemise, by silk stockings and flower-bedecked garters. "For me?"

He was completely clothed and she was almost naked. He had brought her to ecstasy twice, and he still maintained control. Yet he stared, color sweeping up into his face, then ebbing away, stared so hard she could almost feel the heat of his gaze on the nipple that peeked through her chemise, on the swathe of bare thigh above her stockings. Oh, yes, he maintained mastery, but one little taunt, one glance of encouragement would bring him on her.

She almost did it.

But inviting him to take her meant more than just intercourse, and in some dim, still-functioning part of her mind, she knew it. She could do as her body urged and as he so obviously desired, and join their bodies in a celebration of the lust that scrambled her defenses whenever he was near. But if she invited him, she was inviting more than just lust. She would be saying "yes" to everything he wanted—marriage, children, a life spent growing closer until somehow, some way, sorrow ripped them apart.

No. She shuddered. She couldn't do it.

He saw the refusal to give in to what was between them, for his jaw tightened and in his eyes burned a blue, wrathful flame. He wanted more than she had to give, and for one moment she thought he would turn away.

Then he blinked, and his animosity was wiped away. He smiled, and tentatively she smiled back. He nodded, and she nodded back. It was, as she saw it, a tacit agreement that they could lust without pledge. Thank God, he had decided to be reasonable.

As the tension drained from her, she wobbled, and he interpreted that with deliberate inaccuracy. "You can't walk, poor thing." He picked her up, out of the puddle of clothing at her feet, and carried her across the room. As he stepped into the path of the setting sun, it bathed them in flaxen light. Then, as he continued across the chamber, sullen shadow caught them. Darkness would arrive soon, darkness with all its sorrows and its needs.

Yes, she needed him tonight. Only tonight.

His starched shirtfront and waistcoat prickled her bare skin, but she put her hands around his neck and hoped he read that as willingness, but not submission.

"See how I serve you?" he asked. "I am your valet, your

horse, your carriage. Whatever deed you wish performed, I will do, for you are my lady."

His extravagant homage fed a need in her soul, one she wouldn't acknowledge.

So she blushed, and as they came to stand above the bench arranged with the sheepskin, she wondered—why hadn't he removed her thin leather slippers, silk stockings, and flowered garters? She didn't want to ask; it would sound as if she were anxious to be naked. But she was naked, except for . . .

"Sit here."

Her eyes narrowed as he lowered her to the seat. *Had* he planned this? Yes, her servants, directed by the wicked Sima, had locked them in, but had he been in league with those devils?

Then the sensation of fleece, warm and soft, touched her bottom, and she forgot suspicion. Curious now, she sank farther into the curly coat. It yielded beneath her weight, then rebounded to caress her. When she moved on it, it tickled, and the lanolin in the wool smoothed her like lotion.

"You like it," he observed.

His tone gave her pause. He'd placed her here for a reason, to titillate her. If she admitted he'd succeeded, a bit more of her resistance had been chipped away.

Leaning down, he unlaced her chemise completely and pulled it off, leaving her in only her stockings. With his hand on her shoulder, he pushed her back until she lay flat and the pelt caressed her neck, her back, her bottom. Her feet still rested on the floor, like a lady riding sidesaddle.

But without being told, she knew the next thing he would want.

He would want her to put one leg on each side of the bench, and when she did, he would look.

He'd like it, she knew. He already liked it. He glowed

with satisfaction at having her doing his bidding. He glowed with the heat of desire. He glowed because he was a man and he spied victory, but he'd proved on the table that he considered it victory only if she won, too.

"You still have all your clothes on." He was armored; she was almost completely bare. If he removed his clothes, he'd be as self-conscious as she was.

At least, that's what she hoped until he stepped up beside her and said, "Unbutton me and take me out. Put your hands on me. Make me feel what you're feeling."

"Embarrassment?" she asked tartly.

A smile tugged at the corner of his mouth. "Is that *all* you're feeling?"

Of course, it wasn't. Conflicting emotions tore through her. She wanted him nude, and she feared him nude. She wanted to yield, but she resisted unreasonably.

And why did she resist? This was just lust.

"If you want something, Andra, you have to reach out and take it. If you want me, you have to take at least one step in my direction. Just one step."

She opened his breeches, fumbling with one button at a time. He stood patiently, waiting, watching. He wasn't wearing drawers, which shocked her and made her wonder if he ever wore them, or if he'd been so confident of her, he'd left them off.

Maybe it hadn't been a case of being confident of her, but of himself. Maybe he could give himself completely because he had no dark places in his soul, no ugly scars that he feared to show, no reason for the ghosts to haunt him like her lost menfolk haunted her.

It took all her nerve to slide his breeches down, and she realized—no, Hadden was hiding nothing. He was so proud of himself, all of himself, and he thought that when he'd cajoled her out of her shyness, she'd be as proud as he.

Well, maybe she would be—of her body. Her soul she'd keep sacrosanct, but he'd be satisfied with her body. She'd give him that, for now.

On that resolution, she ran her fingers along the length of him. She didn't know if she'd made him feel what she felt, but his half-closed eyes and indrawn breath bestowed optimism upon her. While he was distracted, she raised one foot onto the bench, keeping her knee bent and trying to strike a casual pose.

He noticed anyway. "I love these little flowers." As he knelt beside her, his fingers flirted with the rosette on her garter. "They give a hint of what's higher."

Gently he caressed the center of the rosebud, and that touch vibrated into the center of her. Almost without her volition, her hips rippled in answer.

"Move again," he urged. "Just watching you move makes me . . ." In a sudden flurry of activity, he stripped his clothes from his lower body.

From this range and this angle, everything about him looked bold and muscular. His lightly haired thighs gave witness to his years of riding; his rippling stomach proclaimed him a man of action; and . . . she traced one long muscle from his groin to his knee. "Aren't you going to remove your coat?"

"What?" He seemed distracted by her action.

She smiled a secretive smile and dared ask for another memory to store away. "If you would, I would be your valet."

That snapped his attention away from his gratification and back to her. "One more step?"

A big step, she thought as she cautiously sat up. The first step she had taken without suggestion or coaxing. Hadden seemed especially enthralled, his eyes following her, when she reached up and tugged hard to strip the coat from his shoulders. She peeled him free, then inspected his cravat, waistcoat and shirt. With her hands on his cravat, she said, "I shall expect a very large tip for this."

"You'll get one," he promised as she unclothed him completely.

He wasn't talking about money. When she'd flung his garments across the room and he was as bare as she, he said, "I would like you to try something different."

"Different?" This was all different.

"When you lie down, lie down face first, and feel the way the fleece caresses your breasts and your stomach."

"Face first? That won't work."

He fought a grin, and she knew she'd said something silly. "There are more ways to make love than there are nights to experiment with them. But I assure you, we will do our scientific best to attempt them all."

"Oh." As she thought about it, her hands wandered down his chest and cupped him once again. He was ready, very ready, and with the proper positioning . . . "Yes," she speculated. "It might be possible." It might be enjoyable, too. With elaborate nonchalance, she stretched herself facedown onto the bench.

"Move on it." He smoothed each one of her buttocks, then nudged her legs apart. When her feet settled on the floor, he urged again, "Move. It feels good."

She might have been a babe, exposed to his gaze, but she didn't feel like a babe, especially when she did as he instructed and moved. Her belly relished the comfort of the fleece while her nipples tightened with its stimulus. Her eyes closed as she concentrated on the sensations, and his soft laughter sounded from behind her. "That's it." His fingers explored her, brushing the short, curly hair over her nether lips, languidly parting them while she waited in aroused suspense. When she whimpered, he clutched her hips, moved closer, and held her still. Leaning into her, he penetrated her in a slow, firm, relentless motion, and when he had buried himself to the hilt, he said, "You're mine."

"No." But had he heard her? She could scarcely speak. Her system hummed, overloaded with the sense of abundance, of being more, of taking his span and returning joy.

"Can you feel me?" he asked.

"Yes."

"Really feel me? I'm not lying on you, you're not lying on me, and only one part of each of us is touching." He moved in her. "This part. There's only the pull to invoke passion for you."

In and out, in and out, he created friction in her flesh with his action, and friction in her mind with his words.

"Do you feel more if I touch you?"

His stomach pressed against her bottom, and he lifted her a little. His fingers winnowed into her thatch of hair, into her cleft. He found the button he sought and pressed.

Sensitized by expectancy, desire, by two climaxes already achieved, she bucked and almost succeeded in jumping away from him.

"Too much, Andra?" His touch lightened, became less than a whisper, yet louder than a drum. "Is that better?"

"Don't need you." She couldn't even articulate a whole sentence, and she tried again. "I don't . . ."

Catching her hand, he brought it down and replaced his own with hers. "You do it," he urged. "Show me what you like."

The touch of Hadden made her live, and his wholehearted approval of her craving made it grow like a flower deprived of water and now given a drink.

"I don't need more," she managed to say. Grabbing handfuls of the fleece, she spasmed, swept away by sensuality indulged.

"I can feel . . . everything. Your inner muscles"—he sucked in a breath—"they hold me, grip me." His fingers slid around her buttocks, directing their course, reaching where she would not. "Do it again."

His hoarse voice told the tale. He was trying to give her satisfaction while he retained dominion.

He infuriated her. How dare he retain control when all her vaunted discipline disappeared at the first sight of him?

Vengefully, she touched not herself, but him. She circled the base of his penis with her fingers and gripped him.

And he roared like a rutting stallion, carrying her with him as he half stood for his climax.

The motion brought her eye-to-eye with a small statue of a stallion, in a state of exaggerated excitement. For one horrified moment, she stared at the blatant fertility symbol in dismay.

Then another, cataclysmic climax swept her. Lowering her head, she buried her face in the sheepskin and muffled her cries in the fleece.

Eight

Hadden was an ordinary man with ordinary needs and an ordinary temperament. This is to say, he was kind, understanding, hardworking, good-tempered, and logical. Especially logical.

But as he and Andra collapsed to the sheepskin, it was too vividly borne in on him that, where she was concerned, his logic failed him. Her stubborn insistence on independence stirred him into a brew of frustration, anger, and sexual insanity.

In fact, every kind of insanity. And it was no wonder, because although Andra was generous, conscientious, and tender, she was at the same time the most unreasonable, emotional, immature creature on the face of the earth.

They straddled the bench, the sheepskin cradled them, and Andra took long breaths as the tension of orgasm slowly eased. He smoothed his hand down the curve of her spine. "Are you all right, darling?"

She rubbed her cheek against the fleece. "Hmm?"

He smiled. She was exhausted, and he felt almost sorry for her and almost remorseful himself for subjecting her to such a barrage of carnal stimulation.

But, damn it, how else was he supposed to make her sit still long enough to listen to him, except to tempt her and pleasure her until she was too limp to run away? As heaven was his witness, he'd tried everything on his first visit. He'd kissed. He'd cajoled. He'd promised. He'd begged. He'd tried sound reasoning, although in the entire history of civilization, such a tactic had never worked on a woman. Nothing succeeded. Andra fled commitment like a rabbit fled a hawk.

And what woman in her right mind would flee commitment with him? She had to be as insane as she made him.

Gently, regretfully, he separated their bodies. If it were up to him, he would stay inside her forever, bringing them both to passion's explosive release time and again. But the sun had set. Light was rapidly fading. He glanced at the closed trapdoor. He didn't know Sima's plan—hadn't even known she had one—but he would guess she had no intention of letting them out tonight. What was it she had said as she urged them to eat hearty? *'Tis a long time until mornin', and a fair climb t' the top o' the tower.*

He'd been too angry to guess her plot then . . . but if he had, he would have been a willing participant. Somehow, no matter how vigorously Andra denied him, he had been determined to find out what he had done—or said—that had frightened her.

His hand flexed where it rested on the sweet curve of her buttock. He'd found out, all right.

He'd shouldered a measly few of her responsibilities. He'd been fool enough to try and make himself indispensable.

Now, as the heat of the day died, she shivered, and he knew that, no matter how he wished to settle this matter of their union before she could recover her composure, he had to care for her while he could see well enough to do what must be done. "Rest, darling, and let me care for you."

Her head half rose off the bench in instinctive rejection.

He was taking responsibility again. Well, she would just have to get used to it. Pressing his hand to her cheek, he said again, "Rest."

She sighed and relaxed. Perhaps because she had begun to accept him as her consort. Most likely because she was too tired to struggle.

Swinging one leg over the bench, he stood, strode to the trapdoor, and pulled on it. As he expected, as he hoped, the lock held firm. They had to remain here for the night. He had the night to convince her she was his.

Working quickly, he gathered the lengths of cloth Andra had dropped beside the trunk. In the corner, he made a mattress of tartans and a bolster for their heads. He folded two at the foot to use as covers. Pressing his hand on the softness of the makeshift bed, he decided that once he placed Andra between him and the wall, she would not get to leave until they had finished this affair—to *his* satisfaction this time.

Making his way to Andra's side, he found her sitting, weaving just a little, wrapped in the sheepskin. "That's good." He slid his arm under her knees and across her back and lifted her. "We'll use this beneath us, too." Laying her down in the middle of the makeshift bed, he spread out the sheepskin, then climbed in beside her.

He felt her trying to gather herself to do something— what, he couldn't imagine, but it was always that way with Andra. Whatever he couldn't imagine, she did, and he wouldn't let the reins change hands now. So he pulled the covers over them and said, "It was just as you suspected."

"What was?"

Slipping his arm beneath her neck, he hugged her head to his chest. "The marriage kilt was just an excuse to come to you." He heard her draw breath, but he continued without pause. "I'm grateful to Lady Valéry for that, although I imagine she sent me off for no other reason than the fact she was heartily sick of having me stomp around her home. You see, the recording of Scottish traditions is the only thing that moves me to passion." With his hand on her back, he urged her closer. "Or, shall I say, the only thing that had *formerly* moved me to passion."

Andra cleared her throat before she spoke, and she sounded tremulous and unsure. "I haven't said, but I think it's a noble thing you do."

It didn't surprise him that she avoided any mention of his ardor for her, and it much pleased him that she snuggled against him without a struggle. Her mind had not accepted the truth of her new circumstances, but her body understood very well. "I don't know that loving you is noble, since I have no choice, but it is challenging."

Her hand hovered over his chest, touching down several times before settling on the place over his heart. "I didn't mean—"

"The thing is, I couldn't comprehend why you had rejected me in such a callous manner, but now that you've explained, I see the problem."

"I explained?" Her fingers clutched the hair on his chest.

Gently, he loosened them. "So—references. I'm willing to get you references."

"For what?" Her voice rose a pitch.

"To say that I am a steady man, not given to flights of fancy nor fits of infatuation." The darkness of a Scottish night in the midst of the Highlands was blacker than any Hadden had ever encountered, and that darkness cloaked the tower now. He could see nothing but the square of star-be-speckled night sky through the window, but he read Andra's confusion and fear without difficulty. "Lady Valéry, who has known me since I came into her household at the age of nine, would give me such a reference."

"Lady Valéry."

Andra's parrotlike performance made him grin. He'd

turned her upside down. Now he was shaking her, and if he were lucky, when she regained her balance she would see their future as he saw it. Discreetly keeping all amusement out of his tone, he said, "You've met Lady Valéry, I believe, on one of her jaunts through the Highlands, and would admit that she is a woman of honor."

She squirmed. "Of course, but I don't understand why you think these references would be important to me."

He ignored that. She did know, and if she wanted to play the dunce, then he could do the same. "I can also offer Sebastian Durant, Viscount Whitfield. Now you might not know him, but I assure you—"

"I met him at the christening of the MacLeod son."

"Ah." She knew Ian and Alanna. Another link between them. "Ian MacLeod is my cousin."

"He's charming."

Hadden could hear the smile in her voice, and he didn't like it. He didn't like it one bit. "Only if you like dark-haired, handsome men with a shade too much seductiveness."

She slid one leg across and nestled her calf between his. "I didn't think he was *too* seductive."

"I had to thrash Ian once when he tried to take advantage of my sister." Hadden caught her thigh and pulled her tightly against him. "I can do it again."

"So you're given to violence."

She still wore her garters, he realized, and he untied the one. "I defend my own."

She gave a funny little trill, and he realized she was giggling. "He's married, Hadden, and he can't take his gaze off his wife. If you trounce him, he'd likely wonder why."

"Humph." He knew she was right. Ian didn't give a damn about anything except Alanna and their children and Fionnaway Manor. But, damn it . . .

"Viscount Whitfield?" she prompted.

He couldn't allow himself to be distracted by an absurd

surge of jealousy. Not when his goal loomed so close. "Sebastian." He rubbed his chin on the top of her head and tried hard to focus. "One introduction to Sebastian, that's all it takes, and you know he is a hard man with very little tolerance for injustice."

"He scared me," she admitted. "He's too intense, and he watches his wife—"

"My sister."

Andra's head came up so fast, she cracked his jaw with her skull. "She's your sister?" She rubbed her head. "Ow."

"Yes. Ow." He rubbed his chin. She was communicating, talking about his family, his friends, and not resisting him with every fiber of her being. A cracked jaw was a small price to pay.

"Of course." She sounded excited. "You look like her! The hair and the eyes and the . . . you're both handsome."

"Well-formed?"

"Extremely," she answered. "But unlike you, your sister is not conceited."

"Ow," he said again, although he wasn't offended. She was teasing, treating him as normally as she had before he'd uttered those fatal words—*marry me*. It was another breakdown in her defenses, and he began to think that perhaps, just perhaps, his plan would succeed. "So Sebastian is my brother-in-law, and you might think he is prejudiced in my favor. But I assure you, he detests the Fairchilds—remember, I told you the family is the most dissolute bunch of blackguards you'll find this side of Hell—and if I were like them, he would have no compassion for my suit. He would tell you I was unworthy and blast me for daring to court a lady of integrity. But he helped me go to university, and since then I've worked with him and for him, and you can trust him to tell you the truth."

He paused and waited until she acknowledged, "I'm sure that he would tell nothing but the truth."

"Exactly. And finally, I must offer my sister. There is no one else alive who has known me my whole life, so it has to be her."

"For what reason?"

"Mary will gladly testify that I have never proposed to a woman before, not even when I was five and fancied myself quite a ladies' man."

"Oh."

It was a tiny sound, and one he found infinitely fulfilling. "There's Ian and Alanna I can call on to write me a reference. And the men and women I met and worked with in India, although those letters will take time to reach us, but all of them will say much the same thing."

"That you're not flighty in matters of the heart, and that you can be depended upon?"

"Very good." He cradled her in both his arms, holding her as close as he could in the hope that, if the words did not reach her, the closeness would. "I will not leave you, no matter how you try to drive me away. I'm not your father or your brother or your uncle; I'm Hadden Fairchild, and I've never loved another woman, Andra, and I never will."

She didn't say anything. She didn't return his vow of love, or say that she would read his references, or that she believed that he would remain with her always.

Yet neither did she protest his insight that the abandonment of her menfolk had created her terror of the bonds of affection.

He wasn't satisfied, of course. What he sought was her absolute surrender. But he couldn't force that, and he knew that he'd planted a new thought inside her head. That he was the man she could depend on.

Andra heard Hadden's breath deepen as he slid into sleep. She noted that his grip on her did not loosen, and she was reminded of that other night they had shared. Even in the depths of sleep, the man held what he cherished. Did she believe he would do the same in the light of day when faced with the hardships of the life she led? He was a fine, well-traveled English gentleman, used to amenities. Even if he were to throw his fortune into Castle MacNachtan, it would be years before the conditions would be more than just tolerable. Did she believe he would remain with her regardless of the rugged living conditions? More important, could he shoulder the responsibilities of being her husband without shirking? And when they fought, as all married folk must, would he not flee back to London, but still come to her bed and kiss her good night?

She didn't know the answers. Not really. Not even if she accepted the references he urged on her. Not even if she considered the man himself and all she knew of him. No matter what decision she made, she might lose.

Could she bear that? To perhaps once again see the back of a man she loved as he rode down the road away from her?

But one thing was certain: if she rejected his suit, she would see the back of him anyway.

With a sigh, she eased herself out of his embrace and slid over the top of him.

He came awake immediately and grabbed at her. "What are you doing?"

It might not be that easy to reject him, she realized. In fact—she bit her lip against a laugh—he'd even taken the extreme measure of spreading those fertility goddesses throughout the tower. If they worked . . .

"Andra," he snapped, "where are you going?"

"I'm cold. I'm going to get another cover."

He still held her as he debated, but he must have decided she couldn't escape, for his fingers slid away and he grudgingly gave permission. "Don't be long."

"Gracious," she muttered as she made her way across the room, and when she came back, tartan in hand, she wasn't surprised when his hands came up to meet her.

*   *   *

Morning sunshine and the babble of voices assaulted Hadden, and he lay with his eyes and ears closed tightly against them. He didn't care to be assaulted after a night spent on the floor on a makeshift bed trying to sleep with one eye open in case Andra made a dash for it.

She hadn't. After that one trip after an extra blanket, she had curled up at his side and slept the sleep of the innocent.

Blasted woman. After waking up a few dozen times, he would have welcomed a wrestling match.

Now he was hungry and grumpy. Andra still warmed his side, so who the hell was running up and down the stairs and talking in those loud tones?

He opened his eyes—and made a grab for the tartans. "Mary, what are you doing here?"

"I could ask you the same thing," his loving sister answered.

Her critical blue gaze made him aware of his expanse of bare chest, and he glared at her as he pulled up the blankets. Then his gaze shifted to encompass Sebastian and Ian, and he prudently arranged the tartans over the already-covered Andra, adjusting them to her chin. "Where did everyone come from?" His mind leaped from suspicion to suspicion. "Is this Lady Valéry's doing?"

"A woman of her age can't climb the stairs." Alanna held Ian's arm and stroked the mound of her belly. "But she sent you her regards, and she invites you to bring your complaints to her."

"If I were the lady Andra's brother, I'd be forced to beat you for debauching so gentle a maid." Sebastian rubbed his chin as if remembering a former trouncing.

"I'd help." Ian rubbed his fist into his palm as if the thought pleased him.

Both the men owed him a drubbing, but Andra was tapping his shoulder, and Hadden didn't have time for silly, manly challenges.

"Hadden," Andra whispered, "what are all these people doing here?"

He almost groaned. How was he going to explain this to her when he couldn't explain it to himself? The tower could scarcely contain the crowd; his relatives, some Scottish dignitaries he barely recognized, and Sima, Douglas, and the house servants.

"I couldn't venture to say," he mumured.

Taking in the scene, she decreed, "We need some privacy." With careful deliberation, she reached out, grasped the edge of one of the tartans, and pulled it over their heads.

The plaid was so thin that the light leaked through, and he could see Andra on the bolster beside him—Andra with her wild-woman hair and sleepy eyes and puckish smile.

"There it is," he said inconsequentially.

She looked puzzled. "What?"

"Your smile. I was afraid you'd lost it."

Her smile trembled and grew, and her eyes began to shine with the kind of light that gave him a smidgen of hope. "Are they here for the wedding?" she whispered.

My God, was she talking about what he thought she was talking about?

"Our wedding," she clarified. "A wedding is usually the only reason you'll see my cousin Malcolm anywhere near Castle MacNachtan. He's afraid I'll ask for money. And a wedding is free food and drink." Hadden was still too dumbfounded to speak, so she added, "I saw his whole family out there. He's very thrifty, you ken."

Hadden caught her hand in his. "Andra, I swear I never planned this."

"I'll acquit you."

"I seized the chance I was offered, and without regret, too, to tell you—"

She put her finger over his lips. "And tell me you did, in more ways than one. It's a lot of sense you made, Hadden

Fairchild, and while I am still afraid, I love you enough to take the gamble."

His heart, frozen and constricted for too long, expanded with joy. Taking her wrists, he reeled her in. "Andra . . ."

"If you'd look, you'd see that I've already accepted your proposal."

He glanced around but could see nothing. Nothing except—he laughed aloud—over his head, the black and red and blue MacNachtan marriage kilt.

On a recent trip to Scotland, my family and I went looking for Brigadoon.

We didn't find it. The mythical village that appears out of the mist only one day out of every hundred years proved elusive to us, but Scotland holds many treasures. In the Lowlands we found Lady Valéry's eighteenth-century manor (or one much like I imagined), the original setting of Mary Fairchild's story in *A Well Pleasured Lady*. On the wild west coast we explored an estate much like the one Ian Fairchild won—along with his wife—in *A Well Favored Gentleman*. Finally, in the midst of the Highlands, we discovered a moldering castle, and I remembered, Mary's brother Hadden, a man badly in need of a story. When I came home to Texas, the stones of that castle rose in my mind, and I created Andra to be a mate to the incomparable Hadden.

I hope you enjoyed this tale, and as well as the Fairchild tales.

And I'll see you in Brigadoon.

Rose in Bloom

Stephanie Laurens

One

Ballynashiels, Argyllshire

June 17, 1826

"What the devil are you *doing here?"*

Duncan Roderick Macintyre, third earl of Strathyre, stared, stupefied, at the willowy form bent over the piano stool in his drawing room. Sheer shock, liberally laced with disbelief, held him frozen on the threshold. A lesser man would have goggled.

Rose Millicent Mackenzie-Craddock, bane of his life, most insistent, persistent thorn in his flesh, lifted her head and looked up—and smiled at him, with the same, slightly lopsided smile with which she'd taunted him for decades. Her large, light-brown eyes twinkled.

"Good morning, Duncan. I'd heard you'd arrived."

Her soft, lilting brogue washed over him, a warm caress beneath his skin. His gaze locked on the expanse of creamy breasts now on display, Duncan stiffened—all over. The reaction was as much a surprise as finding Rose here—and every bit as unwelcome. His jaw locked. Fingers clenched about the doorknob, he hesitated, then frowned, stepped into the room and shut the door.

And advanced on his nemesis with a prowling gait.

Holding the sheets of music she'd been sorting, Rose straightened as he neared—and wondered why the devil she couldn't breathe. Why she felt as if she did not dare take her eyes from Duncan's face, shift her gaze from his eyes. It was as if they were playing tag and she needed to read his intent in the cool blue, still as chilly as the waters of the loch rippling beyond the drawing-room windows.

They weren't children any longer, but she sensed, quite definitely, that they were still playing some game.

Excitement flashed down her nerves; anticipation pulled them taut. The room was large and long; even with her gaze fixed on Duncan's face, she had ample time to appreciate the changes the last twelve years had wrought. He was larger, for a start—much larger. His shoulders were wider; he was at least two inches taller. And he was harder—all over—from his face to the long muscles of his legs. He looked dangerous—he *felt* dangerous. An aura of male aggression lapped about him, tangible in his stride, in the tension investing his long frame.

The lock of black hair lying rakishly across his forehead, the harsh angularity of his features and his stubbornly square chin—and the male arrogance in his blue eyes—were the same, yet much sharper, more clearly defined. As if the years had stripped away the superficial softness and exposed the granite core beneath.

He halted a mere two feet away. His black brows were drawn down in a scowl.

Forced to look up, Rose tilted her head—and let her lips curve, again.

His scowl grew blacker. "I repeat"—he bit off the words—"what the *devil* are you doing here?"

Rose let her smile deepen, let laughter ripple through her voice. "I'm here for Midsummer, of course."

His eyes remained locked on hers; his scowl eased to a frown. "Mama invited you."

It wasn't a question; she answered nevertheless. "Yes. But I always visit every summer."

"You do?"

"Hmm." Looking down, she dropped the lid of the piano stool, then shuffled the music sheets together and stacked them on the piano.

"I must have missed you."

She looked up. "You haven't been here all that much these last years."

"I've been tending to business."

Rose nodded and quelled a craven impulse to edge toward the windows, to put some space between them. She had never been frightened of Duncan before; this couldn't be fright she felt now. She tossed her head back and looked him in the eye. "So I've heard. Away in London, resurrecting the Macintyre fortunes."

He shrugged. "The Macintyre fortunes are well and truly resurrected." His gaze sharpened. "And I haven't forgotten what you did twelve years ago."

Twelve years ago, when last they'd met. He'd been a painfully fashionable twenty-three, with the highest, starchiest shirtpoints north of the border. Even south of it. She hadn't been able to resist. Half an hour before he'd gone up to dress for his mother's Hunt Ball, she'd slipped into his room and steamed all his collars. He'd been forced to appear slightly less than sartorially perfect. Unrepentant still, Rose grinned. "If only you could have seen yourself . . ."

"Don't remind me." His gaze searched her face, then returned to her eyes. His narrowed. "You're twenty-seven—why haven't you married?"

Rose met his gaze directly, and coolly raised her brows.

"Because I haven't yet met a man I wish to marry, of course. But you're thirty-five, and you haven't married either—although that's about to change, I understand."

Exasperation colored his frown. His lips thinned. "Possibly. I haven't yet made up my mind."

"But you've invited her here, with her parents, haven't you?"

"Yes—no. Mama invited them."

"At your instruction." When she got no response beyond a further tightening of his lips, Rose dared a teasing grin. She wasn't entirely sure it was safe to play her old game, but the old tricks still seemed to work. The change was infinitesimal, yet he tensed in response to her smile.

She'd known Duncan literally all her life. As the only child of aging and wealthy parents, her childhood had been one of indulgence and cossetting, but also of severe restrictions. As her father's heiress, she'd been groomed and watched over; only during the summers, during the long blissful weeks she had spent here, at Ballynashiels, had she been allowed to be herself. Her wild, carefree, hoydenish self. Her mother had been a close friend and cousin of Duncan's mother, Lady Hermione Macintyre; together with her parents, she'd spent every summer of her childhood here, in precious freedom. After her mother's death five years ago, it had been natural to continue her visits, with or without her father; Lady Hermione was a surrogate mother and a dearly loved haven of sense in a world that was, too often for Rose's taste, governed by sensibility.

She did not have a "sensible" bone in her body, a fact to which Duncan could attest. Eight years her senior, he'd been the only other child here through those long-ago summers; naturally, she'd attached herself to him. Being insensible—or, more accurately, stubborn, willful and not easily cowed—she'd ignored all his attempts to dislodge her from his heels.

She'd dogged his every step; she was quite sure she knew more about Duncan than anyone else alive.

Which meant that, more than anyone else, she'd been aware of his driving obsession, his desire to be the best, to perform to the highest standards, to achieve the very best in all things—the perfectionism that drove him. And, being her irreverent self, she had never been able to resist teasing him, pricking and prodding him whenever his obssession overstepped the bounds of her trenchant common sense.

Teasing "Duncan the perfect" had become first a game, then a habit. Through the years, she'd perfected her skills, guided by the insight no other had ever had of him; her ability to successfully strike through his defenses was now the strongest memory either had of the other.

Which explained his black scowl and his watchful wariness. She couldn't, however, explain the tension that held him, the tension that tightened her own nerves, restricting her breathing and setting her skin flickering. *That* was entirely new.

He still stood before her, frowning down at her. She raised a haughty brow. "I gather your last years have been crowned with success; from all I've heard, you've reason to feel quite smug."

With a light shrug, he dismissed it—the endeavor to which she knew he'd devoted all his energies for the last ten years. "Things fell into place. The future of Ballynashiels is now assured. That was what I wanted—it was what I achieved."

Rose smiled warmly, sincerely. "You should enjoy your success. There aren't many estates in the Highlands so comfortably underwritten."

On inheriting both title and estate, Duncan had accepted, as few of his peers had, that the rugged country of the Argyll would not provide more than a subsistence. In typical fashion, driven by his need to excell, he'd taken the bit between his teeth and plunged into business. According to the pundits, he was now fabulously wealthy, with a solid income deriving from trade with the Indies and a sizable nest egg derived from shrewd speculation. Rose was not at all surprised. Knowing as she did his devotion to his heritage, and the inherent responsibilities, she felt a subtle pride in his achievements. At a time when many Highland estates were suffering, Ballynashiels was safe.

For that, she was truly grateful.

Her eyes still on his, stubbornly ignoring the inner voice clamoring that before her stood danger, she tilted her head and let amused understanding light her eyes. "So, now Ballynashiels is secure, it's time to get a wife?"

A muscle in his jaw locked; his eyes narrowed.

Duncan fought to concentrate on her words, struggled to find some quip to put her in her place or, better yet, send her fleeing from the house. His reeling mind could supply neither. He'd never before understood what being "bowled over" entailed—now he knew.

And it was Rose who'd done it.

He wasn't sure if he should feel horror at that discovery, or whether, given their history, he should have expected it. From the instant when, bent over the piano stool, she'd looked up at him, his wits had scrambled. Not, perhaps, surprising, considering the view he'd had. He doubted many men could think clearly when faced with a view like that.

Rose, his little thorn, had grown. Bloomed. In the most amazing way.

Since letting go of the doorknob, he'd kept his eyes glued to hers. It hadn't helped. He was acutely aware of the soft curves of her breasts, warm ivory mounds enticingly displayed by the scooped neckline of her morning gown. In soft, pale-green muslin sprigged with tiny gold leaves, the gown clung to shapely hips and long, sleek legs. It took real effort not to drop his gaze and check just how long those

legs were; his wayward mind insistently reminded him that
Rose had always been tall.

She'd been gangly. Awkward. A scrawny ugly duckling,
with huge, soft brown eyes far too large for her face, lips too
wide for it, too, wild hair that had usually resembled a bird's
nest, straight brown brows too severe for a female and a nose
too upturned and far too pert for beauty. And a barbed tongue
that had stung him far too often.

Keeping his expression unchanged, Duncan inwardly
cursed. Who would have imagined all those oddly disparate
parts would, with the years, meld into the vision before him?
Her eyes were as before, but now they fitted her face, the
perfect vehicles for her always-direct gaze. Her brows were
still straight, uncompromising, but their line was now softened by her hair, still faintly frizzy but so abundant and rich
in color, it made any male with blood in his veins itch to sink
his hands into it. She wore it loosely braided and coiled; he
wondered how long it was.

And despite the insistence of his common sense, telling
him to move back, to put more distance between them so he
could no longer detect her perfume—a subtle blend of violet
and rose—if he moved farther back, he doubted he could
stave off the urge to let his eyes feast on her figure, no longer
scrawny in the least. Every curve was full, ripe, alluring.
And those legs—his imagination was already running riot,
but he had a sneaking feeling the reality might prove even
more interesting.

Even more arousing.

Which was the last thing he needed; he was in pain as it was.

Yet remaining so close to her, within easy reach, wasn't
any cure. Her lips, despite her teasing, lopsided smile, were
temptation incarnate. No longer overlarge, they were generous—not just feminine but womanly, their full curves
promising all manner of sensual delights. And as for the
teasing, provocative light in her eyes . . . a burning urge

gripped him, compelling him to raise his hand, frame her face and kiss her, taste her . . .

And that way lay madness. This was Rose, the thorn in his flesh.

Her words finally penetrated the fog of lust shrouding his mind; Duncan inwardly groaned. Nothing had changed.

He was acutely uncomfortable, and growing more so with every passing second.

Which meant he was in trouble. Serious trouble.

He'd returned to Ballynashiels with his intended in tow, only to find . . .

"Damn it—why *aren't* you married?" And safe beyond his reach, some other man's problem, not his. "Where on God's earth have you been spending the years, in a convent?"

Predictably, she smirked—a little twist of her lips that could bring a man to his knees—and smoothly glided past him. "Oh, I've been busy enough in that sphere, but there's been nothing that's taken my fancy."

Duncan smothered a snort; he could just imagine. Rose was an heiress; her suitors had to be legion. He swung to watch her as she halted before the windows—oh, yes, her legs were long . . . long, long, long . . . He swallowed. And scowled. "Your father's too lenient—he should have seen you married years ago."

She shrugged lightly. "I've spent the last nine Seasons in Edinburgh and Glasgow—it's hardly my fault if the gentlemen haven't measured up."

Half turning her head, she sent an artful glance his way; it began at his boots and traveled slowly—very slowly—upward . . . By the time she reached his face, Duncan felt like strangling her. After he'd ravished her.

Abruptly he swung away, fervently praying that she hadn't noticed his reaction, unfortunately visible given that he was dressed in skintight inexpressibles. Ready to greet his intended.

"I'm going to see Mama." Glancing back, he saw Rose's brows fly high. "How long are you staying?"

She considered him; he prayed a good deal harder. Then she shrugged. "We haven't decided. At least until Midsummer."

Duncan frowned. "Your father's here?"

She hesitated, then inclined her head.

Duncan nodded curtly and strode for the door. "I'll see you later."

He would much rather not see her ever again, but that, he knew, was unlikely.

When it came to Rose, fate had never been kind.

"Damn it, Mama! *Why* did you have to invite Rose?"

Duncan shut his mother's dressing-room door with unnecessary force.

Lady Hermione Macintyre, seated before her dressing table rouging her cheeks, blinked at him in the mirror. "Really, dear! What a peculiar question. The Mackenzie-Craddocks have always visited in summer; you know that."

She returned her attention to her cheeks, unperturbed by the sight of her only offspring pacing like a trapped leopard at her back. After a moment, she murmured, "Besides, I thought you wanted a goodly number of family and friends here, so the arrival of Miss Edmonton and her parents wouldn't appear too particular?"

"I'm perfectly well aware I gave you a *carte blanche*. I just didn't expect to find Rose gracing the drawing room." Bent over the piano stool.

Lady Hermione sighed fondly. "The dear girl offered to sort the music sheets—they were in a such a muddle."

"She's done it," Duncan snapped. And shattered his complacency, and shot his plans to hell.

"I really can't see," Lady Hermione continued, lifting a brush to her lips, "why you're so exercised by Rose's presence."

Duncan uttered a silent prayer in appreciation of small mercies. He missed the shrewd glance his mother directed his way.

"Besides," she continued, "in the circumstances, I wanted to meet Mr. Penecuik."

"Penecuik?" Frowning, Duncan halted. "Who's he?"

Lady Hermione opened her eyes wide. "Why, the gentleman Rose is considering marrying. Didn't she tell you?"

Duncan felt his face blank; his emotions blanked, too, as if they'd fallen into a void. Then he remembered Rose's words on marriage. He glanced sharply at his mother. "She's considering accepting him?"

"Indeed." Lady Hermione nodded. "She'd be a fool not to—and Rose was never a fool."

"Humph!" Duncan resumed his pacing. After a long moment, he asked, "So, who is he, this Penecuik?"

"Mr. Jeremy Penecuik, son of Joshua Penecuik, who is first cousin to the duke of Perth. Mr. Penecuik the elder is the duke's sole heir, which means, in time, Jeremy will inherit the dukedom. So Rose has quite a decision to make. It's not every day a girl is offered a dukedom with both wealth and establishments intact. Perth is doing quite well, I understand."

"Hmm." His gaze on the rug, Duncan paced on.

Lady Hermione laid down her brush and peered at her face in the mirror. "You needn't fear being called upon to pass judgement on Mr. Penecuik. Rose is quite capable of making up her own mind."

"Given she's twenty-seven and still unwed, I'm surprised you don't think she needs a push." Duncan glanced at his mother.

Turning on her stool, she met his gaze calmly. "Nonsense, dear. Rose may be twenty-seven, but she's hardly on the shelf. Nor, if I read the signs aright, is she likely to be for long."

A fist clutched his heart—Duncan told himself it was anticipation, anticipation that Rose would soon be a thorn in someone else's side.

"But that's enough of Rose." Lady Hermione smiled. "The lady you're considering making your countess will arrive any minute. That's what you should be concentrating on."

That *was* what he was concentrating on—Miss Clarissa Edmonton's arrival, and all the disasters that might ensue. Very likely *would* ensue now that Rose was here—now that Rose was as she was. She might finally succeed in driving him demented; that had always seemed her principal goal in life.

Teeth gritted, Duncan strode to the window and pushed aside the lace curtain. And glimpsed a flash of reflected light. A second later, he saw a heavy traveling carriage rounding the far end of the loch.

"They're here."

He delivered the words as if prophesying their doom; his mother calmly turned back to her mirror.

Duncan watched the carriage draw nearer and dismissed the wild plans he'd been formulating to rid himself of Rose and her disturbing presence. Fate had left him no time, no room to maneuver. He was going to have to greet his intended and decide whether or not she was, indeed, the lady he wanted to wife—with Rose Millicent Mackenzie-Craddock, ten times more distracting than she'd ever been, looking on. In glee, he had not a doubt.

What he had done to deserve such a fate, he had absolutely no idea.

By the time the carriage rocked to a halt before the front steps, Duncan was on the front porch. He strolled down the marble steps and met Mr. Edmonton as he descended.

A short, rotund gentleman, Charles Edmonton shook his hand, his expression noticeably easing as he took in the magnificence of Ballynashiels. Masking his cynicism, Duncan greeted him urbanely, then gave Mrs. Edmonton his arm from the carriage.

A matronly woman dressed in the height of fashion, she looked up before her foot touched the marble; her expression was even more transparent than her husband's. After a quick scan of the long facade, she beamed at Duncan. "I do declare, my lord, your home is quite the most imposing house I've ever seen."

"How kind of you to say so." Duncan smoothly handed her on to her husband and turned to give his arm to the vision that next filled the carriage doorway.

A princess in pale blue, Miss Clarissa Edmonton was the epitome of feminine perfection. She was slim and slender, with sleek, pale-blond hair neatly gathered in a fashionable chignon. Of average height, she was classically beautiful, with regular, perfectly symmetrical features set in an oval face. Her complexion was unblemished alabaster, her eyes the same cornflower blue as her gown.

She met Duncan's eyes and smiled sweetly, demurely. Putting her hand in his, she let him help her to the ground. Then she looked at the house. Her perusal took a good deal longer than her parents'; Duncan couldn't help wondering if she was counting the windows.

Then she smiled up at him. "Why—it's so big, I hadn't imagined . . ." A graceful gesture filled in the rest of her sentence.

He returned her smile and offered his arm. "My mother is waiting in the drawing room."

She was, with at least half the company she had assembled to celebrate the Midsummer revels.

"So very glad you could join us," Lady Hermione informed the Edmontons. She smiled graciously at Clarissa. "After all Strathyre has told me, I've been positively eager to make your acquaintance. I do hope you enjoy your stay here.

We'll be having a ball on Midsummer's Eve—it's a major celebration in these parts."

Duncan listened as his mother rattled on, grateful that she refrained from describing the details of the local Midsummer revels. Dancing around the Midsummer's Eve bonfire was a traditional activity for all the young people, and if, as the fire died, some slipped away into the shadows, well . . . that was life. It was expected that, in August and September, there'd be a rash of unexpected weddings—and that was life, too. Life in the Highlands—brash, braw and simple.

Midsummer was a time for mating, a time when weddings were arranged by the simplest of criteria.

That was not, however, how his wedding would be arranged; the fact that it was Midsummer was merely coincidence.

His mother introduced the Edmontons to a range of relatives and family friends. Duncan listened with half an ear—until she came to Rose. Focusing abruptly, he saw Rose smile, assured and confident, at Clarissa.

"An unexpected pleasure, Miss Edmonton." Rose's smile deepened as she released Clarissa's fingers. "Though perhaps I may call you Clarissa, and you can call me Rose, as it seems we're the only unmarried ladies present."

Her gaze lifted to Duncan's face; only he saw the laughing, teasing light in her eyes. Tearing his gaze free, he scanned the room—and heard, from beside him, Clarissa reply, "Indeed, yes. I would be very grateful for your company, Miss . . . I mean, Rose."

Stunned by the revelation that his mother, who most certainly knew better, had neglected to invite any of his younger relatives to provide screening company for himself and Clarissa, Duncan looked down in time to see Clarissa smile sweetly at Rose. "I gather you know the house quite well—I'll look to you for help in finding my way, if I may."

Rose smiled. "Indeed—"

"Clarissa—" Duncan cut in.

"Rose?"

That last had them all turning as a slender gentleman of about thirty joined them. He was quietly elegant, with wavy brown hair, a soft, almost feminine mouth and an easygoing expression.

Rose turned her smile on him. "Jeremy." She let him take her hand and place it on his sleeve. "Allow me to present you to Strathyre." She looked up and met Duncan's eyes. "Mr. Jeremy Penecuik."

Obliged to nod politely and shake Jeremy Penecuik's hand, Duncan fought down an urge to dismiss him instead. He had enough distractions already to hand without the additional irritation of seeing Jeremy Penecuik draw Rose close, as if he had some recognized claim on her.

Aware that in the present company, he could not scowl— not at Rose or Penecuik—he was forced to stand silently while Clarissa and Rose chatted. Penecuik contributed the odd observation; for his part, Duncan said nothing at all. While one part of his mind would dearly have loved to commandeer the conversation, and spirit Clarissa out of Rose's orbit, another part of his mind—the dominant part of his mind—was engrossed in yet another discovery.

It was impossible to assess Clarissa with Rose standing by, because, if Rose was within twenty feet of him, his attention deflected to her.

Clarissa, at nineteen, perfect princess that she was, stood not a chance against the attraction Rose exuded, the earthy sensuality of a mature woman, compounded, in his case, by memories legion, by shared childhoods—and a soul-deep remembrance of the timbre of her voice.

It had always had that huskiness, soft and deep, like a lover's caress. Age had perfected the siren's song; the years had heightened his sensitivity.

So he stood there, silently, and listened to her voice, to the lilting brogue which, he suddenly realized, was the sound of home to him.

His butler, Falthorpe, rescued him from total confusion by announcing that luncheon was served.

Luncheon, with Rose and Penecuik at the other end of the table, allowed Duncan to refocus on the matter at hand: Clarissa Edmonton. As she and her parents were clearly taken with the house, he seized the opportunity and offered to take them on a tour; they left directly from the luncheon room.

He made the tour a lengthy one. As they were returning through the east wing, Mrs. Edmonton commented, "It's such a monstrous pile, it must be hard to keep it heated in winter."

Duncan shrugged lightly. "There are fireplaces in every room."

"Anyway, Mama"—Clarissa flashed a smile at her mother—"it's not as if Duncan would spend much of the winter here. There's the Season, and all his business to attend to in London, after all."

She turned her bright, rather eager expression on Duncan; he responded with a calm, noncommittal smile.

And wondered whether he should explain that, contrary to Clarissa's expectations, now he'd secured Ballynashiels' future, he expected to spend all his days—not just the winter—within the arms of the narrow valley that held his home.

They passed a large window and he glanced out—and saw the loch, wind-whipped blue under the wide sky, saw the tall crags encircling the fertile plain bisected by the narrow ribbon of the river that both fed and drained the loch. In the center of the loch lay an island on which the remains of a turreted castle, first home of the Macintyres in this place, stood surrounded by the greens of birch and hazel.

His ancestors had lived in this valley for generations; he

would live here, too. With his wife, and the family they would raise.

The view fell behind as they strolled on; Duncan glanced down at Clarissa, eyes wide as she took in the old tapestries, the velvet curtains, the portraits of Macintyres long gone. He had chosen her because she was perfect—perfect in face, perfect in figure, perfect in deportment, in her connections, her breeding, in her ability to be the perfect wife. He'd chosen her in London, and she had been perfect there.

But here?

Looking ahead, he reflected that he had said nothing, made no promises, no commitment. Couples like the Edmontons, well-connected but not wealthy, knew how things were done: when the visit ended, if he made no offer, they would shrug and move on to the next likely candidate.

There would be no drama; he knew beyond doubt that there were no feelings involved, not on his part or Clarissa's. When he'd chosen her, he'd counted that in her favor, that her feelings would never go beyond mere affection, so she would not interfere too deeply in his life.

Looking ahead, he inwardly sighed. He'd learned over his years of trading to deal with mistakes decisively, to recognize them quickly, admit them and go forward. They reached the top of the stairs; his expression impassive, he started down. "All the reception rooms bar the ballroom are on the ground floor."

He showed them the formal dining room, then took them on a circuit of the well-stocked library. Exiting by one of the lesser doors, he led the way down a secondary corridor. And heard laughter coming from behind the door at its end.

Rose's laughter, warm, infectious—he recognized it instantly. It was followed immediately by the rumble of a male voice.

Duncan turned left and steered the unsuspecting Edmontons into the conservatory.

"Oh!" Clarissa clapped her hands at the sight of the ferns, palms and exotic blooms artfully arranged about the room. "This is just perfect. So pretty!"

Mentally toying with the possibilities of what Rose was up to in the billiard room, Duncan didn't smile. "I can take no credit, I fear—this area is Mama's domain."

"I must remember to commend her ladyship." Mrs. Edmonton sailed down the long room, admiring the display. Clarissa followed more slowly.

Duncan turned to Mr. Edmonton. "If you don't mind, I'll leave you here. There's some business I need to attend to."

Mr. Edmonton smiled. "Indeed, my lord. You've been most kind in giving us your time."

"Not at all." Duncan inclined his head. "Dinner will be at seven."

His "business" took him straight to the billiard room. He opened the door—and beheld a sight similar to the one that had stopped him in his tracks earlier in the day. This time, Rose was leaning over the billiard table, laughter spilling from her bright eyes, her ivory breasts all but spilling from the neckline of her dress. Jeremy Penecuik was beside her, his hands wrapped about the cue Rose was angling.

That much, Duncan had expected. What he hadn't foreseen was that it was Rose teaching Penecuik, not the other way about.

Rose's smile, predictably, widened at the sight of him; to his relief, she straightened.

"Duncan—*perfect.* You're just the man we need."

With an imperious wave, she gestured him in. Belatedly wary, Duncan complied. If Penecuik had not been there, he would have been tempted to retreat; he'd learned to distrust that particular light in Rose's eye.

"Jeremy can't play, and I'm finding it impossible to demonstrate—he's left-handed." As she spoke, Rose crossed to the rack holding the cues and took down another. Then she turned and, head on one side, regarded Duncan. "If you and I play an exhibition match, Jeremy can see how it's done."

Then her eyes twinkled.

"Are you game?"

Duncan's jaw locked; he was crossing the room toward her before he'd had time to think. Then he thought—and it made no difference; he was incapable of walking away from her challenge.

He stopped by her side; looking down at her, he took the cue from her hand. "What form?"

She smiled, and her dimples winked. "Just the usual."

They proceed to play; he knew she played well—he'd taught her himself, one day long ago, when she hadn't driven him to distraction first. Now . . . he watched from across the table as she sighted along her cue, and tried to remember to breathe.

She potted two balls, then rounded the table; dragging in a quick breath, Duncan stayed where he was, leaning on his cue. Only to be treated to an equally mesmerizing sight: that of the ripe hemispheres of Rose's luscious bottom, outlined beneath her thin gown as she leaned over the table. His mouth dried like a desert.

Rose missed and cursed lightly; forcing his eyes to the balls, Duncan approached the table to take his shot. Rose leaned one hip on the table beside him. Duncan bent low. He gritted his teeth and concentrated on the ball—and tried to block out her perfume, and the more subtle scent that was her and her alone. He drew in a tight breath; her scent wreathed through his brain.

His gut locked; his hand trembled.

He missed the shot.

Rose raised her brows. "Hmm." She slanted Duncan a provocative glance. "You can't have been practicing in London."

She circled the table and selected a ball; as she bent over

her cue, at the edge of her vision, she saw Duncan tense. Inwardly frowning, she sighted this way, then that, wondering at his response. She wasn't teasing him just now, so why was he tensing?

By the time she sank three balls, she'd worked it out—but it still made no sense. Duncan was thirty-five; she was quite sure he'd seen more than a few female breasts in his time, all considerably more bare than hers. She had a great deal more claim to being a nun than he had of being a monk. Yet the conclusion was inescapable.

Interestingly, Jeremy, for all he was watching avidly, showed no signs of the same susceptibility.

And when she missed and Duncan took charge of the table again, his every muscle locked when she settled close beside him.

The discovery was curious—and utterly fascinating.

She thrashed him resoundingly.

Curiosity, Rose had often been told, was her besetting sin. The observation had never stopped her before; it was not going to stop her now. But the size of the house party, and the consequent length of the dining table, forced her to restrain her besetting sin until the gentlemen rejoined the ladies in the drawing room after concluding their ritual with the port.

Her fell intent—to further probe Duncan's sudden and amazing susceptibility—was, to her surprise, aided and abetted by Clarissa Edmonton. The girl—Rose could not think of her otherwise, she seemed so very young—linked arms with her as soon as the gentlemen appeared, and steered her directly toward Duncan, who had helpfully entered at Jeremy's side.

Clarissa smiled sweetly as they bore down on their victim; Rose's smile held a different promise.

"I thought we should plan what we will do tomorrow," Clarissa innocently suggested.

Duncan looked down at her, his expression unreadable, then he glanced at the still-uncurtained windows, through which the loch with its backdrop of craggy peaks was visible. "There's a mist coming down; it'll most likely be damp, drizzle if not rain, at least for most of the morning. Not the best weather for riding."

"Oh." Clarissa followed his gaze. "But I hadn't meant . . ." Turning back, she smiled at Duncan. "I must admit, I don't ride all that well, so you must not think you need make up a riding party just for me. And the scenery hereabouts is a trifle bleak—the mountains seem to close in on one so, don't you think?—so I thought perhaps we might play charades or have a musical morning, singing songs."

She looked up, into Duncan's face, her expression sweetly eager. Rose bit her tongue, swallowed her laughter and equally eagerly fixed her gaze on Duncan—and waited, breath bated, for his reaction.

His lips thinned, his face hardened, but his voice remained urbanely even. "I'm afraid I only arrived late last night and have urgent business I must see to in the morning. You'll have to excuse me"— his gaze lifted to Rose and Jeremy—"but no doubt the others will be happy to join you."

Rose wasn't having that. "Actually," she purred, catching Duncan's gaze and smiling knowingly, "I rather think Lady Hermione intends to exhort us to music here and now."

The words proved prophetic. They all glanced at Lady Hermione; she saw and imperiously beckoned them. Mrs. Edmonton sat beside her on the *chaise*.

"Clarissa, my dear, your mother has been telling me how wonderfully you play the pianoforte; I do so enjoy a well-rendered air. I really must entreat you to entertain us all—just a few pieces to enliven the evening."

"Oh. Well . . ." Clarissa blushed and demurred prettily.

Prompted by a look from his mother, Duncan politely

added his entreaties. "The company would be honored." He offered his arm. "Come, I'll open the pianoforte."

Clarissa gifted him with a too-sweet look; his expression impassive, Duncan led her to the piano, sited between two long windows overlooking the terrace. He handed her to her seat; Jeremy opened the piano while Rose handed Clarissa the stacked music sheets. The rest of the company eagerly gathered around, shifting chairs and *chaises* to get a better view. After sorting through the music, Clarissa chose two pieces; Rose restacked the rest on the piano, then joined Jeremy and Duncan at the side of the room.

Frowning slightly, Clarissa shifted the stool, reshuffled the music, then shifted the stool again. Finally, she laid her hands on the keys.

And played.

Predictably perfectly.

After three minutes, two of Duncan's aunts resumed their conversation, whispering softly. Beside Rose, Jeremy shifted his weight, once, twice; then he straightened and, with a murmured "Excuse me," drifted off to study a cabinet filled with Dresden miniatures.

Rose, as partial to good music as Lady Hermione, willed herself to concentrate, yet even she found her mind wandering. Clarissa's performance was technically flawless but emotionally barren. Every note was struck correctly, but there was no heart, no soul—no feeling—to bring the music alive.

Surrendering to the inevitable, Rose stopped trying to listen and let the notes flow past her; she scanned the company, most now distracted, then glanced at Duncan beside her.

In time to see him stifle a yawn.

She stifled a grin and leaned closer. "Seriously, you aren't going to marry her, are you?"

He looked down at her, then replied through gritted teeth, "Mind your own business."

Rose let her grin show; his expression only grew harder. She looked away, across the room—Clarissa's first piece was reaching its penultimate crescendo. Deliberately, Rose leaned lightly against Duncan, letting their bodies touch fractionally as she brushed past him, across him, on her way to Lady Hermione's *chaise.*

She heard the swift hiss of his indrawn breath, felt the sudden, brutally powerful seizing of his muscles.

Lips curving lightly, Rose headed straight for the safety of his mother's presence; reaching the *chaise,* she nodded to Lady Hermione, then turned and gazed innocently about the room, studiously refusing to let her eyes flick to Duncan, still standing, rigid, by the wall.

From the corner of her eye, she could see his hands were fisted, that his gaze had followed her; it remained fixed, intent, on her. She suspected he was envisaging throttling her, closing his long, strong fingers about her neck and wringing it—his usual response to her teasing.

To her considerable surprise, he straightened; fists relaxing, he prowled toward her.

Rose quelled a frown; when she teased him, Duncan usually avoided her. He ran; she chased—that's how it had always been.

Not this time.

As Clarissa concluded her first piece, Duncan strolled up and halted directly behind her, slightly to one side. Trapping her between the back of the *chaise* and him. His strolling prowl had appeared nonchalant, yet Rose could sense his tension, the controlled, steely power behind every movement.

Clarissa held the final chords, then lifted her fingers from the keys. Everyone applauded politely; Rose clapped distractedly. Duncan clapped slowly, softly, deliberately, directly behind her right shoulder—she got the distinct impression he was applauding *her* performance, not Clarissa's.

After favoring the company with a suitably demure smile,

Clarissa looked at her mother, then Lady Hermione, and then at Rose and Duncan. Rose summoned an encouraging smile; she knew without looking that Duncan was watching Clarissa, virtually over her own head. Clarissa smiled and turned back to the piano, and started her second piece.

Rose struggled to breathe, struggled to ignore the vise that, once again, had clamped about her lungs. Her senses flickered wildly, in a state unnervingly akin to panic, her mind wholly focused not on the music, but on Duncan, so close, so still, so silent behind her.

The first sweep of heat along the side of her neck and shoulder, exposed by her gown, caught her unawares. She frowned slightly, then banished the expression as the sensation ceased.

It returned a moment later, hotter, stronger, extending over more of her, from her shoulder to the swells of her breasts, bare above her neckline.

And it was her turn to drag in a quick breath and hold it, as she realized it was Duncan's gaze that she could feel. He was . . .

Rose inwardly cursed and gritted her teeth against the wave of sensation washing over her, through her, pooling heat within her . . .

In desperation, she searched for salvation. Lady Hermione was sitting before her and could not see; all the older guests were busy chatting. Even Jeremy had deserted her. He was now deep in discussion with Mr. Edmonton.

Duncan shifted—closer.

Rose's knees quaked. She gripped the back of the *chaise* as unprecedented giddiness threatened.

Clarissa ended her short piece. She lifted her hands from the keys and looked up—and Rose was safe. As everyone applauded, Rose breathed again, released from Duncan's gaze.

He stepped away from her as Clarissa, escorted from the piano by Jeremy, drew near. Before Rose could gather her wits and slide around the opposite end of the *chaise,* Duncan turned and smiled, in a languid, general fashion, at his mother, and her.

"Perhaps Rose would care to play next?"

Lady Hermione immediately swiveled to beam up at Rose. "Indeed. Rose, dear, I haven't heard you play for an age—do oblige us."

Rose knew a trap when she saw one, but, as others turned to her and added their pleas, she had to smile and graciously agree. She looked at Jerermy. "Would you turn the pages for me?"

Jeremy smiled warmly and offered his arm. Rose took it, quelling a twinge of guilt; she'd only asked him to ensure that Duncan wouldn't hover at her shoulder while she played. If he did, she was quite sure her fingers would tie themselves into knots; if that had been his plan, she'd spiked his guns.

With barely muted pride, Jeremy led her to the piano stool. Duncan, with Clarissa on his arm, followed more slowly. Rose quickly selected her piece—a sonata, one of Lady Hermione's favorites. She settled the music on the stand; Jeremy took up his stance beside her.

Rose drew in a deep breath, then laid her fingers on the keys and let them free. She kept her eyes on the music, yet she played from memory; she had no need of the sheets to guide her. Which was just as well.

Duncan had led Clarissa around the piano; they now stood directly before her, watching her play.

To Rose's immense relief, the music protected her, acted as her shield as she lost herself in it. The delicate, haunting air, so evocative of the wild country surrounding them, rose up and wreathed about her, then wrapped her in its spell. She let her lids fall and gave herself up to it, to the magic of the wildness, the compelling beauty of the sound.

About the room, not a whisper was heard; not a cough or

shuffle marred the magic. Rose held the entire company in thrall, effortlessly harnessing the power Clarissa, for all her technical perfection, had not been able to command.

For Duncan, his gaze fixed on Rose, the comparison was inescapable. Without thought or consideration, Rose gave her heart and soul; she played with an emotional abandon which, he inwardly acknowledged, was an inherent part of her, the Rose he had known quite literally since her birth. The realization affected him powerfully.

His jaw hardened—all of him hardened; possessive lust ripped through him. He wanted her—desired her—driven by the sure knowledge that Rose would love in exactly the same way. With her heart and soul. With complete and utter abandon.

He dragged in a tight breath and found it insufficient to deaden the sudden pounding in his blood. He set his teeth and tried to wrench his gaze from her—and failed. Beyond his will, his eyes devoured her—the rich abundance of her coiled hair, the warm cream of her complexion, the soft, suggestive curves so temptingly arrayed in amber silk.

Mesmerized, he let his gaze linger; under the fine fabric, her nipples peaked. He glanced up and saw her lashes tremble. Lust roared again; with an inward curse, he swallowed it whole and fought to unfocus his gaze. They were in his mother's drawing room, under the eyes of more than thirty of his relatives, as well as his no-longer intended and her parents, and Rose's prospective husband and her father.

She was driving him demented, but for the first time in their shared lives, it wasn't—entirely—her fault.

Duncan gritted his teeth and endured.

Eventually, the sonata came to an end. Rose struck the last chords lovingly; a sigh rippled through the room. As she lifted her fingers from the keys, the company returned to life.

So did Rose, thankful that she didn't blush all that readily. She smiled and looked around, everywhere but at Duncan.

She even managed to exchange a mild glance with Clarissa without focusing on him.

"Rose, dear!"

She swiveled on the stool to face Lady Hermione.

Who smiled beguilingly. "If you would, dear—*The Raven's Song*. There's four of you to sing it."

Rose blinked, then inclined her head. "Yes, of course." Swinging back to the piano, she looked at Jeremy. "Do you know it?" Her gaze moved on to include Clarissa; both she and Jeremy nodded. Rose didn't bother asking Duncan; his mother's favorite song was as imprinted on his brain as it was on hers. At the edge of her vision—where she carefully kept him—she saw him shift, drifting around the piano to her left. Clarissa drifted right, until she stood beside Jeremy.

Rose set her teeth and reached for the keys. If Duncan ogled her breasts again, she would hit him. A second later, the introduction rolled out. They all started in time and went carefully through the first verse, all listening, gauging each other's voices. Jeremy's was a mild tenor, restrained and light; Clarissa's soprano was thin and reedy, wavering a little on the sustained high notes.

Duncan's singing voice was as she remembered it: a deep baritone, rich and powerful, capable of imparting a surging cadence reminiscent of the sea. Rose heard it and, for the life of her, could not stop her own voice, a warm contralto, from merging, interweaving, soaring above, then sliding into the resonance of his.

They'd sung this song, together, in this very room, for years; as memory was overlaid by new experience, Rose could hear the difference, the added depth and power in Duncan's voice, the softer, more rounded, more sensual tones of hers, melding into an even finer, richer, more compelling aural tapestry than they'd previously managed to create.

She concentrated on the notes, and sensed him following

her. By the time they started the final verse, their voices dominated, stronger, more assured, more enduring.

They held the final note, then, by perfect, unspoken, mutual accord, let it die.

The room erupted with wild applause.

Rose laughed; smiling, she glanced up—and met Duncan's eyes. His lips were curved, but his eyes weren't laughing—they were focused, intently, on her. A thrill streaked through her and left her lightheaded—she told herself it was simply exhilaration, compounded by breathlessness. Turning toward Jeremy, she swung about on the stool and stood.

Giddiness struck—she swayed.

And Duncan was there, by her side, steadying her, shielding her from the room. His fingers gripped her elbow—and burned her like a brand. Rose sucked in a breath and looked up. And was trapped in his eyes, in the cool blue that now burned with a million tiny flames.

Flames?

Rose blinked and looked away. She'd never seen fire in Duncan's eyes before. Drawing a determined breath, she steeled herself and looked again.

He met her gaze with a look of limpid innocence.

Not a flame in sight.

Rose resisted the urge to narrow her eyes at him. Instead, keeping a firm hold on her curiosity, she retrieved her arm and, with an airy nonchalance that was entirely feigned, glided away from him.

She tried not to notice how fast her heart was racing.

Two

Duncan's prediction proved accurate; the next day
dawned drizzly and gray. Drifts of fine mist shrouded the
mountains, enhancing the aura of isolation, of being cut off
from the world.

Gazing out of the parlor windows, Rose drank in the
sight, the atmosphere, the deep sense of peace. Behind her,
in the cozy parlor, the ladies had assembled to pass the
morning in gentle companionship, some setting the odd
stitch in their embroideries, others too idle to even bother
with the facade. Murmuring conversations drifted up and
down the room, mirroring the drift of the clouds outside.

For her, it was a comfortable gathering; all those present,
bar Jeremy and the Edmontons, had known her for years,
most since her birth. Already that morning, she had spoken
with each of Duncan's six aunts, catching up with the exploits
of his cousins. The older ladies were now exchanging social
gossip, mostly of Edinburgh society, with a few relevant tales
from London thrown in. She had little interest in such stories;
if truth be told, she had little interest in society at all.

To her left, some way from the house, she saw a group of

gentlemen heading out for a walk along the path about the loch. Her father was there, as was Jeremy—it wasn't hard to pick him out; he was the one wearing the brand-new deer-stalker and a many-caped cloak. Despite his connection with the dukedom of Perth, he'd lived all his life in Edinburgh.

Rose watched the men enter the trees. The sight of Jeremy, striding along among them, was a pointed reminder of why she'd come to Ballynashiels at this particular time, with him in tow. He wanted to marry her. At twenty-seven, having turned down so many young men, to have a candidate of Jeremy's caliber go down on his knees was not something she could dismiss with a smiling laugh. Jeremy deserved consideration. Aside from anything else, she actually liked him, in a mild sort of way. She could, she supposed, imagine setting up house with him. He would be a kind and considerate husband; of that she had not a doubt, but still . . .

She'd answered Duncan truly: she hadn't married because she'd yet to meet a man she wanted to wed. She had a very definite idea of how she would feel if the right candidate appeared—swept away by some force greater than her own will. For years, she'd rationalized that this had not happened because she was so willful, so strong-willed. It hadn't happened yet, and it wouldn't with Jeremy, but at twenty-seven she had to consider her options. Which was what had brought her here.

Lady Hermione's invitation had been a godsend, giving her a reason to bring Jeremy to Ballynashiels, to the one place on earth she felt most alive, most truly herself. Most clearly, strongly sure of herself. She'd reasoned that if there were any possibility that she and Jeremy could make a match of it, she'd know it here, at Ballynashiels.

Rose smiled wryly, resignedly. She'd promised Jeremy she would give him her answer on Midsummer's Day, but she'd already made up her mind: Jeremy made less impression on her here than he had in the ballrooms of Edinburgh. It was not he who had captured her interest, focused her attention.

She stood at the window, gazing unseeing outside, for a full five minutes before she realized where her thoughts had gone. To whom they'd gone.

Duncan the perfect.

He'd always effortlessly captured her attention—he still did. She'd always been interested in his exploits, his thoughts, his achievements—now, after twelve years absence from her life, he intrigued her.

After last night, however, intrigue was tempered by caution. He'd seriously unnerved her; as she'd climbed into bed, she'd promised herself she would avoid him for the rest of her stay. He'd changed. He was no longer the boy she'd teased, the youth she'd taunted—all with absolute impunity. The boy, the youth, had never struck back; this Duncan did. With a weapon she did not precisely understand, and against which, it seemed, she had no defence.

Which was definitely not fair.

That had been last night. This morning, she was bored. Teasing Duncan had always enlivened her life; she'd always felt excitement in his presence. As she had last night. Rose stared at the cloud-shrouded crags. Perhaps she simply needed a little experience to become used to the sort of excitement Duncan now evoked.

Her normal response when faced with a new challenge was to confront it, overcome it. Dealing with Duncan at thirty-five was certainly a new challenge, but, very likely, all she needed to do to overcome her silly susceptibility, to conquer that unnerving feeling that had assailed her yesterday evening, was to confront him. Face him.

Tease him as she used to.

Except, of course, they weren't children anymore.

Shifting, Rose glanced down the room to where Clarissa sat in an armchair, industriously embroidering. She was the only woman in the room so engrossed, the very picture of maidenly occupation.

Rose inwardly grimaced. She was not the sort of woman to interfere in another's life, but Clarissa was clearly not a suitable wife for Duncan. If he didn't already know that, he should, so she could tease him with a clear conscience. And while in wider society her teasing might be seen as something else, all those gathered here would know there was nothing in it—that it was simply the way she and Duncan had always dealt.

Vivid memories of the excitement she'd experienced last night, the sharp, tingling tension that had laid seige to her nerves, slid through her mind and beckoned. Abandoning the window, Rose crossed to where Lady Hermione reclined on a *chaise*. Her ladyship looked up inquiringly.

"I need a distraction." Rose smiled ingenuously. "I think I'll fetch a book."

Lady Hermione's smile was serene. "Indeed, dear. An excellent idea."

Duncan was deep in a ledger of accounts when the library door opened. Assuming it was one of the guests looking for a book, he did not look up. Then he realized which guest it was, and looked up—quickly.

His heart stopped—just for a second—long enough to bring home the danger. Rose sensed his gaze; she turned her head and threw him a teasing smile. Then, with airy grace, she wandered along the wall lined with bookcases, fingers lightly trailing along the spines.

Duncan set his teeth, shifted in his seat—and tried not to think of how those teasing fingertips would feel trailing across his bare chest. She was wearing a muslin morning gown; the fabric clung lovingly to her hips and thighs as she strolled slowly down the room. For long, silent minutes, he watched her search for a book. And gave serious thought to the question of whether she really wanted to read, or if she was deliberately baiting him. He wasn't sure those alternatives were mutually exclusive.

Whatever, he could not take his eyes from her. At least part of that compulsion derived from their past, from deep-seated self-preservation. He'd learned from experience that Rose could be startlingly inventive; keeping an eye on her whenever she got close had always been wise.

Keeping an eye on her now might not be so wise, but he couldn't stop himself, couldn't wrench his gaze from her. He still couldn't get over her transformation. In years past, keeping a wary eye on her had been a necessary chore; keeping an eye on her now was no hardship at all. The only hardship involved was in keeping his hands off her—he'd only just succeeded in toeing the line thus far. Heaven help him if he lost that fight.

God only knew what she would do to him then.

The thought froze his mind—and freed his imagination. He was deep in salacious fantasies when a crackle of paper to his right recalled him to the present. He glanced fleetingly at Henderson, his steward and old friend; seated on a chair by the side of the desk, Henderson was poring over another ledger. They'd been there for two hours; all the important business was done.

Henderson had barely glanced up when Rose had entered. As she'd visited every summer, his staff had presumably become used to her as she now was; Duncan was the only one who'd been shaken to his toes.

He looked back at his nemesis-turned-siren, and shifted in his seat again.

He'd spent all night thinking of her, thinking about all she now was. Lusting after all she now was. And brooding about where that might land him. For despite all else, she still was

Rose—the woman who'd made his life hell from the moment she'd first entered it.

She was and always had been a thorn in his flesh. If he gave rein to the compulsion that gripped him every time she swanned into his sight, would he exorcise her, pluck her out of his life forever, or simply drive her deeper in?

Watching her perusing the first pages of a novel, Duncan inwardly cursed. He was in agony as it was; he might as well discover what fate had in store for him—the pain couldn't be any worse.

Pushing back his chair, he glanced at Henderson. "We'll finish this tomorrow." He stood, then considered. "On second thoughts, let's leave it until after Midsummer." When his mind might be free of its present distraction.

Henderson readily acquiesced and gathered up the ledgers. Duncan waited until he was headed for the door before strolling around the desk. And setting out in the wake of his nemesis.

By any rational standard, he should have spent at least some time in the last twelve hours considering Clarissa, detailing his arguments and making his final decision. Instead, his decision seemed to have been made for him, by some part of his mind that he couldn't override. He would not marry Clarissa.

Who he *would* marry was a different question, one he had not, yet, dwelled much upon. With Rose about, distracting him, attracting him, he couldn't think clearly enough to even focus on the point.

The door shut softly behind Henderson. A second later, when Duncan was still ten paces from her, Rose glanced up—too quickly—from her book. Duncan suppressed a feral grin. She swung to face him; he stopped directly before her. Ducking slightly, he checked the title of the book she held, shieldlike, between them. "You've already read that."

She blinked at him. "That was years ago." She paused, then added, her eyes on his, "I thought I might revisit old playgrounds."

Duncan held her gaze. "Indeed?" Propping one shoulder against the bookshelves, he looked down at her. "You need to be wary of old playgrounds."

"Oh?"

There was just enough teasing laughter in her voice to bring out the rake in him. Duncan let his intent infuse his eyes. "The ground might have shifted—and even if you do stay on your feet, you might find the rules of the games changed."

A light flush touched her cheeks; he half expected her to fluster—instead, she arched a brow at him. "I've always learned quickly." Her throaty purr slid under his skin, heating him. She searched his eyes, then that teasing brow rose higher. "And I doubt there's anything I need fear."

She turned away on the comment—one he would have believed was expressly designed to tempt him to some act of madness, except that Rose knew him not. She did not know what he was, what he had become, how he had changed over the last twelve years. She did not know what his principal recreational activity now was. If he told her it was riding, she'd probably imagine horses.

Duncan watched her return the book to the shelf and considered how best to break the news to her.

She picked out another volume and slanted him a glance. "Have you finished with Henderson? I'm sure Clarissa would be delighted to see you; she's in the parlor keeping busy with her needle."

"If she's absorbed, I don't think we need bother her."

Tawny brown eyes opened wide. "But don't you think you should spend more time with her?"

He held her innocent gaze for a fraught second, then flicked a glance at the clock on the mantelpiece. And sighed artistically. "There's just enough time for a game of charades."

His gaze returned to her; she didn't miss his implication. "You abhor charades."

Duncan smiled. "So do you."

She eyed him measuringly, then shrugged lightly and, taking her selected book, strolled toward one of the long windows. Duncan trailed behind, perfectly content to follow, his eyes glued to her hips, watching their seductive swaying. She stopped directly before the window; he continued past her to prop his shoulders against the window frame—he thrust his hands into his trouser pockets to keep them from her curves.

"I dare say Clarissa will do well enough"—holding the book at her waist, Rose studied the landscape—"although I confess I don't understand why she would find the mountains oppressive."

"Hmm."

"And just because you ride every day, there's really no reason she needs to."

"Ah-huh."

"And as for the size of the house and all the servants, I know she feels a little overwhelmed, but I'm sure she'll get used to it."

"She won't have to."

"What?"

Her head came around so fast, Duncan had trouble suppressing his grin; he looked down.

"You're going to live mostly in *London?*"

He looked up—and swallowed his contemptuous denial just in time. Rose's eyes were huge; her expression, aghast—she was stunned at the thought, and off balance. Duncan narrowed his eyes. "Have you accepted Penecuik?"

She blinked, then pulled back; with a haughty glance, she resumed her study of the scenery. "I'm still considering."

The abject relief that flooded him was unnerving; frowning, Duncan straightened. "Considering what? His future prospects?"

"Future prospects, your mother informed me, are to be highly regarded in a prospective husband."

Duncan's soft snort communicated his opinion of his mother's wisdom. "You'll lead him by the nose for the term of his natural life—is that the sort of husband you want?"

Her gaze on the mountains, she actually considered it. While she did, he reached out and tugged the book from her grasp. She surrendered it absentmindedly; Duncan glanced at the title, then dropped it on a nearby table.

Rose heard the soft thud and turned as Duncan turned back to her. Their gazes met; he raised a brow. She replied with a provocative glance. "It might be rather nice to have one's opinion revered."

His eyes held hers. "Most wives would prefer that their husbands worshipped something other than their opinions."

His tone was even more provocative than her glance.

"Indeed?" Rose smiled brightly. "I must remember to discuss the point with Jeremy." Her eyes still on Duncan's, she gestured airily. "Who knows what else about me he might feel moved to worship?"

Something changed in Duncan's eyes. For an instant, she thought the flames were back—before she could be sure, his gaze dropped from hers. She felt it sweep over her like a warm summer wind.

Her nerves tightened; excitement flickered across her skin.

"I think," he drawled, his voice two tones lower, "that I could make an educated guess." His gaze slowly rose; reaching her face, it locked with hers. He stepped toward her.

Eyes flying wide, Rose stepped back. And came up against the window frame. Duncan continued to advance; she hauled in a desperate breath. "Indeed?" It took effort not to squeak.

His gaze dropped to her bodice, which was straining as she couldn't release the breath she'd sucked in. "Hmm."

He halted directly before her, with a bare inch between

them. With her spine plastered to the window frame, Rose struggled not to quiver. "Well? What?"

Slowly, he lifted his head—until his gaze locked with hers again. Rose forgot her struggle to breathe, forgot not to quiver—she lost all ability to think. A tangible force, his maleness reached for her, wrapped around her, locked—and held her at his mercy. She couldn't blink, could not break free—like mesmerized prey, quivering to the core, she watched his darkened eyes and the glint within them that she'd mistaken for flames.

Then his lips curved—teasingly. "I've forgotten the question."

He looked down on the words—at her lips.

Rose felt them soften, felt them part.

Slowly, Duncan lowered his head—

They both heard the step outside the door an instant before it swung open. Jerermy entered.

"Ah!" His face lit up. "There you are."

Supported by the window frame, Rose fought down the urge to press a hand to her heaving breast. "Yes—" Her vocal chords seized. Nodding, she cleared her throat and tried again. "Here I am." She steadfastly ignored the potent presence lounging against the other side of the window.

"We were just discussing," he purred, "the prospects for riding."

Rose shot him a scandalized look; he turned to her and grinned. "Not today, I fear—perhaps tomorrow?"

The question was so pointed, she had to answer. "I sincerely doubt it," she managed.

"Oh, I don't know," Jeremy chimed in. "Nothing like a brisk gallop to stir the blood."

"Indeed," Duncan agreed.

"You were looking for me?" Rose determinedly cut in. She managed to keep her tone light, if brittle.

Jeremy smiled engagingly. "It started to rain, so we cut

short our walk. I wondered if we might pass the time to lunch about the billiard table."

Rose smiled. "An excellent idea." Deciding her legs were now steady enough to risk walking, she started across the room.

"Rose."

Duncan's tone sent tingling shivers streaking down her spine. Rose halted; slowly, she turned back.

"You forgot your book." He held it up.

Rose looked at it, clasped in his long, strong fingers, then looked at him. He made no move to bring the book to her. She drew in a quick breath. "I'm no longer interested in reading it."

With that, she swung around—and saw Jeremy smile at Duncan. "Care to join us, Strathyre?"

Rose froze; she could hear her heart beating. After what seemed an interminable age, she heard Duncan's voice, cool, but with an undertone just for her: "I think not. I have other skills to hone."

Almost giddy with relief, Rose nodded vaguely in his direction—and escaped before he could change his mind.

By dinnertime, she'd convinced herself she'd made too much of the entire episode. No matter what the circumstances, no matter what the provocation—no matter what her fevered brain might have imagined—Duncan would never lay a finger, much less a lip, on her. He certainly wouldn't ravish her. Not Duncan. He might threaten all manner of retribution, but he'd never, in all their shared years, ever physically retaliated.

Except once, but that had been a sort of mistake.

As she waited in the drawing room for the gentlemen to return, her impatience hidden behind a serene mask, Rose reviewed all she had seen of Duncan from lunchtime onward.

The clouds had broken by then; the weather had progressively improved. As she and Jeremy had risen from the luncheon table, Duncan had come up, Clarissa on his arm, and suggested a stroll through the gardens. She'd smiled and kept her hand firmly on Jeremy's arm. But Duncan had been charming—and nothing more. At no time during the long, thoroughly enjoyable ramble, nor during the protracted afternoon tea in the parlor once they'd got back, had she seen so much as a fleeting glimpse of the prowling predator she'd faced in the library.

Which meant he'd been teasing her, scaring her—putting on a very good show to intimidate her into keeping out of his hair, keeping her distance and keeping her tongue between her teeth, at least with respect to his proposed marriage.

She swallowed an indignant *humph* as Clarissa came to join her before the open window.

Clarissa frowned at the soft twilight outside, and shivered delicately. "It's sort of eerie, isn't it—that odd light? Not proper daylight, but not night." She flashed a gentle smile at Rose. "I fear I'm rather sensitive to atmosphere. I find all this"—she gestured to the mountain peaks looming over the valley—"dreadfully cold."

Rose bit her tongue, swallowing the advice that Clarissa should not inform Duncan that she thought his home "dreadfully cold."

"Luckily, there doesn't seem to be any real reason Strathyre needs to spend time here—the estate contributes very little to his wealth, I understand." Clarissa turned and scanned the long, elegantly appointed room. "The house, of course, is magnificent—such a pity it isn't in Kent, or Surrey, or even Northamptonshire. Still"—Clarissa flashed another of her sweet, confiding looks at Rose—"I dare say, seeing it's so grand a residence, it won't be too hard to find a tenant."

Rose only just managed not to choke. "Hmm" was all she felt it safe to say. Clarissa remained beside her, idling away the time until the gentlemen joined them; Rose considered long and hard but, in the end, said nothing.

It wasn't her place to puncture Clarissa's bubble, and, given Clarissa's open lack of appreciation for Duncan's home—his ancestral seat—she couldn't believe he would be such a nitwit as to offer for the girl. In all logical matters, she had absolute confidence in his good sense. If nothing else, his drive for perfection—especially strong where his home was concerned—would see him, and Ballynashiels, safe from the tragedy of him marrying Clarissa. She didn't need to say anything more on that score.

Which should make things simpler. It wasn't on account of Clarissa that she intended to beard the prowling leopard tonight.

From the corner of her eye, she spied movement by the door; together with Clarissa, she turned as the gentlemen strolled in. Duncan was the last, in company with her father. Inwardly grinning, Rose turned aside, a smile curving her lips as Jeremy approached.

She neither looked at, nor smiled at, Duncan. She wanted to get him alone; she had a shrewd idea how to manage it.

Clarissa drifted away, pausing by the *chaise* where her parents sat; Duncan joined her there. Rose bided her time until the tea had been dispensed, and some of the older members of the party had retired, before leaning closer to Jeremy and suggesting, "Let's stroll on the terrace. It's stuffy in here, and the breeze is so mild."

She directed Jeremy's gaze to where French doors stood open to the deepening twilight, fine curtains wafting on the breeze. "The terrace stretches down the side of the house— there's a lovely view of the loch from the end." She started to stroll, steering him, unresisting, toward the French doors.

"I suppose . . ." He looked down at her. "As long as you don't think it improper?"

Rose smiled, very warmly, up at him. "I'm quite sure no one will even imagine we have any impropriety in mind."

Except Duncan.

They strolled past him as he conversed with Mrs. Edmonton and one of his aunts, Clarissa still on his arm. Without so much as a glance in his direction, with her gaze—indeed, all her attention—apparently fixed on Jeremy, Rose allowed her escort to hold back the curtains and hand her onto the terrace.

The air was cool, the breeze as mild as she'd intimated; the sky was a wash of muted pastels, with soft clouds gathering about the peaks. Strolling the flags, Rose closed her eyes and drew in a deep breath, scented with pine and spruce, and wondered how Clarissa could fail to appreciate the magic of Ballynashiels.

"It's such a peaceful place."

Rose opened her eyes and smiled at Jeremy. Together, they stopped by the balustrade and looked out across the well-tended lawn, host to a grouping of old shade trees. Beyond lay the shrubbery, a conglomeration of deepening shadows.

"You seem . . ."—Jeremy gestured—"very much at home here."

Rose grinned. "I am." Removing her hand from his sleeve, she leaned on the balustrade. "Ballynashiels feels like home."

"But you live in Edinburgh with your father, don't you?"

"Yes, but—" Rose broke off; she and Jeremy both turned at the sound of a footstep.

Rose met Duncan's dark gaze and smiled serenely. "Have you come to take the air? Come and join us." She waved him forward. "I was just telling Jeremy how I used to spend the summers here."

Duncan hesitated, then strolled over. "I see."

"Indeed." Exuding guileless innocence, Rose flashed him a smile. "Even you must remember." She turned her laughing glance on Jeremy. "I was forever under Duncan's feet." She proceed to describe, in terms both humorous and brief, an abridged but not untruthful history of her visits. Jeremy was entranced, as she'd intended him to be; Duncan listened silently—the suspicious cynicism in his gaze, only she could see.

"So that's how I know Ballynashiels so well."

Jeremy smiled his understanding; he glanced at Duncan. "She must have been quite a handful."

Duncan looked at him, then looked at Rose. "Not as much as you might think."

Rose responded with a look of mild amusement, then turned her back on him and faced the mountains once more. With a graceful sweep of her arm, she encompassed the landscape. "It's so wild and beautiful—and untamed."

His gaze on the mountains, Jeremy murmured in agreement.

His gaze on Rose, Duncan said nothing at all.

Suddenly, she shivered, just as Jeremy turned back to her. "I say," he said. "You're cold. We'd best go inside."

"Oh, no!" Chafing her bare arms, Rose smiled pleadingly. "It's so pleasant out here."

Jeremy frowned. "But you might catch a chill."

"Perhaps"—Rose tilted her head—"if you were to fetch my shawl . . ."

"Of course." Jeremy straightened. "Where is it?"

"I think . . ." Rose frowned. "I *think* I left it in the drawing room."

Jeremy grinned. "Never fear, I'll find it." With a bright smile, he strode for the French doors and disappeared inside.

Duncan watched him go, then turned his gaze on Rose. "What are you up to?"

"Up to?" For one instant, her face remained a picture of

abject innocence, then she dropped her facade and smiled at him, with that teasing, taunting smile she reserved just for him. Turning, still smiling, fingers lightly trailing the balustrade, she strolled down the terrace. "Why do you imagine I'm up to anything?"

Duncan watched her retreating form, then inwardly shrugged and strolled after her. "Wild, beautiful and untamed. You may fool all others with your social facade, but I know you, remember?"

"You've missed twelve years—you don't know me at all."

"I could quote that back at you, with greater accuracy, but some things never change."

"Indeed?" Rose stopped at the end of the terrace, where the balustrade curved in a semicircle, and swung to face him.

Duncan slowed as he neared, struck by the vision of her, set against the backdrop of the darkening mountains, the slate waters of the loch. A familiar tension had infused his every muscle by the time he stopped, directly before her. He looked down at her, studying her eyes. "You're as recklessly hoydenish as ever."

Rose grinned. And wondered, now that she'd got him where she wanted him, just what to do next—how to lure the leopard into revealing his spots.

His attempt to intimidate her in the library had whetted her curiosity, raising it to impossible heights. She'd never encountered the particular power he now wielded; she wanted to learn more—at least enough to counter it, or, better yet, enough to wield it herself. At the moment, she felt at a disadvantage, as if he'd found some special place in the countryside and hadn't yet shown her. She intended to drag his secret from him.

Turning back to the view, she slanted him a considering glance. "I have to say I was taken aback by your choice of Clarissa; she seems so cool, so reserved. Not at all the sort of lady with whom I'd imagined you dallying."

When Duncan said nothing, she risked a quick glance at his face; his gaze was fixed on her, his expression unreadable. He appeared, to her chagrin, to be entirely at ease—not precisely relaxed, but definitely in control, his lord-of-the-manor mask firmly in place.

Her eyes on his, she raised a deliberately arch brow and let teasing amusement lace her tones. "Somehow, I imagined the ladies you would favor as having a little more fire."

"The ladies I favor generally do."

The flat statement was a clear refusal to be drawn; Rose abruptly changed tack. "Actually," she said, leaning closer and lowering her voice, "I wanted to cast myself on your mercy." With a lilting smile, she raised her eyes to his. "Draw on your experience."

He raised a brow. "My experience?"

Her smile deepened. "In matters of . . . dalliance." Her lashes drifted lower, and she looked away. "I wanted to inquire as to your educated guess."

Duncan frowned. "Guess?"

"Hmm. About what aspects of myself Jeremy might worship." Turning slightly, Rose faced him, with less than a foot between them. And smiled, warmly, enticingly—provocatively. "I wanted to know what, in your opinion, a gentleman might find most alluring in me."

Her eyes, when they met his, didn't twinkle; they smoldered. Duncan drew a slow, steady breath and held firm against the impulse to react, to allow the tension surging inside him to show, to transmute into physical expression in his eyes, his face, his body. She was as transparent as rippling water; she was up to something, but he couldn't see what. She was purposely tempting him, and doing a very good job of it—that much he knew. Luckily, he was in control. They were on the open terrace, not in the library; within twenty feet sat hordes of his relatives, her father, her prospective husband, and his own prospective bride and her parents. And

Penecuik would return any second with her shawl. She didn't have the first idea how to conduct a seduction. He'd have to teach her, but not here, not now. "I wouldn't presume to hazard a guess as to what Penecuik might find attractive."

Rose favored him with a sultry glance. "You do have some idea—you said so." She leaned closer; her fragrance wreathed his senses, her warm curves a handsbreadth away. She tipped her face up and met his eyes. "So what is it—my eyes? My lips? My body?"

All that, and a great deal more. Duncan stiffened, and refused to let his demons loose. He remembered, vividly, the one and only time he'd touched Rose with any physical intent, when, an adolescent fourteen, he'd reacted to one of her barbs. Together with two friends from Eton, he'd gone hiking in the woods, with Rose at his heels, unmercifully cheeky as usual. One of her comments had struck too close to a bone; he'd swung about and clipped her over the ear. He hadn't struck her hard, but she'd fallen to the ground, more from shock than the blow. That had been when, to his horror, he'd discovered that Rose didn't cry like other girls. She didn't screw up her face and bawl; instead, her huge eyes had silently filled with tears, then overflowed. She'd lain there, one palm to her ear, tears rolling down her cheeks—with a look in her eyes, in her face, that had slain him.

He'd been on his knees beside her, stammering an incoherent apology, trying awkwardly to comfort her—all in front of his utterly bemused friends.

Afterward, he'd vowed he'd never again put himself at her mercy; he'd never physically responded to her taunts again.

He looked into her eyes, warm golden brown, enticing and inciting, and steadfastly reminded himself that he was strong enough to withstand anything she threw at him.

She moved closer, bridging the last inches between them; her breasts brushed his coat, pressed lightly against his chest; her hip settled, a warm weight, against his thigh. The light in her eyes as she lifted them to his, and lifted a hand to lay it, palm flat, slim fingers extended, on his chest, was beyond teasing—pure, unadulterated temptation glowed in the soft brown.

The heat of her hand sank through his fine shirt; inwardly, Duncan quaked.

"You do know," she whispered, her brogue a soft caress. "So . . . tell me."

He looked into her eyes, drew in a less-than-steady breath—and dispensed with all caution. He had to put an end to her game; she was driving him demented. Again. Dropping his impassive mask, he fixed her with a narrow-eyed glare. "What is it you're really after?"

His clipped accents had the desired effect; she blinked, and straightened away from him—Duncan fought down the urge to pull her back, to draw her soft warmth back against him.

Rose read his eyes, read his face—and frowned. Her attack wasn't working; he appeared impervious to her teasing, her taunts—to every move she made. Not that she had any experience inciting gentlemen, but her failure, nevertheless, irked mightily. Disgruntled, she scanned his long frame, down all the way to his shoes, then up, slowly. When she reached his face, she shook her head.

Not a single *hint* of the tension she wanted to provoke showed. It was that she wanted to learn about—that odd tension of his that transferred itself to her, tightening her nerves, leaving her tingling with a sensation she could only call excitement.

She met his eyes—crystal hard in the moonlight—and sighed in disgust. "If you must know, I wanted to know what it was that . . . that came over you in the library." When he didn't immediately react, she prodded a finger into his chest. "What made you so tense." She wrapped her fingers about the steely muscles of his upper arm and tried to squeeze. "What that something was that . . . that made me feel like you were going to eat me!"

Duncan managed not to groan, only because his teeth had set. "That particular response," he informed her through them, "is fully described by a single four-letter word starting with L." He heard his words, and quickly added, "L-U-S-T."

Rose stared at him. *"Lust?"* she eventually got out. "That's *lust?*"

"Precisely—the overwhelming urge to have you, preferably naked in my bed." He was losing the fight; the reins were slipping from his grasp. Duncan could feel his body tensing, feel it heating. Rose's widening eyes didn't help. He pointed a finger at her nose. "And you needn't look so shocked—you feel it, too."

She stiffened. "Nonsense!" She shifted her gaze from his face; looking past his shoulder, she gestured skittishly. "I was merely curious—"

"That I believe."

"It was no more than that."

"Liar."

At the soft, purring taunt, she snapped her gaze back to his. "I do not want . . ."—dragging in a breath, she lifted her head—"to be *in lust* with you."

With that, she went to step around him; Duncan put out a hand to stop her. Rose didn't see it in time. She walked into it—pressed her left breast firmly into his right palm.

Reflexively, Duncan's fingers cupped the soft weight.

Rose's knees buckled.

Instinctively, he caught her, supporting her against him. And felt the deep shudder—of surrender, of pure need—that slid through her. He did not withdraw his hand; instead, his thumb brushed the warm flesh, found and circled her pebbled nipple.

He heard her breath shiver, felt shimmering desire rise within her; she held herself stiffly for one moment longer, then sank against him, leaning her forehead against his collarbone.

"Don't."

She whispered the word without any conviction.

"Why?" He kneaded her breast, and felt the flesh firm. "You like it."

She shivered and pressed closer, her body saying what she would not. Bending his head, Duncan pressed a kiss to the top of her forehead. Instinctively, she turned her face up. And he covered her lips with his.

He gave her no choice, no chance to think—no chance to tease him and drive him insane. Her lips were as luscious as he'd imagined, soft, hauntingly sweet, breathtakingly generous. He sampled them thoroughly, then wanted more. Shifting slightly, he slid the hand at her back down, over her hips, over her gorgeously ripe bottom, then filled his palm with her heated flesh and drew her fully against him.

She gasped—her lips parted. He slid his tongue between and tasted her, and felt his heart skip a beat, felt desire soar, felt a ravenous hunger grip him. He angled his head, deepened the kiss—and ravished her. Voraciously.

And she responded. Tentatively at first, then with greater urgency, pressing her own demands. Hot, wild, untempered, abandoned, her passion poured through them; he felt her hands steal up his chest, over his shoulders, until her fingers locked in his hair. And as she'd always done, she taunted and teased; even though he knew she had no idea what she was doing—or perhaps because of that—he was powerless to tame his own response, an urgent, ruthless, primitive need to take her, claim her. Make her his.

Rose sensed it, knew it, and reveled in the knowledge. Beyond thought, beyond sense, with only sensation and emotion to guide her, she sank into the kiss, seized the moment and him, and gave herself up to the delight, the challenge, the insatiable need to appease him, ease his hunger, satisfy and soothe the raging tempest that had somehow sprung up between them.

It was a whirlwind of legendary proportions, a cataclysmic force that tensed his every muscle, and left her melting against him. Heat rose between them—she gasped as it flared. Duncan drank the sound, taking it from her along with her breath. She drew him deep and returned the pleasure, stirred to her toes when she felt his breath hitch.

She was deep in the kiss, sunk in delight, hostage to spiraling sensation, when a feminine gasp not her own fell on her ears.

"Oh! I say!"

It was Jeremy's voice.

Reeling, Rose pulled back; Duncan released her lips, but slowly. Even more slowly, he drew his hands from her, closing them about her waist in a warning squeeze before he released her. Straightening, he turned; her hands falling from him, dazed and close to stupefied, Rose blinked at Jeremy and Clarissa.

Round-eyed, slack-jawed, they stared back.

"Ah . . ." Rose cleared her throat and rushed into speech. "Duncan and I are cousins, you know—it was just a cousinly kiss. As a . . . a thank-you." She shot a glance at Duncan; he was watching her, his expression inscrutable. Rose resisted the urge to wring her hands—or his neck. Dragging in a breath, she drew herself up and looked directly at Jeremy and Clarissa. "I was just thanking Duncan for finding a book for me to read. I like to read before I fall asleep."

"Oh." Jeremy's expression cleared; he smiled ingenuously. Then he held out her shawl. "I had to get your maid to fetch it from your room—you must have forgotten to bring it down."

Rose gave thanks for the faint light, too weak to show her blush. Ignoring the cynical quirk of Duncan's brow, she smiled graciously and stepped forward and turned; Jeremy draped the shawl over her shoulders. It was clear he'd accepted her excuse; equally clearly, Clarissa, still shooting sharp glances from Duncan to her and back again, had not.

Avoiding Duncan's eye, still light-headed and fervently praying she wouldn't faint, Rose smiled at Jeremy. "I think we should go inside."

They did; Duncan and Clarissa trailed in behind them. Only a few members of the party were still in the drawing room; they looked up and smiled and nodded their good nights.

As a group, the four of them climbed the stairs; Rose could feel Clarissa's gimlet gaze on her back. From the gallery, they would go their separate ways; Rose calmly bade both Jeremy and Clarissa good night, then turned to Duncan.

He turned from Clarissa and inclined his head. "Don't forget my present." His eyes met hers, his gaze limpid, unthreatening—totally untrustworthy. "By all means dwell on it once you've slipped between the sheets, but don't be surprised if it keeps you awake."

She had to smile serenely, had to incline her head graciously. From the corner of her eye, she saw Clarissa blink, saw her glance quickly at Duncan, saw her suspicions fade. Exercising the wisdom of Solomon, Rose declined to tempt fate—or Duncan—further. "Good night, my lord." She let her gaze slide from his as she turned. "Sleep well."

Duncan watched her glide away, her hips gently swaying. Only the presence of Jeremy Penecuik, and thirty-odd others he mentally wished at the Devil, prevented him from following—and ensuring he did.

Three

Rose began the next day determined to keep her distance from Duncan, at least until she could understand just what was going on. Lust—particularly with him—was not something she'd come prepared for. She'd spent most of the night in a mental tizz, a state that had never afflicted her before.

Then again, no man had kissed her like that before.

She entered the breakfast parlor more wary, more uncertain, than ever before in her life. She took her place beside Jeremy, close to the foot of the table, not far from the comforting presence of Lady Hermione—and a long way from Duncan.

Only to have Duncan prowl up, with Clarissa, once more sweetly smiling, on his arm. Duncan just looked, a distinctly feral glint in his eyes; it was Clarissa who spoke.

"We thought, seeing the weather's amenable, to take a punt out on the lake." Both coy and clinging, Clarissa smiled up at Duncan. "I'm quite partial to the activity"—she turned her ingenuous gaze back to Jeremy and Rose—"but we really need a party or it wouldn't be at all the thing."

Her naivete robbed her speech of any insult. Jeremy smiled brightly. "That sounds an excellent idea." He looked at Rose.

Who reached for her teacup and took a long sip. She could feel their gazes on her, but she could *feel* Duncan's the most. Only a small part of the loch was suitable for punting; the rest was too deep. Punting meant hugging the banks, with the shrubs and trees and the flat loch for views, not the soaring mountains, the wild peaks. To appreciate those, you needed a rowboat, needed to go farther out on the loch or, better yet, to the island.

Punting was boring. And possibly dangerous, although she couldn't imagine how. But Jeremy wouldn't go without her, and Clarissa couldn't go with Duncan alone.

"The new punt will hold four easily."

Lady Hermione's matronly comment sent a clear message; Rose couldn't ignore it. Stifling a sigh, she looked up and smiled. "Yes, of course. Let's go punting."

Her gaze met Duncan's; she could read nothing in his eyes, his expression, other than a certain smugness which made her itch to . . .

Determinedly, she stood and gestured to the window, to the loch, smooth and glassy under a pale gray sky. "Shall we?"

They quit the house and strolled down the lawn, then through the extensive pinetum. The punt was waiting at the small jetty directly below the house; Duncan must have given orders for it to be brought around from the boathouse.

That was when they discovered that Clarissa, partial to the activity or not, was frightened of stepping down into the gently bobbing punt. Duncan tried to hand her in—she shied and skittishly backed, for all the world like a horse facing a float for the first time. Rose squelched the unflattering comparison and tried to encourage her. Wild eyes fixed not on

the punt, but on the wide waters of the loch, Clarissa shook
her head. "It's so big!" she gasped.

Jeremy went down the jetty; unlooping the rope that secured the punt, he shortened it, holding the narrow boat
steady. "Try now."

Duncan gently urged Clarissa forward; she smiled tightly.
Shuffling forward, she paused, poised on the edge of the
jetty, drew a deep breath, then another—and turned to Rose.
"Perhaps . . . if you could go first?"

Rose smiled reassuringly and held out her hand. Duncan
took it and handed her in; she stepped down into the punt
without the slightest mishap. She smiled up at Clarissa. "See?
It's no different than on a river." So saying, she carefully
stepped over the benches to the seat in the punt's prow; sub-
siding, she settled her skirts, gracefully reclined against the
cushions and, still smiling serenely, waved Clarissa down.

Duncan tried to hand Clarissa in; again, she balked.

"Just a minute," she said breathlessly. "I'll take off my
hat." Reaching up, she pulled her hat pin free and removed
her stylish villager bonnet—and promptly dropped it.

"Oh!" She turned to grab it, only to kick it farther. On her
other side, Duncan couldn't help. The hat skated down the
jetty, heading for the water. Dropping the punt's rope, Jeremy dove to his right and snagged it.

"No!"

The admonition burst from Duncan and Rose simultane-
ously. Stunned, both Jeremy and Clarissa turned uncompre-
hendingly to Duncan. Then they followed his fixed gaze to
where the punt was swinging wide, gripped by some powerful current. As they watched, it revolved once, then headed
smoothly out over the loch.

Carrying Rose away. Her face, unshaded by any hat, wore
an expression of aghast incredulity Duncan suspected he
would treasure all his life.

"Oh, dear!" Beside him, Clarissa stifled a nervous titter. "How dreadful." She did not sound overly concerned.

Not so Jeremy, rising from the planks of the jetty, Clarissa's bonnet dangling from one hand. "I say." The knowledge that he had been the one who dropped the rope— to rescue Clarissa's hat—showed in his expression. He turned to Duncan. "Is she in any danger?"

His narrowed gaze fixed consideringly on the punt, on Rose's rapidly dwindling figure, Duncan didn't answer.

"Don't be silly." Clarissa laid a hand on Jeremy's sleeve and squeezed reassuringly. "The punt will just go out, then come in to shore again, somewhere farther along." She glanced at Duncan. "Won't it?"

"Actually, no." Duncan turned to face them. "But Rose knows where the punt will fetch up—she won't be worried on that score."

Jeremy frowned. "Where will it fetch up?"

Duncan looked out, over the loch. "On the island."

"Ah." Jeremy studied the small island, covered with trees, situated in the center of the widest part of the loch. "We'll have to go and rescue her, then."

"Why? The pole's in the boat." Clarissa sounded close to pouting. "All she need do is exert herself a little, and she'll get herself back to shore."

"No." His gaze still on Rose, sitting upright, staring back at the shore, Duncan wondered how long it would take her to work it out, to see what was bound to happen next. "The main part of the loch is too deep for punting, and there are no oars in the punt. We'll need to get the rowboat and go after her."

"Right, then." Manfully squaring his shoulders, Jeremy looked along the shoreline. "Where's the boathouse?"

"I can't go in any rowboat—not across all that!" The panic in Clarissa's voice rang clearly. Duncan and Jeremy both looked at her; wild-eyed, she stared back. "It's too wide. Too big." She glanced at the loch and shuddered. "I couldn't *possibly*."

"Well, that's all right." Jeremy spoke calmingly. "Strathyre and I will go after her. You can go back to the house."

Clarissa cast a horrified glance back up the slope. "Through the trees?" She shivered. "I couldn't—there might be someone in the shadows. And anyway"—her chin trembled—"Mama wouldn't like me walking about alone."

Jeremy frowned at her.

Duncan spoke decisively. "Penecuik, if you would escort Miss Edmonton back to the house, I'll get the rowboat and fetch Rose."

Jeremy looked up. "If you can show me the boathouse, I'll go and get her; after all, it was I who dropped the rope."

Duncan shook his head. "No—the loch isn't a river. The currents are complex." He looked out at the punt, shrinking in the distance. "I'll go after Rose."

"Oh." Jeremy half grimaced but accepted his fate. He offered an arm to Clarissa; she leaned on it as if she were in imminent danger of collapse.

She flashed a weak smile at both Jeremy and Duncan. "All this excitement! I fear I'll need to rest once we get back to the house."

Duncan merely nodded, and they parted, Clarissa and Jeremy heading back through the trees. Duncan turned and studied Rose's tiny figure; she was still staring at the shore. Lips twitching, he swung about and headed for the boathouse.

And heard, from far across the water, an anguished wail.

"Nooooo!"

He looked at the punt, but Rose had slumped back on the cushions, out of sight. Duncan grinned, unrestrainedly triumphant, and lengthened his stride.

* * *

Sand crunched as he beached the rowboat on the island forty minutes later. Stepping out into the shallows, he hauled the boat up the narrow beach, a crescent of gravel edging a small cove, until the boat was safe from any shifting currents. The punt, empty, bobbed nearby. Duncan waded over, grabbed the prow and towed it to the rowboat. After lashing the punt to the rowboat's stern, he turned and surveyed the trees.

Which was all he could see. No Rose.

Duncan considered, then climbed up the beach onto the path that led to his forefathers' castle. He hadn't been on the island for years—not, now he thought about it, since the days he and Rose had run wild over the Strathyre lands. The years hadn't changed the basic geography, but trees he remembered as saplings were now full-grown; bushes of hazel had turned to thickets. The paths, however, although rock-strewn, remained easily navigable.

Ten minutes later, he rounded a corner of the old keep and found Rose precisely where he'd expected her to be. She was seated on a huge slab of weathered gray rock, a long-ago part of the battlements. As children, that particular spot had been their especial place. In the past, she'd usually scrambled up, skirts hiked to her knees, and sat cross-legged—an engaging if irritating imp—to view their domain. That had been their customary game here—to start at the far right and name all the peaks, noting any changes the seasons had wrought, traveling the horizon, all the way to the far left.

She looked liked she was doing that now, except that her legs were now so long she could sit properly on the stone. Her hands were clasped in her lap; although he made no sound, she sensed him as he neared, and looked around.

"I've just reached Mackillanie."

Her voice, soft, lilting, with the endearing rounded roughness of the Highlands, was a memory he'd never forgotten. She smiled—softly, easily, without teasing or restraint—and

time stood still. A willing captive to the web she'd so effortlessly thrown over him, Duncan returned the smile, then sat
beside her on the stone. And squinted up at the distant
mountains, all part of his lands. "Gilly Macall rebuilt his
cottage. In a slightly different spot."

They both scanned the relevant slope. "There!" Rose
pointed.

Duncan squinted, then nodded. They started all over
again, at the far right, matching what they could see with
changes one or the other recalled.

As they did, Duncan could almost sense a growing, building, strengthening of his connection with his lands; he
should have done this before, more often. This particular
view, from the old forecourt of his ancestors' home, encompassed the very essence of his being, all that he was. He was
Strathyre, head of one branch of the Macintyres, keeper of
this place, defender, protector and owner of these lands.

He felt the same compelling awe, the same mystique that
used to grip him as a child. As an adult, he still couldn't fully
describe the emotion—a sense of belonging, of deep and
abiding love for his lands. It was that that had sent him to
London for ten years, to ensure that Ballynashiels was safe.

Safe for the next generation.

And beside him sat someone who understood all that,
even though they'd never discussed it. Rose loved these
peaks as he did; she understood the beauty, the awe, the belonging—the sheer magic of Ballynashiels.

She leaned across him, pointing out a fallen boulder on a
distant slope; Duncan looked, briefly at the boulder, rather
longer at her. He waited until they reached the end of their
catechism, until a gentle, peaceful silence held sway, before
asking, his words soft, low, quiet, "Will you accept Penecuik?"

Rose flicked him a glance, then, looking back at the soaring peaks, sighed. "No."

"Not even for a dukedom—a duchess's tiara?"

Rose grinned. "Not even for the tiara." She stared at the mountains; her smile slowly faded. "He's nice enough, I suppose, but Perth is hale and hearty, and Jeremy's father more so. If I married Jeremy, we'd live in Edinburgh for most of our lives."

"And you wouldn't like that?"

"I couldn't *bear* that." Rose considered the statement and knew it was true. She glanced at Duncan. "What about you? Are you going to offer for Clarissa?"

He grimaced exasperatedly. "When the mountains scare her and she can't even look out over the loch without getting panicky? No, I thank you. I require rather more fortitude in a wife."

Rose choked, then chuckled; Duncan met her gaze and grinned. Their gazes held, locked; each studied the other, looking deep, seeing far beyond each other's social mask. The moment stretched—Rose suddenly realized she couldn't breathe. Breaking the contact, she smoothed her skirt. "We really should be getting back, or Jeremy will raise the alarm."

"When are you going to put the poor blighter out of his misery?"

Rose cocked her head and studied Duncan as he stood, stretching mightily. "Strange to tell," she answered, her usual haughty tones resurfacing, "I don't believe there'll be any misery involved; that's not why he wants to marry me."

"Oh?" Brows rising, Duncan looked down at her.

Rose spread her arms wide. "I'm suitable—wealthy, well-born and wise." Duncan choked; Rose smiled wryly. "I agreed to make my announcement on Midsummer's Day, which seems the best strategy. Otherwise, the rest of his stay might be a trifle awkward."

Duncan's brows rose higher. "Indeed." He cast a last glance at the towering peaks, then nodded, once, to himself. And turned back to Rose. "We'd better get going."

With that, he bent and hoisted her into his arms.

"Duncan!" Rose immediately struggled—and rapidly came to the same conclusion she'd reached years ago: there was never any point fighting Duncan physically; he was far stronger than she. "Put me down." She didn't pause to see if he would comply—she knew he wouldn't. He was striding along; held against his chest, she swayed against him. "What the devil are you about?"

He glanced down at her, his expression one of utter reasonableness. "My duty as a host."

"What?"

"I'm ensuring that you don't get a chance to play ghost-in-the-ruins and make me chase you through them. They're too dangerous; you might get hurt."

Rose snapped her mouth shut. "I haven't done that for more than a decade."

Ducking a branch that guarded the path to the cove, he met her gaze. "You haven't changed that much."

Rose drew in a deep breath—and struggled to ignore the increased pressure between her breast and his chest. "I am not about to play chase in the ruins."

"So you say now. But how do I know when you'll change your mind?"

Rose knew better than to swear an oath on it; he probably wouldn't accept that, either. "Duncan—this has gone far enough." She was starting to feel light-headed. "Put me down at once!"

"Stop fashin'." His voice took on the cadence of the local accent, sliding beneath her skin; his tone—one of endearment—made her inwardly quiver. Then he reverted to his normal voice. "Besides, you've only got slippers on, and the path's rocky."

"I got to the stone, didn't I?" Rose grumbled, none too gratefully.

"As your host, I should do all I can to ease your stay."

And drive her witless. Rose could feel the rumble of every word reverberating through his chest, could feel each and every one of his fingers as they gripped her—one set across her midriff, just beneath one breast, the other set wrapped around one thigh. Held firmly, effortlessly—far too easily—she felt increasingly helpless, increasingly vulnerable, in a distinctly unnerving way.

Just thinking about it made her breath seize.

She tried a last wriggle; he only tightened his hold. "Just hold still—we're only a few minutes from the beach."

Would she reach it sane?

When Duncan's boots crunched on the gravelly shore and he lowered her into the rowboat, Rose wasn't at all sure how competent her mind was. Her senses were rioting, in excellent health. Rational thought, however, when close to Duncan—especially when in contact with Duncan—seemed beyond her.

Not a comforting prospect. Especially as, settled in the prow of the boat watching him bend to the oars, she had a strong suspicion he knew it. There was nothing to be read in his face, however, nor in his eyes. Affecting a calmness she was far from feeling, she lay back and enjoyed the scenery. Soaring peaks, rippling muscles and all.

The peaks were impressive; the man who rowed her to shore, no less so. The boat glided powerfully across the water, impelled by steely muscles that flexed and relaxed, then flexed and relaxed again; the rhythm was both soothing and, at a different level, evocative.

Evocative enough to remind her of the extent of Duncan's physical prowess: he was an excellent rider, an expert marksman, a skillful climber, a noted whip. His need to excel had always found expression in physical pursuits; she'd bet her life he was also a superb lover.

Feeling heat in her cheeks, Rose shifted her gaze to the

craggy peaks. Despite Clarissa's conviction, they were far less threatening.

Duncan rowed directly to the boathouse, easing the rowboat into its berth, leaving the punt bobbing astern. The loch was at its summer level; he had to haul himself up to the wooden wharf. He accomplished the deed easily, then tied the rowboat up. And turned to Rose.

In time to catch the distinctly nervous look in her eyes. The sight tempted him to smile in rakish anticipation; ruthlessly, he suppressed the impulse. Rose could read him too easily, and he had no intention of pushing her into doing something unpredictable, into attempting to escape just now, just when he almost had his hands on her.

He'd spent the journey from the island carefully planning what came next. And ignoring the way she'd been watching him, the way she reacted to him. He was far too experienced to consider a rowboat in the middle of an open loch—overlooked by a house full of guests, no less—as an acceptable venue for what he had in mind.

He was determined to take things slowly—to stretch the moments, to appreciate each and every encounter to the full. Rose had teased and taunted him for years. Now it was his turn.

He waved her to her feet, then, with an impatience not entirely feigned, gestured her nearer. She edged to the center of the boat to stand before him, her expression an attempt at prosaic practicality. She lifted her arms and extended her hands to him.

Duncan grinned, stooped and swooped; gripping her under her arms, he hoisted her.

Rose gasped and clung wildly. Duncan lifted her out of the boat as if she were a child, then swung her to the wharf. But he didn't put her down. The wharf was a narrow walkway lining the wall of the boathouse; holding her before

him, her toes clear of the planks, Duncan turned, took one
step—and pinned her against the wall.

Rose's eyes flew wide. One look into his revealed the
danger. *"Dunc—!"*

That was all she got to say before his lips sealed hers.

Seared hers.

He proceeded to set her alight.

Rose tried to hold aloof, tried to hold firm, tried to main-
tain some degree of control . . . and failed on all counts. His
lips were commanding, demanding. Ruthlessly, he captured
her awareness and held it—appalled, aghast, excruciatingly
awakened—totally focused on their kiss. On the hot melding
of their lips, the searing sweep of his tongue, the heavy
weight of his chest, his hips, pressed against her much softer
flesh. The artful, evocative temptation he pressed on her
held her captive, unable to think, unable to act—able only to
feel.

The thought of physically struggling never entered Rose's
head; hands gripping his upper arms, she tried to mentally
pull back from the engagement, to regain some degree of
equilibrium, only to discover her wits scattered, her senses
reeling.

He immediately drew her back, into the maelstrom, with
even more evocative kisses, with heat, and yet more heat,
until she felt like she was fighting a losing battle against a
wildfire out of control. Flames licked greedily, now here,
now there—she doused one outbreak, only to see another
flare.

Then he caught her, and she burned, kissing him back
with the same heat, the same passion, the same wild and
reckless urgency. The pressure of their lips, the wild tangle
of their tongues, only heightened the physical need.

It was then that he finally set her down. Slid her down until her toes just touched the floor, his hard thigh parting, then

wedging firmly between hers. She gasped; he drank the sound, then angled his head and deepened their kiss.

And closed both hands over her breasts.

She melted—there was no other way to describe the sensation, the pure wave of hot desire that flooded her, liquefied her bones, pounded through her veins and pooled deep within her. His fingers firmed, kneaded, caressed—all too knowingly. She arched and offered herself up to them, to him, beyond thought, beyond reason, totally engrossed in the passion that burned so hotly between them. Locking her fingers in his hair, she pressed herself against him and thought she heard him groan. Releasing her breasts, he swept his hands down her body, over her hips, then closed both hands about her bottom and lifted her to him.

Rose couldn't believe the compulsion that battered her, the sheer, driving need to lift her long legs and wrap them about him. Her skirts defeated it, saved her from that too-revealing act, but she knew it in her bones—and so did he.

And it was that that saved her; as Duncan slowly eased back from their kiss, soothed and dampened the fires, doused their burning flames, she knew that as truth. And any doubts she might have been inclined to develop were laid to rest when she opened her eyes—and stared into his, darkened and burning. His lips, wicked things, kicked up at the ends; he bent his head and brushed them lightly across hers, swollen and aching, in a final caress, then drew back and trapped her gaze.

One dark brow rose, teasingly, tauntingly. "Just so we know where we stand."

The words reverberated through her; Rose managed not to gape. She knew precisely where she was standing at present. Across his thigh.

With another wicked glance, he stepped back—he steadied her when her legs quaked. For one long instant, Rose could do nothing but stare at him, trying to take it all in, trying to reestablish reality when her world had turned upside down.

He, of course, just watched her—like a very large jungle cat. Rose dragged in a deep breath. Her head still spun, but she didn't dare take her eyes from his. She'd very nearly offered him an invitation she had never offered any man. She couldn't take that in, could not believe it—could not understand the force that had warped her common sense and driven her to it. The man before her was Duncan—yet he wasn't.

This *wasn't* the youth she'd grown up with—and the difference was significant.

Before she could follow that thought to any logical conclusion, the gong for lunch boomed in the distance.

Duncan grinned—the very essence of male wickedness— and held out his hand. "Much as I'd rather have you instead of a cold collation, I suspect we'd better go in."

Rose sucked in a breath and drew herself up, but didn't take his hand. "Indeed."

She swung about and marched to the door. And continued to march up the slope to the house, all too aware of Duncan prowling easily beside her.

He was dangerous. She felt it in the air, a premonition that set her nerves quivering. He was dangerous in the way men like him were dangerous to ladies like her. She'd known it after he'd kissed her on the terrace; he'd now confirmed it beyond doubt.

How he now viewed her, she couldn't imagine—any more than she could guess what he might do next. Was he simply teasing her, now he'd discovered he could? Paying her back for all the years through which she'd had the upper hand and exercised it ruthlessly?

He was as ruthless as she in that respect; the thought made her quiver even more.

A wayward thought wafted through her distracted mind; she stifled a disgusted snort. She had to be still distracted or she'd never have thought of it. Duncan could not be interested in her as a wife; she was nowhere near perfect enough for him.

She'd lived all her life knowing that; she'd never thought otherwise. Duncan would marry perfection. Not even Clarissa had lived up to his standards. But he would keep looking, and someday he would find her, the perfect wife for him. He was nothing if not persistent, dogged, incapable of accepting failure—just witness his efforts to save Ballynashiels.

He'd find his perfect wife and marry her, which was all very well. That didn't explain—give her any clue—as to what he thought he was about with her. And she could no longer handle him; she was no match for him, had no counter to his experience in this particular sphere.

She didn't have a clue what he thought, what he wanted, what he might do—to her, with her—next.

The house loomed before them. Rose lifted her head, squared her shoulders and refused to even glance at Duncan. Sliding back into their old ways, their old relationship, was no longer a viable option. She would have to act in the only way she could.

Avoid him—possibly forever.

Four

Clarissa retired immediately after luncheon, appar-
ently still fragile after the events of the morning. From the
other end of the room, Rose watched her go, and started
thinking—fast.

"I really need to write some letters," Jeremy confessed—
just as Duncan strolled up.

"Make use of the desk in the library," Duncan offered, the
epitome of the urbane host. "You'll find everything you need
there."

Jeremy hesitated. "You're sure I won't be putting you
out?"

"No, no." With an easy smile, Duncan waved the suggestion aside. "I've completed all the estate business necessary." His gaze swung to Rose. "I rather think I'm more in
need of relaxation." The timbre of his voice altered subtly;
his gaze, holding hers, grew more intent. "I was thinking of
a game of croquet."

Rose didn't bat an eye. "Croquet?"

"Hmm. Somewhat combative for a lady, I know, but I
wouldn't have thought that would deter you."

He was pricking her deliberately, challenging her, doubtless in the hope that she'd rise to his bait and forget that the croquet lawn, while not far from the house, was surrounded by a screening hedge—a completely private enclosure for a game that, unless she missed her guess, would have very little to do with hoops and mallets. Not unless she used one on him.

Rose smiled and rose—and limped around her chair. "So sorry to disappoint you, but I seem to have turned my ankle."

"I say." Solicitously, Jeremy offered his arm. "Is it serious?"

"Oh, no," Rose replied. "But I think I should rest it for the afternoon."

"How did it happen?" Jeremy asked as she leaned on his arm.

Rose shrugged lightly and looked at Duncan. "Perhaps on the island—it was rather rocky."

"Or perhaps," Duncan said, his tone carrying an implication Jeremy heard but couldn't interpret, "it happened in the boathouse—you seemed to experience some difficulty there."

Rose stared at him calmly, then lightly shrugged again. "Perhaps," she said, her eyes on his. "But I'm afraid I won't be able to accommodate you." She let a second elapse before adding, "With a croquet game."

With that, and a calm look just for him, she hobbled off on Jeremy's arm.

She made very sure she was not alone at any time for the rest of the day, and the whole of the evening. Lady Hermione gave her a very odd look when she offered to play and sing for the company. Rose ignored it; she had already decided that being on the piano stool, under the eyes of the entire company, was about as safe as she could be.

All she had to bear with from Duncan was a quirking brow and a look she tried hard not to notice. She survived

the evening and retired without any further challenge from
him.

Midsummer's Eve dawned, full of promise for the next
day and the evening's revels. The sun shone, and the air was
crisp and clear, as it could be only in the Highlands.

Strolling into the breakfast parlor, Duncan was surprised
to discover Rose and Clarissa already there, heads together.
A more unlikely pair he could not imagine—Clarissa so innocent, Rose anything but. They looked up and greeted him,
both smiling—Clarissa sweetly, Rose somewhat smugly.
She explained that last as he sat.

"Clarissa has always wanted to learn how such a large es-
tablishment runs. I've offered to show her about."

"We're to start in the stillroom," Clarissa eagerly informed him.

"Hmm." Rose's smile was serene. "And then we'll go
through the buttery and the dairy—and, of course, the succession houses."

"And after that, Lady Hermione has offered to demonstrate how she tends her special plants."

Duncan smiled easily, but the glance he sent Rose held a
warning and a promise.

Rose noted it, but, her confidence resurrected, felt sure she
could outwit him—at least until Midsummer, when she could
release Jeremy and then decide whether to stand or flee.

She wasn't up to making that decision yet; she had to live
through Midsummer's Eve first.

Luckily, her confidence had yet to reach the cocksure; as
they left the breakfast parlor, Clarissa suggested and she
concurred that they'd need wraps to brave the cool of the
stillroom. Clarissa's room was in a different wing; leaving
her own minutes later, Rose headed for the side gallery, the
shortest route to the stillroom.

She never knew what warned her—perhaps a shifting

shadow or a whiff of sandalwood. Some sixth sense alerted, she stopped, quivering, on the threshold of the long, narrow gallery.

And knew Duncan was close—very close.

With a smothered shriek, she whirled and ran. Behind her, she heard him curse. She hied straight down the main corridor of bedrooms; in her soft slippers, light on her feet, she made very little sound. Duncan, so much heavier, could not follow, not fast—if he ran, he'd have everyone on the floor poking their heads out of their doors and asking what was wrong. Rose reached the end of the corridor and slowed, then skipped lightly down a narrow side stair. She gained the bottom, slipped out a side door and started across a flagged terrace.

Halfway across, she looked up—and saw Duncan watching her from the gallery above.

She waved; he scowled.

Smiling even more brightly, she headed for the stillroom, conscious of exhilaration streaking down her veins, conscious of the pounding of her heart.

They were no longer children—but they could still play games.

"I really think it's time I took you for a ride."

Duncan uttered the words in his most charming voice—to Clarissa, not Rose.

"Oh, yes!" Clarissa smiled brightly and turned to Rose, beside her. "That will fill in the afternoon nicely, don't you think?"

Slowly, her eyes on Duncan's innocent face, Rose nodded. "Indeed." She could see no danger in a ride; on the back of her customary mount, while she couldn't outride Duncan, she could at least outmaneuver him. And she'd have Clarissa and Jeremy near. She nodded more definitely. "A ride sounds an excellent idea."

Getting changed and sorting out mounts and saddles filled the next half hour—it was midafternoon before they were away. It was rapidly apparent that while Rose and Duncan were superlative riders, the others were much less accomplished. Jeremy handled his chestnut with confidence but insufficient skill; Clarissa was clearly uncomfortable above a slow canter.

Exchanging a long-suffering look with Rose, Duncan dropped back to ride beside Clarissa, leaving Rose to entertain Jeremy. While she pointed out various peaks and other spots of interest, she listened to the murmurs behind her. And inwardly approved. Duncan's manner was that of a host, considerate of his guest's enjoyment; Clarissa was full of that evening's ball, of her gown, of the anticipated dancing—Duncan indulged her with an avuncular air.

As they rounded the loch and, hooves clacking, crossed the stone bridge spanning the river, Rose felt much more in charity with Duncan than she had for days. He was behaving exactly as he should.

They rode on through the lush meadows, and on into the foothills, eventually reining in on a bluff looking out over the valley. From the valley floor, the view was deceptive: although from the house the bluff looked quite close, it was actually miles away. That became apparent when they looked back at the house, small and white on the opposite side of the loch.

Clarissa viewed the wide expanse, broken only by a few scattered cottages and copses, with something akin to dismay. "Oh!" She blinked. "Good heavens—well!" She glanced at Jeremy.

Who was drinking in the view. "Quite spectacular," he averred. Turning, he looked behind them, at the gradual rise of the foothills, lapping the feet of the towering crags. "It's amazing how much arable land there is—you wouldn't think it from the house."

He and Duncan fell to discussing the various farms that made up the estate.

Clarissa bit her lip and looked down, nervously plaiting her mare's mane. Rose, on the other side of Jeremy, inwardly sighed and held her tongue.

"Shouldn't we be getting back?" Clarissa abruptly suggested, silencing both men. They looked at her; then Duncan inclined his head.

"Of course—you'll be eager to dress for the ball."

The smile Clarissa beamed at him was truly ingenuous; Rose resisted the urge to shake her head. Picking up her reins, she was about to swing her mare's head for home when she saw Duncan frown and cock his head.

She stilled and listened. And heard what he had: a distant mewling, carried on the light breeze.

Both Jeremy and Clarissa, noticing their absorption, listened, too.

"It's a cat." Clarissa tightened her reins. "It's probably just mousing."

Neither Rose, Duncan nor Jeremy replied; they all frowned abstractedly, concentrating on the sound. It came again, louder—a wail, ending on a telltale sob.

"A child." Rose scanned the nearby slope, then, eyes widening, looked down the rocky bluff, a tumble of boulders angling down to the valley floor. "Oh, God! Duncan—you don't think . . . ?"

Face set, he was already dismounting. "They must be in the caves."

"Yes, but which one?" Pushing aside the skirts of her habit, Rose kicked free of her saddle and slid to the ground.

Duncan shot out a hand to steady her. "Heaven only knows."

Jeremy frowned as they both tethered their mounts to nearby bushes. "Can't you simply follow the sound?"

"Echoes." His face grim, Duncan strode to the lip of the

bluff. "The entire rock face is riddled with caves. They're all joined—any sound made in one echoes throughout the system. It's damned hard to locate the source of any sound."

"Oh."

"But . . . ," Clarissa frowned as she studied Duncan, who stood, hands on hips, looking down the cliff. "Shouldn't we head back, then?"

"Back?" Duncan glanced at her, clearly at a loss.

"So we can send someone for the child," Clarissa artlessly explained. "We can send a groom to the farms around here to let them know one of their children is lost in the caves, so the parents can get them out."

Rose kept her gaze on Duncan's face, ready to intervene if need be. She sensed his reactive rage; to her relief, he mastered it. And, in a voice devoid of inflection, explained, "By the time we ride back and a groom rides out again, it'll be twilight. Despite its appearance, this area is not a wilderness—there're cottages and crofters' huts scattered all over. And it's Midsummer's Eve—everyone will be everywhere, getting ready for the festivities."

"Precisely," Clarissa returned. "And your mother's ball is the most *important* festivity—you can't possibly mean to be late."

Rose grabbed Duncan's sleeve, not that he seemed to notice. Jeremy's horse shifted uneasily.

"Ahem," Jeremy said, drawing Clarissa's attention. "I rather think Strathyre means that it's potentially too dangerous to delay going to the child's aid."

Clarissa stared at him. "But it's only some shepherd's brat. They've probably just twisted their ankle. It will serve them right—teach them a lesson—to stay out all night and miss the Midsummer's Eve revels. I don't see," she concluded, elevating her nose haughtily, "how any *gentleman* could possibly suggest that because of some uncouth brat's misdemeanors, *I* should be forced to be late for the ball."

That speech held Jeremy, Rose and Duncan silent for a full minute. Clarissa looked belligerently back at them; it was patently clear she meant every word.

His expression grim, Duncan looked at Jeremy. "I would be much obliged, Penecuik, if you would escort Miss Edmonton back to the house."

Jeremy frowned. "Shouldn't I stay? What if you need help?"

Duncan glanced at Rose, standing beside him. "Rose knows the caves as well as I do." He looked back at Jeremy. "I need her with me"—he nodded at Clarissa—"and Miss Edmonton requires an escort."

Jeremy's expression stated very clearly what he thought of Clarissa's demands, but he was too much the gentleman to argue further. "Should I send any others out to help?"

Duncan glanced at the sky. "No. If we need help, we'll find it nearer to hand."

Jeremy nodded, then wheeled his horse and waved Clarissa to join him. She sniffed and did so; they set off down the track. Rose and Duncan turned back to the cliff's edge. Ears straining into the quiet, they waited—and finally heard the distant crying again.

"It's so weak." Without hesitation, Rose started down the cliff, climbing down between two boulders. "They're a long way down, don't you think?"

Duncan nodded. "I think." He grimaced. "But they could simply be deep in the system. If they're young, they might have gone even farther than we ever did."

"Heaven forbid," Rose whispered.

The cliff was not sheer but a steep, boulder-pocked rock face. They climbed down without talking, Duncan quickly outstripping Rose and swinging across beneath her. Rose noted the protective measure but said nothing. Gradually, the soft, thin wail grew louder.

Duncan stopped and waited for Rose to reach him. When

she was standing beside him, he whispered in her ear, "Call to them—if I do, they might panic and shut up."

Rose nodded. "Sweetheart," she called, her voice soft and comforting, "where are you? It's Rose from the big house— you remember me, don't you?"

Silence—then, as if fearing some trick of nature, came a hesitant, "Miss Rose?"

"That's right. A friend and I are going to get you out. What's your name, sweetheart?"

"Jem, miss. Jem Swinson."

"Are you all right, Jem—not hurt?"

Silence again, then, in a tearful voice, Jem blurted, "I've just got a few scratches—but it's m'brother, Petey, miss. He's fallen down a hole and he's lying so *still!*"

Jem's voice broke on a sob; beside Rose, Duncan cursed. "Keep him talking."

Rose nodded. Jem was seven years old, his brother Petey only four. "Jem?" No answer. "Jem, you must keep talking so we can find you and help Petey."

After a moment, they heard Jem clear his throat. "What do you want me to say?"

"Can you come out of the cave and show us where it is?"

"No." Jem sobbed, then collected himself. "I slid into the hole to try and help Petey, and now I can't get out."

"Ask him to describe the cave entrance," Duncan hissed as he helped Rose past a particularly large boulder. Rose complied; Jem described an opening that could have been one of at least ten on the rock face.

"Can you still see the entrance?" Rose asked.

"No. We went around a corner—all I can see is a glow if I look back that way."

Rose frowned. "How far did you go in before you came to the corner?"

"Far?"

"Think in steps—how many steps did you take before you went around the corner?"

Duncan threw Rose a questioning look; she ignored it, waiting for Jem's answer.

"About four?" Jem tentatively suggested. "It wasn't very far."

Rose smiled beatifically. "They must be in that cave I used to use to trick you, remember?"

Duncan threw her a glance that said he remembered all too well. And changed direction. "It was over there, wasn't it?"

Rose looked across the valley, to where the first lights were being lit at Ballynashiels, then back at the slope, gauging positions. "Yes." She nodded decisively. "Farther down and farther across—just beyond that boulder with the bush at its base."

They skidded and slid in their haste to reach the spot; Rose continued to talk to Jem, confidence ringing in her tone. The boy responded, sounding less and less worried with every exchange. Crossing a stretch of loose rock, Rose slipped. Duncan cursed and slapped a hand to her bottom, steadying her, then easing her descent. There was nothing sexual in his touch; not even when, reaching the ledge where he stood in an ungainly rush, Rose cannoned into him, did either of them so much as blink. They were both totally focused on rescuing Jem and Petey; in that instant, nothing existed beyond that.

"Yes!" Rose all but jigged when they reached the mouth of the suspect cave and heard Jem's voice ring strong and true. "Jem, we're here. We're going to get you out."

Silence. Then: "I don't want to leave Petey." Jem's voice started to waver. "He followed me in—he's always following me about—I should of looked out for 'im better."

"Now, Jem. Petey will be all right." Rose prayed that was so. "We're going to get him out, too, so you needn't worry."

The cave entrance was low and just wide enough for Rose to squeeze through. She knew the narrow passage widened just past the entrance, then turned sharply to the right. She was about to kneel down and wriggle in, when Duncan's hand closed on her shoulder; he spun her around.

"Here." He pushed her hands through the armholes of his jacket, the wrong way around.

"What?" Rose frowned at the jacket.

Ruthlessly, Duncan hauled the jacket up her arms and around her, buttoning it up at the back. "They're presumably down that hole you used to disappear into. I can probably get into the passage, but I don't think I'll be able to get around the corner."

Rose glanced at him, at the width of his shoulders: there was indeed a great deal more of him than there had been all those years ago.

"So," Duncan continued, speaking fast and low, "you lead the way in. We'll get Jem out and get him back into the passage; then you'll have to slide into the hole and lift Petey out to me."

Rose nodded. "So why the jacket?" She examined her new coat; because of the width of his shoulders and back, it did not restrict her movements.

"Because," Duncan tersely explained, "you're no longer a scrawny fifteen—you won't be able to simply wriggle, chest and belly to the rock, out of that hole like you used to."

Rose's expression blanked. "Oh."

"Indeed." Duncan gestured her inside as Jem called out again. "I'll have to haul you out—and I don't want any of your anatomy damaged in the process."

Rose couldn't help a grin, but she sobered the instant she scraped through the entrance—and discovered she couldn't even stand upright in the passage. "We're nearly there, Jem. Don't be frightened."

The light in the cave was poor; Rose blinked rapidly, then

headed for the corner. Duncan wriggled through the entrance behind her; she heard a rip as his shirt did not quite make it through with him.

Then she eased around the corner, through a narrow constriction; looking hard, she could just discern the pool of shadow on the dusty floor—which was, in fact, a large hole. Crouching down, she looked in and saw the pale moon of a face looking up at her.

"Oh, miss!"

At Jem's tearful wail, Rose reached down and tousled his hair. "Come on, now. We'll need to get you out first." She held out her hands to him. "Take them, and sort of walk up the side of the hole."

The hole was nearly six feet deep; when Jem's hands found hers, Rose reached farther and wrapped her fingers around his wrists. "Now, up you come."

She braced herself to take his weight; luckily, he wasn't that heavy. With a grunt and a sob, he was in her arms; Rose hugged him briefly, then pushed him toward the main passage. "Go on now, so we can get Petey out."

Clearly torn, Jem looked back at the small body, only just visible in the darkness at the bottom of the hole.

"Jem—come on."

Jem looked up, blinking as Duncan, still in the entrance passage, beckoned him out. "Come out here, and let Rose get to Petey. She'll lift him out to me; then we'll need you to watch him while I get Rose out—all right?"

The plan, including a part for him, reassured Jem. He gulped, nodded and slipped back into the main passage. In the dark, he didn't recognize Duncan; Duncan gripped his shoulder reassuringly, then sent him to sit by the entrance.

Looking around the corner again, Duncan saw—nothing. Precisely what he always used to see. Rose would taunt him, then slip into the cave and disappear; it had taken him forever to realize there was a hole there.

Just then, her head popped up; she looked at him over the lip of the hole. "Broken bones—his arm at least, maybe more. He's unconscious."

Duncan nodded. "Nothing for it—we'll have to lift him out. Can you manage it?"

Rose disappeared again—and came up with a small, twisted body in her arms. "Here." It was an effort: she straining to support Petey, a dead weight on her arms, stretching as far as she could; Duncan, wedged as deeply into the contriction as possible, reaching, straining to get a good grip on the small body. Teeth gritted, he managed it and lifted Petey from Rose. Backing took a moment or two, easing out of the trap he'd forced himself into.

"Don't," he said to Rose, seeing her place her palms on the lip of the hole. "Just wait, dammit."

He took Petey to Jem, and laid him down gently, then returned to find Rose trying unsuccessfully to hike herself out of the hole. "Here—give me your hands."

She did. It was the work of a minute for him to haul her out; his coat, of course, would never be the same, but it had gone in a good cause.

Returning to the boys, he clasped Jem's shoulder; when Rose joined them, he sent her out, then Jem, then handed Petey through and followed.

They splinted Petey's broken bones as best they could using strips torn from Rose's petticoat. Then they set about the difficult task of climbing back up the cliff face, Rose leading Jem, Duncan carrying Petey. Rose insisted that Duncan go ahead; he tried to argue, but she refused to budge. It was full twilight by the time they reached the horses, and edging into night before the long, necessarily slow ride, with Rose carrying Jem before her, and Duncan carrying Petey—thankfully still unconscious—came to an end at the Swinson farm.

The family hadn't gone to join the festivities down by the

loch; they'd been frantically searching every burn, every field, every hayrick.

"Oh, thank the Lord!" Meg Swinson, the boys' mother, spotting them as they neared the gate, came running, arms reaching. Her face fell when she saw Petey so still.

Duncan quickly explained; then Rose reined in beside him and set Jem down. Meg pounced on him and enveloped him in a bone-crushing hug; Doug Swinson, the boys' father, gently lifted Petey from Duncan's arms. Rose quickly reassured him, relieved when she saw the boys' grandmother, Martha, squinting from the farmhouse door.

The Swinsons hurried their lost lambs into the farmhouse; Malachi, Doug's brother, nodded to Duncan and Rose. "Don't know as how we'll ever be able to thank you enough, m'lord, Miss Rose. But if ye'd like a pint o'ale and some biscuits before ye set out back, we'd be proud to supply both."

They hadn't eaten since luncheon; Duncan slanted a glance at Rose, who kicked her feet free of her stirrups and slid down. "Just a small glass for me, Malachi, but I'm sure his lordship would like a pot."

They sat on the bench beside the front door, their backs to the wall, and sipped their ale, their gazes roaming the valley spread before them, a mass of dark, not-yet-black shadows, with the loch a smooth slate under the light of the rising moon.

Behind them, inside the cottage, the Swinsons fussed and fretted; Petey had yet to regain consciousness. Duncan rolled the ale on his tongue, then swallowed. "Do you think he'll be all right?"

Rose leaned her shoulder briefly against his. "Old Martha Swinson knows what she's about—if she says Petey will be all right, he will be."

Night slowly fell; a deep silence enveloped them, not empty, but enriched with the glow of shared achievement from a challenge successfully met, of harmony from shared goals successfully served. Neither moved; neither needed to look to sense what the other felt.

And in that timeless moment, Duncan finally understood all that Rose meant to him. She was terror and delight, irritation and gratification—a thorn in his flesh who had bloomed into his Rose. His. She had always matched him so effortlessly, so instinctively, it had been easy not to notice. Yet when she was by his side, his life was whole, complete, somehow richer—he never wanted another day to dawn when she wouldn't be by his side.

The night deepened, and still they sat, each quietly savoring their mutual contentment, neither wanting to break the spell, the magic of perfect accord.

Beside the loch, on the bank close to the bridge, a torch flared; then a bonfire surged to life. The Midsummer's Eve revels had begun.

Then a reedy wail issued from the cottage; a minute later, Doug Swinson emerged. "Praise be, but he seems well enough." The big man grinned with relief. "Two broken bones, Ma says, but clean breaks—and she's already set them, thanks be. Once he drinks some of her sleeping potion, he'll be down for the night. Safe, thanks to you."

Duncan shrugged and stood. "Just luck that we were there." He drained his tankard.

Rose grinned and handed Doug her empty glass. "Tell Meg her biscuits were delicious as always, and her ale as well. I hope you both get some time to join in the fun." Scrambling into her saddle, she nodded to the bonfire, now a roaring blaze leaping into the night.

"Oh, aye." Doug looked at her and Duncan. "But I'm thinking it's you should stop at the bonfire."

Mounting, Duncan laughed; atop her mare, Rose laughed, too, rather less sincerely. "Good night, Doug." With a wave, she headed the mare out of the gate; Duncan's powerful chestnut quickly came up alongside.

She felt his gaze on her face. After a long moment, he asked, "Want to stop by the bonfire?"

It was tempting, so tempting. But . . . "Your mother would wring your neck—and mine—if we did."

"Actually . . . I don't know about that."

"With half the Argyll waiting in your ballroom? It's a certainty."

"Hmm." Duncan grimaced. "Well, if we must, we'd better hurry. As it is, we'll be lucky to make the last waltz."

Rose shot him a glance. "Race you."

She sprang her mare on the words; Duncan whooped and followed. They thundered over the fields, down tracks they didn't need to see to follow, tracks engraved in their memories. Duncan had the more powerful horse, but he rode much heavier; over the distance and terrain, they were evenly matched.

The ride was wild, neither giving an inch or expecting any quarter. They rode like demons, on through the night, skirting the loch, the glittering magnificence of his home their ultimate goal. Their route took them close by the bonfire—roaring, spitting flames high into the night. Despite their streaking progress, or perhaps because of it, they were recognized. People called and waved; by unspoken accord, they reined to a walk as they approached the bridge and waved back.

Some of the men called suggestions through the night; breathing quickly, her blood stirred by the ride, Rose blushed and set her mare onto the bridge. She reined in at the center and sensed Duncan doing the same, to look down the length of the loch, at the reflection of the lights of Ballynashiels dancing on its dark surface.

Her heart thudded; her nerves tingled, sensitized to the

excitement flickering in the air, the anticipation evoked by traditions older than time. Her wayward senses reached for Duncan—and he reached for her.

One arm snaked about her waist, lifting her from her saddle, locking her against him; his other hand framed her face as she turned, gasping—and his lips covered hers.

The kiss was as wild as their ride—untamed, unrestrained, hot and demanding. He took her mouth and she gave it, sinking into his embrace, returning every caress greedily, avidly, unable to mask the desire he evoked, incapable of reining it in. She had more chance of stopping the moon in its orbit than controlling the passion he unleashed in her.

Sensations battered her; compulsion dragged at her. Her wits, what was left of them, reeled. Where they were headed, she had no idea, but they were still riding far too fast.

When his hand dropped to her breast, already swollen and aching, she dragged her lips free. And groaned, moaned, then managed to gasp, "Duncan—we *have* to go home, remember?"

If they'd stopped anywhere but on the bridge, if there'd been grass beneath them rather than stone, he would have taken her down, off her horse, and taken her, then and there. She sensed it, knew it—heard it in his eventual, reluctant groan.

Breathing deeply, his chest expanding dramatically, he rested his forehead against hers. "Am I *forever* destined to have to let you go?"

She managed a shaky laugh, but gave no other answer.

With a frustrated sigh, Duncan set her back in her saddle. He was prepared to wager a significant sum that both his mother and her father would rejoice if he stayed out all Midsummer's Eve with Rose, but there were benefits to be had in returning to Ballynashiels. A bed, among others. He picked up his reins. "Let's go."

No longer racing, they still rode like the wind, neither seeing any reason to do otherwise. It was indeed late; to make any appearance at the ball at all, they needed to fly.

They clattered into the stableyard. Duncan leapt from his saddle; Rose all but fell out of hers. Duncan caught her hand and hauled her upright; grinning widely, ignoring his startled stablemen, he raced across the cobbles, dragging Rose, giggling, behind him.

They erupted into the servants' hall. Duncan flung orders left and right, striding without pause for the back stairs, leaving chaos in his wake. Maids and his valet fell over their toes in their rush to follow; the housekeeper set houseboys drawing hot water from the kettles and dispatched burly footmen to fetch the copper baths.

Duncan didn't wait; he hauled Rose, giggling helplessly, up the stairs to the second floor. He stopped in the private gallery—and kissed her witless.

When he raised his head, she was reeling. Eyes glittering, he looked down at her face. "Hurry—I'll wait for you here."

With that, he let her go. The first of the maids bustled up the stairs; turning on his heel, he strode for his room.

Rose watched him go, then laughed, pirouetted once— and dashed for hers.

The next half hour was the essence of madness. A bevy of maids helped her strip; others filled the bath; still others raided her wardrobe at her instruction. Her own maid, Lucy, stood at the room's center issuing directions. Everyone grinned—a sense of wild excitement had infected them all. Rose bathed, dressed and had her hair coiffed in record time. Lucy scurried behind her, still fastening the clasp of her necklace as she headed out of the door.

"Your shawl, miss!" One of the maids dashed out of the

room and quickly arranged the spangled silk over Rose's arms.

Flashing her, and all the others gathering in the doorway to watch her go off, a wide and grateful smile, Rose glided toward the gallery.

Duncan was waiting, so tall and darkly handsome that Rose's heart skipped a beat. In sheer self-defense, she sent him a teasing, sultry, knowingly alluring glance.

Taking her arm, he ducked his head and ran his lips along the edge of her earlobe. "Later," he murmured.

Rose shivered—and shot him a warning look.

Duncan grinned, wolfishly, and headed for the main stairs.

Older guests thronged the ballroom's foyer, chatting and gossiping; all heads turned as Duncan, proud and assured, descended, Rose poised and elegant on his arm. Smiles greeted them, along with nods of approval; they were known by everyone. Whispered comments abounded; as they reached the tiled foyer and slipped effortlessly into their social roles, Rose heard someone say, "Aye—a striking couple. They've always dealt well when they're not scrapping."

Rose smiled. She curtsied and touched cheeks with two of the local *grandes dames*. Music drifted from the ballroom— the evocative strains of a waltz. Yielding to the pressure of Duncan's fingers about her elbow, Rose excused herself. Duncan led her to the arched door of the ballroom; they swept in as the last waltz died.

Duncan slanted her a glance. "Too late." His murmur was swamped as his mother descended, a host of neighbors in her wake.

Lady Hermione was all gracious absolution, insisting that they relate the whole tale, then declaring that she herself would visit the injured culprits on the morrow. Their neighbors understood completely; all nodded approvingly—they would have reacted in exactly the same way. Clan—or any for whom one was responsible—always had first claim on a chieftain's time.

Only Clarissa, hanging back at the edge of the crowd, appeared less than impressed. Eyes on Duncan, she all but glowered; then she noticed Jeremy standing quietly to one side, softly smiling at Rose. Clarissa's eyes narrowed; after a moment, she headed his way.

Some time later, Rose slipped from Duncan's side and joined Jeremy and Clarissa. Jeremy smiled. "You were successful, it seems."

"Yes, thank heavens." Rose returned his smile. "There were two of them."

"We've heard," Clarissa acidly informed her.

Rose looked at her, without comment, then smiled again at Jeremy. "But it's late—I won't keep you."

"Indeed," Clarissa stated. "I was about to ask Jeremy to escort me upstairs."

Jeremy's eyes did not leave Rose. "I'll speak with you tomorrow."

Smoothly, Rose inclined her head. "Tomorrow."

"Rose!" They all turned to see Lady Hermione beckoning.

They parted, and Rose rejoined Duncan and his mother— the guests were leaving. As a trio, they stood on the front steps and waved them away, Rose on Duncan's right, Lady Hermione on his other side.

As the last carriage rumbled away, Lady Hermione sighed. "That's over." She nodded decisively and picked up her skirts. "And I'm for bed, my dears. Good night."

With a regal nod, she swept indoors and straight on up the stairs. Duncan, with Rose on his arm, followed more slowly, his gaze resting thoughtfully on his mother's retreating back.

He halted in the front hall; behind them, Falthorpe shot the bolts home. Duncan looked down at Rose; she looked up at him and lifted a brow. He grinned. "I'm famished."

Rose's dimples winked. "So am I."

They raided the buffet in the supper room, then carried their piled plates into the ballroom so the staff could get on with their clearing. They lounged on a *chaise* and ate as they talked, comparing notes of who had been present and said what, helping themselves to morsels from each other's plate at will. About them, staff set the room to rights, straightening furniture, pushing wide brooms across the polished floor. Footmen used ladders to snuff out the candles in the chandeliers and wall sconces; Duncan shook his head when asked if he wanted any candles left burning. Gradually, all activity about them ceased, leaving them in peace, the room lit by wide swathes of moonlight slanting through the windows.

When they'd devoured every last crumb, Rose licked her fingers, and, looking out over the dance floor, sighed. "It's a pity we missed the last waltz."

Duncan shot her a glance, then reached out, relieved her of her empty plate, set it aside, fluidly stood—and swept her an elegant bow. "My dance, I believe."

Rose chuckled and gave him her hand. He drew her to her feet, into his arms, into the slow revolutions of a waltz. Rose hummed softly and let him sweep her away; they dipped and swayed in perfect accord, physically in tune, in time, in step. She felt the strength in the arm about her, felt the lean, steely length of him pressed against her, the hard column of his thigh parting hers as he swept her through the turns.

Moonlight bathed them, a shimmering silvery glow—the essence of midsummer magic. A deep silence held them, filled with the beat of their hearts and a breathless anticipation.

How long they revolved, Rose couldn't have said; when Duncan slowed and halted before one of the long windows, she was far past breathless.

She looked up and saw the dark glow in his eyes; she

reached up and traced the harsh line of one cheekbone. Then she stretched up—and lifted her lips to his as he bent his head to kiss her.

They kissed simply, sincerely, without barriers, limits or restraints, simply sinking into the other until there was only one. One sense, one heartbeat, one emotion, one longing.

Rose eventually drew back; she had to breathe. Eyes closed, she leaned her forehead against Duncan's shoulder. "We should go to bed."

"Hmm—my thought exactly."

Duncan turned her; his arm around her, her head on his shoulder, they slowly climbed the stairs. They reached the private gallery; Rose started to turn toward her room. Duncan's arm tightened; inexorably, he led her on—toward his.

Rose blinked, suddenly wide awake. Her heart jerked to life, then raced. In a mental scramble, she replayed their last exchanges, the tenor of his reply . . . "Ah—" She had to clear her throat. "I meant in separate beds."

"I know." Duncan glanced down at her. "*I* meant in mine."

Rose looked into his eyes and read his intent clearly; he wasn't going to let her go this time. She felt the steel in the arm about her, the strength in the body prowling beside her. She dragged in a quick breath and forced her feet to stop. "Duncan, I don't know—"

"I know—so why don't you do what you've always done?" He stopped and swung to face her; his gaze trapping hers, he drew her closer. "Just follow my lead—and let me teach you."

His head swooped and his lips found hers—no gentle kiss this time, but a searing, passion-laden incitement to madness. A soul-stirring challenge; as his lips moved on to trace fire down her throat, Rose realized what he was doing. "Good God!" she gasped. "You're seducing me!"

He chuckled, the sound wickedly evocative. "Am I succeeding?"

Yes—oh, yes! Rose bit her tongue and held back the admission, but she couldn't hold back a soft moan as his lips trailed lower, into the deep valley between her breasts, then over the exposed upper curves, while one thumb artfully brushed, tantalizingly to and fro, over one silk-clad nipple.

"Rose." He breathed her name against her flushed skin. "Come spend Midsummer's Eve with me—come taste the magic. I'll take you on a ride more wild than the last. There's another landscape you've never seen, peaks you've never climbed—come let me show you. Come ride with me."

How could she resist him? Rose discovered she couldn't, discovered that there did indeed exist a compulsion strong enough to sweep aside all caution, all sanity, strong enough to insist that this was not only right, but meant to be. The next thing she discovered was that, somehow, they'd crossed the threshold of Duncan's room and now stood beside his four-poster bed. "This is madness," she murmured. Obedient to his tugging, she lowered her arms so he could draw the sleeves of her gown down. Revealing her naked breasts.

"Oh!" she blushed vividly and crossed her arms protectively. "I was in such a rush, I forgot my chemise."

"Don't apologize on my account." Curling his fingers about her wrists, Duncan drew her arms down. She would have resisted, but he gave her no choice; drawing her arms out and down, then lacing his fingers with hers, he stared, apparently mesmerized, at what he'd revealed.

Rose cleared her throat. "They are rather large, I know."

Duncan choked on a groan, then his eyes lifted to hers. "Sweet Rose—you're beautiful." He raised his hands and gently, tenderly, cupped the firm mounds; thumbs slowly circling the sensitive peaks, he backed her until her legs hit the bed. Rose was glad to feel it behind her; if her legs gave way, as they were threatening to do, at least she wouldn't hit the floor.

Eyes dark, Duncan concentrated on her breasts, fondling, gently kneading. "You're beautiful, generous. And mine." With that, he bent his head and took one tight peak into his mouth.

Rose gasped; she swayed—she would have crumpled in a heap if he hadn't caught her and lifted her against him. She clung to him, fingers sliding from his shoulders to twine frantically in his hair as he pressed wet kisses over her soft flesh. His mouth was so hot, she felt sure he was burning her, then his tongue rasped her nipple, and she nearly died.

She might even have screamed—she wasn't sure she could hear anything over the pounding of her own heartbeat, over the roar of savage desire. He feasted on her as if he were famished; she panted, squirmed and writhed in his arms.

The hand at her back shifted, pressing her more firmly against him, then sliding possessively down, slipping beneath the folds of her gown gathered at her waist, over naked skin, to her bottom, to trace, to tantalize, then to fondle far too knowingly. She arched in his arms, pressing her hips even more firmly to his; she felt the heated ridge, the blatant evidence of his arousal, hard against her lower belly.

There was fire in her veins; he had set it there. He caught one aching nipple and suckled fiercely—and she went up in flames.

And then he was laying her across the big bed, on sheets cool to her fevered flesh. He drew her gown down, over her hips, down her long legs, flipping off her slippers as he went. She lost all the breath she still possessed when, sitting beside her, he surveyed her—totally naked but for her stockings, gartered above her knees. His perusal started at her toes, traveled slowly upward, lingered for a moment on her garters, then rose higher. She should have been overcome with maidenly modesty; instead, freed by the fire in his eyes, she felt wanton, wild, abandoned—blissfully excited. She burned as he studied her thighs, her hips, the soft, bronzy thatch at the base of her quivering belly. Then his gaze, heated and hot, swept upward, over her breasts, swollen and marked by his attentions, to her lips, parted and swollen, too.

The smile that curved his lips, the dark glint that lit his eyes, left her quivering.

"One more item."

His voice was deep, gravelly with desire. Expecting him to reach for her garters, she blinked in surprise when he leaned over—and reached for her hair. He speared his fingers into the coiled tresses, then spread them, scattering pins left and right. He brushed them away, then fell to unravelling the plaited braids. She studied his face, the hard edge that desire had set to the already-angular planes. The tension that invested his whole frame, that held her fast in its grip, naked and quivering, wanting and waiting, held an excitement she'd never known, that she wanted to experience more than she wanted to breathe.

Finally freeing her hair, he tossed it about her head and shoulders, arranging it to frame her face. Gripped by an urgency she didn't understand, she slid one hand down to her garters.

"No." Duncan caught her hand, then, capturing her gaze, raised it to his lips. "Leave them." The puzzled question in her eyes nearly made him groan. "Trust me." Letting go of her hand, he sat up and started to undo the buttons on his shirt.

She moved so quickly, he had no time to react. He heard the swish as she swung her legs about, then she was pressed against him, breasts to his back, reaching around him to help with his shirt. Her lips nuzzled his ear. "Why do you want me to keep my stockings on?"

Duncan closed his eyes and bit back a groan. "It's a secret."

"A secret?"

He might as well have invited her to tease him; her fingers found their way beneath his shirt and trailed, as tantalizingly as he'd imagined, over his chest, then down, over his ridged stomach. Then down . . .

Fighting free of his cuffs, he abruptly stood and shrugged off the shirt. Rounding on Rose, he caught her hands and bore her back onto the bed. "I think," he said, trapping her beneath him, "it's time to start your tuition."

"Oh?" She squirmed beneath him, her breasts caressing his chest, her thighs caressing his aching erection.

Duncan gritted his teeth and used his full weight to subdue her. "If I have my way," he ground out, "it'll be an extended first lesson."

He could but try.

He kissed her long and hard, until he felt her soften beneath him. Then he shifted his attentions to her breasts, until she was hot and aching, arching sweetly in his arms. Relinquishing her breasts, he slid lower, trailing open-mouthed kisses over her waist, pausing at her navel to probe evocatively with his tongue, until she sobbed and sank her fingers into his shoulders.

Then he shifted lower.

He thought she was going to scream when he traced the top of each garter with his tongue. She gasped and tensed when he parted her thighs and dotted kisses up their sensitive inner faces. And when he parted her, and kissed the soft petals as she bloomed for him, she called out his name on a sob of pure desire.

He gave her what she wanted, experience and much more. With each caress more intimate than the last, he opened doors she hadn't imagined existed, showed her delights she was only just able to comprehend. He tasted, licked, probed and suckled; she threshed her head wildly, fingers clamped to his skull, her body in full flower, open and aching—and all his.

Dragging in a deep breath, her perfume sinking deep, wreathing through his mind, he shifted back and sat on the edge of the bed, replacing his lips and tongue with the fingers of one hand. With the other, he unbuttoned his trousers.

Freed of his weight, yet still captive to his fingers, which probed her heat with a slow, steady rhythm, Rose breathed rapidly, deeply, then cracked open her lids. Duncan saw her eyes glint from beneath her long lashes. Saw her watching what he was about. Then she licked her lips.

"Why the stockings?"

He couldn't even begin to explain—that he'd fantasized about her legs, about having them wrapped about him, leaving her wide open, his to fill. "You'll see in a minute."

He stripped off his trousers, kicked them off and turned to her; her eyes flew wide. She started to sit; he knelt between her thighs, caught her hands and bore her down again. And covered her—covered her lips—before she could say whatever she'd been about to; he was sure he didn't need to hear it.

The kiss turned into a struggle for supremacy; they both lost when desire came out of nowhere and captured them both. Rose squirmed beneath him—not to get away, but to press herself closer. Duncan drew back and gasped, "Wrap your legs about my hips."

She did, instantly—and he returned to ravage her mouth, wanting to be filling her there when he entered her below. She welcomed him in, sweet and hot in both places. He flexed his hips and sank into her, filling her, stretching her. Her breath caught; she arched beneath him. Duncan drew back and thrust deep, through the slight resistance. She tensed, shocked, then, two heartbeats later, melted around him. They both lay still, savoring the moment, the glorious intimacy, the sensation of their hearts beating in time.

Rose moved first, compelled by some impulse she didn't know or understand. Duncan responded immediately, giving her what she hadn't known she wanted, riding easily within her. The sensations that swirled through her were startling, riveting, totally addictive—she wanted to feel them again and again. Duncan obliged, and she suddenly realized what he'd meant by a new landscape—one filled with warm waves of pleasure, lapping peaks of exquisite delight. They rode into it, at a steady gallop, escalating into urgency as the waves rose higher and the peaks pierced the sun.

Only it wasn't the sun; it was pure oblivion. He rode her right into it, into a malestrom of sensations, emotions, and on into a vale of unutterable bliss.

Braced above her, Duncan watched her face as she fractured about him, watched the tension ease and melt away, even as she melted beneath him. Her womb throbbed and contracted; instinctively, she tensed about him.

He gasped, closed his eyes and, filling her one last time, joined her in sweet oblivion.

Rose woke early, before the sun was up. She knew that from the deep peace that pervaded the house; not even a tweeny was stirring. Eyes closed, she settled more comfortably, dreamily wondering why her pillow was so hard. A hair tickled her nose; cracking open her lids, she brushed at it—and woke up with a start.

Eyes wide, she surveyed her pillow—Duncan's bare chest. Her mind, scrambling to attention, slowly filled in the rest—the long body lying intimately wrapped about hers, both naked beneath the covers. She couldn't even remember getting beneath the covers.

She could, however, remember the oblivion that had overtaken her—and what had led up to it.

Cheeks burning, she struggled to think—of where she now was, where she now stood—lay—with him. And discovered that, with his heart thudding in her ear and his hair-dusted limbs trapping hers, she couldn't formulate a single coherent thought.

Escape was imperative.

Very gently, she eased away from his chest, then, slowly and smoothly, lifted the hand that lay over her waist, and rolled away. Onto his other arm. He breathed in deeply; she froze, but when nothing happened, she edged her legs—still clad in her silk stockings, for heaven's sake!—to the side of the bed, then lifted her shoulders from his arm and started to slide to safety—

His hands clamped about her waist before she reached it.

"Duncan! Let me go."

She sat up fully and tried to wriggle free; he chuckled—an intensely wicked sound—slid his hands down to close over her hips and drew her inexorably back into the bed.

Rose wasn't having it. She yielded to his pull, then flipped onto her stomach, expecting to break his hold and slide away. He read her mind and swung over her as she flipped, straddling her legs, trapping her between his rock-hard thighs.

"Ah-huh—you can't run away before your second lesson."

Rose lifted her face from the pillows. "What second lesson?"

She felt him lean forward; his chest grazed her back, his lips grazed her nape, as he slid one hand beneath her stomach—then the other between her thighs. She gasped; he whispered softly, "Your second lesson in being mine."

Her body heated instantly; her breathing seized. "Dunc—*ooooh!*" His name dissolved into a long-drawn sigh—of delight, of anticipation. His fingers artfully delved; then he drew her back, onto her knees.

She went willingly, eagerly, caught in his spell. He caressed the firm globes of her bottom, and she shivered. He grasped her hips, nudged her knees apart and slid into her—slowly, thoroughly, mind-numbingly deep.

And taught her how to feel all over again, taught her about delight, rapture and earthly bliss. The constant slide of his body into hers, the rhythmic rocking as he filled her—fully, repeatedly—filled her mind, overwhelmed her senses, imprinted him deeply on her soul.

The ride was slow and long; she was sobbing before it ended. Sobbing his name, sobbing with joy, mindless in ecstasy. And, this time, when he drove her over the last peak, he followed immediately. Before oblivion swamped her, she felt his warmth flood her and heard his helpless groan, as he collapsed upon her.

Duncan woke, a good two hours later, unsurprised to find himself alone in his bed. By any normal standards, the woman who'd shared his bed throughout the night and into the early morning shouldn't have been able to crawl, much less walk, out, but Rose had somehow made good her escape.

He wished he'd been awake to see it.

Lips curving in a wolfish, thoroughly satisfied smile, he stretched, then crossed his arms behind his head and wondered what she was doing now.

Two minutes later, he was out of bed and dressing. If the years had taught him anything, it was never to underestimate Rose.

All was quiet downstairs, the household in the grip of the usual aftermath of a major ball. Duncan doubted his mother or any of the other ladies were yet about, which focused his mind even more acutely on finding Rose.

Striding down the long corridor leading from the front hall, he heard voices. Halting, he listened and identified Rose—and Penecuik.

Duncan dragged in a deep breath and held it; through the half-open door of the breakfast parlor, he glimpsed Rose and her suitor on the terrace. Rose had her back to the room, gesturing as she spoke. Penecuik was frowning, concentrating on her words.

Duncan reminded himself that they had a right to privacy, that Rose wasn't yet formally his. That he should give her the opportunity to deal with Penecuik on her own. None of his arguments stood a chance of persuading him; quietly, silently, he passed on to the morning room next door, opened the door and slipped inside.

"You're not listening, Jeremy." Rose looked her erstwhile suitor in the eye and tried, once more, to convince him of his position. "I am not going to marry you. I have decided I do not wish to, and that is all there is to it."

Jeremy eyed her stubbornly, even mulishly. Then started, once again, to enumerate all the reasons why she couldn't possibly think that.

Rose struggled not to roll her eyes to the skies, struggled to listen civilly. He'd waylaid her before she'd even had a chance to break her fast, to restore her failing strength—drained very effectively by Duncan—and now Jeremy was being unbelievably difficult, obtuse and refractory. He wouldn't accept his dismissal.

Which mattered not a jot, because he was going to have to. She'd finally discovered that something she'd been looking for all her adult life—that force stronger that her will that would sweep her into some man's arms—and she wasn't about to turn her back on it. Not that she understood it yet, given it had been Duncan's arms into which it had swept her.

She hadn't, thanks first to Duncan and now Jeremy, yet had a chance to consider that aspect, or very much else. It was Midsummer, and she'd promised Jeremy her answer. Now she'd given it him, the least he could do was accept it with good grace.

Suppressing an urge to tell him so—plainly—she waited until he reached the end of his predictable list, then drew a deep breath and earnestly said, "Jeremy, this is not a matter of who you are, or what you own, or what benefits might accrue to your wife. This decision is about me, and what *I* am." She fixed him with a direct gaze and willed him to understand. "I'm not yours."

She was Duncan's.

Jeremy sighed, as if arguing with a child. "Rose, I really don't think you're weighing this decision as you should. Your feelings for me, personally, shouldn't sit so heavily in the scale." He smiled at her. "You and I get along well enough; that's all that's required. But the rest—the duchy, the estate—"

"My fortune."

He nodded. "That, too. All these are the principal reasons behind my proposal, and I think you need to consider things from the same perspective."

Jaw set against a scream, Rose folded her arms and glared at him.

And heard a deep sigh from the morning room to her left. Both she and Jeremy stared as Duncan strolled languidly through the open French doors. He nodded to Jeremy. "Excuse me, Penecuik, but I have an urgent matter to discuss with my countess-to-be."

Jeremy frowned. "Your countess-to-be?"

"Ah, yes—I'm sure you would have eventually winkled it out of her"—Duncan slid his arm about Rose's waist and, drawing her against him, smiled down into her eyes—"but the truth is, Rose has decided not to be a duchess-in-waiting. She's going to be a countess instead."

Her mouth open, Rose simply stared at him, utterly flabbergasted and not a little chagrined. Duncan committed the sight to memory, then flicked a glance at Penecuik. "If you'll excuse us, Penecuik—that urgent something . . ." Letting his words trail off, Duncan gathered Rose into his arms, lowered his head and kissed her—deeply, ravenously. Convincingly.

As was fast becoming her habit, she melted into his arms and returned the kiss avidly. From beneath his lashes, Duncan saw Jeremy's face blank, then he glared, assumed a petulantly supercilious expression and stomped off along the terrace.

Rose didn't hear him go—her mental processes had frozen at the words "countess-to-be." When Duncan finally consented to lift his head and let her drag in a breath, she stared into his face, then narrowed her eyes. "I had visions, you realize, of having you on your knees."

Duncan grinned. "As I've already had you on yours, that seems a trifle redundant."

Rose quelled a delicious shiver and sternly studied his eyes. He lifted an inquiring brow; she lifted one back. "I'm not perfect, you know."

Duncan held her gaze steadily. "Perfection is in the eye of the beholder."

No one had ever considered her in any way perfect—the wild wanton in socially acceptable disguise. And Duncan knew all of her, the wild wanton as well as the lady. The look in his eyes, cool blue but glowing so warmly, assured her of his sincerity, his conviction, his single-minded determination. He thought her perfect for the role of his countess.

Rose smiled, slowly, seductively; the light in her eyes that Duncan had always distrusted gleamed provocatively. "Are you sure," she murmured, stretching up and wrapping her arms about his neck, "that you've seen enough of me to be sure?"

Duncan frowned, admitted his memory could do with a little refreshing—and took her straight back to his bed.

* * *

And as they rolled amongst his sheets, from far across the fields the kirk bells rang out, welcoming in Midsummer.

Four weeks later, the bells rang again, even more joyously, when the thorn in Duncan Macintyre's flesh became . . . his perfect Rose.

After years of enjoying Regency romances as an escape from the dry world of professional science, and suddenly finding herself desperate for reading material, STEPHANIE LAURENS turned to writing. The hobby became a career, and after eight Regencies, her first historical romance, *Captain Jack's Woman*, was published by Avon Books. This was followed by *Devil's Bride*, the first in a series about the sexy, irresistible Cynster cousins.

Living in a leafy, bayside suburb of Melbourne, Australia, Stephanie divides her free time between her husband, two teenage daughters, and an affable idiot of a hound. She also enjoys gardening and needlework.

She welcomes readers' comments. Letters can be sent c/o the Publicity Department, Avon Books, Inc., 10 East 53rd Street, New York, NY 10022-5299, or via e-mail at *www.stephanielaurens.com*.

Gretna Greene

Julia Quinn

For Jason Weinstein,
whose phone calls never fail to brighten my day.

And for Paul, even though he doesn't believe me
when I insist we're not zoned for llamas.

One

Gretna Green, Scotland

1804

*Margaret Pennypacker had chased her brother half-*way across a nation.

She had ridden like the very devil through Lancashire, discovering when she dismounted that she possessed muscles she didn't even know existed—and that every one of them was bone-sore.

She had squeezed herself into an overcrowded hired coach in Cumbria and tried not to breathe when she realized that her fellow passengers apparently did not share her fondness for bathing.

She had endured the bumps and jolts of a mule-drawn wooden cart as it made its way across the last five miles of English soil before she was unceremoniously dropped at the Scottish border by a farmer who warned her that she was entering the devil's own country.

All to end up here, at Gretna Green, wet and tired, with

little more than the coat on her back and two coins in her pocket. Because—

In Lancashire, she'd been thrown from her horse when it stepped on a stone, and then the dratted thing—so well-trained by her errant brother—had turned and run for home.

On the Cumbria coach, someone had had the temerity to steal her reticule, leaving her with only the coins that had slipped out and settled into the deepest recesses of her pocket.

And on that last leg of the journey, while riding in the farmer's cart that had given her splinters, bruises, and probably—with the way her luck was running—some sort of chicken disease, it had started to rain.

Margaret Pennypacker was definitely not in good temper. And when she found her brother, she was going to *kill* him.

It had to be the cruelest sort of irony, but neither thieves nor storms nor runaway horses had managed to deprive her of the sheet of paper that had forced her journey to Scotland. Edward's sparsely worded missive hardly deserved a rereading, but Margaret was so furious with him that she couldn't stop her fingers from reaching into her pocket for the hundredth time and pulling out the crumpled, hastily scrawled note.

It had been folded and refolded, and it was probably getting wet as she huddled under the overhang of a building, but the message was still clear. Edward was eloping.

"Bloody idiot," Margaret muttered under her breath. "And who the devil is he marrying, I'd like to know. Couldn't he have seen fit to have told me *that?*"

As best as Margaret could guess, there were three likely candidates, and she wasn't looking forward to welcoming any of them into the Pennypacker family. Annabel Fornby was a hideous snob, Camilla Ferrige had no sense of humor, and Penelope Fitch was as dumb as a post. Margaret had once heard Penelope recite the alphabet and leave out *J* and *Q*.

All she could hope was that she wasn't too late. Edward Pennypacker was not getting married—not if his older sister had any say in the matter.

Angus Greene was a strong, powerful man, widely reputed to be handsome as sin, and with a devilishly charming smile that belied an occasionally ferocious temper. When he rode his prized stallion into a new town, he tended to elicit fear among the men, rapid heartbeats among the women, and wide-eyed fascination among the children—who always seemed to notice that both man and beast shared the same black hair and piercing dark eyes.

His arrival in Gretna Green, however, caused no comment at all, because everyone with a lick of sense—and Angus liked to think that the one virtue common to all Scots was sense—was inside that night, bundled up and warm, and, most importantly, out of the driving rain.

But not Angus. No, Angus was—thanks to his exasperating younger sister, whom he was beginning to think might be the only Scot since the dawn of time to be completely devoid of common sense—stuck out here in the hard rain, shivering and cold, and establishing what had to be a new national record for the greatest use of the words "damn," "bloody," and "bugger" in a single evening.

He'd hoped to get farther than the border this evening, but the rain was slowing him down, and even with gloves, his fingers were too cold to properly grip the reins. Plus, it wasn't fair to Orpheus; he was a good horse and didn't deserve this sort of abuse. This was yet another transgression for which Anne would have to take the blame, Angus thought grimly. He didn't care if his sister was only eighteen years old. When he found that girl, he was going to *kill* her.

He took some comfort in the fact that if he had been slowed down by the weather, then Anne would have been forced to a complete stop. She was traveling by carriage—

his carriage, which she'd had the temerity to "borrow"—and would certainly be unable to move southward with the roads muddied and clogged.

And if there was any luck floating about in the damp air, Anne might even be stranded here, at Gretna Green. As a possibility, it was fairly remote, but as long as he was stuck for the night, it seemed foolish not to look for her.

He let out a weary sigh and wiped his wet face with the back of his sleeve. It didn't do any good, of course; his coat was already completely sodden.

At his master's loud exhale, Orpheus instinctively drew to a halt, waiting for the next command. Trouble was, Angus hadn't a clue what to do next. He supposed he could start by searching the inns, although truth be told, he didn't much relish the thought of going through every room in every inn in town. He didn't even want to think about how many innkeepers he was going to have to bribe.

But first things had to come first, and he might as well get himself settled before beginning his search. A quick scan up the street told him that The Canny Man possessed the best quarters for his horse, so Angus spurred Orpheus in the direction of the small inn and public house.

But before Orpheus had managed to move even three of his four feet, a loud scream pierced the air.

A feminine scream.

Angus's heart stopped beating. Anne? If anyone had touched so much as the hem of her dress . . .

He galloped down the street and then around the far corner, just in time to see three men attempting to drag a lady into a dark building. She was struggling mightily, and from the amount of mud on her dress, it looked as if she had been dragged a fair distance.

"Let go of me, you cretin!" she yelled, elbowing one of them in the neck.

It wasn't Anne, that was for sure. Anne would never have known enough to knee the second man in the groin.

Angus jumped down and dashed to the lady's aid, arriving just in time to grab the third villain by the collar, pull him off of his intended victim, and toss him headfirst into the street.

"Back off, sod!" one of the men growled. "We found her first."

"That is unfortunate," Angus said calmly, then bashed his fist into the man's face. He stared at the two remaining men, one of whom was still sprawled in the street. The other one, who had been doubled over on the ground and clutching at his nether regions ever since the lady had kneed him, looked at Angus as if he wanted to say something. But before he could make a sound, Angus planted his boot in a rather painful area and looked down.

"There is something you should know about me," he said, his voice unnaturally soft. "I don't like to see women hurt. When it happens, or even when I think it *might* happen, I—" He stopped talking for a moment and cocked his head slowly to the side, pretending to search for the right words. "I go a wee bit mad."

The man sprawled on the cobbles found his feet with remarkable speed and ran off into the night. His companion looked as if he dearly wanted to follow, but Angus's boot had him a bit too securely pinned to the ground.

Angus stroked his chin. "I think we understand each other."

The man nodded frantically.

"Good. I'm sure I don't need to tell you what will happen should we ever again cross paths."

Another pained nod.

Angus moved his foot and the man ran off, squealing all the way.

With the threat finally removed—the third villain, after

all, was still unconscious—Angus finally turned his attention to the young lady he had possibly saved from a fate worse than death. She was still sitting on the cobbles, staring up at him as if he were a ghost. Her hair was wet and sticking to her face, but even in the dim light shining from the nearby buildings, he could tell that it was some sort of shade of brown. Her eyes were light in color, and utterly huge and unblinking. And her lips—well, they were blue from the cold, and shivering to boot, so they really shouldn't have been so appealing, but Angus found himself instinctively moving toward her, and he had the oddest notion that if he kissed her . . .

He gave his head a little shake. "Idiot," he muttered. He was here to find Anne, not dally with some misplaced young Englishwoman. And speaking of which, what the devil was she doing here, anyway, alone on a darkened street?

He leveled his sternest stare at her. "What the devil are you doing here?" he demanded, then added for good measure, "Alone on a darkened street?"

Her eyes, which he thought couldn't possible get any more huge, widened, and she started to scoot away, her bottom skimming along the ground as she used the palms of her hands to support her. Angus thought she looked a bit like a monkey he'd seen in a menagerie.

"Don't tell me you're frightened of *me*," he said incredulously.

Her shaking lips managed something that could never be called a smile, although Angus had the distinct impression that she was trying to placate him. "Not at all," she quavered, her accent confirming his earlier supposition that she was English. "It's just that I—well, you must understand—" She stood so suddenly that her foot caught on the hem of her dress, and she nearly fell over. "I really have someplace I have to be," she blurted out.

And then, with a wary glance in his direction, she started

walking away, moving sideways so that she could keep one eye on him and one on wherever it was she thought she was going.

"For the love of—" He cut himself off before he blasphemed in front of this chit, who was already looking at him as if she were trying to decide whether he more resembled the devil or Attila the Hun. "I am not the villain in this piece," he bit off.

Margaret clutched at the folds of her skirt and chewed nervously on the inside of her cheek. She had been terrified when those men had grabbed her, and she still hadn't managed to stop the uncontrollable shaking of her hands. At four-and-twenty, she was still an innocent, but she'd lived long enough to know their intentions. The man standing in front of her had saved her, but for what purpose? She didn't think he wanted to hurt her—his comment about protecting women was a bit too heartfelt to have been an act. But did that mean she could trust him?

As if sensing her thoughts, he snorted and jerked his head slightly. "For the love of God, woman, I saved your bloody life."

Margaret winced. The big Scotsman was probably correct, and she knew her deceased mother would have ordered her to get down on her hands and knees just to thank him, but the truth was—he looked a little unbalanced. His eyes were hot and flashing with temper, and there was something about him—something strange and indescribable—that made her insides quiver.

But she wasn't a coward, and she had spent enough years trying to instill good manners in her younger siblings that she wasn't about to prove herself a hypocrite and behave rudely herself. "Thank you," she said quickly, her racing heart causing her words to tumble from her mouth. "That was . . . uh . . . very well done of you, and I . . . thank you, and I believe I can speak for my family when I say that they also thank you, and I'm certain that if I ever found myself wed, my husband would thank you as well."

Her savior (or was it nemesis?—Margaret just wasn't sure) smiled slowly and said, "Then you're not married."

She took a few steps back. "Uh, no, uh, I really must be going."

His eyes narrowed. "You're not here to elope, are you? Because that's *always* a bad idea. I have a friend with property in the area, and he tells me that the inns are full of women who have been compromised on the way to Gretna Green but never wed."

"I am certainly *not* eloping," she said testily. "Do I really look that foolish?"

"No, you don't. But forget I asked. I really don't care." He shook his head wearily. "I've ridden all day, I'm sore as hell, and I still haven't found my sister. I'm glad you're safe, but I don't have time to sit here and—"

Her entire countenance changed. "Your *sister?*" she repeated, charging forward. "You're looking for your sister? Tell me, sir, how old is she, what does she look like, and are you a Fornby, Ferrige, or Fitch?"

He looked at her as if she had suddenly sprouted horns. "What the devil are you talking about, woman? My name is Angus Greene."

"Damn," she muttered, surprising even herself with her use of profanity. "I had been hoping you might prove a useful ally."

"If you're not here to elope, what *are* you doing here?"

"My brother," she grumbled. "The nitwit thinks he wants to marry, but his brides are completely unsuitable."

"Brides, plural? Bigamy is still illegal in England, is it not?"

She scowled at him. "I don't know which one he eloped with. He didn't say. But they're all just horrible." She shuddered, looking as if she had just swallowed an antidote. "Horrible."

A fresh burst of rain fell upon them, and without even thinking, Angus took her arm and pulled her under the deep overhang. She kept on talking through the entire maneuver.

"When I get my hands on Edward, I'm going to bloody well kill him," she was saying. "I was quite busy in Lancashire, you know. It's not as if I had time to drop everything and chase him to Scotland. I've a sister to care for, and a wedding to plan. She's getting married in three months, after all. The last thing I needed was to travel up here and—"

His hand tightened around her arm. "Wait one moment," he said in a tone that immediately shut her mouth. "Don't tell me you traveled to Scotland by yourself." His brows pulled together, and he looked as if he were in pain. "Do not tell me that."

She caught sight of the fire burning in his dark eyes, and drew back as far as his heavy grip would let her. "I knew that you were crazy," she said, looking from side to side as if searching for someone to save her from this lunatic.

Angus yanked her in closer, purposefully using his size and strength to intimidate her. "Did you or did you not embark upon a long-distance journey without an escort?"

"Yes?" she said, the single syllable coming out like a question.

"Good God, woman!" he exploded. "Are you insane? Do you have any idea what happens to women traveling alone? Did you give no thought to your own safety?"

Margaret's mouth fell open.

He let go of her and started to pace. "When I think about what might have happened . . ." He gave his head a shuddering shake, muttering, "Jesus, whiskey, and Robert the Bruce. The woman is daft."

Margaret blinked rapidly, trying to make sense of all this. "Sir," she began cautiously, "you don't even know me."

He whirled around. "What the hell is your name?"

"Margaret Pennypacker," she answered before it occurred to her that maybe he really *was* a lunatic, and maybe she shouldn't have told him the truth.

"Fine," he spat out. "Now I know you. And you're a fool. On a fool's errand."

"Just wait one moment!" she burst out, stepping forward and waving her arm at him. "I happen to be engaged in an extremely serious mission. My brother's very happiness might be at stake. Who are you to judge me?"

"The man who saved you from rape."

"Well!" Margaret responded, mostly because that was all she could think to say.

He raked his hand through his hair. "What are your plans for tonight?"

"That's none of your business!"

"You became my business the minute I saw you being dragged off by—" Angus whipped his head around, realizing that he'd forgotten about the man he'd knocked unconscious. The fellow had woken up and was slowly rising to his feet, obviously trying to move as silently as possible.

"Don't move," Angus snapped at Margaret. He was in front of the burly man in two steps, then grabbed his collar and hauled him up until his feet dangled in the air. "Do you have anything to say to this woman?" he growled.

The man shook his head.

"I think you do."

"I certainly have nothing to say to *him,*" Margaret put in, trying to be helpful.

Angus ignored her. "An apology, perhaps? An abject apology with ample use of the phrase 'I'm a miserable cur' might lessen my temper and save your pathetic life."

The man started to shake. "I'msorryI'msorryI'msorry."

"Really, Mr. Greene," Margaret said quickly, "I think we're quite finished. Perhaps you ought to let him go."

"Do you want to hurt him?"

Margaret was so surprised, she started to cough. "I beg your pardon," she finally managed to get out.

His voice was hard and strangely flat as he repeated his question. "Do you want to hurt him? He would have dishonored you."

Margaret blinked uncontrollably at the odd light in his eyes, and she had the most horrifying feeling that he would kill the man if she just gave the word. "I'm fine," she choked out. "I believe I managed a few blows earlier in the evening. It quite satisfied my meager bloodlust."

"Not this one," Angus replied. "You hurt the other two."

"I'm fine, really."

"A woman has a right to her revenge."

"There's really no need, I assure you." Margaret glanced quickly about, trying to assess her chances for escape. She was going to have to make a run for it soon. This Angus Greene fellow might have saved her life, but he was completely mad.

Angus dropped the man and pushed him forward. "Get out of here before I kill you."

Margaret began to tiptoe in the opposite direction.

"You!" he boomed. "Don't move."

She froze. She might not like this huge Scotsman, but she was no idiot. He was twice her size, after all.

"Where do you think you're going?"

She decided not to answer that one.

He quickly closed the distance between them, crossed his arms, and glowered down at her. "I believe you were about to advise me of your plans for the evening."

"I regret to inform you, sir, but my intentions were not following that particular line of—"

"Tell me!" he roared.

"I was going to look for my brother," she blurted out, deciding that maybe she was a coward, after all. Cowardice, she decided, wasn't really such a bad thing when faced with a mad Scot.

He shook his head. "You're coming with me."

"Oh, please," she scoffed. "If you think—"

"Miss Pennypacker," he interrupted, "I might as well inform you that when I make a decision, I rarely change my mind."

"Mr. Greene," she replied with equal resolve, "I am not your responsibility."

"Perhaps, but I have never been the sort of man who could leave a lone woman to her own defenses. Therefore, you are coming with me, and we will decide what to do with you in the morning."

"I thought you were looking for your sister," she said, her irritation clear in her tone of voice.

"My sister certainly isn't getting any farther away from me in this weather. I'm sure she's tucked away in some inn, probably not even here at Gretna Green."

"Shouldn't you search the inns for her this eve?"

"Anne is not an early riser. If she is indeed here, she will not resume her journey any earlier than ten. I have no qualms about delaying my search for her until the morning. Anne, I'm sure, is safe this eve. You, on the other hand, I have my doubts about."

Margaret nearly stamped her foot. "There is no need—"

"My advice, Miss Pennypacker, is for you to accept your fate. Once you think about it, you'll realize it's not such a bad one. A warm bed, a good meal—how can those be so very offensive?"

"Why are you doing this?" she asked suspiciously. "What is in it for you?"

"Nothing," he admitted with a lopsided smile. "But have you ever studied Chinese history?"

She shot him a wry look. As if English girls were ever actually allowed to study more than embroidery and the occasional history lesson—British history, of course.

"There's a proverb," he said, his eyes growing reminiscent. "I don't remember how it goes precisely, but it is something about how once you save a life, you are responsible for it forever."

Margaret choked on her breath. Good God, the man didn't think to watch over her forever, did he?

Angus caught her expression and nearly doubled over in laughter. "Oh, do not worry, Miss Pennypacker," he said. "I have no plans to install myself as your permanent protector. I'll see you through until daylight and make certain you're settled, and then you may go on your merry way."

"Very well," Margaret said grudgingly. It was difficult to argue with someone who had one's best interests at heart. "I do appreciate your concern, and perhaps we might search for our errant siblings together. It should make the job a bit easier, I should think."

He touched her chin, startling her with his gentleness. "That's the spirit. Now then, shall we be off?"

She nodded, thinking that perhaps she ought to make a peace offering of her own. After all, the man had saved her from a horrible fate, and she had responded by calling him a lunatic. "You have a scrape," she said, touching his right temple. It had always been easier for her to show her gratitude through deeds, rather than words. "Why don't you let me tend to that? It's not very deep, but you ought to have it cleaned."

He nodded and took her arm. "I would appreciate that."

Margaret caught her breath, a bit surprised by how much larger he seemed when he was standing right next to her. "Have you secured a room yet?"

He shook his head. "Have you?"

"No, but I saw a vacancy sign at The Rose and Thistle."

"The Canny Man is better. Cleaner, and the food is hot. We'll see if they have room first."

"Cleanliness is good," she commented, more than happy to forgive his arrogance if it meant clean sheets.

"Do you have a bag?"

"Not anymore," she said ruefully.

"You were robbed?"

"I'm afraid so." At his darkening look, she added quickly, "But I didn't bring anything of value."

He sighed. "Well, there's nothing to be done about it now. Come with me. We'll discuss what to do about your brother and my sister once we're warm and fed."

And then he grasped her arm a bit more securely and led her down the street.

Two

Their truce lasted all of two minutes. Margaret wasn't exactly certain how it came about, but before they were even halfway to The Canny Man, they were bickering like children.

He couldn't resist reminding her that she'd been beyond foolish in setting out for Scotland by herself.

She just *had* to call him an arrogant boor as he propelled her up the front steps and into the inn.

But none of that—not one single snippy word—could have prepared her for what happened when they stood before the innkeeper.

"My wife and I require rooms for the night," Angus said.

Wife?

By sheer force of will, Margaret managed to keep her jaw from dropping to her knees. Or maybe it was an act of God; she didn't much think her will was strong enough to keep her from smacking Angus Greene in the arm for his impertinence.

"We have only one room available," the innkeeper informed them.

"We'll take that, then," Angus replied.

This time she *knew* she was subject to divine intervention, because there could be no other explanation for her restraint in the face of her massive desire to box his ears.

The innkeeper nodded approvingly and said, "Follow me. I'll show you up. And if you would like a meal—"

"We would," Angus cut in. "Something warm and filling."

"I'm afraid all we have at this late hour is cold meat pie."

Angus pulled a coin from his coat and held it forward. "My wife is very cold, and given her delicate condition, I would like to see that she receives a good meal."

"My condition?" Margaret gasped.

Angus smiled down at her and winked. "Come now, darling, surely you didn't think you would be able to hide it forever."

"Congratulations to you both!" the innkeeper boomed. "Is this your first?"

Angus nodded. "So you see why I'm so protective." He snaked his arm around Margaret's shoulders. "She's such a delicate woman."

That "delicate" woman promptly bent her arm and jabbed her elbow into Angus's hip. Hard.

The innkeeper must not have heard the ensuing grunt of pain, because he just took the coin and rolled it around in his hand. "Of course, of course," he murmured. "I'll have to wake my wife, but I'm sure we can find something hot."

"Excellent."

The innkeeper moved forward, and Angus made to follow, but Margaret grabbed the hem of his coat and yanked. "Are you mad?" she whispered.

"I thought you had already questioned my sanity and found it acceptable."

"I have reconsidered," she ground out.

He patted her on the shoulder. "Try not to overset yourself. It's not good for the baby."

Margaret's arms were sticks at her sides as she tried to keep herself from pummeling him. "Stop talking about the baby," she hissed, "and I am not going to share a room with you."

"I really don't see what other choice you have."

"I would rather—"

He held up a hand. "Don't tell me you'd rather wait out in the rain. I simply won't believe you."

"*You* can wait out in the rain."

Angus ducked and peered out a window. Raindrops were beating loudly against the glass. "I think not."

"If you were a gentleman . . ."

He chuckled. "Ah, but I never said I was a gentleman."

"What was all that about protecting women, then?" Margaret demanded.

"I said I don't like to see women hurt and abused. I never said I was willing to sleep in the rain and give myself a raging case of lung disease for you."

The innkeeper, who had walked on ahead, stopped and turned around when he realized that his guests had not followed. "Are you coming?" he inquired.

"Yes, yes," Angus replied. "Just having a small discussion with my wife. It seems she is having a remarkable craving for haggis."

Margaret's mouth fell open, and it took several attempts at speech before she managed to say, "I don't like haggis."

Angus grinned. "I do."

"Och!" the innkeeper exclaimed with a broad smile. "Just like my wife. She ate haggis every day while she was expecting, and she gave me four fine boys."

"Brilliant," Angus said with a cocky smile. "I shall have to remember that. A man needs a son."

"Four," the innkeeper reminded him, his chest puffing out with pride. "I've got four."

Angus slapped Margaret on the back. "She'll give me five. Mark my words."

"Men," she spat out, stumbling from the force of his friendly pat. "A bunch of strutting roosters, the lot of you."

But the two men were too involved in their manly game of one-upmanship—Margaret fully expected them to start arguing about who could toss a caber farther any moment now—and clearly didn't hear her.

She stood there with her arms crossed for a full minute, trying not to listen to a thing they were saying, when Angus suddenly patted her on the back and said, "Haggis, then, for dinner, my love?"

"I'm going to kill you," she hissed. "And I'm going to do it slowly." Then Angus jabbed her in the ribs and glanced at the innkeeper. "I'd love some," she choked out. "My very favorite."

The innkeeper beamed. "A woman after my own heart. Nothing protects one from the spirits like a good haggis."

"The smell alone would scare off the devil," Margaret muttered.

Angus chuckled and gave her hand a squeeze.

"You must be a Scotswoman, then," the innkeeper said, "if you love the haggis."

"Actually," Margaret said primly, yanking her hand back. "I'm English."

"Pity." The innkeeper then turned to Angus and said, "But I suppose if you had to marry a Sassenach, at least you picked one with a taste for haggis."

"I refused to ask for her hand until she tasted it," Angus said solemnly. "And then I wouldn't go through with the ceremony until I was convinced that she liked it."

Margaret walloped him in the shoulder.

"And a temper, too!" the innkeeper chortled. "We'll make a good Scotswoman out of her yet."

"I'm hoping," Angus agreed, his accent suddenly growing stronger to Margaret's ear. "I'm thinking she ought to learn to throw a better punch, though."

"Didn't hurt, eh?" the innkeeper said with a knowing smile.

"Not a bit."

Margaret ground her teeth together. "Sir," she said as sweetly as she could muster, "could you please show me to my room? I'm a terrible mess, and I would so like to tidy myself before supper."

"Of course." The innkeeper resumed his trek up the stairs, Margaret right on his heels. Angus loitered a few steps behind, no doubt grinning at her expense.

"Here it is," the innkeeper said, opening the door to reveal a small but clean room with a washbasin, a chamber pot, and a single bed.

"Thank you, sir," she said with a polite nod. "I am most appreciative." Then she marched into the room and slammed the door.

Angus howled with laughter. He couldn't help himself.

"Och, you're in trouble now," the innkeeper said.

Angus's laughter settled down into a few choice chuckles. "What's your name, good sir?"

"McCallum. George McCallum."

"Well, George, I think you're right."

"Having a wife," George pontificated, "is a delicate balancing act."

"I never knew how much until this very day."

"Luckily for you," George said with a devious smile, "I still have the key."

Angus grinned and tossed another coin at him, then caught the key when George flipped it through the air. "You're a good man, George McCallum."

"Aye," George said as he walked off, "that's what I keep telling my wife."

Angus chuckled to himself and put the key in his pocket. He opened the door only a few inches, then called out, "Are you dressed?"

Her reply was a loud thump against the door. Probably her shoe.

"If you don't tell me otherwise, I'm coming in." He poked his head inside the room, then pulled it out just in time to avoid her other shoe, which came sailing at him with deadly aim.

He poked back in, ascertained that she had nothing else to throw at him, and then entered the room.

"Would you mind," she said with barely controlled fury, "telling me what the devil that was about?"

"Which bit of it?" he stalled.

She answered him with a glare. Angus thought she looked rather fetching with her cheeks all red with anger but wisely decided that now was not the time to compliment her on such things.

"I see," he said, unable to prevent the corners of his mouth from twitching with mirth. "Well, one would think it would be self-explanatory, but if I must explain—"

"You must."

He shrugged. "You wouldn't have a roof over your head right now if George didn't think you were my wife."

"That's not true, and who is George?"

"The innkeeper, and yes, it most certainly is true. He wouldn't have given this room to an unmarried couple."

"Of course not," she snapped. "He would have given it to me and tossed you out on your ear."

Angus scratched his head thoughtfully. "I'm not so sure about that, Miss Pennypacker. After all, I'm the one with the money."

She glared at him so hard, her eyes so wide and angry, that Angus finally noticed what color they were. Green. A rather lovely, grassy shade of green.

"Ah," he said at her silence. "Then you agree with me."

"I have money," she muttered.

"How much?"

"Enough!"

"Didn't you say you'd been robbed?"

"Yes," she said, so grudgingly that Angus thought it a wonder she didn't choke on the word, "but I still have a few coins."

"Enough for a hot meal? Hot water? A private dining room?"

"That's really not the point," she argued, "and the worst part of it is, you were acting as if you were having fun."

Angus grinned. "I *was* having fun."

"Why would you do this?" she said, shaking her hands at him. "We could have gone to another inn."

A loud clap of thunder shook the room. God, Angus decided, was on his side. "In this weather?" he asked. "Forgive me if I lack the inclination to venture back outside."

"Even if we had to masquerade as husband and wife," she conceded, "did you have to poke so much fun at my expense?"

His dark eyes grew tender. "I never meant to insult you. Surely you know that."

Margaret found her resolve weakening under his warm and concerned gaze. "You didn't have to tell the innkeeper that I was pregnant," she said, her cheeks growing furiously red as she uttered that last word.

He let out a sigh. "All I can do is apologize. My only explanation is that I was merely getting into the spirit of the ruse. I have spent the last two days riding the length of Scotland. I'm cold, wet, and hungry, and this little masquerade is the first amusing thing I've done in days. Forgive me if I over-enjoyed myself."

Margaret just stared at him, her hands fisted at her sides. She knew she ought to accept his apology, but the truth was, she needed a few more minutes to calm down.

Angus raised his hands in an overture of conciliation. "You may keep your stony silence all you want," he said with an amused smile, "but it won't wash. You, my dear Miss Pennypacker, are a better sport than you think you are."

The look she gave him was doubtful at best and sarcastic at worst. "Why, because I didn't strangle you right there in the hall?"

"Well, there's that, but I was actually referring to your unwillingness to hurt the innkeeper's feelings by disparaging his cooking."

"I did disparage his cooking," she pointed out.

"Yes, but you didn't do it loudly." He saw her open her mouth and held up his hand. "Ah, ah, ah, no more protests. You're determined to make me dislike you, but I'm afraid it won't work."

"You're insane," she breathed.

Angus peeled off his sodden coat. "That particular refrain is growing tedious."

"It's difficult to argue with the truth," she muttered. Then she looked up and saw what he was doing. "And don't remove your coat!"

"The alternative is death by pneumonia," he said mildly. "I suggest you remove yours as well."

"Only if you leave the room."

"And stand naked in the hall? I don't think so."

Margaret starting pacing and searching the room, opening the wardrobe and pulling out drawers. "There has to be a dressing screen here somewhere. There has to be."

"You're not likely to find one in the bureau," he said helpfully.

She stood stock-still for several moments, desperately trying not to let go of her anger. All her life she'd had to be responsible, to set a good example, and temper tantrums were not acceptable behavior. But this time . . . She looked over her shoulder and saw him grinning at her. This time was different.

She slammed the drawer shut, which should have given her some measure of satisfaction had she not caught the tip of her middle finger. "Yooooooowwwwww!" she howled, immediately stuffing her throbbing finger into her mouth.

"Are you all right?" Angus asked, moving quickly to her side.

She nodded. "Go away," she mumbled around her finger.

"Are you certain? You might have broken a bone."

"I didn't. Go away."

He took her hand and gently pulled her finger out of her mouth. "It looks fine," he said in a concerned voice, "but truly, I'm no expert on these matters."

"Why?" she moaned. "Why?"

"Why am I no expert?" he echoed, blinking in a rather confused manner. "I wasn't under the impression you thought I'd received medical training, but the truth is, I'm more of a farmer than anything else. A gentleman farmer, to be sure—"

"Why are you torturing me?" she yelled.

"Why, Miss Pennypacker, is that what you think I'm doing?"

She snatched her hand out of his grasp. "I swear to God above, I don't know why I am being punished in this way. I cannot imagine what sin I have committed to warrant such—"

"Margaret," he said loudly, halting her speech with his use of her given name, "perhaps you are making a wee bit too much out of this matter."

She stood there, barely moving, next to the bureau, for a full minute. Her breath was uneven, and she was swallowing more than normal, and then she started blinking.

"Oh, no," Angus said, closing his eyes in agony. "Don't cry."

—*Sniff*—"I'm not going to cry."

He opened his eyes. "Jesus, whiskey, and Robert the Bruce," he muttered. She certainly *looked* as if she were going to cry. He cleared his throat. "Are you certain?"

She nodded, once, but firmly. "I never cry."

He breathed a heartfelt sigh of relief. "Good, because I never know what to do when—oh, blast, you're crying."

"No. I'm. Not." Each word came out like its own little sentence, punctuated by loud gasps for air.

"Stop," he begged, shifting awkwardly from foot to foot. Nothing made him feel more like an incompetent, awkward clod than a woman's tears. Worse, he was fairly certain this woman hadn't cried in over a decade. And even *worse,* he was the cause.

"All I wanted to do—" she gasped. "All I wanted to do—"

"Was . . . ?" he prompted, desperate to keep her talking—anything to keep her from crying.

"Stop my brother." She took a deep, shuddering sigh and flopped onto the bed. "I know what's best for him. I know that sounds condescending, but I really do. I've been caring for him since I was seventeen."

Angus crossed the room and sat down next to her, but not so close as to make her nervous. "Have you?" he asked softly. He'd known from the moment she'd kneed that man in the groin that she was no ordinary woman, but he was coming to realize that she was more than a stubborn temper and a quick wit. Margaret Pennypacker cared deeply, was loyal to a fault, and would lay down her own life for those she loved without even a second's hesitation.

The realization made him smile wryly—and at the same time terrified him to the core. Because in terms of loyalty, caring, and devotion to family, Margaret Pennypacker might have been a female version of himself. And Angus had never before met a woman who matched those standards he held for himself.

And now that he had—well, what was he to do with her?

She interrupted his thoughts with a very loud sniffle. "Are you listening to me?"

"Your brother," he prompted.

She nodded and took a deep breath. Then she suddenly looked up from her lap and turned her gaze on him. "I'm not going to cry."

He patted her shoulder. "Of course not."

"If he marries one of those awful girls, his life will be ruined forever."

"Are you certain?" Angus asked gently. Sisters had a way of thinking they knew best.

"One of them doesn't even know the entire alphabet!"

He made a sound that came out rather like "Eeee," and his head recoiled slightly in commiseration. "That *is* bad."

She nodded again, this time with more vigor. "Do you see? Do you see what I mean?"

"How old is your brother?"

"He's only eighteen."

Angus let out a whoosh of air. "You're right, then. He has no idea what he's doing. No boy of eighteen does. Come to think of it, no girl of eighteen does, either."

Margaret nodded her agreement. "Is that how old your sister is? What's her name? Anne?"

"Yes, on both counts."

"Why are you chasing after her? What did she do?"

"Ran off to London."

"By herself?" Margaret asked, clearly aghast with horror.

Angus looked over at her with a bemused expression. "Might I remind you that you ran off to Scotland by yourself?"

"Well, yes," she sputtered, "but it's entirely different. London is . . . London."

"As it happens, she's not entirely by herself. She stole my carriage and three of my best servants, one of whom is a former pugilist, which is the only reason I'm not terrified out of my skull right now."

"But what does she plan to do?"

"Throw herself upon the mercy of my great-aunt." He shrugged. "Anne wants a Season."

"And is there a reason she cannot have one?"

Angus's expression grew stern. "I told her she could have one next year. We have been renovating our home, and I'm far too busy to drop everything and head to London."

"Ah."

His hands went to his hips. "What do you mean, ah?"

She moved her hands in a gesture that was somehow self-deprecating and all-knowing, all at once. "Just that it seems to me that you are putting your needs before hers."

"I am doing no such thing! There is no reason she cannot wait a year. You, yourself, agreed that eighteen-year-olds know nothing."

"You're probably right," she concurred, "but it's different for men and for women."

His face moved a fraction of an inch closer to hers. "Would you care to explain how?"

"I suppose it's true that eighteen-year-old girls know nothing. But eighteen-year-old boys know *less* than nothing."

To her great surprise, Angus started to laugh, falling back upon the bed and shaking the mattress with his chuckles. "Oh, I should be insulted," he gasped, "but I fear you're right."

"I know I'm right!" she retorted, a smile sneaking across her face.

"Oh, dear Lord," he sighed. "What a night. What a sorry, miserable, wonderful night."

Margaret's head snapped up at his words. What did he mean by that? "Yes, I know," she said—just a touch hesitantly, since she wasn't quite sure what she was agreeing with. "It's a muck. What are we to do?"

"Join forces, I suppose, and look for both of our errant siblings at once. And as for tonight, I can sleep on the floor."

A tension that Margaret hadn't even realized she was carrying slid right out of her. "Thank you," she said with great feeling. "I appreciate your generosity."

He sat up. "And you, my dear Margaret, are going to have to enjoy the life of an actress. At least for a day."

An actress? Didn't they run about half-dressed and take lovers? Margaret caught her breath, feeling her cheeks—and a rather lot of other bits—grow warm. "What do you mean?" she asked, horrified by how breathy she sounded.

"Merely that if you want to eat tonight—and I'm fairly certain there will be more than haggis on the menu, so you may breathe easier in that respect—then you will have to pretend to be Lady Angus Greene."

She frowned.

"And," he added with a roll of his eyes, "you're going to have to pretend that the position is not quite so disagreeable. After all, we *did* manage to get you with child. We can't dislike each other so very much."

Margaret blushed. "If you don't stop talking about that infernal nonexistent baby, I swear I shall close the drawer on *your* fingers."

He clasped his hands behind his back and grinned. "I am quaking with terror."

She shot him an irritated look, then blinked. "Did you say *Lady* Greene?"

"Does it matter?" Angus quipped.

"Well, *yes!*"

For a moment Angus just stared at her, disappointment spreading in his chest. His was a minor title—just a baronetcy with a small but lovely piece of land—but still women viewed him as a prize to be won. Marriage seemed to be some sort of contest to the ladies he knew. She who catches the title and money, wins.

Margaret placed her hand over her heart. "I place great stock in good manners."

Angus found his interest renewed. "Yes?"

"I shouldn't have called you Mr. Greene if you're truly Lord Greene."

"It's actually Sir Greene," he said, his lips twitching back into a smile, "but I can assure you that I am not offended."

"My mother must be turning over in her grave." She shook her head and sighed. "I've tried to teach Edward and Alicia—my sister—what my parents would have wanted. I've tried to live my life the same way. But sometimes I think I'm just not good enough."

"Don't say that," Angus said with great feeling. "If you're not good enough, then I have serious fears for my own soul."

Margaret offered him a wobbly smile. "You may have the ability to make me so furious that I can't even see straight, but I shouldn't worry about your soul, Angus Greene."

He leaned toward her, his black eyes dancing with humor, mischief, and just a touch of desire. "Are you trying to compliment me, Miss Pennypacker?"

Margaret caught her breath, her entire body growing oddly warm. He was so close, his lips mere inches away, and she had the sudden, bizarre thought that she might like to be a brazen woman for once in her life. If she just leaned forward, swayed toward him for only a second, would he take the initiative and kiss her? Would he sweep her into his arms, pull the pins from her hair, and make her feel as if she were the star of a Shakespearean sonnet?

Margaret leaned.

She swayed.

She fell right off the bed.

Three

Margaret yelped in surprise as she slid through the
air. It wasn't a long slide; the floor practically jumped to
meet her hip, which was (of course) already bruised from
her ride in the farmer's cart. She was sitting there, somewhat
stunned at her sudden change of position, when Angus's
face appeared over the edge of the bed.

"Are you all right?" he asked.

"I, er, lost my balance," she muttered.

"I see," he said, so solemnly that she couldn't possibly believe him.

"I frequently lose my balance," she lied, trying to make
the incident seem as unremarkable as possible. It wasn't
every day she fell off a bed while swaying into a kiss with a
complete stranger. "Don't you?"

"Never."

"That's not possible."

"Well," he mused, scratching his chin, "I suppose that's
not entirely true. There are times . . ."

Margaret's eyes fixed on his fingers as they stroked the
stubbled skin of his jaw. Something about the movement

transfixed her. She could see each little whisker, and with a horrified gasp she realized that her hand had already crossed half the distance between them.

Good Lord, she wanted to touch the man.

"Margaret?" he asked, his eyes amused. "Are you listening to me?"

She blinked. "Of course. I'm just—" Her mind flailed for something to say. "Well, it's obvious that I'm sitting on the floor."

"And this interferes with your auditory skills?"

"No! I—" She clamped her lips together in an irritated line. "What were you saying?"

"Are you certain you don't want to come back up on the bed so you can hear me better?"

"No, thank you. I'm perfectly comfortable, thank you."

He reached down, clamped one of his large hands around her arm, and hauled her up onto the bed. "I might have believed you if you'd left it at one 'thank you.' "

She grimaced. If she had a fatal flaw, it was trying too hard, protesting too much, arguing too loud. She never knew when to stop. Her siblings had told her so for years, and deep in her heart, she knew she could be the worst sort of pest when she was single-mindedly fixed on a goal.

She wasn't about to inflate his ego any further by agreeing with him, though, so instead she sniffed and said, "Is there anything distasteful about good manners? Most people appreciate a word of thanks every now and then."

He leaned forward, shocking her with his nearness. "Do you know how I know you weren't listening to me?"

She shook her head, her normally ready wit flying out the window—which was no inconsiderable feat, considering that the window was closed.

"You had asked me if I ever felt off-balance," he said, his voice dropping to a husky murmur, "and I said no, but then—" He lifted his powerful shoulders and let them fall in an oddly graceful shrug. "Then," he added, "I reconsidered."

"Be-because I told you that's not possible," she just barely managed to say.

"Well, yes," he mused, "but you see, sitting here with you, I had a sudden flash of memory."

"You did?"

He nodded slowly, and when he spoke, he drew each word out with mesmerizing intensity. "I can't speak for other men . . ."

She found herself caught in his hot gaze, and she could no more look away than she could stop breathing. Her skin tingled and her lips parted, and then she swallowed convulsively, suddenly certain that she'd been better off on the floor.

He touched one finger to the corner of his mouth, stroking his skin as he continued his lazy speech. " . . . but when I am overcome with desire, drunk on it—"

She shot off the bed like a Chinese firecracker. "Maybe," she said, her voice sounding strangely thick, "we should see about getting that supper."

"Right." Angus stood so suddenly that the bed rocked. "Sustenance is what we need." He grinned at her. "Don't you think?"

Margaret just stared at him, amazed by his shift in mien. He'd been attempting to seduce her—she was sure of it. Or if he wasn't, he was definitely trying to fluster her. He'd already as much as admitted that he enjoyed doing so.

And he'd succeeded. Her stomach was flipping about, her throat seemed to have grown three large lumps, and she kept having to grab hold of the furniture to keep her balance.

And yet here he was, completely composed—smiling, even! Either he hadn't been the least bit affected by their nearness, or the dratted man belonged on the Shakespearean stage.

"Margaret?"

"Food is good," she blurted out.

"I'm glad you agree with me," he said, looking utterly amused by her loss of composure. "But first you must take off that wet coat."

She shook her head, hugging her arms to her chest. "I don't have anything else."

He tossed a garment in her direction. "You can wear my spare."

"But then what will you wear?"

"I'll be fine in a shirt."

Impulsively, she reached out and touched his forearm, which was exposed by a rolled-up sleeve. "You're freezing. Is your other shirt made of linen? It won't be heavy enough." When he didn't reply, she added firmly, "You cannot give me your coat. I won't accept it."

Angus took one look down at her tiny hand on his arm and started imagining it traveling up to his shoulder, then across his chest . . .

He didn't feel cold.

"Sir Greene?" she asked softly. "Are you quite all right?"

He tore his eyes off her hand and then made the colossal mistake of looking at her eyes. Those grassy green orbs, which had, in the course of the evening, gazed upon him with fright, irritation, embarrassment, and, most recently, innocent desire, were now brimming with concern and compassion.

And it quite unmanned him.

Angus felt himself fill with an age-old male terror—as if somehow his body knew what his mind refused to consider—that she might be The One, that somehow, no matter how hard he fought, she'd be pestering him for all eternity.

And worse, that if she ever took it upon herself to stop pestering him, he might have to track her down and chain her to his side until she started up again.

Jesus, whiskey, and Robert the Bruce, it was a terrifying fate.

He tore off his shirt, furious with his reaction to her. It had started with just a hand on his arm, and the next thing he knew, he'd seen his entire life stretched out before him.

He finished dressing and stomped to the door. "I'll wait in the hall until you're ready," he said.

She was staring at him, her body trembling with tiny shivers.

"And take off all of those damned wet clothes," he ordered.

"I can't just wear your coat with nothing under it," she protested.

"You can and you will. I won't be responsible for your catching a lung fever."

He saw her shoulders straighten and her eyes fill with steel. "You can't order me about," she retorted.

He raised a brow. "You can take off your wet shirt, or I'll do it for you. It's your choice."

She grumbled something under her breath. Angus didn't quite hear all of the words, but the ones he *did* catch weren't terribly ladylike.

He smiled. "Someone ought to scold you for your language."

"Someone ought to scold you for your arrogance."

"You've been trying all night," he pointed out.

She made an unintelligible sound, and Angus just barely managed to duck out the door before she threw another shoe at him.

When Margaret stuck her head out the bedroom door, Angus was nowhere to be seen. This surprised her. She hadn't known the huge Scotsman for more than a few hours, but she was fairly certain he wasn't the sort to leave a gently bred lady to fend for herself in a public inn.

She shut the door behind her quietly, not wanting to draw attention to herself, and tiptoed down the hall. She was prob-

ably safe from unwanted attention here at The Canny Man—
Angus had loudly proclaimed her his wife, after all, and
only a fool would provoke a man of his size. But the trials of
the day had left her cautious.

In retrospect, it had probably been a foolish endeavor to
trek all the way to Gretna Green by herself, but what other
choice did she have? She couldn't let Edward marry one of
those awful girls he'd been courting.

She reached the stairwell and peered down.

"Hungry?"

Margaret jumped about a foot and let out a short, yet quite
remarkably loud, scream.

Angus grinned. "Didn't mean to startle you."

"Yes, you did."

"Very well," he admitted. "I did. But you certainly had
your revenge on my ears."

"It serves you right," she muttered. "Hiding in the stairwell."

"Actually," he said, offering her his arm, "I hadn't intended to hide. I would never have left the hall, except that I
thought I heard my sister's voice."

"You did? Did you find her? Was it she?"

Angus raised a bushy black brow. "You sound rather excited about the prospect of finding someone you don't even
know."

"I know you," she pointed out, dodging a lamp as they
moved through The Canny Man's main room, "and much as
you vex me, I would like to see you locate your sister."

His lips spread into an easy grin. "Why, Miss Pennypacker, I think you might have just admitted that you like
me."

"I *said*," she said pointedly, "that you vex me."

"Well, of course. I do it on purpose."

That earned him a glare.

He leaned forward and chucked her chin. "Vexing you is the most fun I've had in ages."

"It isn't fun for me," she muttered.

"Of course it is," he said jovially, leading her into the small dining room. "I'll wager I'm the only person you know who dares to contradict you."

"You make me sound like a termagant."

He pulled out a chair for her. "Am I correct?"

"Yes," she mumbled, "but I'm not a termagant."

"Of course not." He sat down across from her. "But you *are* used to having your own way."

"So are *you*," she retorted.

"Touché."

"In fact," she said, leaning forward with a knowing gleam in her green eyes, "that's why your sister's disobedience is so galling. You cannot bear that she's gone against your wishes."

Angus squirmed in his chair. It was all fun and well when he was analyzing Margaret's personality, but this was unacceptable. "Anne has been going against my wishes since the day she was born."

"I didn't say she was meek and mild and did everything you say—"

"Jesus, whiskey, and Robert the Bruce," he said under his breath, "I would that were true . . ."

She ignored his odd expletive. "But Angus," she said animatedly, using her hands to punctuate her words, "has she ever before disobeyed you on such a grand scale? Done something that so completely disrupted your life?"

For a second, he didn't move; then he shook his head.

"See?" Margaret smiled, looking terribly pleased with herself. "That's why you're in such a dither."

His expression moved to the comical side of haughty. "Men do not dither."

Her expression moved to the ridiculous side of arch. "I beg your pardon, but I am looking at a dithering male as we speak."

They stared at each other across the table for several seconds, until Angus finally said, "If you raise your eyebrows any farther, I'm going to have to physically retrieve them from your hairline."

Margaret tried to respond in kind—he could see it in her eyes—but her humor got the best of her, and she burst out laughing.

Margaret Pennypacker consumed with laughter was a sight to behold, and Angus had never been so perfectly content to sit back and watch another person. Her mouth formed an enchanting, open-mouthed smile, and her eyes glowed with pure mirth. Her entire body shook, and she gasped for air, finally letting her brow drop down into one supporting hand.

"Oh, my goodness," she said, pushing aside a lock of gently curving brown hair. "Oh, my hair."

Angus smiled. "Does your coiffure always come undone when you laugh? Because I must say, it's a rather endearing quirk."

She reached up and self-consciously patted her hair. "It's mussed from the day, I'm sure. I didn't have time to re-pin it before we came down to supper and—"

"You don't need to reassure me. I have every confidence that on a normal day, every hair on your head is in place."

Margaret frowned. She had always prided herself on a neat and tidy appearance, but Angus's words—which were surely meant as a compliment—somehow made her feel like the veriest stodge.

She was saved from further contemplation on this issue, however, by the arrival of George, the innkeeper.

"Och, there you are!" he boomed, slapping down a large earthenware dish on their table. "All dried off, are you?"

"As best as can be expected," Angus replied, with one of

those nods that men shared when they thought they were commiserating over something.

Margaret rolled her eyes.

"Weel, you're in for a treat," George said, "because my wife, she had some haggis made and ready to go for tomorrow. Had to boil it up, of course. Can't have a cold haggis."

Margaret didn't particularly think the hot haggis looked terribly appetizing, but she forbore to offer an opinion on the matter.

Angus wafted the aroma—or fumes, as Margaret was wont to call them—in his direction and took a ceremonial sniff. "Och, McCallum," he said, sounding more Scottish than he had all day, "if this tastes anything like it smells, your wife is a blooming genius."

"Of course she is," George replied, grabbing two plates off a side table and setting them in front of his guests. "She married me, didn't she?"

Angus laughed heartily and gave the innkeeper a convivial slap on the back. Margaret felt a retort welling up in her throat and coughed to keep it down.

"Just a moment," George said. "I need to get a proper knife."

Margaret watched him leave, then leaned across the table and hissed, "What is *in* this thing?"

"You don't know?" Angus asked, obviously enjoying her distress.

"I *know* it smells hideous."

"Tsk, tsk. Were you so gravely insulting my nation's cuisine earlier this evening without even knowing of what you speak?"

"Just tell me the ingredients," she ground out.

"Heart, minced with liver and lights," he replied, drawing the words out in all their gory detail. "Then add some good suet, onions, and oatmeal—stuffed into the stomach of a sheep."

"What," Margaret asked to the air around her, "have I done to deserve this?"

"Och," Angus said dismissively. "You'll love it. You English always love your organ meats."

"I don't. I never have."

He choked back a laugh. "Then you might be in a wee bit of trouble."

Margaret's eyes grew panicked. "I can't eat this."

"You don't want to insult George, do you?"

"No, but—"

"You told me you placed great stock in good manners, didn't you?"

"Yes, but—"

"Are you ready?" George asked, sweeping back into the room with blazing eyes. "Because I'll be giving you God's own haggis." With that, he whipped out a knife with such flair that Margaret was compelled to lurch back a good half a foot or risk having her nose permanently shortened.

George belted out a few bars from a rather pompous and overblown hymn—foreshadowing the actual meal, Margaret was sure—then, with a wide, proud swipe of his arm, sliced into the haggis, opening it for all the world to see.

And smell.

"Oh, God," Margaret gasped, and never before had she uttered such a heartfelt prayer.

"Have you ever seen a thing so lovely?" George rhapsodized.

"I'll take half on my plate right now," Angus said.

Margaret smiled weakly, trying not to breathe.

"She'll take a small portion," Angus said for her. "Her appetite's not what it once was."

"Och, yes," George replied, "the babe. You'll be in your early months, then, eh?"

Margaret supposed that "early" could be construed to mean pre-pregnancy, so she nodded.

Angus lifted a brow in approval. Margaret scowled at him, irritated that he was so impressed that she had finally participated in this ridiculous lie.

"The smell might make you a bit queasy," George said, "but there's nothing for a babe like a good haggis, so you should at least try, as my great-aunt Millie calls it, a no-thank-you-portion."

"That would be lovely," Margaret managed to choke out.

"Here you are," George said, scooping her a healthy amount.

Margaret stared at the mass of food on her plate, trying not to retch. If this was no-thank-you, she shuddered to imagine yes-please. "Tell me," she said, as demurely as possible, "what did your Aunt Millie look like?"

"Och, a lovely woman. Strong as an ox. And as large as one, too."

Margaret's eyes fell back to her dinner. "Yes," she murmured, "I thought as much."

"Try it," George urged. "If you like it, I'll have my wife make hugga-muggie tomorrow."

"Hugga-muggie?"

"Same thing as haggis," Angus said helpfully, "but made with a fish stomach instead of sheep."

"How . . . lovely."

"Och, I'll tell her to stuff one up, then," George assured her.

Margaret watched in horror as the innkeeper pranced back to the kitchen. "We *cannot* eat here tomorrow," she hissed across the table. "I don't care if we have to change inns."

"So don't eat the hugga-muggie." Angus forked a huge bite into his mouth and chewed.

"And how am I supposed to avoid that, when you've been prattling on about what good manners it is to praise the innkeeper's food?"

Angus was still chewing, so he managed to avoid answering. Then he took a long swig of the ale that one of George's servants had slipped onto the table. "Aren't you even going to try it?" he asked, motioning to the untouched haggis on her plate.

She shook her head, her huge green eyes looking somewhat panicked.

"Try a bite," he urged, attacking his own portion with great relish.

"I can't. Angus, I tell you, it's the oddest thing, and I don't know how I know this, but if I eat one bite of this haggis, I *will* die."

He washed down the haggis with another sip of ale, looked up at her with all the seriousness he could muster, and asked, "You're sure of this?"

She nodded.

"Well, if that's the case . . ." He reached over, took her plate, and slid the entire contents onto his own. "Can't let a good haggis go to waste."

Margaret starting glancing around the room. "I wonder if he has any bread."

"Hungry?"

"Famished."

"If you think you can manage for ten more minutes without perishing, old George will most likely bring out some cheese and pudding."

The sigh Margaret let out was heartfelt in the extreme.

"You'll like our Scots desserts," Angus said. "Not an organ meat to be found."

But Margaret's eyes were strangely fixed on the window across the room.

Assuming she was merely glazing over from hunger, he said, "If we're lucky, they'll have cranachan. You'll never taste a finer pudding."

She made no reply, so he just shrugged and shoveled the rest of the haggis into his mouth. Jesus, whiskey, and Robert the Bruce, it tasted good. He hadn't realized how hungry he'd been, and there was truly nothing like a good haggis. Margaret had no idea what she was missing.

Speaking of Margaret . . . He looked back at her. She was now squinting at the window. Angus wondered if she needed spectacles.

"My mum made the sweetest cranachan this side of Loch Lomond," he said, figuring that *one* of them had to keep up the conversation. "Cream, oatmeal, sugar, rum. Makes my mouth water just—"

Margaret gasped. Angus dropped his fork. Something about the sound of her breath rushing through her lips made his blood run cold.

"Edward," she whispered. Then her countenance turned from surprise to something considerably blacker, and with a scowl that would have vanquished the dragon of Loch Ness, she shot to her feet and stormed out of the room.

Angus set down his fork and groaned. The sweet aroma of cranachan wafted in from the kitchen. Angus wanted to bang his head against the table in frustration.

Margaret? (He looked at the door through which she had just exited.)

Or cranachan? (He looked longingly at the door to the kitchen.)

Margaret?

Or cranachan?

"Damn," he muttered, rising to his feet. It was going to have to be Margaret.

And as he walked away from the cranachan, he had the sinking feeling that his choice had somehow sealed his fate.

Four

The rain had subsided, but the damp night air was a slap in the face as Margaret dashed through the front door of The Canny Man. She looked wildly about, twisting her neck to the left and the right. She'd seen Edward through the window. She was sure of it.

Out of the corner of her eye, she saw a couple moving quickly across the street. Edward. The man's golden blond hair was a dead giveaway.

"Edward!" she called, scurrying in his direction. "Edward Pennypacker!"

He made no indication of having heard her, so she picked up her skirts and ran into the street, yelling his name as she closed the distance between them.

"Edward!"

He turned around.

And she did not know him.

"I-I-I'm so sorry," she stuttered, stumbling back a step. "I mistook you for my brother."

The handsome blond man inclined his head graciously. "It's quite all right."

"It's a foggy night," Margaret explained, "and I was looking out the window . . ."

"There is no harm done, I assure you. But if you will excuse me"—the young man put his arm around the shoulder of the woman at his side and drew her near—"my wife and I must be on our way."

Margaret nodded and watched them disappear around the corner. They were newlyweds. From the way his voice had warmed over the word "wife," she knew it had to be so.

They were newlyweds, and like everyone else here at Gretna Green, they'd probably eloped, and their families were probably furious with them. But they looked so very happy, and Margaret suddenly felt unbearably tired, and forlorn, and old, and all those sad, lonely things she'd never thought she'd be.

"Did you have to leave right before the pudding?"

She blinked and turned around. Angus—how the devil did such a large man move so quietly?—was looming over her, arms akimbo, eyes glowering. Margaret didn't say anything. She didn't have the energy to say anything.

"I assume that wasn't your brother you saw."

She shook her head.

"Then for the love of God, woman, can we finish our meal?"

An unwilling smile danced across her lips. No recriminations, no "You stupid woman, why did you go running off into the night?" Just "Can we finish our meal?"

What a man.

"That would be a fine idea," she replied, taking his arm when he offered it. "And I might even taste the haggis. Just a taste, mind you. I'm sure I won't like it, but as you said, it's only polite to try."

He raised a brow, and something about his face, with those big, bushy eyebrows, dark eyes, and slightly crooked nose, made Margaret's heart skip two beats.

"Och," he grunted, stepping toward the inn. "Will wonders never cease? Are you telling me that you were actually listening to me?"

"I listen to almost everything you say!"

"You're only offering to try the haggis because you know I ate your portion."

Margaret's blush gave her away.

"A-ha." His smile was positively wolfish. "Just for that, I'm going to make you eat hugga-muggie tomorrow."

"Can't I just try that cranopoly that you were talking about? The one with the cream and the sugar?"

"It's called cranachan, and if you endeavor not to nag me the entire way back to the inn, I might be inclined to ask Mr. McCallum to serve you some."

"Och, you're ever gracious," she said sarcastically.

Angus stopped in his tracks. "Did you just say 'och?'"

Margaret blinked in surprise. "I don't know. I might have done."

"Jesus, whiskey, and Robert the Bruce, you're beginning to sound like a Scotswoman."

"Why do you keep saying that?"

It was his turn to blink in surprise. "I'm quite certain I've never mistaken you for a Scot until this very moment."

"Don't be obtuse. I meant the bit about the son of God, heathen spirits, and your Scottish hero."

He shrugged and pushed open the door to The Canny Man. "It's my own little prayer."

"Somehow, I doubt your vicar would find that particularly sacrosanct."

"We call them ministers up here, and who the devil do you think taught it to me?"

Margaret nearly tripped over his foot as they reentered the small dining room. "You're joking."

"If you plan to spend any time in Scotland, you're going

to have to learn that we're a more pragmatic people than ye of warmer climes."

"I've never heard 'warmer climes' used as an insult," Margaret muttered, "but I believe you've just managed it."

Angus pulled her chair out for her, seated himself, and then continued with his pontification. "Any man worth his salt quickly learns that in times of great need, he must turn to the things he can trust best, things he can depend upon."

Margaret stared at him with a mix of incredulity and disgust. "What on earth are you talking about?"

"When I feel the need to summon a higher power, I say, 'Jesus, whiskey, and Robert the Bruce.' It makes perfect sense."

"You're a stark, raving lunatic."

"If I were a less easygoing man," he said, signaling to the innkeeper to bring them some cheese, "I might take offense at that."

"You can't pray to Robert the Bruce," she persisted.

"Och, and why not? I'm sure he's more time to watch over me than Jesus. After all, Jesus has the whole bleeding world to look after, even Sassenachs like you."

"It's wrong," Margaret said firmly, her head shaking with her words. "It's just wrong."

Angus looked at her, scratched his temple, and said, "Have some cheese."

Margaret's eyes widened in surprise, but she took the cheese and put some in her mouth. "Tasty."

"I'd comment on the superiority of Scottish cheese, but I'm sure you'll already be feeling a wee bit insecure about your nation's cuisine."

"After the haggis?"

"There's a reason we Scots are bigger and stronger than the English."

She let out a ladylike snort. "You're insufferable."

Angus sat back, resting his head in his hands, with his arms bent out at the elbows. He looked like a well-sated man, a well-confident man, one who knew who he was and what he meant to do with his life.

Margaret couldn't take her eyes off of him.

"Perhaps," he allowed, "but everyone loves me so well."

She threw a piece of cheese at him.

He caught it and popped it into his mouth, grinning wolfishly as he chewed. "You do like to throw things, don't you?"

"Funny that I never felt the inclination to do so until I met *you.*"

"And here everyone told me I brought out the best in them."

Margaret started to say something and then just sighed.

"What now?" Angus asked, clearly amused.

"I was *about* to insult you."

"Not that I'm surprised, but why did you think the better of it?"

She shrugged. "I don't even *know* you. And here we are, bickering like an old married couple. It's quite incomprehensible."

Angus eyed her thoughtfully. She looked tired and weary, and just a little bit baffled, as if she had finally slowed down enough for her brain to realize that she was in Scotland, dining with a stranger who had very nearly kissed her not an hour earlier.

The subject of his perusal broke into his thoughts with a persistent, "Don't you think?"

Angus smiled guilelessly. "Was I supposed to make a comment?"

That earned him a rather fierce scowl.

"Very well," he said, "here is what I think. I think that friendship blossoms most quickly under extreme circumstances. Given the events that have unfolded this evening and, indeed, the common purpose that unites us, it's not surprising that we are sitting here enjoying our meal as if we have known each other for years."

"Yes, but—"

Angus briefly considered how splendid his life would be with the removal of the words, "yes" and "but" from the English language, then interrupted with, "Ask me anything."

She blinked several times before replying, "I beg your pardon?"

"You wanted to know more about me? Here is your chance. Ask me anything."

Margaret grew thoughtful. Twice she parted her lips, a question on the tip of her tongue, only to close them again. Finally she leaned forward and said, "Very well. Why are you so protective of women?"

Tiny white lines appeared around his mouth. It was a small reaction, and well controlled, but Margaret had been watching him closely. Her question had unnerved him.

His hand tightened around his mug of ale, and he said, "Any gentleman would come to a lady's aid."

Margaret shook her head, recalling the wild, almost feral look of him when he'd dispatched the men who'd attacked her. "There is more to it than that, and we both know it. Something happened to you." Her voice grew softer, more soothing. "Or perhaps to someone you love."

There was an achingly long silence, and then Angus said, "I had a cousin."

Margaret said nothing, unnerved by the flatness of his voice.

"She was older," he continued, staring at the swirling liquid in his mug of ale. "Seventeen to my nine. But we were very close."

"It sounds as if you were fortunate to have her in your life."

He nodded. "My parents were frequently in Edinburgh. They rarely took me with them."

"I'm sorry," Margaret murmured. She knew what it was like to miss one's parents.

"Don't be. I was never lonely. I had Catriona." He took a sip of his ale. "She took me fishing, she let me tag along on her errands, she taught me my multiplication tables when my tutors threw up their arms in despair." Angus looked up sharply; then a wistful smile crossed his face. "She wove them into songs. Funny how the only way I could remember that six by seven was forty-two was to sing it."

A lump formed in Margaret's throat because she knew this story did not have a happy ending. "What did she look like?" she whispered, not entirely certain why she wanted to know.

A nostalgic chuckle escaped Angus's lips. "Her eyes were much the same color as yours, maybe a touch bluer, and her hair was the richest red you've ever seen. She used to lament that it turned pink at sunset."

He fell silent, and finally Margaret had to voice the question that hung in the air. "What happened to her?"

"One day she didn't come to the house. She always came on Tuesdays. Other days I didn't know if she'd visit or not, but Tuesdays she always came to help me practice my numbers before my tutor arrived. I thought she must be ill, so I went to her house to bring her flowers." He looked up with an oddly regretful expression. "I think I must have been half in love with her. Who ever heard of a nine-year-old boy bringing his cousin flowers?"

"I think it's sweet," Margaret said gently.

"When I arrived, my aunt was in a panic. She wouldn't let me see her. Said I was right, that Catriona was ill. But I went around back and climbed through her window. She was lying in her bed, curled up in the tightest ball you've ever seen. I've never seen anything so—" His voice broke. "I dropped the flowers."

Angus cleared his throat, then took a sip of ale. Margaret noticed that his hands were shaking. "I called her name," he said, "but she didn't respond. I called it again and reached out to touch her, but she flinched and pulled away. And then her eyes cleared, and for a moment she looked like the girl I knew so well, and she said, 'Grow strong, Angus. Grow strong for me.' "

"Two days later, she was dead." He looked up, his eyes bleak. "By her own hand."

"Oh, no . . ." Margaret heard herself say.

"No one told me why," Angus continued. "I suppose they thought me too young for the truth. I knew she'd killed herself, of course. Everyone knew—the church refused to bury her in consecrated ground. It was only years later that I heard the whole story."

Margaret reached across the table and took his hand. She gave it a reassuring squeeze.

Angus looked up, and when he spoke again, his voice sounded brisker, more . . . normal. "I don't know how much you know of Scottish politics, but we've a good many British soldiers roaming our land. We're told they're here to keep the peace."

Margaret felt something queasy growing in the pit of her stomach. "Did one of them . . . was she . . . ?"

He nodded curtly. "All she did was walk from her house to the village. That was her only crime."

"I'm so sorry, Angus."

"It was a path she'd traveled all her life. Except this time, someone saw her, decided he wanted her, and took her."

"Oh, Angus. You do know that this wasn't your fault, don't you?"

He nodded again. "I was nine. What could I have done? And I didn't even learn the truth until I'd reached seventeen—the same age Catriona was when she died. But I promised myself—" His eyes burned dark and fierce. "I promised *God* that I'd not let another woman be hurt the same way."

He smiled lopsidedly. "And so I've found myself the subject of more brawls than I'd care to remember. And I've fought several strangers I'd rather forget. And I don't receive many thanks for my intervention, but I think that *she*—" His eyes flitted heavenward. "I think that she thanks me."

"Oh, Angus," Margaret said, her heart in her voice, "I know she does. And I know I do." She realized she was still holding his hand, and she squeezed it again. "I don't believe I've thanked you properly, but I do appreciate what you did for me this evening. If you hadn't come along, I— I don't even want to think about what I'd be feeling right now."

He shrugged uncomfortably. "It was nothing. You can thank Catriona."

Margaret gave his hand one last squeeze before she pulled hers back to her own side of the table. "I'll thank Catriona for being such a good friend to you when you were small, but I'll thank *you* for saving me this eve."

He pushed some food about on his plate and grunted, "I was happy to do it."

She laughed at his less-than-gracious reply. "You *aren't* used to being thanked, are you? But enough of that; I believe I owe you a question."

He looked up. "I beg your pardon?"

"I got to ask you anything. It's only fair I return the favor."

He waved his hand dismissively. "You don't have to—"

"No, I insist. It wouldn't be sporting of me, otherwise."

"Very well." He thought for a moment. "Are you upset that your younger sister is getting married before you?"

Margaret let out a little cough of surprise. "I . . . how did you know she is getting married?"

"Earlier this evening," Angus replied, "you mentioned it."

She cleared her throat again. "So I did. I . . . well . . . you must know that I love my sister dearly."

"Your devotion to your family is clear in everything you do," Angus said quietly.

She picked up her napkin and twisted it. "I'm thrilled for Alicia. I wish her every happiness in the world."

Angus watched her closely. She wasn't lying, but neither was she telling the truth. "I know you're happy for your sister," he said softly. "You don't have it in you to feel anything else for her. But what do you feel for yourself?"

"I feel . . . I feel . . ." She let out a long, tired breath. "No one has ever asked me this before."

"Maybe it's time."

Margaret nodded. "I feel left behind. I spent so much time raising her. I've devoted my life to this moment, to this end, and somewhere along the way, I forgot about myself. And now it's too late."

Angus raised a dark brow. "You're hardly a toothless crone."

"I know, but to the men in Lancashire, I am firmly on the shelf. When they start thinking of potential brides, they don't think of me."

"Then they're stupid, and you shouldn't want anything to do with them."

She smiled sadly. "You *are* sweet, Angus Greene, no matter how hard you try to hide it. But the truth is, people see what they expect to see, and I've spent so much time chaperoning Alicia that I have been cast in an authoritative role. I sit with the mothers at country dances, and that, I fear, is where I'll stay."

She sighed. "Is it possible to be so happy for one person and at the same time be so sad for oneself?"

"Only the most generous in spirit can manage it. The rest of us don't know how to be happy for another when our own dreams have gone astray."

A single tear pricked Margaret's eye. "Thank you," she said.

"You're a fine woman, Margaret Pennypacker, and—"

"Pennypacker?" The innkeeper came scurrying over. "Did you just call her Margaret Pennypacker?"

Margaret felt her throat close up. She knew she'd get caught in this bloody lie. She'd never been good at fabrication, or even at playacting, for that matter . . .

But Angus just looked George calmly in the eye and said, "It's her maiden name. I use it as an endearment from time to time."

"Well, then, you must be recently married, because there's a messenger traveling from inn to inn, asking after her."

Margaret sat up very straight. "Is he still here? Do you know where he went?"

"He said he was going to try The Mad Rabbit." George jerked his head to the right before turning to walk away. "It's just down the street."

Margaret stood so quickly that she overturned her chair. "Let's go," she said to Angus. "We have to catch up with him. If he checks all the inns and doesn't find me, he might leave the village. And then I'll never get the message, and—"

Angus laid a heavy, comforting hand on her arm. "Who knows you're here?"

"Just my family," she whispered. "Oh, no, what if something dreadful has happened to one of them? I will never forgive myself. Angus, you don't understand. I'm responsible for them, and I could never forgive myself if—"

He squeezed her arm, and somehow the motion helped to settle her racing heart. "Why don't we see what this messenger has to say before we panic?"

Margaret couldn't believe how reassured she was by his use of the word "we." She nodded hurriedly. "Right. Let's be off, then."

He shook his head. "I want you to remain here."

"No. I couldn't possibly. I—"

"Margaret, you're a woman traveling alone, and—" He saw her open her mouth to protest and continued with, "No, don't tell me how capable you are. I've never met a more capable woman in my life, but that doesn't mean that men aren't going to try to take advantage of you. Who knows if this messenger really is a messenger?"

"But if he *is* a messenger, then he won't release the message into your hands. It's addressed to me."

Angus shrugged. "I'll bring him back here, then."

"No, I can't. I can't bear to feel useless. If I stay here—"

"It would make me feel better," he interrupted.

Margaret swallowed convulsively, trying not to pay attention to the warm concern in his voice. Why did the dratted man have to be so bloody nice? And why did she even *care* if her actions could make him "feel better"?

But she did, bugger her eyes.

"All right," she said slowly. "But if you don't return in five minutes, I'm coming after you."

He sighed. "Jesus, whiskey, and Robert the Bruce, do you think you might be able to grant me ten?"

Her lips wobbled into a smile. "Ten, then."

He pointed at her mouth with the jauntiest of fingers. "Caught you grinning. You can't be that angry with me."

"Just get me that message, and I'll love you forever."

"Och, good." He saluted her and walked out the door, pausing only to say, "Don't let George give my cranachan to anyone else."

Margaret blinked, then gasped. Good Lord, had she just told him she'd love him forever?

Angus reentered The Canny Man eight minutes later, message in hand. It hadn't been that difficult to convince the messenger to relinquish the envelope; Angus had merely said—with a certain level of firmness—that he was serving as Miss Pennypacker's protector, and he would see to it that she received the message.

It also didn't hurt that Angus towered over six feet by a good four inches—which gave him nearly a foot over the messenger.

Margaret was sitting where he had left her, tapping her fingers against the table and ignoring the two big bowls of cranachan that George must have set before her.

"Here you are, my lady," he said jovially, handing her the missive.

She must have been in a daze, because she jerked to attention and gave her head a little shake before taking it.

The message was indeed from her family. Angus had managed to obtain that information from the messenger. He wasn't worried about there being an emergency; the messenger—when asked, once again firmly—had told him the message was very important but that the woman who had given it to him hadn't seemed overly panicked.

He watched Margaret carefully as her shaking hands broke the seal. Her green eyes scanned the lines quickly, and when she reached the end, she blinked several times in rapid succession. A strangled, choking sort of sound emerged from her throat, followed by a gasp of "I can't believe he did this."

Angus decided he'd better tread carefully. From her reaction, he couldn't tell whether she was about to start screaming or crying. Men and horses were easy to predict, but God alone understood the workings of the female mind.

He said her name, and she thrust two sheets of paper toward him in reply.

"I'm going to kill him," she bit out. "If he isn't dead yet, I'm going to bloody well kill him."

Angus looked down at the papers in his hand.

"Read the bottom one first," Margaret said bitterly.

He switched the sheets and began to read.

Rutherford House
Pendle, Lancashire

My dearest sister—

This note was delivered to us by Hugo Thrumpton. He said he was under strict orders not to bring it by until you had been departed a full day.
    Please do not hate Edward.
    Godspeed.

yr. loving sister,
Alicia Pennypacker

Angus looked up with questioning eyes. "Who is Hugo Thrumpton?"

"My brother's best friend."

"Ah." He pulled out the second letter, which was written in a decidedly more masculine hand.

Thrumpton Hall
nr. Clitheroe, Lancashire

My dear Margaret—

It is with a heavy heart that I write these words. By now you have received my note advising you of my flight to Gretna Green. If you react as I know you will, you will be in Scotland as you read this.
    But I am not in Scotland, and I never had any intention of eloping. Rather, I leave tomorrow for Liverpool to join the Royal Navy. I shall use my portion to purchase my commission.
    I know you never wanted this life for me, but I am a man now, and as a man I must choose my own fortune.

226 Julia Quinn

*I have always known that I must be destined for the
military life; ever since I played with my pewter soldiers as a young boy have I longed to serve my country.*

*I pray you will forgive my duplicity, but I knew that
you would come after me to Liverpool if you were
aware of my true intentions. Such a farewell would
pain me for the rest of my days.*

It is better this way.

yr. loving brother,
Edward Pennypacker

Angus looked up into Margaret's eyes, which were suspiciously bright. "Did you have any idea?" he asked quietly.

"None," she said, her voice quavering on the word. "Do
you think I would have undertaken this mad journey if I'd
dreamed he'd gone to Liverpool?"

"What do you plan to do next?"

"Return home, I imagine. What else can I do? He's probably halfway to America by now."

She was exaggerating, but Angus figured she'd earned
that right. There wasn't a lot one could say in such a situation, though, so he leaned over and pushed her bowl of pudding a little closer to her. "Have some cranachan."

Margaret looked down at her food. "You want me to eat?"

"I can't think of anything better to do. You didn't touch
your haggis."

She picked up her spoon. "Am I a terrible sister? Am I
such a terrible person?"

"Of course not."

"What kind of person am I that he would feel the need to
send me all the way to Gretna Green just so he could make a
clean escape?"

"A well-loved sister, I imagine," Angus replied, spooning

some cranachan into his mouth. "Damn, this is good. You should try some."

Margaret dipped her spoon, but she didn't raise it to her mouth. "What do you mean?"

"Obviously he loves you too well to endure a painful farewell. And it sounds as if you would have put up quite a fight to his joining the navy had you known his true intentions."

Margaret had been about to retort, "Of course I would!" but instead she just sighed. What was the use defending her position or explaining her feelings? What was done was done, and there was nothing she could do about it.

She sighed again, louder, and lifted her spoon. If there was one thing she hated, it was situations about which she could do nothing.

"Are you going to eat that pudding, or is this some sort of experiment in the science of spoon-balancing?"

Margaret blinked her way out of her daze, but before she could reply, George McCallum appeared at their table.

"We'll be needing to clean up for the night," he said. "I don't mean to toss you out, but my wife is insisting." He grinned at Angus. "You know how it is."

Angus motioned to Margaret. "She hasn't finished her cranachan."

"Take the bowl up to your room. Pity to waste the food."

Angus nodded and stood. "Good idea. Are you ready, my sweet?"

Margaret's spoon slipped out of her hand, landing in her bowl of cranachan with a dull splat. Had he just called her his *sweet?* "I . . . I . . . I . . ."

"She loves me so much," Angus said to George, "sometimes she loses her power of speech."

While Margaret was gaping at him, he lifted his powerful shoulders in a huge, satisfied shrug, and said, "What can I say? I overwhelm her."

George chuckled while Margaret sputtered. "You'd best watch your back," the innkeeper advised Angus, "or you'll be finding yourself washing your hair with my wife's best cranachan."

"A fine idea," Margaret bit out.

Angus laughed as he stood and held out his hand to her. Somehow he'd known that the best way to distract her from her sorrows was to raise her hackles with another joke about her being his devoted wife. If he'd mentioned the baby, she would probably forget her brother altogether.

He started to open his mouth, then caught sight of the furious gleam in her eyes and thought the better of it. A man had to think of his own safety, after all, and Margaret looked ready to do some serious physical harm—or at least fling a bowl of cranachan at him.

Still, he'd gladly take the pudding shot if it meant she could stop thinking about her brother, even for a few moments. "Come along, darling," he said smoothly, "we need to let this good man close up for the night."

Margaret nodded and stood, her lips still clamped tightly together. Angus had a feeling she didn't trust herself to speak.

"Don't forget your cranachan," he said, motioning to the bowl on the table while he picked up his own.

"You might be wanting to carry hers, too," George chortled. "I dinna trust that look in her eye."

Angus took his advice and scooped up the other bowl. "An excellent idea, my good man. My wife will have to walk without the benefit of my arm, but I think she'll manage, don't you?"

"Och, yes. That one doesn't need a man to tell her where to go." George elbowed Margaret in the arm and smiled conspiratorially. "But it's nice nonetheless, eh?"

Angus nudged Margaret out of the room before she killed the innkeeper.

"Why must you persist in teasing me like that?" she growled.

Angus turned the corner and waited for her to start up the stairs before following. "It took your mind off your brother, didn't it?"

"I . . ." Her lips parted in stunned amazement, and she stared at him as if she'd never before seen another human being. "Yes, it did."

He smiled and handed her one of the bowls of pudding while he fished in his pocket for the key to their room. "Surprised?"

"That you would do such a thing for me?" She shook her head. "No."

Angus turned slowly around, the key still sitting in the lock. "I meant, were you surprised you'd forgotten about your brother, but I think I like your answer better."

Margaret smiled wistfully and touched her hand to his arm. "You're a good man, Sir Angus Greene. Insufferable at times . . ." She almost grinned at his mock scowl. "Well, insufferable *most* of the time, if one wants to put a fine point on it, but still a good man."

He pushed the door open, then set his bowl of cranachan on a table inside the room. "Should I not have mentioned your brother just now? Perhaps I should have left you spitting mad and ready to slit my throat?"

"No." She let out a long, tired exhale and sat on the bed, another lock of her long brown hair spilling from her coiffure onto her shoulder. Angus watched her with an aching heart. She looked so small and defenseless, and so damned melancholy. He couldn't bear it.

"Margaret," he said, sitting beside her, "you have done your best to raise your brother for what, how many years?"

"Seven."

"Now it's time to let him grow up and make his own decisions, right or wrong."

"You yourself said no boy of eighteen knows his own mind."

Angus swallowed a groan. There was nothing more detestable than being haunted by one's own words. "I shouldn't want to see him marry at such an age. Good God, if he made a bad choice he'd have to live with it—her!—for rest of his life."

"And if he made a bad choice by entering the military, how long a life will he have to regret it?" Margaret raised her face to his, and her eyes looked unbearably huge in her face. "He could die, Angus. I don't care what people say, there is always a war. Somewhere, some stupid man will feel the need to fight with some other stupid man, and they're going to send my brother to settle it."

"Margaret, any one of us could die tomorrow. I could walk out of this inn and be trampled by a mad cow. You could walk out of this inn and be struck by lightning. We can't live our lives in fear of that moment."

"Yes, but we *can* try to minimize our risks."

Angus lifted his hand to rake it through his crisp hair; it was an action he often repeated when he was tired or exasperated. But somehow his hand moved slightly to the left, and he felt himself touch Margaret's hair instead. It was fine, and straight, and silky smooth, and there seemed to be a lot more of it than he'd originally thought. It slid from its pins and cascaded over his hand, between his fingers.

And as he savored the feel of it, neither of them breathed.

Their eyes locked, green against the darkest, hottest black. Not a word was spoken, but as Angus leaned forward, slowly closing the distance between them, they both knew what was going to happen.

He was going to kiss her.

And she wasn't going to stop him.

Five

His lips brushed against hers slowly, in the barest of touches. If he'd crushed her against him or ground his mouth onto hers, she might have pulled away, but this feather-light caress captured her soul.

Her skin prickled with awareness, and she suddenly felt . . . *different,* as if this body she'd possessed for twenty-four years were no longer her own. Her skin felt too tight, and her heart felt too hungry, and her hands . . . oh, how her hands ached for the touch of his skin.

He'd be warm, she knew, and sculpted. His were not the muscles of a sedentary man. He could crush her with one blow of his fist . . . and somehow that knowledge was thrilling . . . probably because he was holding her now with such gentle reverence.

She pulled away for a moment, so that she could see his eyes. They burned with a need that was unfamiliar, and yet she knew exactly what he wanted.

"Angus," she whispered, lifting her hand to rub the rough skin of his cheek. His dark beard was coming in, thick and coarse and entirely unlike her brother's whiskers on the few occasions she'd seen him unshaven.

He covered her hand with his, then turned his face into her palm, pressing a kiss against her skin. She watched his eyes over the tips of her fingers. They never left hers, and they were asking a silent question, and waiting for her answer.

"How did this happen?" she whispered. "I've never . . . I never even wanted—"

"But you do now," he whispered. "You want me now."

She nodded, shocked by her admission, yet unable to lie to him. There was something about the way he was looking at her, the way his eyes swept over her as if he could see all the way to the very center of her heart. The moment was terrifyingly perfect, and she knew that lies had no place between them. Not in that room, not on that night.

She moistened her lips. "I can't . . ."

Angus touched his finger to her mouth. "Can't you?"

That brought forth a wobbly smile. His teasing tone melted her resistance, and she felt herself swaying toward him, leaning into his strength. More than anything, she wanted to throw aside all of her principles, every last ideal and moral to which she'd held true. She could forget who she was, and what she'd always held dear, and lie with this man. She could stop being Margaret Pennypacker, sister and guardian of Edward and Alicia Pennypacker, daughter of the departed Edmund and Katherine Pennypacker. She could stop being the woman who brought food to the poor, attended church every Sunday, and planted her garden every spring in neat and tidy rows.

She could stop being all of that, and finally be a woman.

It was so tempting.

Angus smoothed one of his callused fingers across her furrowed brow. "You look so serious," he murmured, leaning forward to brush his lips to her forehead. "I want to kiss away these lines, brush away these worries."

"Angus," she said quickly, letting her words tumble out before she lost her ability to reason, "there are things I can't do. Things I want to do, or I think I want to do. I'm not sure, because I've never done, but I can't— Why are you smiling?"

"Was I?"

He knew he was, the bounder.

He shrugged helplessly. "It's only that I've never seen anyone quite so becomingly befuddled as you, Margaret Pennypacker."

She opened her mouth to protest, since she wasn't sure if his words were complimentary, but he placed his finger over her lips.

"Ah, ah, ah," he said. "Hush now, and listen to me. I'm going to kiss you, and that's all."

Her heart soared and fell in a single moment. "Just a kiss?"

"Between us, it will never be just a kiss."

His words sent a shiver through her veins, and she lifted her head, offering her lips to him.

Angus drew in a hoarse breath, staring at her mouth as if it held all the temptations of hell—and all the bliss of heaven. He kissed her again, but this time he held nothing back. His lips took hers in a hungry, possessive dance of desire and need.

She gasped, and he savored her breath, inhaling its warm, sweet essence, as if that might somehow enable her to touch him from the inside out.

He knew he ought to go slowly with her, and much as his body was crying with need, he knew that he would end this night unfulfilled, but he could not deny himself the pleasure of feeling her small body beneath his, and so he lowered her down onto the bed, never once taking his mouth off hers.

If he was just going to kiss her, if that was all he could do, then he was damned if this kiss didn't last the whole night through.

"Oh, Margaret," he moaned, letting his hands roam down

the side of her, past her waist, over her hip, until he cupped the smoothly rounded curve of her buttocks. "My sweet Mar—"

He broke off and lifted his head, flashing her a boyishly lopsided grin. "Can I call you Meggie? Margaret's a bloody mouthful."

She stared up at him, breathing hard, unable to speak.

"Margaret," he continued, trailing his fingers along the edge of her cheek, "is just the sort of woman a man wants by his side. But Meggie . . . now, that's a woman a man wants underneath."

It took her an eighth of a second to say, "You can call me Meggie."

His lips found her ear, as his arms snaked around her. "Welcome to my embrace, Meggie."

She sighed, and the movement sank her deeper into the mattress, and she gave herself up to the moment, to the flickering candle and the sweet scent of the cranachan, and to the strong and powerful man who was covering her body with his.

His lips moved to her neck, whispering along the lines that led down to the crook of her shoulder. He kissed the skin there, so pale against the black wool of his coat. He didn't know how he'd ever wear that garment again, now that it had spent an entire evening brushing against her bare skin. It would smell like her for days, and then, after the scent drifted away, the memory of this moment would still be enough to set his body on fire.

His nimble fingers undid just enough buttons to reveal the barest hint of her cleavage. It was nothing more than a shadow, really, a vague darkening that hinted at the wonders below, but even that was enough to send fire through his veins, tightening a body that he had thought couldn't possibly get any harder.

Two more buttons found their way free, and Angus trailed his mouth down along each new inch of bared skin, whispering the whole time, "It's still a kiss. Just a kiss."

"Just a kiss," Margaret echoed, her voice strange and breathy.

"Just a kiss," he agreed, slipping yet another button through its loophole so that he could fully kiss the deep hollow between her breasts. "I'm still kissing you."

"Yes," she moaned. "Oh, yes. Keep kissing me."

He spread open his coat, baring her small, yet gently rounded breasts. He sucked in his breath. "Good Christ, Meggie, this coat never looked half so good on me."

Margaret stiffened slightly under the intense heat of his gaze. He was staring at her as if she were some strange and wondrous creature, as if she possessed something he'd never seen before. If he touched her, caressed her, or even kissed her, she could melt right back into his embrace and lose herself in the passion of the moment. But with him just staring at her—she was made uncomfortably aware that she was doing something she'd never even dreamed of doing.

She'd known this man only a few short hours, and yet—

Her breath catching, she reached up to cover herself. "What have I done?" she whispered.

Angus leaned down and kissed her forehead. "No regrets, my sweet Meggie. Whatever you feel, don't let regret be a part of it."

Meggie. Meggie didn't adhere to the strictures of society simply because that was the way she was raised. Meggie sought her own fortune and her own pleasure.

Margaret's lips hinted at a smile as she let her hands fall away. Meggie might not lie with a man before marriage, but she would certainly allow herself this moment of passion.

"You're so beautiful," Angus growled, and the last syllable was lost as his mouth closed around the peak of her breast. He made love to her with his lips, worshipping her in every way a man could show his devotion.

And then, just as Margaret felt her last shreds of resistance slipping away, he took a shuddering, deep breath and, with obvious reluctance, closed the folds of his coat around her.

He held the lapels together for a full minute, breathing hard as his eyes fixed on some blank spot on the wall. His face looked almost haggard, and to Margaret's untrained eye, he looked almost as if he were in pain.

"Angus?" she asked hesitantly. She wasn't certain what she was supposed to ask him, so she settled for just his name.

"In a minute." His voice was a touch harsh, but somehow Margaret knew that he bore her no anger. She held silent, waiting until he turned his head back toward her and said, "I need to leave the room."

Her lips parted in surprise. "You do?"

He nodded curtly and tore himself away from her, crossing the distance to the door in two long strokes. He grabbed the doorknob, and Margaret saw the muscles in his forearm flex, but before he pulled the door open, he turned around, his lips starting to form words . . .

. . . that quickly died on his lips.

Margaret followed his gaze back to herself . . . Good God above, the coat had fallen open when he'd let go of it. She snatched the lapels together, thankful that the dim candlelight hid her mortified blush.

"Lock the door behind me," he instructed.

"Yes, of course," she said, rising to her feet. "Here, you do it, and then take the key." She fumbled toward the table with her left hand, clutching the coat together with her right.

He shook his head. "Keep it."

She took a few steps toward him. "Keep the— Are you mad? How will you get back in?"

"I won't. That's the point."

Margaret's mouth opened and closed a few times before she managed to say, "Where will you sleep?"

He leaned toward her, his nearness heating the air. "I won't sleep. That's the problem."

"Oh. I . . ." She wasn't such an innocent that she didn't recognize what he was talking about, but she certainly wasn't experienced enough to know how to respond. "I—"

"Has it started to rain again?" he asked curtly.

Margaret blinked at the rapid change of subject. She cocked her head, listening for the gentle patter of rain against the roof. "I . . . yes, I believe it has."

"Good. It had better be cold."

And with that, he stalked out of the room.

After a second of paralyzing surprise, Margaret ran to the door and poked her head into the hall, just in time to see Angus's large form disappear around the corner. She hung onto the doorframe for a full ten seconds, half in and half out of the room, not precisely certain why she felt so completely stunned. Was it the fact that he'd left so abruptly? Or that she'd allowed him liberties she'd never dreamed of allowing any man who wasn't her husband?

If truth had to be told, she'd never even dreamed that such liberties existed. ·

Or maybe, she thought wildly, maybe what really stunned her was that she'd lain on the bed, looking up at him as he'd stormed across the room, and he'd been so completely . . . well, *delicious* to watch that she hadn't even realized that the coat had fallen open and her breasts were peeking out for all the world to see.

Or at least for Angus to see, and the way he looked at her . . .

Margaret gave herself a little shake and shut the door. After a moment's pause, she locked it as well. Not that she worried about Angus. He might be in a bear of a mood, but he'd never lift a finger against her, and, more importantly, he'd never take advantage of her.

She didn't know how she knew this. She just did.

But one never knew what manner of cutthroats and idiots one might find in a country inn, especially in Gretna Green, which she imagined saw more than its fair share of idiots, what with everyone eloping here all the time.

Margaret sighed and tapped her foot. What to do, what to do. Her stomach let out a loud and vigorous rumble, and it was then that she remembered the cranachan sitting on the table.

Why not? It smelled delicious.

She sat down and ate.

When Angus stumbled back into The Canny Man several hours later, he was cold, wet, and feeling like he ought to be drunk. The rain, of course, had resumed, as had the wind, and his fingers resembled nothing so much as thick icicles attached to the flat snowballs that had used to be his hands.

His feet didn't feel quite his own, and it took him several attempts and many stubbed toes before he made it up the steps to the top floor of the inn. He leaned against the door to his room as he fumbled for the key, then remembered he hadn't brought a key, then turned the doorknob, then let out an irritated grunt when the door didn't budge.

Jesus, whiskey, and Robert the Bruce, why the *hell* had he told her to lock the door? Had he truly been that worried about his self-control? There was no way he could ravish her in this state. His nether regions were so cold, he probably couldn't muster up a reaction if she opened the door without a stitch of clothing on her body.

His muscles made a pathetic attempt at tightening. All right, maybe if she were completely naked . . .

Angus sighed happily, trying to picture it.

The doorknob turned. He was still sighing.

The door swung open. He fell in.

He looked up. Margaret was blinking rapidly as she regarded him. "Were you leaning against the door?" she asked.

"Apparently so."

"You did tell me to lock it."

"Yer a good woman, Margaret Pennypacker. Dutiful 'n' loyal."

Margaret narrowed her eyes. "Are you drunk?"

He shook his head, which had the unfortunate effect of banging his cheekbone against the floor. "Just cold."

"Have you been outside this entire—" She leaned down and touched her hand to his cheek. "Good God, you're freezing!"

He shrugged. "Started to rain again."

She jammed her hands under his arms and tried to heave him to his feet. "Get up. Get up. We have to get you out of these clothes."

His head lolled to the side as he shot her a disarmingly lopsided grin. "At another time—at another temperature— I'd delight in those words."

Margaret tugged at him again and groaned. She hadn't managed to budge him an inch. "Angus, please. You must make an effort to stand. You must be double my weight."

His eyes wandered up and down her frame. "What are you, seven stone?"

"Hardly," she scoffed. "Do I look that insubstantial? Now, please, if you can just get your feet flat on the floor, I can get you to bed."

He sighed. "Another one of those sentences I'd dearly like to misinterpret."

"Angus!"

He wobbled into an upright position, with not-inconsiderable aid from Margaret. "Why is it," he mused, "that I so enjoy being scolded by you?"

"Probably," she retorted, "because you so enjoy vexing me."

He scratched his chin, which was now quite darkened by a day's growth of beard. "Think you might be right."

Margaret ignored him, trying instead to concentrate on the task at hand. If she dumped him onto the bed as he was, he'd soak through the sheets in a matter of minutes. "Angus," she said, "you need to put on some dry clothing. I'll wait outside while you—"

He shook his head. "Don't have any more dry clothes."

"What happened to them?"

"You're"—he jabbed her shoulder with his forefinger—"wearing them."

Margaret uttered a very unladylike word.

"You know, you're right," he said, sounding as if he'd just made a very important discovery. "I *do* enjoy vexing you."

"Angus!"

"Ah, very well. I shall be serious." He made a great show of forcing his features into a frown. "What is it you need?"

"I need you to take off your clothing and get into bed."

His face lit up. "Right now?"

"Of course not," she snapped. "I'll leave the room for a moment, and when I return, I expect you in that bed, with the covers pulled up to your chin."

"Where will you sleep?"

"I won't. I'm going to dry your clothes."

He twisted his neck this way and neck. "At what fireplace?"

"I'll go downstairs."

He straightened to the point where Margaret no longer had to support him. "You are not going down there by yourself in the middle of the night."

"I can't very well dry your clothing over a candle."

"I'll go with you."

"Angus, you'll be naked."

Whatever he'd been about to say—and Margaret was certain, from the indignant thrust of his chin and the fact that he had his mouth open and ready to contradict her, that he'd been about to say *some*thing—was abandoned in favor of a loud and extremely creative string of curses.

Finally, after running through every profane word she'd

ever heard, and a good deal more that were new to her, he grunted, "Wait right here," and stomped out of the room.

Three minutes later, he reappeared. Margaret watched with nothing short of amazement as he kicked open the door and dumped about three dozen candles on the floor. One, she noticed, was still smoking.

She cleared her throat, waiting for his scowl to soften before saying anything. After a few moments, though, it became apparent that his grumpy mood was not going to change in the near future, so she asked, "Where did you get all of these?"

"Let's just say that The Canny Man is going to wake to a very dark morning on the morrow."

Margaret declined to point out that, at well past midnight, it was *already* the morrow, but her conscience did require her to say, "It's *dark* in the morning this time of year."

"I left one or two in the kitchen," Angus grumbled. And then, without a word of warning, he started to peel off his shirt.

Margaret yelped and dashed out into the hall. Blast that man, he knew he was supposed to wait until she was out of the room before stripping to his skin. She waited a full minute, then gave him another thirty seconds on account of the cold. Numb fingers didn't do well with buttons.

Taking a deep breath, she turned around and knocked on the door. "Angus?" she called out. "Are you in bed?" Then, before he could answer, she narrowed her eyes and added, "With the covers pulled up!"

His reply was muffled, but it was definitely in the affirmative, so she twisted the doorknob and pushed.

The door didn't budge.

Her stomach began a dance of panic. The door couldn't be locked. He would never have locked it, and doors didn't lock themselves.

She banged the side of her fist lightly against the wood. "Angus! Angus! I can't open the door!"

Footsteps followed, and when she next heard his voice, it was clearly coming from just on the other side of the door.

"What's wrong?"

"The door won't open."

"I didn't lock it."

"I know. I think it's stuck."

She heard him laugh, which produced an overwhelming desire to stamp her foot—preferably onto *his* foot.

"Now this," he said, "is interesting."

The urge to do him bodily harm was growing more intense.

"Margaret?" he called out. "Are you still there?"

She closed her eyes for a moment as she exhaled through her teeth. "You're going to have to help me open the door."

"I am, of course, naked."

She blushed. It was dark; he couldn't possibly see her reaction, and still she blushed.

"Margaret?"

"The mere sight of you shall probably blind me, anyway," she snapped. "Are you going to help me, or will I have to break the door down myself?"

"It would certainly be a sight to behold. I'd pay good money to—"

"Angus!"

He chuckled again, a warm, rich sound that melted through the door and straight into her bones. "Very well," he said. "On my count of three, push against the door with all of your weight."

Margaret nodded, then remembered that he couldn't see her and said, "I will."

"One . . . two . . ."

She squeezed her eyes shut.

"Three!"

She slammed all her weight against the door, but he must have yanked before she slammed, because her shoulder had barely met the wood before she fell into the room and hit the floor. Hard.

Miraculously, she managed to keep her eyes shut the entire time.

She heard the door click shut, then sensed him bending over her as he inquired, "Are you all right?"

She slapped her hand over her eyes. "Get into bed!"

"Don't worry, I've covered myself."

"I don't believe you."

"I swear. I wrapped the bedsheets around me."

Margaret separated her fore and middle fingers just enough to let in the narrowest strip of vision. Sure enough, there seemed to be something white wrapped around him. She got up and pointedly turned her back on him.

"You are a hard woman, Margaret Pennypacker," he said, but she heard his footsteps taking him back across the room.

"Are you in bed?"

"Yes."

"Do you have the covers pulled up?"

"To my chin."

She heard the smile in his voice, and as exasperated as she was with him, it was still infectious. The corners of her lips wiggled, and it was an effort to keep her voice stern as she said, "I'm turning around now."

"Please do."

"I shall never forgive you if you've been lying to me."

"Jesus, whiskey, and Robert the Bruce, just turn around, woman."

She did. He had the covers pulled up—not quite to the promised level of his chin, but far enough.

"Do I meet with your approval?"

She nodded. "Where are your wet clothes?"

"On the chair."

She followed his line of vision to a soggy pile of fabric, then set about lighting the multitude of candles. "This has to be the most ridiculous endeavor," she muttered to herself. What she needed was some kind of massive toasting fork upon which to spear the garment. As it was, she was likely to burn the shirt, or maybe her hands, or—

A drop of hot wax on her skin cut off her line of thinking, and she quickly stuck the injured finger into her mouth. She used her other hand to keep the flame moving from candle to candle, shaking her head as she watched the room grow brighter and brighter.

He was never going to be able to sleep with so many candles burning. It was bright as day.

She turned around, prepared to point out this lack of foresight in their plans, but her words never made it past her lips.

He was asleep.

Margaret stared for one more minute, taking in the way his unruly hair fell over his forehead and his lashes rested against his cheek. The sheet had slipped slightly, allowing her to watch his muscular chest as it gently rose and fell with each breath.

She'd never known a man like this, never seen a human who was quite so magnificent in repose.

It was a long, long time before she turned back to her candles.

By morning, Margaret had dried all of the clothing, blown out all of the candles, and fallen asleep. When Angus woke up, he found her curled up next to the bed, his coat wadded into a pillow beneath her head.

With gentle hands, he picked her up and laid her down on the bed, pulling the covers to her chin and tucking them around her slender shoulders. Then he settled into the chair next to the bed and watched her sleep.

It was, he decided, the most perfect morning of his recollection.

Six

Margaret came awake the following morning just the way she always did: completely and in an instant.

She sat upright, blinked the sleep from her eyes, and realized three things. One, she was in the bed. Two, Angus was not. And three, he wasn't even in the room.

She hopped to her feet, grimacing at the irreparably wrinkled state of her skirts, and made her way to the small table. The empty cranachan bowls were still there, as were the sturdy pewter spoons, but they had been joined by a folded piece of paper. It was wrinkled and smudged, and looked as if it had been torn from a larger piece of paper. Margaret imagined that Angus had had to search the inn fairly thoroughly just to find this little scrap.

She smoothed it open and read:

Gone for breakfast. Will return shortly.

He hadn't bothered to sign it. Not that that mattered, Margaret thought as she searched the room for something with which she might brush her hair. As if the note could have come from anyone but Angus.

She smiled as she looked down at the bold, confident handwriting. Even if someone else had had the opportunity to slip the note into her room, she would have known it was from him. His personality was right there in the lines of his letters.

There was nothing to use as a brush, so she settled for her fingers as she moved to the window. She pushed the curtains aside and peeked out. The sun had made an appearance, and the cerulean sky was gently dotted with clouds. A perfect day.

Margaret shook her head and sighed as she heaved the window open for some fresh air. Here she was in Scotland—with, as it turned out, no reason to be in Scotland—she had no money, her clothing was stained beyond redemption, and her reputation would probably be in shreds by the time she returned home.

But at least it was a perfect day.

The village had already come awake. Margaret watched a young family cross the street and enter a small shop, then shifted her gaze onto yet one more couple who had clearly just eloped. Then she took to counting all the young couples moving from street to inn and back to street.

She didn't know whether to smile or frown. All this eloping couldn't be a good thing, and yet some romantic corner of her soul had been stirred the previous night. Maybe some of these new brides and grooms weren't the complete idiots she'd called them the night before. It wasn't entirely unreasonable to suppose that some of them actually had good reasons for running off to Scotland to elope.

With an uncharacteristically sentimental sigh, she leaned a little farther out the window and started making up stories for all the couples. That young lady had an overbearing father, and this young man wanted to wed his true love before he joined the army.

She was trying to decide which young lady had the

wicked stepmother, when a thunderous cry shook the building. Margaret looked down just in time to see Angus tearing
out into the street.

"Aaaaaaaaaaaaaannnnnnnnnnnnnne!"

Margaret gasped. His sister!

Sure enough, a tall, black-haired miss was standing on the
other side of the street, looking extremely panicked as she
tried to hide behind an obviously well-maintained carriage.

"Jesus, whiskey, and Robert the Bruce," Margaret whispered. If she didn't get down there soon, Angus was going to
kill his sister. Or at least frighten her into temporary insanity.

Picking up her skirts to well above her ankles, Margaret
dashed out of the room.

Angus had been feeling reasonably cheerful, whistling to
himself as he'd set about finding the perfect Scottish breakfast to bring back to Margaret. Porridge, of course, and a true
Scottish scone were necessities, but Angus wanted to give
her a taste of his country's delectable smoked fish as well.

George had told him that he'd have to go across the street
to the fishmonger in order to get some wild salmon, and so
he'd told the innkeeper that he'd be back in a few minutes
for the porridge and scones, and pushed open the front door.

He hadn't even taken a step into the street when he spied
it. His carriage. Sitting innocently across the street with two
of his best horses hitched up to it.

Which could only mean one thing.

"Aaaaaaaaaaaaaannnnnnnnnnnnnne!"

His sister's head poked out from around the side of the
carriage. Her lips parted with horror, and he saw her mouth
his name.

"Anne Greene," he roared, "don't you take another step!"

She froze. He barreled across the street.

"Angus Greene!" came the shout from behind him.
"Don't you take another step!"

He froze.

Margaret?

Anne stretched out a little farther from behind the carriage, the stark terror in her eyes giving way to curiosity.

Angus turned around. Margaret was racing toward him with all the grace and delicacy of an ox. She was, as always, completely focused on a single subject. Unfortunately, this time that subject was him.

"Angus," she said in that matter-of-fact tone of hers that made him almost think she knew what she was talking about, "you don't want to do anything rash."

"I wasn't planning on doing anything rash," he said with what he would deem saintly patience. "I was just going to strangle her."

Anne gasped.

"He doesn't mean it," Margaret hastened to add. "He's been very worried about you."

"Who are you?" Anne asked.

"I do mean it!" Angus shouted. He jabbed his finger at his sister. "You, young lady, are in very big trouble."

"She has to grow up sometime," Margaret said. "Remember what you said to me last night about Edward."

Anne turned to her brother. "Who is she?"

"Edward was running off to join the navy," Angus growled, "not following a fool's dream to London."

"Oh, and I suppose London is worse than the navy," Margaret scoffed. "At least she isn't going to have her arm shot off by some Portuguese sniper. Besides, a season in London isn't a fool's dream. Not for a girl her age."

Anne's face brightened visibly.

"Look at her," Angus protested, waving his arm at his sister while he stared at Margaret. "Look how beautiful she is. Every rakehell in London will be after her. I'm going to have to beat them off with a stick."

Margaret turned to Angus's sister. Anne was quite pretty, with the same thick black hair and dark eyes that her brother possessed. But she was no one's idea of a classic beauty. No one's but Angus's.

Margaret's heart swelled. She hadn't, until that very minute, realized just how well Angus loved his sister. She laid a hand on his arm. "Maybe it's time to let her grow up," she said softly. "Didn't you say you had a great-aunt in London? She won't be alone."

"Aunt Gertrude has already written that I might stay with her," Anne said. "She said she would like the company. I think she might be lonely."

Angus's chin jutted forward like an angry bull. "Don't try to make this about Aunt Gertrude. You want to go to London because you want to go to London, not because you're worried about Gertrude."

"Of course I want to go to London. I never said I didn't. I was merely trying to point out that my going benefits two people, not just one."

Angus scowled at her, and she scowled back, and Margaret caught her breath at how alike the two siblings looked in that moment. Unfortunately, they also looked as if they might come to blows at any moment, so she deftly stepped between them, looked up (Anne was a good six inches taller than she was, and Angus topped her by well over a foot), and said, "That's very sweet of you, Anne. Angus, don't you think Anne made a good point?"

"Who's side are you on?" Angus growled.

"I'm not on anybody's side. I'm just trying to be reasonable." Margaret pulled on his forearm, drew him aside, and said in a low voice, "Angus, this is exactly the same situation about which you counseled me last night."

"It's not at all the same thing."

"And why not?"

"Your brother is a man. My sister is just a girl."

Margaret glowered at him. "And what is that supposed to mean? Am I 'just a girl' as well?"

"Of course not. You're . . . you're—" He fished the air for words, and his face grew rather agitated. "You're Margaret."

"Why," she drawled, "does that sound like an insult?"

"Of course it isn't an insult," he snapped. "I just complimented your intelligence. You're not the same as other females. You're . . . you're—"

"Then I think you just insulted your sister."

"Yes," Anne piped up, "you just insulted me."

Angus whirled around. "Don't eavesdrop."

"Oh, please," Anne scoffed, "you're talking loud enough to be heard in Glasgow."

"Angus," Margaret said, crossing her arms, "do you think your sister is an intelligent young woman?"

"I *did,* before she ran off."

"Then kindly offer her some respect and trust. She isn't running blindly away. She has already contacted your aunt and has a place to stay and a chaperone who desires her presence."

"She can't choose a husband," he grumbled.

Margaret's eyes narrowed. "And I suppose you could do a better job of it?"

"I'm certainly not going to allow her to marry without my approval of her choice."

"Then go with her," Margaret urged.

Angus let out a long breath. "I can't. Not yet. I told her we could go next year. I can't be away from Greene House during the renovations, and then there is the new irrigation system to oversee . . ."

Anne looked to Margaret pleadingly. "I don't want to wait until next year."

Margaret looked from Greene to Greene, trying to work out a solution. It was probably rather odd that she was here, in the middle of a family squabble. After all, she hadn't even known they existed the previous morning.

But somehow this all seemed very natural, and so she turned to Angus with steady eyes and said, "May I make a suggestion?"

He was still glaring at his sister as he said, "Please do."

Margaret cleared her throat, but he didn't turn around to look at her. She decided to go ahead and speak, anyway. "Why don't you let her go to London now, and you can join her in a month or two? That way, if she's found a man she fancies, you can meet him before things grow serious. And you'll have time to finish your work at home."

Angus frowned.

Margaret persevered. "I know that Anne would never marry without your approval." She turned to Anne with urgent eyes. "Isn't that correct, Anne?"

Anne was taking a little too long to ponder the question, so Margaret elbowed her in the stomach and said again, "Anne? Isn't that correct?"

"Of course," Anne grunted, rubbing her midsection.

Margaret beamed. "You see? It's a perfect solution. Angus? Anne?"

Angus rubbed a weary hand against his brow, grasping his temples as if the pressure would somehow make the entire day go away. It had started out as the perfect morning, gazing upon Margaret as she slept. Breakfast awaited, the sky was blue, and he was certain he would soon find his sister and bring her back home where she belonged.

And now Margaret and Anne were ganging up upon him, trying to convince him that *they*—not he—knew best. As a united front, they were a mighty powerful force.

And Angus feared that as an object, he might not be completely immovable.

He felt his face softening, felt his will weakening, and he knew the women sensed their victory.

"If it makes you feel more comfortable," Margaret said, "I shall accompany Anne. I can't go all the way to London, but I can see her at least to Lancashire."

"NO!"

Margaret started at the forcefulness of his reply. "I beg your pardon?"

Angus planted his hands on his hips and glowered down at her. "You're not going to Lancashire."

"I'm not?"

"She isn't?" Anne queried, then turned to Margaret and asked, "If you don't mind, what *is* your name?"

"Miss Pennypacker, although I should think we may use our given names, don't you? Mine is Margaret."

Anne nodded. "I'd be ever so grateful for your company on the journey to—"

"She's not going," Angus said firmly.

Two pairs of feminine eyes swung around to face him.

Angus felt ill.

"And what," Margaret said, not unkindly, "do you suppose I do instead?"

Angus had no idea where the words came from, no idea even that the thought had formed, but as he looked at Margaret, he suddenly remembered every last moment in her company. He felt her kisses and he heard her laughter. He saw her smile and he touched her soul. She was too bossy, too stubborn, and too short for a man of his proportions, but somehow his heart skipped over all of that, because when she looked up at him with those gorgeously intelligent green eyes, all he could do was blurt out, "Marry me."

Margaret had thought she knew what it felt like to be speechless. It wasn't a condition she often experienced, but she thought she was reasonably familiar with it.

She was wrong.

Her heart pounded, her head grew light, and she started

choking on air. Her mouth grew dry, her eyes grew wet, and her ears began to ring. If there'd been a chair in the vicinity, she would have tried to sit in it, but she'd probably have missed the seat entirely.

Anne leaned forward. "Miss Pennypacker? Margaret? Are you unwell?"

Angus didn't say anything.

Anne turned to her brother. "I think she's going to faint."

"She's not going to faint," he said grimly. "She never faints."

Margaret began to tap the flat of her chest with the flat of her hand, as if that might possibly dislodge the ball of shock that had settled in her throat.

"How long have you known her?" Anne asked suspiciously.

Angus shrugged. "Since last night."

"Then how can you possibly know if she faints or not?"

"I just know."

Anne's mouth settled into a firm line. "Then how— Wait just one second! You want to marry her after one day's acquaintance?!"

"It's a moot question," he bit out, "since it doesn't appear that she's going to say yes."

"Yes!" It was all Margaret could do to choke the word out, but she couldn't bear to see the disappointed look on his face any longer.

Angus's eyes filled hope—and with the most endearing touch of disbelief. "Yes?"

She nodded furiously. "Yes, I'll marry you. You're too bossy, too stubborn, and too tall for a woman of my stature, but I'll marry you, anyway."

"Well, isn't this romantic," Anne muttered. "You should have made him ask on bended knee, at the very least."

Angus ignored her, smiling instead down at Margaret as he touched her cheek with the gentlest of hands. "You do realize," he murmured, "that this is the craziest, most impulsive thing you have ever done in your entire life?"

Margaret nodded. "But also the most perfect."

" 'In her life?' " Anne echoed dubiously. " 'In her life?' How can you know that? You've only known her since yesterday!"

"You," Angus said, spearing his sister with a stare, "are superfluous."

Anne beamed. "Really? Does that mean, then, that I may go to London?"

Six hours later, Anne was well on her way to London. She'd been given a stern lecture from Angus, heaps of sisterly advice from Margaret, and a promise from both that they would come and visit in a month's time.

She'd stayed in Gretna Green, of course, for the wedding. Margaret and Angus were married less than an hour after he'd proposed. Margaret had originally balked, saying that she ought to be married at home, with her family present, but Angus had just raised one of those dark eyebrows and said, "Jesus, whiskey, and Robert the Bruce, you're in Gretna Green, woman. You have to get married."

Margaret had agreed, but only after Angus had leaned over and whispered in her ear, "I'll be bedding you this eve whether or not we've the minister's blessing."

There were benefits, she quickly decided, to a hasty marriage.

And so the happy couple found themselves back in their room at The Canny Man.

"I might have to buy this inn," Angus growled as he carried her over the threshold, "just to make certain this room is never used by anyone else."

"You're that attached to it?" Margaret teased.

"You'll know why by morning."

She blushed.

"Pink cheeks still?" he laughed. "And you, an old married woman."

"I've been married for two hours! I think I still have the right to blush."

He dumped her on the bed and looked down at her as if she were a treat in the bakery window. "Yes," he murmured, "you do."

"My family isn't going to believe this," she said.

Angus slid onto the bed and covered her body with his. "You can worry about them later."

"*I* still can't believe it."

His mouth found her ear, and his breath was hot as he said, "You will. I'll make sure you will." His hands stole around her backside, cupping her and pressing her firmly against his arousal.

Margaret let out a surprised, "Oh!"

"Do you believe it now?"

Where she got her daring, she never knew, but she smiled seductively and murmured, "Not quite."

"Really?" His lips spread into a slow smile. "This isn't enough proof?"

She shook her head.

"Hmmm. It must be all of these clothes."

"Do you think?"

He nodded and went to work on the buttons of his coat, which she was still wearing. "There are far, far too many layers of fabric in this room."

The coat melted away, as did her skirt, and then, before Margaret even had time to feel shy, Angus had doffed his own garments, and all that was left was skin against skin.

It was the strangest sensation. He was touching her everywhere. He was above her and around her, and soon, she realized with breathless wonder, he would be within her.

His mouth moved to the delicate skin of her earlobe, nibbling and nipping as he whispered naughty suggestions that caused her to blush right down to her toes. And then, before she could form any sort of response, he moved away and moved down, and then before she knew it, his tongue was circling her navel, and she knew—absolutely knew—that he was going to perform every one of those naughty acts that very night.

His fingers tickled their way to her womanhood, and Margaret gasped as he slid inside. It should have felt like an invasion, but instead it was more like a completion, and yet it still wasn't enough.

"Do you like that?" he murmured, looking up.

She nodded, her breath coming in shallow, needy gasps.

"Good," he said, looking very male and very pleased with himself. "You'll like this even more."

His mouth slid down to meet his fingers, and Margaret nearly bucked off the bed. "You can't do that!" she exclaimed.

He didn't look up, but she could feel him smiling against the tender skin of her inner thighs. "Yes, I can."

"No, you really—"

"Yes." He raised his head, and his slow, lazy smile melted her bones. "I can."

He made love to her with his mouth, teased her with his fingers, and all the while a low, rumbling pressure built up within her. The need grew until it almost hurt, and yet it felt wickedly delicious.

And then something within her exploded. Some deep, secret place she hadn't even known existed burst into light and pleasure, and her world was reduced to this one bed, with this one man.

It was absolute perfection.

Angus slid his body up the length of hers, wrapping his arms around her as she slowly drifted back to earth. He was still hard, his body tightly coiled with need, and yet somehow he felt strangely fulfilled. It was her, he realized. Margaret. There was nothing in life that couldn't be made better with one of her smiles, and bringing her her first woman's pleasure had touched his very soul.

"Happy?" he murmured.

She nodded, looking drowsy and sated and very, very well-loved.

He leaned in and nuzzled her neck. "There's more."

"Anything more would surely kill me."

"Oh, I think we'll manage." Angus chuckled as he rolled over her, using his powerful arms to hold his body a few inches away from hers.

Her eyes fluttered open, and she smiled up at him. She lifted one of her hands to touch his cheek. "You're such a strong man," she whispered. "Such a *good* man."

He turned his face until his lips found the curve of her palm. "I love you, you know."

Margaret's heart skipped a beat—or maybe it pounded double-time. "You do?"

"It's the strangest damned thing," he said, his smile a touch bewildered and a touch proud. "But it's true."

She stared up at him for several seconds, memorizing his face. She wanted to remember everything about this moment, from the glint in his dark eyes to the way his thick, black hair was falling over his forehead. And then there was the way the light hit his face, and the strong slope of his shoulders, and . . .

Her heart grew warm. She was going to have a lifetime to memorize these things. "I love you, too," she whispered.

Angus leaned down and kissed her. And then he made her his.

Several hours later, they were sitting in bed, enthusiastically partaking of the meal the innkeeper had left outside their door.

"I think," Angus said quite suddenly, "that we made a baby tonight."

Margaret dropped her chicken leg. "Why on earth would you think that?"

He shrugged. "I certainly worked hard enough."

"Oh, and you think that one time—"

"Three." He grinned. "Three times."

Margaret blushed and mumbled, "Four."

"You're right! I forgot all about—"

She swatted him on the shoulder. "That's enough, if you please."

"It will never be enough." He leaned forward and dropped a kiss on her nose. "I've been thinking."

"God help me."

"Seeing as how we are Greenes, and this is Gretna Green, and we ought never to forget how we met . . ."

Margaret groaned. "Stop there, Angus."

"Gretel!" he said with a flourish. "We could name her Gretel. Gretel Greene."

"Jesus, whiskey, and Robert the Bruce, please tell me he's joking."

"Gertrude? Gertrude Greene? It doesn't have quite the same flair, but my aunt will be honored."

Margaret sank into the bed. Resistance was useless.

"Grover? Gregory. You cannot complain about Gregory. Galahad? Giselle . . ."

JULIA QUINN learned to read before she learned to talk, and her family is still trying to figure out if that explains A) why she reads so fast B) why she talks so much or C) both. In addition to writing romances, she practices yoga, grows terrifyingly huge zucchinis, and tries to think up really good reasons why housework is dangerous to her health.

The author of thirteen novels for Avon Books, she is a graduate of Harvard and Radcliffe Colleges and lives in the Pacific Northwest with her husband Paul and two pet rabbits.

Julia also spends way too much time online and can be reached via email at *www.juliaquinn.com*. Regular mail can be sent to the following address:

    c/o Avon Books Publicity Department
    10 East 53rd Street
    New York, New York 10022-5299

The Glenlyon Bride

Karen Ranney

One

**Glenlyon Castle
Scotland, 1772**

"I'll not marry the witch," Lachlan said.

No one paid any attention to his words. Instead, his entire clan seemed entranced by Coinneach MacAuley. The old man considered himself a prophet, a seer, and every man, woman, and child in the hall obliged by being his willing audience.

"I see into the far future," the old man intoned. He stood in the middle of the room, both hands in the air as if his palms pressed against an invisible wall. His full white beard ended in a point at mid-chest. Beneath shaggy white brows were bright blue eyes, too young for the aged face. At the moment, they were fixed on the high ceiling of the hall as if he saw the future written there. "I read the doom of the Sinclairs. I see the chief, the last of his line. He will be no father." His voice rose, carried like an echo through the large room. People might have whispered among themselves, but no one thought to interrupt the prophet. "His sons, all the brave ones, are never born. All the honors they would have brought to the clan Sinclair—only dust in the wind. No future chief will ever rule again. Only barrenness and disaster will be the Sinclairs' future." He turned and pointed one long, wrinkled finger at Lachlan. "Because you ignored the Legend."

Lachlan eyed the old man. It was better to simply wait until the seer was finished with his pronouncements than to interrupt. That would only guarantee a longer harangue.

The finger dropped; the seer bowed his head. "No Sinclair will ever rule Glenlyon again," Coinneach continued. "The castle will lie like a crypt, devoid of life."

One eyebrow rose; then, by force of will, Lachlan smoothed his face of all expression. "Give it up, old man," he said now, his voice carrying as easily as the seer's. "I'll not marry the witch."

Coinneach's voice rose once more, its tone designed to lift the hair from the back of the neck of any Sinclair currently listening. The problem was, *all* of them were rapt with attention. They should have been drinking; it was a night of toasts and slow but certain drunkenness. His cousin, James, had wed, and the happy union was being celebrated. Instead, Coinneach was using this occasion to make mischief, and accomplishing his task well.

"And when it comes to pass that the Sinclair will lament over his fate, and the loss of all his unborn sons, only then will he be allowed to sink into his grave. The last of his possessions will be inherited by a Campbell." At this, there was a collective hiss of disbelief. The Campbells and the Sinclairs had been enemies for as long as any could remember. "I see the Bride standing before me," Coinneach interjected quickly. "She knows the secret of life. She'll be claw-footed and have a voice like a banshee, but she'll save the clan Sinclair."

Lachlan sat up straighter. "Is that what's wrong with her,

old man? She limps and screams? Is that why her father so willingly bargains her?"

Coinneach frowned at him. "He wants an end to the raiding, Lachlan. Your promise for his daughter."

The Sinclairs had been making mischief on the border for generations, but ever since the '45 it had been a sheer pleasure to tweak the nose of the English. In the last year, however, the raids had taken on a desperate turn. The cattle they'd stolen had been less for sport than to augment the dwindling Sinclair herds.

Lachlan settled back against the heavily carved chair that had been his father's and his father's father's. He'd been raised with tales of Sinclair feats since he was a small boy, regaled with the history of his clan in this very room. He was laird, a position that seemed to mean less and less among the clans of late. But it had been a sacred duty to his father, and to all the Sinclairs who'd come before him. And it meant something to him. The responsibility he bore for his clan's survival was a constant burden.

His land was starkly beautiful, a succession of softly undulating hills and deeply shrouded valleys giving way to high, bleak peaks. A place of refuge that had always supported its people even in difficult political times. After the '45, it seemed as if the boot of England had continually been at Scotland's neck. No Scot was allowed to forget that his country had rebelled and lost. Roads were built and marched upon by red-coated English soldiers; forts were erected, and cannon stood ready; tariffs were extracted, and laws were made to banish or ban or expunge all that was a matter of pride to his countrymen.

In the last few years, it seemed as if the fate of the Sinclairs was as dismal as Scotland's. Their cattle had not flourished; their land yielded only barley. No wonder so many of his people were leaving.

All that Lachlan Sinclair saw when he looked out into the

large hall of his home was what needed to be done, not what could be accomplished.

The Legend loomed larger and larger in his mind. Almost every day bore some additional reminder of his responsibilities. He was beginning to believe, like some daft seer himself, that this marriage might be the only way for the Sinclairs to prosper after all.

The Legend of the Glenlyon Bride had been whispered about from his birth. Old Mab, the midwife, had had a dream about his future, it was said, one closely tied to the clan's. The determination had been made that the old woman had dreamed of prophecy, and Coinneach had only exploited the tale. Over the years, however, the Legend had grown in importance. He was sure each member of his clan would admit to believing it. They trusted that a stranger's presence would signal an end to the hardship that had plagued them. It would not be his cunning that lifted his clan away from desperation, or his knowledge, or even his daring. *She* would be the answer, this shadowy figure of a woman who dared to stand on the periphery of his vision as if she mocked him even now. He'd rather raid her land and steal her cattle than wed the witch.

Her father had made the offer but a week before. Already, rumor had furnished him details her father had not. Harriet. Even her name was ugly. Coinneach's words only made fast his fears. A stern harridan of a bride, but with a dowry fat enough to feed his people.

He reached for his cup and drained it. There was no more whiskey; the last of the barrels in the castle cellar had been tapped for this occasion. A Scot without whiskey was like a river without water. One merely enhanced the other. Things were never so bad that a taste of the spirit couldn't make it better. He was very much afraid that the lack of whiskey would be one more sign to his people that the last days of the Sinclairs were here.

Angus had been in charge of the distilling, but Angus had died unexpectedly a month earlier. A tragedy in more ways than one, that. Not only had Lachlan lost a clansman, but he'd lost all the knowledge Angus had possessed, and, therefore, the only thing Lachlan might have been able to smuggle and turn into a tidy profit.

There were always those who would pay dearly for good Scots whiskey. Even Englishmen. But the fact of the matter was that the excise tax stripped even the smallest of profits from such a venture. It was commonplace, therefore, to simply avoid the tax. Some would label it smuggling. Lachlan preferred to call it smart commerce. The buyer was pleased with a superior product. The seller made a reasonable profit. The only people who weren't in favor of forestalling the punitive tax were the excise men.

But without the whiskey, he had nothing else to smuggle, trade, or barter. Glenlyon possessed only two things in abundance: barley and hope.

He stood and toasted his cousin, raising his empty cup high. Laughter followed his greeting to the happy couple. His own smile was more forced. He turned and left the room.

What he needed was a miracle. Or a Legend. He stopped, halted by a physical sensation so sharp it was not unlike a dagger spearing his chest. Certainty, that's what it was. Or destiny. He was going to have to wed the Englishwoman to save his clan.

But he wasn't going to do so until he'd had a look at the witch.

Squire Hanson's House
England

It would be a full moon tonight. A reiver's moon, her father had called it. *A moon for dreaming, lass. Close your eyes and feel it 'neath your lids. 'Tis magic, Janet.* She needed a touch of magic. Anything to dispel this awful feeling of being trapped within her skin. Screaming without a sound.

"Janet, may I fetch you a shawl? You are shivering."

She turned, and Jeremy Hanson was there again. As he was most times. So close she was grateful for the muslin fichu across her bodice. She pulled it up discreetly with two fingers. She shook her head.

"Are you ill?"

"No, just having an errant thought," she said, forcing a smile.

"Then you should not think such troubling things." His smile was sincere; the look in his eyes, one of deep devotion. He was a truly nice young man, tall and slender, with hazel eyes and light brown hair. Everything about Jeremy was agreeable, neither too glaring or out of place. But the truth of the matter was that he was too solicitous of her, a fact that would displease his family greatly if they were to realize. She was no more than a poor relation, a companion to the daughter of the house.

"Jeremy, come and see what I've done. I've quite captured the garden in spring, I think. What do you say?" Harriet called out, separating them.

Janet did not doubt that the other woman had intended it just so. Or perhaps she judged Harriet too sharply. She had spent seven years in service to her, enough time to get to know a person, but understanding still slipped through her fingers like water. There were times at which she thought Harriet genuinely kind, still other occasions when she suspected that Harriet waited until she was feeling her lowest to offer up criticism and censure.

Lately, Harriet's mood had been worse than usual. The reason for it had been hard to discern until she'd overheard a conversation. The manor house was cavernous, so much so that even whispers had a tendency to float from unexpected places. She'd learned, accidentally, that Squire Hanson had made peace with the Scot who had made a practice of coming over the border to bedevil him for the last few years. The squire had offered up his daughter and her dowry as an incentive for the Scot to cease stealing his cattle.

Harriet was to wed the laird of the Sinclairs. Now *that* was a surprise.

Janet could not help but wonder, however, if Harriet's father absented himself until the nuptials a month from now solely to avoid the unpleasantness of Harriet's mood. Her irritation about her upcoming nuptials seemed destined to last until the very day she was wed.

Janet turned back to the window, wishing that she had the power to ease herself through the glass and escape into the night like a shadow. She would hide among the trees, peer around a thick trunk, and run into the woods like a forest creature. Away. Where she could not be told that her accent was common or her coloring odd or her fingers clumsy. Where there was music, perhaps, and the sound of laughter. Happiness, wrapped into a parcel of night and bound together with a bow made of acceptance.

She was so lonely sometimes. But for the first time in seven years, she was promised an end to it. She had learned, the day she'd heard of Harriet's wedding, that she was to accompany Harriet to Scotland after she became a bride. To be home once more, to set her feet on Scottish soil. She anxiously counted the days.

"Come away from that window, Janet. I need you." Harriet's voice once again called her to duty.

Janet moved across the room and sat on the chair beside Harriet. She would be quite attractive, Janet thought, if she was not forever scowling at the world. Harriet had hair of a deep chestnut color that curled despite the weather, and was possessed of the softest blue eyes. She was short of stature and small of frame, giving the impression of weakness or

fragility, something delicate to be protected. Harriet, however, possessed a will of iron. It was never overt, never
demonstrated in screaming fits or tirades. It was simply
there, like the sky or the earth.

"You've been pining all evening. What, some Scots holiday
we've neglected to celebrate? Something altogether holy?"

Janet shook her head. It was better to never respond to one
of Harriet's jibes—a lesson she'd learned in the last seven
years. She had only been fifteen when she'd come to England. Her parents were dead, their village decimated by in-
fluenza. People had begun to leave prior to the epidemic;
afterward, it was as if only ghosts inhabited Tarlogie.

She had been given the choice of being a companion to
Harriet or starving in the streets. There were some days
when she knew she had made the wrong choice.

Still, it could be worse. Her duties were not onerous.
She'd learned to ignore most of Harriet's complaints, even
though the nasal whine of her voice made that almost impossible. She was allowed an hour here and there to spend
among the flowers, to read a book borrowed surreptitiously
from Squire Hanson's library. If she had no prospects or future, it was not Harriet's fault.

"You give yourself airs with my brother," Harriet said
now. Her voice had softened to a grating whisper, inaudible
to Jeremy, who sat on the other side of the room, reading.
Periodically, he would look up and send a sweet smile in
Janet's direction.

"I was but pleasant, I think. He asked me a question; I answered it."

Was disposition passed from father to child? Was that
why Harriet frowned so much and seemed so unhappy? If
so, why was Jeremy not more like his father?

No, that was not quite fair, was it? Harriet's parents were
quite nice people. Squire Hanson was a blustery sort of man
who harrumphed a great deal and who was obviously more

comfortable in the presence of animals than people. Harriet's mother, Louisa Hanson, was bedridden and removed from most of the activity in the house. She was a sweet lady, with a habit of sniffing into a lace handkerchief, and she had always been kind, in a slightly absentminded way. Janet would not have been surprised if the other inhabitants of the house forgot about her presence for long stretches at a time, just as Mrs. Hanson, no doubt, forgot about hers.

"I've seen the way you smile at him, Janet," Harriet said. "As if you would charm him."

"I was but being polite."

"Practice your wiles on the groom, Janet. Or the footmen. Else I will have no choice but to mention your wild behavior to my father."

Wild? A small smile was born secretly. She dipped her head in case it blossomed forth and betrayed her amusement. *Oh, Harriet, if you would know what wildness is, see inside my heart. That is wild.*

There, it was out, then. The truth, unadorned and without pretense. She did not want to be here, in this place, eternally a servant while her life drained away. She wanted to be home again, in Tarlogie. She wanted to hear her father's rich laughter and her mother's sweet voice. Her mother's mother had been English, and it was through her grandmother that she claimed kin to the Hansons and, because of that relation, had a home of any sort. But, oh, it was so difficult to pretend to *like* being English.

All her life, she'd been raised to prize her heritage, to find in herself those things that linked her to a proud people. She was her parents' only child, and one who was beset with curiosity, her father had said. Perhaps that was why he'd let her tag along with him, learning his trade as well as any apprentice. She'd grown too accustomed to saying what she thought, to laughing immoderately, to seeing the best side of life.

To be so again, that's what she wished. To dance among the heather, to see a sunrise over the Highlands. To hear the sound of the Gaelic, to smell the acrid scent of peat smoke. That's what being wild felt like.

During the last seven years, she'd made herself into another person. The Janet who'd lived with her parents in the small village outside Tain had disappeared. She barely remembered her Gaelic, the tunes she'd hummed as a child. But then, there was no further cause for laughter, no reason to smile. Even her speech had changed. She sounded more English than Scots.

Oh, but inside, her heart beat with wildness.

"Are you pouting, Janet? It's very unbecoming in a servant. Hand me my case," Harriet said.

Janet bent to reach the embroidery basket. She offered it up mutely, said nothing as Harriet took her time selecting the next thread to use.

"Hold the basket steady, Janet. Your hands are trembling."

Janet braced the heavy basket on her knees.

"I detest this shade of blue thread you selected. Whatever were you thinking?" Harriet picked through the threads. It was one of Janet's duties to rearrange them every night, to wind them around the little spools arranged for just such a purpose. "Are you hoping to rid yourself of doing errands by showing such poor judgment?"

"It is exactly what you asked for, Harriet. A shade of blue for delphiniums."

Harriet looked over at her, her frown deepening.

"Are you telling me I'm wrong, Janet? I cannot believe you would be so foolish."

"If you do not like the shade I selected, Harriet," she said calmly, "perhaps it would be better if you went to the village the next time."

Janet looked down at the floor, horrified at her own words. A full moon, that's what it was. Had she forgotten her place? Yes, oh, yes, she had. Gloriously so. Enough that for once, she'd spoken the truth. Honesty bubbled up from her toes, capped only through will and prudence. Her words could get her dismissed despite any familial ties. Where would she be then? On the road with less future than she had now.

"Forgive me, Harriet," she said softly.

"You must be ill, Janet, to speak so foolishly. That is it, isn't it? Ring for Mrs. Thomas and have her bring you some Dover's Powder."

"It is nothing, Harriet," she said quickly. "Perhaps I am simply tired." Even if she had been feeling ill, she would have denied it to escape a dosing of Dover's. It made her stomach lurch and then induced the most bizarre dreams. The last time she'd been forced to take it, she'd awakened drenched from her own perspiration and vowing never to succumb to the medicine again.

"Why ever should you be tired? You've done nothing of consequence today." Harriet's smile had an edge of daring to it, one that made Janet choke back the retort that she'd walked to the village and back again, not once but twice, simply because Harriet had forgotten something she wished purchased.

"Perhaps you're correct," Janet said. "I could be sickening."

"How very inconsiderate of you to be ill while in my presence. Leave me, then."

Janet replaced the embroidery chest on the floor beside Harriet and nodded to her. Then, before Jeremy could wish her a soft good night, she escaped.

But not to bed. The night was young; the moon was just rising; the enchantment of an early spring breeze was too alluring to resist. The moment was too precious; the freedom too rare to waste.

She would be wild, if only for a moment.

* * *

A shallow stream ran through the Hansons' property to the east of the house. In the morning, it looked as if it glowed; the rays of the sun struck it just so. It reminded her of Tarlogie and the burn that flowed past their small cottage. It had winked in the morning light just like this one, before disappearing into the ground again.

Now the stream was black, lit only by a glimpse of moon. She turned and faced north, wishing that she might be like a bird and fly over the ground, finding a nest among the trees bordering a loch. She could almost feel Scotland call her from here, as if she knew that one of her children was missing. It was in her blood, this longing, so deep and so sharp that it made her wish to weep sometimes. *You can take a Scot from the land, but never the land from the Scot*—a saying she'd heard as a child, but whose actual meaning she'd never known until separated from the land of her birth.

She sat on the bank of the small stream, on the mossy ground cover. There were trees around her, shading the moonlit darkness still further. The night was welcoming, as if it approved of her escape into wildness. Just this once. A few moments out of seven years. Then she would return to being sober Janet.

She wiggled her toes, freed of shoes and stockings, lifted her serviceable servant's gown above her knees and waded into the stream. It was cold even though it was spring. Maybe it carried its chill from the high mountains of Scotland itself. *Whimsy, Janet.* More likely it was a staid little English stream. All proper and demure, never flooding, never straying from its bank. It would not tunnel through peat and carry a smoky taste. It would tumble over rocks and pebbles in only the most demure fashion.

"Is it hard to mind your manners, brook? Do you find it as difficult as I do? I wish I did not have to be so polite all the time," she said softly.

Suddenly a voice called out of the dark. "Are you a brownie, then, that you would speak to the water?"

Her head jerked up. All she saw was a shadow on the landscape, only a long, dark shape near a tree. Her heart thudded heavily in her chest. Her hands fisted her skirts, holding them above the rippling water. Had she not been in such a position, she might have fled at the sound of him.

Or perhaps not. Maybe she'd come to meet him, then, him with his voice all dark and thick like a summer night. With the sound of Scotland in it.

"A brownie?" She could not help it; she smiled. Doing so seemed to remove the cork from her feelings, held so tight and contained these last years. "If I were a brownie," she said, her voice as soft as his, "then I would be in the house performing the chores of the mistress—doing the supper dishes or plying my skill with a needle."

"Ah, but the candle still shines, so perhaps you wait until all are abed before you begin your chores."

He took a few steps forward, and she remained where she was, the sober Janet trapped by impropriety, a hoyden discovered just as she embarked upon her ill-bred ways. It did not seem quite fair to be caught just as she was about to be wild. She wiggled her toes. The rocks beneath her feet were kind and did not cut her skin, nor did the water seem as cold.

"I wish I had a bit of cheese or a drink of milk to give you," he said.

She followed his shadow, wondered who he was. Or was he even real? Had she conjured him up from loneliness? A dream, perhaps? A phantom, come to share her wicked moments?

"You've some skill in the tempting of brownies, I see," she said. "You must not pay them too much, else their pride is wounded."

"Nor ignore their contribution," he said agreeably, "lest they vanish and never appear again."

He was Scots, and it was a moonlit night, and this was England: three points upon which a conclusion could be drawn.

"You are a border raider, aren't you?"

His laughter surprised her—not the throaty sound of it, but the surprise and delight in the sound. He seemed charmed, and that was both idiotic and oddly vainglorious. Sober Janet, captivating a reiver.

"And I've come to steal you, is that it?"

"Have you?" she asked, shaking one foot before placing it on the gently sloping bank. She stepped out of the stream and dropped her skirt.

"While it's true a lass is a blessing, cattle are more prized. Lust is all well and good, but has never taken the place of a full stomach."

Her laughter came freely. Honesty was a commodity much lacking in her life of late. It was a refreshing thing to hear it, even if the truth was so baldly stated.

"Then I'm sorry I am not a cow, for your sake, sir."

"Oh, I've not come for cattle this time."

A faint skitter of alarm tripped through her. "And what *have* you come for?"

"To learn, perhaps. To seek answers to questions."

Silence, while she waited. When it was apparent he wasn't going to satisfy her curiosity, she tilted her head and frowned into the shadows.

"The moon lights your hair, lass. It looks silver in the light. What color does it appear in the sun?"

She blinked at him, startled by the question and the air of bemusement in his voice. "Brown."

"The brown of the earth after a spring rain?"

"Simply brown, I'm afraid. No better nor worse than that." Her smile was coaxed free again by his practiced charm.

"And your eyes?"

"Blue. And no, not the blue of the skies."

"You lack poetry in your soul, lass."

"And I think you've too much of it for a reiver."

"Harriet!" The sound of Jeremy's voice cut through their banter like a sharpened sword. Janet turned her head in the direction of the house, alarmed. If Jeremy was looking for his sister, that meant Harriet was, no doubt, looking for her. And anger or irritation was the only impetus for Harriet to go abroad at night.

She bent down and grabbed her shoes, then crumpled her stockings into her pocket and crossed the stream with one bounding leap.

She stopped and turned, wishing to say good-bye, but he had already disappeared into the shadows. Indeed, she might have imagined him. Later, in her bed that night, she wondered if she had.

Two

It was raining, a very fine mist that ended almost as soon as it began. But Lachlan stood in it, he and his horse, waiting for her, wondering if a proper English miss would come to meet him in the rain. She should be warm and cozy next to a fire. Would she even sense him here? He sluiced the rain from his face and stared up at the windows of the manor house. Which room was hers?

Don't be daft, Lachlan. The very last thing you need to do is to steal your intended from her bed. But it was a tempting thought, nonetheless. Last night, he'd only a hint of her. A moonbeam had strayed beneath a branch and sent a portrait of her into his mind. Shadows obscured her features, but they seemed fine, indeed. Brown hair, she'd said. And plain blue eyes. He doubted it. With her teasing laugh, she'd rendered him curious indeed. She did not screech as Coinneach had promised, and her hurried return to the house had proven that she did not limp.

Harriet. He did not like that name. It did not seem to fit her somehow.

Why had he thought of her all day? Because she'd teased

him about brownies and stood in the middle of a stream, barefooted. Because her laughter was free and easy and seemed tied to the center of him somehow, as if a string linked them.

Come to me, lass.

Would she hear his thoughts, then? Or was he simply a fool to stand here in the rain, waiting for a sight of a woman he'd be wed to, soon enough?

Janet coughed again, earning herself another fierce look from Harriet. Once more, and the other woman's lips pursed so tightly, they disappeared into her face.

"What possessed you, Janet? To rid yourself of your shoes and cavort in the garden like a common doxy? Is that what I should expect of you Scots?" She lowered her needle-work and stared at Janet. "You deserve to be ill, you know. I should dismiss you out of hand, but Mama had a fondness for your mother and would be distressed."

Another cough; another frown.

"Oh, do remove yourself to your chamber, Janet. I cannot bear the sounds you make."

Janet stood, her hands hidden in the material of her skirt. Her fingers trembled, so she fisted them.

"Thank you, Harriet," she said, her voice barely audible. It sounded, to a casual listener, as if she were indeed sickening with a cold. But the night air had been warm, and she'd suffered more hardship in her life than standing in a cold burn.

You are a terrible person, Janet. To pretend an illness in order to escape Harriet. But, oh, the better to be able to race along the grass of the garden and return to the stream. Perhaps her reiver would be there, the man she'd conjured up from loneliness and longing.

The rain that had misted the air earlier had stopped, but the dampness of the grass soaked into her slippers. She brushed against a low-hanging branch, and droplets beaded her cheek. She smiled. How many times had she stood in a Highland rain, her head tilted back, her face washed clean? *Too many times, but too long ago, Janet.*

The air was scented with the rain still, and the smell of growing things. She stopped and closed her eyes, wondering if she could tell all the various scents apart, one from the other.

You delay because you do not wish to know, Janet, she chided herself. *You do not wish to reach the stream and have him not be there. Why else do you stand in full view of the house and discovery? In order to summon him here with wishes, then?*

"Have you another name?" His voice came from behind a nearby tree. As she watched, a shadow disengaged itself and walked forward. Beside him walked a horse; it, too, only darkness upon darkness. She might have conjured up the man, but had she summoned the horse, too?

"Another name?"

"Not your Christian name."

"Elizabeth," she said, giving him her middle name.

"A nice English name."

"I was named for my grandmother. She was a nice English lady."

"We'll call you the Gaelic, then. Ealasaid."

"Will we?" Should she have imagined a man with such an arrogant nature?

"Do not tell me you'd prefer something more English?" There was a decidedly pained tone in his voice.

"I haven't any objection to my current name," she said.

"It's too harsh for such a lovely lass as yourself."

"And how would you know it?"

"Perhaps I am part brownie."

He tied the reins of his horse to a tree, then walked slowly toward her. She clenched her fists in the material of her shawl. It was not fear she felt at that moment. Fear might have been more prudent. Instead, she felt excitement, perhaps. Daring, of a certainty. She was about to be more than wild. She was to have an adventure, of that she was sure. With a Scots reiver.

"My name is not so unpleasant as yours, lass. Lachlan. Now, doesn't that have a fine ring to it? It flows from the tongue like the burn you waded in last night. Have you had no ill effects from such a daring thing?"

"You must think me puny indeed," she said, her smile enlivened by the gentle teasing in his voice.

"No, simply a lass who should be cosseted, I think. Or protected from her more wayward nature." Was it her imagination, or was there a smile in his voice? He was a vision crafted in mist and shadows. Even the moon had disappeared behind the clouds, as if shrouding him in secrecy.

He was really too close now, his voice curled around her like a dark, silken ribbon. It was almost heaven to hear the sound of it, the lilting tones of its teasing. He played with her, she knew. Daring he was, almost as much as she. But he knew the way of wildness, and she was new to it.

"So, you've not come to steal cattle tonight?"

"You accuse me without proof, Ealasaid. What have I stolen? Cannot I be a simple Scot wandering over the border for the sake of it? England's made it clear we belong to them. Is it only one-sided, then?"

"Then are you seeking answers, still?"

"No," he said, his voice closer than before. "I think I've found what I needed to know."

His fingers touched her cheek, and she jerked, startled. Instead of removing his hand, he continued his exploration, learning the texture of her skin, the shape of her face. She should have moved away or, barring that, asked him to refrain from such intimacies. But she did nothing, only stood, silent and enmeshed within a spell woven around them by the night

and the mist. No, more than that. A longing for moments like
this, with her breath coming in sharp little gasps and her heart
racing. His fingers were rough; his touch, gentle.

His thumb rested upon her chin, dipped beneath her jaw
and pushed her face up. She closed her eyes and tilted her
head back, waiting in terrified wonder for the touch of his
lips on hers, the magical and forbidden taste of wickedness.

Instead, he spoke, his breath brushing against the tendrils
of hair at her temple. "Why did you come, lass?"

Her eyes opened. He stood so close, she could feel his
breath upon her cheek. Push him back, or be enfolded in his
arms. That's how close they stood.

"I couldn't stay away." The simple truth of it frightened
her. She'd done nothing but think of him all day, wondering
if she'd dreamed their first encounter.

"Neither could I, lass. A good omen, I think." There was
that hint of a smile in his voice again, as if he was amused by
her. It should not have coaxed free her own smile. It might
have been better if she'd feared him.

"Give me your hand, Ealasaid."

She reached out her arm, until her fingers brushed his
chest. The hand that encompassed hers was large; his palm,
roughened. He laughed then, an odd sound in the darkness,
and pulled her with him.

Three

He had thought about her all day, this woman with the ill-fitting name. She wasn't timid. A timid miss might ask where he was taking her. But then, a timid miss would not be in the dark with him, or stand in a stream with her skirts to her knees.

Her voice was melodic, almost as if she had the sound of Scotland trapped within her speech. She was fleet of foot as she followed him, skipping every once in a while to keep her steps equal to his.

"Are you certain you've not come to steal?" she asked, her voice breathless.

"Are you feared I would ride with you across the border, lass? Hide you in my castle and demand a ransom for you?"

"Have you a castle?" She sounded fascinated.

Did she not know who he was? A thought without merit at this particular moment. But still, a thread of doubt crept through his mind. He'd never thought she wouldn't know him. Lachlan was a good Scots name, but not very common.

"I'm Sinclair," he said, wondering how she would receive

the news that the man who held her hand and pulled her through the forest was her future husband.

"Oh." A small sound, for all that. Still, she did not protest.

They traveled slower, winding through the thick woods. He waited for her to speak, wondered what her questions would be.

"Could you tell me about the castle?"

"Glenlyon?"

"Yes. It's to be my home, so I would like to know."

"It's a castle," he said. "It's old and grows cold in the winter, though passably cool in the summer. You don't expect me to tell you what color the curtains are or some such?"

Her laughter surprised him. So, too, the fact that it seemed tied to his own smile, as if she'd the power to summon it.

"Can you not wait until you see it, then?"

"You're right; I should wait. It is only a month."

Her hand still rested trustingly in his, and she'd said those words that had calmed his sudden jealousy without a clue that it had been there at all. *It's to be my home.* She'd known who he was, then, and had not simply come with him to have an adventure before marrying. He wanted to kiss her, some recompense, some reward for her hesitant honesty, for her gift of tremulous anticipation. There had been fear in her words, barely audible, but then he'd had some experience with learning that emotion in the past few years. He was occasionally afraid of the future, afraid he might not be able to save his clan. He turned his mind from such dour thoughts.

He brought her hand to his face, kissed the inside of her wrist. He did not wish to startle her; they were newly met, however destined their future together might be. She seemed silenced by his gesture, the pounding of her blood beneath her skin the only communication between them. Perhaps not a timid woman, but one of shyness still, of uncertainty. It was there in the way her breathing had escalated, in the small step she took away from him; almost, but not quite, pulling her hand from his stewardship.

He said nothing, simply walked on, his route one learned years ago when he had first begun to visit this place. The waterfall was the headwater for the small stream she'd bathed in last night.

The sound of the rushing water drowned out her words. She pulled free of his grasp and stood on the mossy bank overlooking the pool formed by the rapids. The moon chose that moment to peek out from behind the lowering clouds, and he was treated to the sight of her, bathed by silvered light.

She took his breath away.

She turned, her smile as radiant as the moon, the night no match for her beauty. Were all women as such when seen for the first time, or had it been his singular blessing to view her in the moonlight? Had Fate, who'd decreed the Sinclairs such a sorry lot these past years, felt only pity and sorrow for his condition, then? Had he been given this woman in order to right so many wrongs? A woman with a child in her heart, who gamboled in streams and raced like a fawn, whose laughter taunted him to smile and whose face made him thankful for Old Mab and the Legend. And perhaps even Coinneach.

Her lips were full, the lower lip more so than the upper. Her eyes were large; her cheeks, high. Her chin was neither squared nor pointed, but tapering in a way that chins do. And her nose was neither beaked nor sharp, but ended with a small upturn to it. Her hair curled over her shoulders in riotous disarray, and he wanted to know if the mist made it such, or if she was beset with curls every day. A question he'd have answered after their wedding.

He bent finally, and she cupped her hands around his ear so that he might hear her words over the roar of the water. "I've never known such a place existed," she said.

His own words were said in a similar manner. He hesitated as his hands brushed over her hair, feeling the thickness of it, wishing that it might be provident to thread his fingers through it. "You've led a sheltered life, then, lass. Did you never go exploring?"

She shook her head. He didn't need sunlight to see the sparkle of her eyes. He needed no urging for her to grip his hand. They followed the edge of the pool until they came to the waterfall. He turned and looked at her, as if to measure the extent of her daring, then calmly picked her up and walked into the gap between waterfall and stone.

He slowly lowered her to her feet and reluctantly stepped away. What he wanted to do was get so much closer. But they had all the time in the world to learn of the other. These moments hollowed from time and circumstance were sacred to themselves. He wanted to know things that a bridegroom might dismiss. Why she seemed so un-English for one, and why she'd never ventured far from her garden. Were her parents strict? Had she been mistreated, then? A surge of protectiveness for her thudded through him.

The cave was little more than a hollowed-out rock behind the waterfall, deep enough that they could stand with their back to it and watch the silvery curtain in front of them. He wished it were daylight, so he could see the expression on her face. She was little more than a shadow. A breath of substance.

"I shouldn't be here," she said, addressing the waterfall. Her voice was faint enough, but it was oddly less noisy here than in front of the cascade of water. Did she stand so still because she sensed him in the same way he did her? He wanted some connection of flesh to flesh, so he placed his hand on her shoulder. He felt her shiver, a strange sensation that was neither in response to cold nor aversion to his touch. Instead, it was as if every part of her body stilled in that instant, became aware of how close he stood to her, how near they were to each other, how their very breathing seemed in tandem.

"What better place, Ealasaid?"

"In my bed. Asleep."

"Dreaming?"

"Yes," she said. The word sounded sorrowful.

"And what do you dream about, lass?" He had not moved his hand, imagining he could feel the texture of her skin beneath her shawl, her dress.

"I dream of the past," she said. Her voice seemed as soft as a whisper; yet if it had been, he could not have heard it over the sound of the waterfall. "I dream of Scotland."

"Does it frighten you that much?"

"It does not frighten me at all."

"Yet we're an impressive bunch, for all that. I think you a brave lass, to be standing here in the dark with a Scot."

"Which is why I shouldn't be here."

"Do you question your courage, or my honor?"

"My own perversity, perhaps, that I would wish to be nowhere but here, even as I know it's not right or well done of me."

His smile broadened. "I'll not harm you."

She didn't answer him, just looked around the cave as if she could see into the nooks and crannies of it.

"Is this where you hide from the patrols?"

"I've put my wayward life behind me."

"Or encouraged me to join it."

"Is that what you've been dreaming of? The life of a border reiver?"

"It seems a bit more exciting than the life I've led," she admitted. "I've little liking for embroidery threads and sketching."

"Are you craving an adventure, lass?"

She glanced at him. "I think you are my grandest escapade of all."

* * *

She should not be here. It was one thing to be discovered barefooted and racing into the house; another to be missing when she'd convinced Harriet she was ill. She did not doubt that Harriet would send a servant to check on her or go herself to render condemnation and compassion in one breath.

The rain had come as if to wash the sky clean and then disappeared, leaving it dazzling with stars and deep-black night. The moon had been a lantern, illuminating her foolishness, and then his face.

Lachlan Sinclair. One of the Sinclairs. His name alone had sent a thrill through her. She would see him again, then, after Harriet wed. They would live in the same place, know the same people. And perhaps they could meet again, as they did now, stretching the boundaries of the restrictions that held them in place.

An unmarried woman did not eagerly grasp the hand of a man she did not know. She did not race into the woods with her lips clenched tight as if to muffle the sounds of excitement. She certainly did not stand upon the edge of a pool grown black and silver with moonlight and gape at the face of a man she'd never met.

She'd known he was tall, and his breadth had been hinted at in the shape of his shadowed form. But she had not known that his face would be so strong, that the moonlight would dance upon his features and give shape and hollows to them. It was a face of extremes, softened by a mouth that seemed adrift in smiles. She had stared at him as if she'd lost her wits. And perhaps she had, for in that moment, when the moon had encapsulated him in radiance, she'd wanted to touch him. Her fingers ached to dance over the skin of his cheekbones, to see if they were as sharp as moonlight made them. Was his nose that strong, his lips that full? His hair that thick?

Last night she'd thought herself wild. Tonight she knew herself wanton.

She brushed by him. Without another word, she'd found her way from the cave and back to the bank of the pool.

"Ealasaid?"

She looked back, and he stood there, his arm outstretched, his hand palm up. She shook her head. He was too much a lure, and she had learned caution and survival in the past years. She should wait until they met again in Scotland. It would be more properly done. Less tempting than seeing him in the moonlight. Even as she told herself to leave, she did not wish to. A clue, then, to how wild she truly was.

"Meet me here, tomorrow."

Did she just imagine his words? *Wishful thinking, Janet, or a dream?* Or perhaps an echo of wildness?

Four

Janet slept heavily and woke late. She had crept to her room by the servants' stair, had felt only a giddy sense of relief not to have been discovered. But sleep had not come easily. Instead, she had remembered every moment of the hour she'd spent with Lachlan. She spoke his words over and over in her mind, as if to fix them there.

The day passed with aching slowness, a warm spring day that lured her and beckoned her outdoors. She had no errands to perform, no visits to the village, no lists of items to procure at the various shops. Instead, she sat in the large and sunny parlor and read to Harriet while she sewed. Every sentence or so she was halted and made to read another passage, to obscure any hint of accent from her voice. She longed to ask Harriet what she planned to do once she was in Scotland. Was she going to make every Scot repeat his words until his speech sounded more English?

"You are looking peaked, Janet," Harriet said now, her gaze sharp. "Are you still ailing?"

"No, Harriet. Shall I continue to read?"

"You don't like it when I correct you, do you?"

Janet kept her face carefully blank of expression. Honesty was not truly wanted at this moment. She had learned, on too many previous occasions, that it was better to simply pretend to have no thoughts at all.

"I do it for your sake, you know. You'd sound like a barbarian otherwise. But sometimes you look at me as if you dislike my efforts to improve you. You mustn't do so, you know. Servants should always have their eyes downcast when they are being reprimanded."

"Yes, Harriet."

"You dislike me, don't you, Janet?"

She looked over at Harriet. The question surprised her, but it should not have. Harriet did not avoid confrontation; she embraced it. Indeed, there were times at which Janet had thought Harriet that spoiled for a fight, not unlike a young bully she'd known at Tarlogie. Robbie had had just that look about the eyes, that daring glitter.

Now there was a small smile on Harriet's lips, and her gaze was fixed on Janet as if relishing the discomfort she felt.

Did Harriet wish her to fawn? She could not. In truth, she did not know how to answer. She had never thought of Harriet in terms of friendship. Their relationship was built too strictly on servitude, a position Harriet had made clear the first day they'd met, seven years ago.

"You're to be my maid when she's taking her half day, and my footman if none is available. You'll do errands for me and fetch me tea if I require it. If your voice and your ability are agreeable, you will read to me. If not, you will be expected to sit quietly and not speak. Do you understand?"

She had only nodded in response.

"It is not important," Harriet said now. "You are my companion, after all. That is all that's needed."

Janet lowered the book to her lap. "Do you want us to be friends, Harriet?"

"Why ever would I want that? You're hardly my social equal despite our dubious relationship." Harriet's smile carried a brittle edge to it. "I am to be married Janet. Did you know?" Harriet seemed to study her. "But of course you do. Servants always know what is happening in a house. I had decided to take you to Scotland with me, but I believe now that another female will do just as well. In fact, more adequately, I'm sure."

Janet gripped the book so tightly, she thought her fingers might be embedded into the tooled leather. She clamped her lips over words that would plead. She would implore, and Harriet would only smile. Perhaps. Or maybe the price to go home to Scotland was her pride. Was she willing to sacrifice it? The gleam in Harriet's eyes seemed to ask the question.

"Please, Harriet," she said softly. "I very much want to go. Won't you reconsider?"

No words seemed capable of warming that icy smile. If anything, it seemed to soften into contempt. "Do not look so stricken, Janet. Mama will find you a position among the ladies she knows. Someone elderly, perhaps, who nods off during the day and will not mind your odd accent and your moodiness."

This, then, was the punishment for not toadying. For her silence, she was being penalized.

"Please, Harriet." She gave her another part of her pride, delivered in a voice that quivered, but only barely.

Her future, the one that seemed to be changing, now seemed bleak as ash. The cold and empty fireplace held more brightness. Lachlan. She'd never see Lachlan now, never spend time with him, never grow to know him. His home would be a mystery to her just as it was now, a castle that existed only in her imagination. And she would never see Scotland again. Sunsets so vivid they made the heart weep, skies the color of slate, a stark and solemn landscape rendered beautiful by touches of color. A shade of heather, a brown capercaillie and her yellowish chicks.

She didn't think she could bear it.

Did Harriet know how desperately she'd wanted to return to Scotland? If so, this was a wonderful punishment, delivered with a small smile. She felt something tear within her, a veil that hid her tears.

"Do not shame us both with your toadying, Janet." Harriet's voice seemed to come from far away. As far away as Scotland.

Janet began to read again, forcing the words past the constriction in her throat. The last remnants of her pride came to her rescue.

She would not cry in front of Harriet. Nor would she beg further. *O sgiala bronach!* The Gaelic seemed so perfect for this moment. Oh, sad news, sad news.

Where was Coinneach now? If the old man could read the future so well, why hadn't he been able to foretell this disaster?

"What happened, James?" Lachlan stood at the cavern entrance. A thick, milky substance clung to the rock walls and fell in rivulets to pool on the stone floor. It stunk of scorched barley, yet also smelled sickeningly sweet.

James was covered in a similar fashion, as were half the men who stood before him. It was not simply their appearance, he reasoned, that made them hold their heads averted or look at the ceiling or the floor. They looked like children who had been caught at some forbidden game. "What happened?" he said again, and this time, his voice ricocheted back to him. He did not sound pleased.

"We thought we might up the mixture a bit, Lachlan. We discharged the still, and it was a puny brew. Hardly worth tasting."

Twenty heads nodded.

"So you thought you might increase the fire a bit more, is that it?"

"Well, that, and the other," James said.

"What would the other be?"

"We drained off a little more of the water, Lachlan."

"You should have seen it, laird. The kettle looked to have the burps, it did." That was contributed by a small voice from the rear. As he watched, young Alex peeped around his father's legs. Barely six years old, and already learning the ways of a conspirator. Lachlan bit back a smile.

"I take it there's no more potent result. Except for this mess."

James shook his head.

"And no one injured?"

Another negative shake.

Lachlan surveyed the inside of the cavern again. The space was carved into a hill only a short distance from Glenlyon and had served as a hidey-hole for generations. In the last several years, they'd erected their pot still here, where it was sure to escape detection from the English excise officers. A series of pipes and vents ending in a crofter's cottage on the other side of the hill carried the steam from the still. The fact was that although the cottage was sparkling clean and dusted often, set up with furniture, a cookstove, and pots and dishes, it had never actually been inhabited. But the steam that billowed from its chimney would be seen as nothing more than a peat fire. If it smelled a bit too hearty and forever bore the scent of barley, it was in keeping with the Sinclair diet. As it was, they ate barley from morning until night—barley bannocks and barley soup, barley stuffing, barley bread, barley stew.

This venture might very well save them. His bride's dowry would be a blessing, but his clan could not live on it for long. The only thing that would save them was the income from their distillery.

It seemed a good enough plan. The problem was the hundred-pound copper pot. It had been paid for with the last of their ready coin, but it had arrived after Angus' death. No one had been able to coax a palatable brew from it. His clansmen were dedicated, especially since they'd learned there was no more whiskey to be had, but their experience ran to small stills secreted in bed chambers and under piles of peat. They knew nothing about distilling in such a large and imposing vessel. Angus had been closemouthed and guarded his secrets well, so much so that none of their individual or collective efforts had resulted in anything approaching drinkable whiskey. And this afternoon, in an effort to make more powerful the mixture, they'd succeeded in dimpling the expensive pot and bending the tubes that fed into and out of it.

Lachlan stood in the middle of the cave and wondered if the actions of ancestral Sinclair lairds had been so heinous that he was still being punished for it. Surely it was not justice to starve innocents such as young Alex, or cause women to go about with a soft and worried look?

The only bright spot in the gloom of his horizon was Ealasaid. She had been on his mind all night, and she resided there even now as he strode through the cavern, mentally separating those pieces of pipe that could be saved.

"Lachlan?" He looked down, and it was Alex again, this time with his hands tucked manfully into his trousers, his posture not unlike that of his father. His dark brown eyes were the same as most of the Sinclairs; so, too, his dark hair. But it was the stubborn set to his jaw that marked him as a true member of the clan. That and a sweet smile. Lachlan's mother had told him that it was the downfall of many a shy Sinclair lass, that smile. But she'd laughed as she'd said it and looked over at his father fondly. He missed them both. Perhaps part of his sense of responsibility was the notion that his parents were somehow watching him, gauging his merits as laird. If so, they were no doubt disappointed.

"What will we do now, laird?" Lachlan found it disconcerting to be on the receiving end of an intent stare, especially since it was leveled by a six-year-old. But the question the boy asked was one that each man had in his eyes.

"We'll clean up this mess, Alex, and try again. That's what. And if that fails, we'll do it again."

It was an optimism he barely felt, but that must be voiced for the sake of the people standing in front of him. It was the only thing he could give them. That, and the gift of himself, freely given. A sacrifice of marriage. Only it did not feel as much of a loss as it had before he'd met Ealasaid.

Five

She could not wait for darkness; it could not come quickly enough. The sun hung upon the horizon like a recalcitrant child unwilling to find his bed. She urged it on with thoughts and words spoken only in her heart. But it did not pass any quicker.

Finally, it was night. The birds signaled dusk with their warbling. No rain marred the sky, but the moon was no longer full. Shadows graced the garden as the hour grew more advanced. She had learned her lesson during the daylight and did not bid time to hurry, only endured it as she could, her mind blocked to the sound of Harriet's criticism, her smile absent when she nodded to Jeremy.

Harriet had complained to her bedridden mother about her this afternoon. Janet could not help but wonder if it had been planned that she hear the exchange. She was, evidently, clumsy and aloof and rude. A barbarian who had been barely civilized. She had left the chamber rather than overhear any more.

She had worked beside her father for years, had watched as his hands had coaxed magic from the earth's bounty. He was a man who'd taught willingly, naturally, sharing his knowledge with any who asked. It was he who'd explained to her the virtue of patience, that it was possible to hasten a thing to its disaster. He was the one, too, who'd shown her how to measure pressure, who taught her to gauge steam, the pattern it made as it floated toward the ceiling, how it gurgled in the pipes. Only then could one vat be combined with another, a mixture of agitation and one of reserve resulting in the perfect fermentation.

Janet felt the same right at this moment. She was outwardly calm, inwardly furious. But it did not show on her face, and her eyes were kept downcast in case their expression betrayed her rage.

Aloof—she was that and proud of it. She'd channeled her temper these past years. Grief and fury and worry and longing had no place in a fight for survival. She'd cooled them beneath a crust of ice lest they burn her.

Clumsy? She'd no words to fight that accusation. True, she'd tripped more than once on the small rugs scattered over the floor, and she was forever catching something that had fallen from a table or the mantle or a shelf. But the rooms were crowded with bric-a-brac, statuary, small pots, and dainty little doilies that collected dust and grabbed at sleeves.

Rude? Until yesterday, she'd restrained herself, held tight all those feelings she'd had for Harriet. Until yesterday, she'd said nothing when she'd walked the three miles to the village, because it had been an escape of sorts. Nor did she complain when Harriet had handed her mud-stained boots and demanded they be polished, or chastised her for the way she'd done her hair. She'd heard criticisms day and night, and if there was nothing to criticize, there was, at the last, her own being to condemn. She was Scots, a position and a heritage that, according to Harriet, was no more important than being a cur.

What Harriet called barbarism was no more than ignorance. While it was true she'd no knowledge of all the English table ceremony, she'd learned quickly. She wasn't a crude person. Her mother had been a parson's daughter, not schooled in the ways of gentry. But even if she had been it was doubtful that their three-room cottage would have boasted silver salvers and urns.

But that humble cottage had always looked more welcoming than this crowded house with its evidence of wealth.

Harriet said something, and she nodded, knowing an assent was necessary. In truth, she didn't hear the words, didn't care about them. All she was capable of was mastering her temper at this moment, holding it tight to her, so that it was not visible.

When finally the evening was done, she escaped to her room on the third floor and waited again. When she was certain the household was asleep, she tiptoed down the stairs and through the back parlor, into the hallway and to the garden walk beside the stables. Only then did she run. Toward the waterfall, toward Lachlan. And rebellion of the most daring sort.

He *was* daft; that's what he was. It was the only explanation for a man to stand outside a house waiting for a woman who might never appear. She hadn't, after all, said that she would come.

Was he going to make a practice of doing this for the next month?

He could go up those steps and demand to see her, but to do so would be to reveal his need for her. The squire was a canny man, and Lachlan had no doubt that he would savor the fact that the Scot who'd made his life miserable now pined for his daughter. He wouldn't put it past the man to extract his own revenge, possibly even delay the wedding, if only to balance the scales a bit.

He wished she would come to him now, before the night grew later. Every hour that passed was an hour wasted.

A few minutes later, she exited the house, slipping over the garden grass with the grace of an elf. He smiled even more broadly when he realized that she was going in the direction of the waterfall. She'd find a surprise there, his lass.

Six

The light of the full moon had made the path easier to navigate the night before. But the moon waned now, and it took her twice as long to find her way to the waterfall. In fact, she was nearly at the pool before she realized it lay before her. It was the light that alerted her; the faint hint of fire sparkling behind the sheet of water.

She walked around the rim of the pool, stepped carefully over the two stepping stones, and ducked behind the waterfall. She entered the cave, then smiled at the sight in front of her. A blanket had been laid upon the stone floor, and a candle placed at one edge of it, its glow protected from the fine mist by a glass shield.

A bower for a princess. All it lacked was a flower and a prince.

A rose was extended over her shoulder, held out by a large, tanned hand. A perfect pink rose, no doubt purloined from Harriet's garden. Her smile broadened as she turned. A prince, then, darkly enchanting in this place.

The moon had made of him a statue of gray and black. In truth, he was crafted of earth colors. His hair was the color of oak, deeply brown and rich. His eyes were that of Scots whiskey, sparkling with depth and power. A strong face. No, the moon had not lied about that. But had she noticed before how strangely alluring his mouth was, or how squared his chin?

"Ealasaid," he softly said, and the sound of it seemed to flow over her skin.

"Lachlan." It was a simple greeting. Why, then, did it seem an entreaty?

He extended his hand. His grip was strong and warm and gentle. He led her to the blanket, and she sat upon it, silent in the face of her surprising sorrow. She did not know this man, had only spent a few hours over the course of two nights with him. But her waking hours had been filled with thoughts of him, and her dreams were rife with events that had never occurred and would never have a chance to happen now.

How silly she was. But was it so foolish to wish for something that made her heart leap and made her blood pulse? Even servant girls had dreams and wishes.

She folded up her knees, wrapped her arms around them, and looked outward toward the sheen of water. The air was damp, but not unpleasantly so. He did not speak, and she turned her head to find him studying her. He sat back against the stone, his arms crossed in front of him, one foot over the other. His boots were dusty; his trousers, the same. His shirt was dark, befitting a man engaged in illicit activities. His hair was worn long; his face appeared tanned even by the light of a lone candle.

He was a border raider, a reiver, and she sat alone with him in a secluded spot and felt no danger.

Oh, she was foolish, wasn't she? As he watched her, his face unsmiling, his gaze never leaving her, she felt the urge to smile. Her heart beat too loudly; her fingers trembled in the folds of her skirt. She should feel only shame for all her wicked thoughts. The first, that she should wish to be nowhere but here. The second, that she should wonder at the reason for his unerring study of her, or wish that she had a newer dress to wear, something edged with tatting or adorned with ribbons.

She brushed her hair away from her face. It was forever coming undone from its pins.

"What do you do during the day, lass? What occupations fill your hours?"

She tilted her head and looked at him. Women, not men, were supposed to be lovely in candlelight. But the flickering shadows seemed to make his breadth more solid and granted shading to the strong angles of his face. He looked like a man accustomed to the night, one who was familiar with the shape of it, the mystery of darkness. "Errands to the village, embroidery," she said. "I confess to having little patience for fine needlework. I read when I can, and I make myself useful. And you, Lachlan? What do you do?"

"I wait impatiently for night," he said, his voice soft. She looked away, her cheeks warming.

"You lied, lass," he said, a smile softening his words. "You've eyes the color of a loch. And hair that's almost red."

"Is that why you brought the candle? To see me more clearly?"

"A brownie did it," he teased. "Frowned at me quite bitterly when I said I much preferred the dark."

"Do you?"

"No. But until you come to my land, this will have to do."

Grief speared her so quickly, she had no warning of it. She wanted to tell him that she would not be coming, that there would be nothing further between them but these moments. She would never see Scotland again, never see the land of the Sinclairs. But she did not, unwilling to mar these moments with him. There would be time enough to long for what could not be. She would not waste these moments.

She looked around at the dimensions of the cave, made more clear by candlelight. It was deeper than she'd thought, a cozy nook for anyone escaping from the border patrols. When she said as much, he only smiled.

"Did you have no thought of this place, lass? Never?"

"I've never explored this far," she confessed.

One of his eyebrows arched upward. His smile seemed to follow it. "A man might think you timid, Ealasaid. But your presence here gives lie to that."

"A maiden and a reiver?"

"I've given up my past," he said, his smile growing in scope, his eyes seeming to spark in the candle's light. "I've been naught but proper for nearly a month now."

Of course, he would be, especially if his laird was due to marry Harriet. It would not be a proper thing to steal from the laird's future wife.

"Could you not be coaxed to being improper again?"

His laughter surprised her. "Those are words a man should say to a maid, Ealasaid. What matter of impropriety would you urge on me?"

"What is it like, being a reiver?"

His look was almost kind. "Occasionally terrifying, lass. If I sought excitement for the fact of it, it wouldn't be to steal a cow."

"Then it isn't exciting?"

"I didn't say that. It has its moments. Especially when the patrols are not far away." A small smile played on his lips as if he knew what she hinted at, the daring question she ached to ask him.

Finally, it slipped free. "Would you take me raiding?"

"And what would we raid?"

"Is there no fat cow you could take home as prize? If it's beef you're tired of, then I know where the henhouse is. Or the sty."

He did laugh then, the booming sound of it echoing through the cave and beyond, to the night-shrouded landscape.

"What a picture you would paint of me, lass, a few fine squawking hens tied to my saddle, or holding a pig on my lap."

Her smile was rueful. In all honesty, she could see nothing of the sort. He seemed the type, instead, to carry a dirk between his teeth or be the vanguard of a raiding party, screaming a curse at the top of his lungs in warning to all who might doubt their murderous intent. Another reason she should not have felt so comfortable sitting here with him.

"I think what you want is not so much adventure, Ealasaid, as a touch of danger itself."

"Next you'll say that's why I'm here."

His eyes met hers. "Isn't it? Search your mind for the truth of it, lass."

"You make me sound too innocent."

He shrugged. "I've seen naught to lead me to think otherwise. In truth, I would not want you jaded."

"An innocent would not be here with you, Lachlan."

"Do you wish my word as a border raider that you are safe with me?"

She tilted her head and studied him. "That's a contradiction, isn't it?"

"Perhaps. Shall I pledge my clan's honor, instead?"

"Should I make you? Would an innocent take your word so easily?"

"Yes," he said, "but then, so would a woman well versed in adventure and danger."

"I'll never be that."

"Come," he said to her surprise. He stood and held out his hand. "If you would wish to be a woman experienced in excitement, we shall attempt to find some for you."

She stood and tucked her hand in his. "Truly?"

He looked down at her. She thought he was going to say something, but he clamped his lips over the words. Instead, he smiled. "Truly, lass."

Seven

She looked so happy standing there with a smile on her face, as if he'd given her the moon and all the stars. Did she know how little he was actually bringing to her? A run-down castle, worn-out land, a distillery that didn't distill, all countered by his intelligence and the strength of his limbs and an almost maniacal belief in the optimism of the future. But would that be enough?

Perhaps that was why he led her to his horse and helped her mount. To give her something that she wanted. Or maybe he'd simply breathed in too many of the noxious fumes in the cavern this morning.

Either way, they were on their way deeper into England before he could recite the Sinclair motto. *Bi gleidhteach air do dheagh run.* Be guarded with your good intentions.

He found the herd in a pasture not far away. He wasn't sure if they belonged to her father or not. At this point, it didn't matter. One Englishman's cow was going to be sacrificed.

They stood on the edge of the field, looking at the night-darkened shapes. It was something out of an eerie nightmare. Occasionally, one of the cows would make a sound, a cross between a moo and a grunt. Another would echo it. Then one would slowly walk a few feet, disturbing the sleep of a group huddled beneath a tree. And through it all, Ealasaid sat silent behind him.

"Are you going to charge them?" she whispered.

"Hush, I'm thinking."

"Are you waiting for something?"

"Not courage, if that's what you imagine."

"I didn't, really. I just wondered what your next action might be."

"Wondering if I'm daft indeed," he said, looking about him. "I've normally a few men with me."

"Well, should I dismount and wake them up? You can't go about making off with something that's sound asleep."

"You lack the proper respect for these doings, lass," he said, forcing his voice to be stern.

"Then pretend that I'm a fellow raider, Lachlan. What would happen next?"

"It would be a full moon, for one. We would be able to see better. A few men would stand as lookouts, and a few would cull the cows from the herd."

"We've no moonlight; can we not simply pick out a cow?"

"I've no wish to break my horse's leg, Ealasaid," he explained, "by riding over a unknown field."

"Oh."

"Unless, of course," he offered, "you wish to examine it. I could stand here while you crisscross the field."

"And step in dung?"

"Lass, where is your daring?"

"Not in my slippers, Lachlan."

In truth, he felt more like laughing than reiving.

"Then what shall we do?"

He slid from the horse and held his arms out for her.

"We're more surefooted," he said, as she lowered herself into his embrace. Again, he was tempted to hold her against him. Instead, he regretfully stepped back. "And we'll walk carefully."

A few minutes later, he spoke again. "Which one?" he whispered, as they crept up on the herd of cows clustered beneath the tree.

"I'm to pick one?"

"This is your raid, lass. Which beast looks longing for travel?"

"An English cow with a yen for Scotland?"

"There, I knew you would learn the trick of it."

"The rather large one over by the fence."

"That one looks to be in the mother way, lass. The journey might be too rough on her."

"Oh." A moment later, she spoke again. "How can you tell?"

He could not quite stifle his laughter. "Look at her belly, lass. And her teats."

"Is that one acceptable?" She pointed stiffly to another cow. He turned and smiled at her even though it was probably too dark for her to see him. She was embarrassed, but weren't such things discussed among farmers? Not, evidently, between the squire and his daughter.

"That one does looks restless. Bored, too, don't you think? Shall we go and invite her for the journey, then?"

"We're just going to walk up to one?"

"We are. Have you a handkerchief, lass?"

She pulled her handkerchief from her pocket and handed it over to him. It was the only thing to be seen in the darkness, a white flag. Lachlan used it to muffle the bell that hung around the cow's neck.

Once that was done, he gripped the bell rope firmly and led the unresisting cow to the edge of the pasture, opening the fence with one hand while Ealasaid followed him.

"It doesn't seem very adventurous, Lachlan."

"Oh, it's not the cows that mind being raided, lass. It's the people you have to watch for."

He was just congratulating himself on the success of their venture when a shout was heard from the side of the field. More than one man, by the sound of it.

He pulled her behind the trunk of the tree, looked at the looming shadows of his horse and their soon-to-be-stolen cow on the other side and cursed. Unless those men were blind, they would see them in only moments.

"Who is that?" Ealasaid whispered.

"Guards, no doubt."

"I'd not thought to look for one." Her voice sounded horrified.

"That's because you're new to this," he said. "It's a stupid thing we've done, lass, but I hold myself to blame. They use dogs a bit, and guns."

"Guns?"

"You sounded like a mouse then, Ealasaid. Is it that you're afraid?"

"I've no wish to be shot for a cow."

"Ah, then you'd be bored with being a reiver, lass."

"You don't like it either, do you, Lachlan?"

He thought about it for a moment, considered not answering her. But when he did, it was with the truth. "I've no liking for taking that which doesn't belong to me. I've tallied all that I've borrowed over the years and know to whom I owe it. My ancestors would, no doubt, be cursing me from their stones if they knew I was such a failure at thievery."

"And you really didn't want to steal this one, did you?"

"As I said, it's easier when my men are with me."

She gently pulled the bell rope from his hand.

"What are you about, lass?"

"If we leave her behind, then we won't have done anything wrong."

"Still, I doubt an Englishman truly shies at shooting a Scot, lass." She had the oddest ability to summon forth his humor.

She peeked out from behind the tree, led the cow to the opening in the fence, and then pulled the handkerchief from the bell and slapped the cow on the rump. She ambled back to her companions without much encouragement, her bell clanking loudly.

Ealasaid closed the fence behind her and raced back to the tree. Lachlan had mounted by that time, and he pulled her up behind him.

"Isn't this about the time you headed for safety?" she asked, her voice breathless.

The journey back to her home was filled with the sound of their laughter.

They rode to the side of the house, where the shadows loomed the darkest. He dismounted and held his hands out for her again. When her feet touched the ground, he stepped closer, reached out with his hands and framed her face. "It seems, lass, that I still owe you an adventure."

Silence, while she looked up at him and framed her question.

"Would you show me Glenlyon?" she finally asked, reaching out to touch his arm with a trembling hand. The request was rash, perhaps, but patience had been burned away by her earlier anger and her present grief. That, and a longing she should not have had, yet could not help but feel. She wanted to see his home, the land he called his. She wanted to see the place she'd dreamed of for two whole nights, and wished for even before that. She wanted, too, with a true feeling of wickedness, for him to kiss her.

"Show you?"

He slowly stepped back, dropped his hands. She missed

their presence, their warmth, the feeling his touch gave her.

"The moon is no longer full, but it's light enough to see, is it not?"

He nodded.

"And your horse is strong enough to bear the burden of another rider."

He smiled. "As well you know. Do you wish to study the color of the curtains, then?"

"No," she said, smiling. "Only to see it. Is it far?"

"An hour, no more, of fast riding."

His fingers reached out and touched her face again, brushed back her hair, tucked it behind her ear. It was a gesture of intimacy, one of gentleness. She should have been shocked at it, if not offended. But she turned her head so that her cheek cradled his palm, held herself still in that moment when she heard his indrawn breath.

"I owe you a bit of excitement, don't I, lass? For the boredom of stealing cows. You want to see my home?"

She looked up at him, defenseless in that instant of truth. "With all my heart," she said. For a few hours, to be home in Scotland. To be someone she'd not been for seven years. "If we left when the night was young, could we not return before dawn?"

"There's naught to see at night, Ealasaid."

"Then you will have to describe the scenery to me," she said. "Or I can close my eyes and envision it myself."

"We could do that now, could we not? If you close your eyes, I'll tell you about Glenlyon."

"Please take me there, Lachlan. You may sling me over your saddle if you wish, and I'll pretend to be booty from your raids."

He tapped his finger on the tip of her nose. "You'd soften a stone with such pleading, lass. I've but a warning for you: there's more hardship than beauty about my land."

"I know that well, Lachlan. I need to see it. Will you take me?"

"Yes, lass, I will. Tomorrow."

A feeling he could not identify seemed lodged in his chest. He could not help but grin broadly all the way home. For the first time since he'd known Coinneach MacAuley, he blessed the seer.

His journey was interspersed by a chuckle from time to time. It was happiness; that's what it was. He felt as if all the hardships he'd undergone in the past few years were for a reason, the better to understand the fortune of his future.

She wanted to see his home. She yearned for a sight of Glenlyon. No typical English miss, this. Even her voice was different, acquiring a richness to it. Or maybe that was simply wishful thinking. He felt like a boy again, adrift in memories of the woman he'd left behind him.

Oh, lass, if you only knew. It's more than a sight of my home I've a longing to give you. He grinned again and leaned into the wind.

Eight

Not even Harriet could spoil her mood. Nor could Jeremy, although today he seemed even more attentive than usual. The day also seemed to cooperate, not passing with that aching slowness as it was wont to, but sliding from morning to night with gratifying speed. One thought seemed to accentuate its passage. *I am going to Glenlyon. I am going to Glenlyon.*

She sat through their evening meal with patience, her mind not on the lecture being delivered by Harriet nor on the long looks from Jeremy, but on the night ahead. She wished she had something daring to wear, something to echo her heart's wish. Something red, perhaps, or startling green. Something blue, to match the sky's tint, or even yellow to act as a harbinger of day. But she'd only her serviceable browns and blacks, and a shawl of ivory that had once been Harriet's. It would have to be enough for this grand adventure.

But she could wish, could she not? Or hope that her hair would behave just this once? An impossibility, it seemed, but even that fact could not destroy her happiness.

Time ticked by on slow, ponderous feet as she waited for the household to quiet. She stood at her door, her hand pressed against the wood of it, heard the ringing of Mrs. Hanson's bell as she summoned her maidservant to her. Harriet's voice came in response to some remark from Jeremy; a murmur from a servant answered someone's question. Then the night seemed to enfold them, pressing down to silence the entire world.

Everything but the beat of her heart.

She waited an hour more, then sped from the house, her leather slippers flying across the night-shaded grass. She did not realize she had passed him until Lachlan's hand reached out and caught her arm, propelling her into his embrace so forcefully that they both landed hard against the trunk of a tree.

"It's eager you are, lass?"

His chuckle warmed her heart, banished any errant thought cautioning her that such actions were improvident and risky. Instead, she looked up at his shadowed face, felt for the edge of his smile with her fingers, and knew herself to be more welcomed here than in any place she'd been these last seven years.

"Aye, Lachlan," she teased. "I am."

"Then the night awaits, my border lass." He pulled her to where he'd tied his horse and helped her mount behind him.

Glenlyon Castle was a mammoth black shadow that guarded a series of valleys and a small loch. A torch here and there marked its boundaries, seemed to accentuate its size. Lachlan called out a greeting, and they rode through a narrow gate and into the courtyard. The sounds of fiddles and flutes colored the air, as did the laughter of those gathered there.

He reached up his hands to help Janet dismount. A faint smile played on her lips; her eyes held questions as she looked about her. The courtyard was crowded with people, and the rich smiles of his clan masked the poverty of his home. There were few things of beauty left at Glenlyon, but there was the castle itself, an old, imposing fortress that loomed gray on the horizon.

"They've been told you were coming," he explained. "And they play for your arrival."

Her face seemed to bloom at the idea of that. Her smile became one of true happiness; her cheeks turned pink. She was such a surprise, his Ealasaid. One moment daring, the next almost shy.

He bent his elbow, placed her hand on the bend of his arm, and escorted her into the Great Hall. While it was true that the castle had seen better days, there was none to say a Sinclair could not make a party when the occasion warranted it. At their entrance, the fiddles came to a stop, and a signal to the flute player called forth a trilling note that faded into the distance.

He turned to her, his words silenced by the sight of her. One candle had not done her justice. There was true red in her hair, and her eyes were the blue of Scotland's skies. Her skin was pale but enlivened by the blush that seemed to grow as he watched. She was not a tiny woman; her chin would rest upon his shoulder. Her lips were full and seemed to beckon a kiss. Would he shock or please his clan if he bestowed one upon them here and now?

Before he could question the propriety of doing so, he bent his head and kissed her. He heard the collective mutterings of his clan, the sound of approval, a masculine laugh—then nothing more as he seemed to spiral down into the kiss. He had wished for a taste of her and instead had become enchanted.

He pulled away, wondering if the ceiling tilted or if it was only him. Nor did Ealasaid seem immune to the power of that kiss. Her fingers pressed against her lips; her eyes were wide, but not shocked. Wondering, perhaps, but not horrified. He smiled, thinking that they were a pair, indeed. One of them too knowing, yet feeling acutely naïve at this moment. The other, truly innocent, but with the aplomb of a born enchantress. Hardly fair, but decidedly interesting.

Instead of introducing her, which would have caused no end of interruptions that he did not want to tolerate at this moment, he walked with her to the middle of the room, then signaled to the fiddlers to begin a reel.

She shook her head vigorously and would not take his hand.

"What is it, Ealasaid?"

"It's been forever since I danced, Lachlan, and in truth, I've no skill at it." Her voice was a husky whisper that seemed tied to his loins somehow. Had she always sounded so alluring, or had her effect upon him tripled with their kiss? If that were the case, he doubted the ride back to her home would be as uneventful as the journey here. He would have to stop at least three or four times to kiss her again.

"I doubt that, lass. You seem light on your feet. Shall we not try it?"

"Must we?" She looked around at the crowd eagerly watching the two of them, then sent a helpless look in his direction.

"I'm afraid we must," he said.

Five minutes later, he wanted to laugh but refrained from doing so in case it hurt her feelings. Ealasaid had not lied, nor had she exaggerated in order to solicit a compliment. He held her hand and showed her where to turn, the reel being danced in a lively fashion with no regard to steps. But even so, she stepped on his feet twice and stumbled upon her own on one occasion at least. With each aching moment, her flush seemed to accentuate, and her discomfort become even more unbearable.

Finally, the dance was over. He pulled her into his arms and without regard to those who crowded around them, kissed her again. It was neither to make her feel better or to take her mind from the disaster of her dancing. It was that he could not bear another few moments to pass without tasting her again. Strange, how the thought of a month had seemed too quick, and now seemed eons away.

"You cannot sing, either, can you, Ealasaid?" he asked with a smile. The words of the prophecy came back to him. *She'll be claw-footed and have a voice like a banshee, but she'll save the clan Sinclair.*

She shook her head.

He leaned his forehead against hers and smiled. "Still and all, there are other things to wish for in a woman."

Her face bloomed with color again, a fact that made his smile grow larger. It was a strange thing, but he felt like laughing at this moment, or holding her in the air and twirling with her.

He nodded to Coinneach MacAuley, who looked pleased with himself. As well he might, Lachlan thought. So far, every one of his prophecies had come true. But there were things Coinneach had never mentioned. He had never said, for example, that the Glenlyon Bride would be a lovely woman with a laugh that made Lachlan smile, that she would have a voice that was as soft as raindrops, and that her form and her walk would give him dreams.

He twirled her into another reel, uncaring that his feet were at her mercy or that she cringed each time she took a wrong step. Some things were important. Others were not.

He could always teach Ealasaid to dance, but no one could incite a woman to be charming or to lure him to her through miles of darkness. He estimated that he'd had less than three hours of sleep in each of the past few nights, yet he felt more enlivened than at any other time in his life. Why was that? The very same reason the ceiling tilted, he suspected.

Nine

Lachlan whirled her in such a tight circle that the room spun, but she didn't care. Even if she had been standing still, the world would be rocking. Her heart was beating almost too loud to hear her thoughts; her stomach rolled in glorious wonder.

He had kissed her, and that alone was shocking enough. But to do so in full view of the clan was a momentous thing. At least, she thought it was. There were so many rituals and customs of her country that she'd never learned; the last seven years felt as if they had been stolen from her. But discounting the significance of it, the kiss had been momentous enough. Her first, and with such a man as Lachlan Sinclair. But then, to say such a thing to her. Was she awake? Or was this just one of her Dover's Powder dreams? *Please don't let it be a dream. Please.*

The dance was finally and blessedly ended. Lachlan led her to the corner, deliberately faced away from the center of the room—a repudiation or a warning to others to keep clear. It seemed a strange thing to do, until he slowly walked her back against the wall, grinning at her the whole time. He might not wish to indulge in thievery, but in all other ways he was a rogue. She knew it by the sparkle in his brown eyes, by the way his lips turned up at the corner. The last thought she had for several moments was that he should not look so self-assured.

When he raised his head, she sighed, and kept her eyes closed. Surely something so wickedly fine should be outlawed. Lachlan kissed very well. Even in her innocence, she could recognize talent. A kiss from Lachlan Sinclair was almost as strong as the spirits her father had made in Tarlogie.

The man who stepped between them smelled of peat smoke. His hair was long and white, and he carried a staff nearly the equal of his height, gripped in one hand. A long cloak covered his trousers and frayed shirt, and his boots were no more than flapping pieces of leather, laced together.

His bright blue eyes stared at her; his mouth quirked beneath his beard. Janet had the oddest feeling that he was laughing at some hidden jest that had her at its center. She frowned in response, which seemed to only amuse him further.

He turned to Lachlan. "So, lad, you've softened, then."

It was a question that demanded an honest answer.

"Aye," Lachlan said, smiling.

"You'll promise, then?"

Lachlan studied the old man in the silence. The room seemed to have stilled, as if waiting for something. He knew only too well what the clan anticipated: his acceptance of a marriage, but not just an English union. That would take place in its time. They wanted to see a Scots wedding, one here and now, amidst the music and the laughter.

He looked down at Ealasaid. There were many sacrifices he'd make for his clan, but he was truly blessed in the knowledge that this was not one of them. She was his own true love.

He smiled broadly. "You're a schemer, old man, but I'll concede to you this victory."

"It is not mine, lad," Coinneach said. "It's ordained by Fate."

Lachlan stepped aside, reached for Janet's hand and held it solemnly between the two of his. He smiled down into her eyes. "I'll be yours, lass, if you'll have me. This I promise."

Janet stared up at him, bemused, then over at the old man who seemed as happy as a proud father at this occasion. She nodded, and the room erupted in cheering and laughter.

One moment, she was standing there holding Lachlan's hand; the next, she was being pushed from person to person, her cheeks being kissed heartily. Once she was pinched; another time, enfolded in the arms of an old woman who was nearly toothless. She was like a leaf in a stream, incapable of doing more than being carried along. Words that she caught only pieces of seemed to float above her. *A bheil thu toilichte*—something about happiness. *Mi sgith.* Tired? It had been years since she'd spoken Gaelic. She was rusty with it, remembering only a few phrases, but she thought she could understand that much.

As quickly as they had entered the hall, they were out of it again. Instead of mounting Lachlan's tired horse, they slipped into the courtyard and down a path, barely illuminated by the torch mounted on the wall above them.

"Lachlan?" She stopped in the middle of the path and waited until he turned. "Where are we going?"

"Someplace where we can be alone, lass."

"You're going to kiss me again, aren't you?"

"Well, I've thought of it. Have you any objections?"

She turned away, frowned down into the darkness.

"What is it, lass?" He returned to her. His finger traced a path from shoulder to bared elbow. She pulled her shawl down to cover her skin. He was so close that she could feel him breathe, his dark shirt moving against her back, his breath warm upon her neck. "I can't think when you kiss me, you know," she said softly, the words a confession. One that pleased him, if his soft chuckle was any indication.

"It would be a pity if you could. It would mean I wasn't doing it right."

"I think you do it very well indeed, Lachlan." Her voice sounded cross.

His laughter should not have been so charming. He turned her in his arms.

She stared up into his face, darkened by shadows, lit by the faint sliver of moon. "Did you ask me to marry you, Lachlan?"

"Not exactly, lass."

"Oh."

"You sound disappointed. Are you?" He bent down and kissed the spot in front of her ear. It made her skin shiver. She leaned into him.

"I've only known you for ten hours, Lachlan," she mumbled.

"You've counted it, have you?"

She nodded.

"Too soon for declarations and kisses, is that it, Ealasaid?"

Again she nodded.

"Have you always been so proper, lass? So English?" The question preceded another kiss. This one was even more potent than the ones they'd shared in the Great Hall. The top of her head felt as if it was lifting. She could almost see steam behind her eyelids. It drifted up toward the stars, taking all her bones with it. She blinked, slumped against Lachlan, and blinked again.

The oddest sound penetrated the cloud that enveloped her. Plaintive and stirring, it seemed as if the earth itself had been given voice. She tilted her head and listened. It was a rough growl of unearthly beauty, raw and oddly sweet.

" 'Tis the pipes, Ealasaid."

She'd never heard the sound of bagpipes—they had been outlawed since before she was born—but sometimes she thought she might be able to imagine them, so pure and so true that the ache of them could be felt to her bones.

"Are they not forbidden?"

She felt, rather than saw, the shrug of his shoulders. "That's an English law, and an old one. Who is to know what we do here?"

"What are they playing?"

"The Sinclairs' lament. Would you like to know the words?"

She nodded.

"Here is my heart a-calling, now when the night is falling; all the proud Sinclairs greet you here in this glen. Home is the smile to meet you; home is this land to hold you; home is Glenlyon and the spirit of her men." His hands pressed against her back, bringing her closer to him. "It's a catchy tune, lass, but there are some who say it's played a bit much. Still and all, it's our pipes, and we've a right to them."

She was struck by a sense of loss so profound that it nearly defeated her. She reached up, blindly, and curved her hand around his neck. She laid her forehead against his chest; her other hand rested upon his shoulder. She would never be here again. And circumstance would send her far from Glenlyon, far from the border, perhaps even to London.

But she had tonight. It would have to be enough.

Ten

His fingers threaded through the hair at her temples; his palms flattened on her cheeks. He bent until only an inch separated their lips. Her flesh beneath his hands seemed to warm as he waited, patient. Her breath caught, such a small sound to mark the moment. It was one of complicity more than surrender.

How long had he wanted her? Since he'd first seen her, or even before that? From the beginning of his life? It seemed that long.

"Ealasaid," he murmured against her lips. Their kiss was a welcoming, to more than passion. To belonging. To love.

He pulled back, finally, and laid his forehead against hers. Her breathing was fast, her hands gripped his arms tightly, and her cheek was hot where he touched it with gentle fingers. Anticipation was part of loving, and he wanted her to feel every measure of the pleasure and pain of it.

As he did. His blood was as heated, his breath as harsh, and his flesh was hard and straining against his trousers.

He pulled away and knelt before her, his hands reaching for her shoes.

"Lachlan?" The question was there in her voice, but she didn't step back.

He placed his hand on the back of her ankle. A soft tug, and she raised her foot. He quickly removed her shoe.

"You've lovely feet, Ealasaid."

"Thank you," she said.

So polite, his Ealasaid. Would she thank him, later, in her proper English voice? He grinned. If he did it right, she would.

Another movement, and the other shoe was removed. He burrowed beneath her skirt, trailed his hands up one leg to the top of her stockings. He looked up at her. She was staring down at him, but she did not step away. A slight tremor raced under her skin, as if she were awakening to his touch one slow inch at a time.

"I've wanted my hands on you since the night I first saw you, Ealasaid." His hands met at her knee. He was prevented from touching her skin by the coarse weave of her stockings. Why didn't she wear silk and fine ribbons? And why were her clothes of less fine quality than those of a rich English miss? This observation amused him, since the only real concern he had for clothing right at this moment was to remove hers as soon as possible. Other questions would be asked and answered at a later time.

He began rolling the hem of her skirt up slowly. He was a man with a notion of seduction on his mind. And she seemed in tune with it, her arms fallen to her sides, her gaze not moving from his hands. He reached up and gently folded her hand around the edge of her skirt. Complicity was so much more heady than dominance. He wanted her to be his partner in this act.

Once her legs were visible, he trailed his fingers to the top of one stocking and hooked his thumb inside it, feeling her skin for the first time. Soft and warm. A sound like a growl emerged from between his lips, some male noise that was both appreciation and warning to her if she but knew it. He rolled the stocking down her leg, taking his time with it.

When her leg was bared, he bent forward and kissed her naked knee. Her hand fluttered out—whether in protest or from sensation, he didn't know. But her only words were a soft gasp of sound, a tiny whimper.

"Ealasaid," he said, tracing her name in a soft kiss against her skin.

He reached for her other stocking and rolled it down. Instead of kissing her, he reared back and looked at her. One of her hands was on her mouth, knuckles pressed against her full lips. The other was clasped to her waist, holding her skirt from falling.

"You look just as you did the night I first saw you, wading in the burn and pretending to be a brownie," he said, the sound of his voice harsher than he intended. She had no comment for that, but then, he didn't expect one.

He bent forward and kissed the knee recently bared, trailed his fingers up the back of her leg from ankle to knee. She trembled beneath his touch.

"Your skin is almost hot, as if a fever burns you."

They were well matched in that. He was consumed in fire, hiding it only by the greatest of wills. Had he not, he would be inside her now, with her legs wrapped around him, easing this damnable ache of too many days' duration. But she was innocent and she was his, and he would have her pleasured and sighing in his arms by daybreak.

By such vows were Sinclairs known.

His hands made the slow progression from her knees to her thighs, burrowing under fabric, pushing it aside. His fingers skimmed over the smoothness of her skin, sweeping over curves and then repeating the gesture in appreciation for her sweetly rounded flesh. Again, a small gasp from her. It seemed to measure both her innocence and his daring.

His hands slid beneath fabric, traced even farther upward

until they reached her hips. His thumbs met and brushed against the curls at the juncture of her thighs. Not intrusive, only teasing.

He looked up. Her eyes were closed.

"You feel warm here, too, Ealasaid," he said softly.

Her knees trembled. Her fist pressed tight against her lips as if to restrain a sound.

He reached up and pulled her down to him, and she sank like a feather into his arms. Kissing her was like falling into a void where the only constants were her hands gripping him and the surge of blood in his veins. His body thrummed, shouting messages of *hurry!* and *now!* His mind seemed to have similarly lost its sanity and sided with his flesh. Both feverishly urged him to ease himself into her.

Patience, Lachlan.

He laid her down on the grass of Glenlyon, bent over her and unlaced her dress.

"I'm of a mind to make you mine this moment, Ealasaid," he said, his voice having lost its teasing edge. "Tell me you're not afraid." *Please.*

She only shook her head from side to side. Her hands were clenched in the material of her skirt, and he gently pried it from her grip. His fingers fumbled with her clothing, his experience forgotten, his haste and hunger only too apparent in the trembling of his fingers and his rapid breath.

Somehow in the last few minutes, even silent, even still, she'd transformed him into a ravening beast. When his hands found her breasts and cupped around them, he uttered a gusty, relieved sigh. Appeasement was close.

He pushed her dress up until it was wadded around her torso. Half in desperation, half with humor, he swore venomously. He was rescued by Ealasaid sitting up and sliding the material over her head.

Another moment, and she did the same with her undergarments. She was finally, gloriously, naked.

In another minute, so was he.

A proper woman would have stayed his hands, or moved away, or told him no when he announced his intent. But she had lost those careful markers that showed the way to a circumspect life. Censure simply did not matter. Pride was buried beneath future loneliness. Consequences did not hold as much power as curiosity. She was desperately lonely, an expatriate offered a night of freedom with those of her kind. To hear the Gaelic and the pipes, to be a Scottish lass for these moments, seemed a blessed gift. She wanted all that was hers to want, all those things she'd been told to put aside, emotions too volatile for polite company, passions too strong for her position. She wanted, for a few hours, to be the woman she could have been, had not circumstance altered her life.

And most of all, she wanted him.

She wished she could have been perfumed in roses for him, with her hair brushed until it shined, and her gown one of silk. But she would not have changed the hour or the time or the setting of this joining. Let it be here, at Glenlyon, with the sound of the pipes a soft and wistful backdrop. She would remember it always.

His hands cupped her breasts; his finger traced from a full curve to the length of her nipple, measuring it. Her back arched in surprise at the touch of his lips there, and her body seemed to heat even further.

A low keening sigh slipped from her as he suckled her. Her hands reached up to bracket his head, fingers spearing into the thickness of his hair. With suddenly demanding hands, she brought his mouth to hers, instantly changing his soft chuckle to a guttural moan.

No woman had ever embraced her ruination with such hunger.

His teeth grazed the underside of her breast, and his fingers smoothed over her belly. She made a sound, a pairing of groan and entreaty, and gripped his arms with trembling hands.

Her body felt as if it was weeping. She ached in places rarely felt, and she needed something she'd only dreamed about in the last few days. Him. Lachlan.

His fingers stroked her intimately, urging her to whimper in his arms. When she did, he bent down and whispered into her ear, some harsh and lovely words in Gaelic. The sound of it was right for this place, for this moment, beneath the skies with only the earth and the stars as witness.

He was heavy against her, his flesh hard and hot and insistent. She widened her legs in wordless invitation. He accepted it instantly, lowered himself over her, and entered her with a sudden, sharp thrust.

Her soft moan of pain stopped him. He braced his hands on either side of her arms and lowered his head, his breath coming in great, shuddering gasps.

"There's a time and a place to be grateful for your innocence, Ealasaid, but I cannot tell you that now is one of them."

It was an odd time to feel a spike of humor.

She surged up beneath him, clamping her hands upon his hips and driving him into her. His low and fevered curse accompanied the pain of his full entry. She ached with it, but it was not unbearable, even with him settled in her, hard as iron and almost as heavy.

"My innocence is no longer an encumbrance," she murmured, trying to hide her smile. But he began to kiss her then, only to rear back and look at her. In the dark, his expression was hidden. Was he angry?

"It could be that we've wasted a few days," he said, his voice amused.

"And precious moments now," she said, her fingers trailing over his arms.

He surged more fully within her. His fingers clamped on

either side of her head, kept her steady for his kiss. Amusement abruptly faded beneath the hunger again. He gripped her hands and entwined their fingers, their elbows grinding into the grass.

"Come with me, my Ealasaid, because I cannot wait." He began thrusting into her, a long, slow, measured invasion that counted off a cadence as old as time.

Her gaze was on his face, even though he was draped in shadow. She knew he watched her, as well.

Each time he thrust against her, an answering spark seemed to glow. Flickers of sensation began to mask the ache and grow within it, rendering it unimportant. A small wildfire began to race along her spine; a cord within her was lit, and the flames traveled up and over and through her. They were colored orange and red and blue and a fiery orchid, and all the hues and tints she could imagine.

She closed her eyes, helpless in the face of it. Lachlan leaned forward, kissed her, and whispered words into her ear. *Tha gaol agam ort.* She knew the words well, had heard them from her parents often: *I love you.* His skin was slick with sweat, and his hands clamped on her hips as he drove deep.

She cried out, and he swallowed her cry, his kiss urging her on to touch all the colors of this magical rainbow, to become part of him as he was even now part of her.

He took her, this reiver, to a place she'd never been before, one in which there was no silence and no loneliness, only weeping joy and a belonging of the flesh and mind and heart.

When it was over, and after the night had reluctantly given way to the first creeping rays of dawn, she held him in her arms and loved him again, feeling neither shyness nor regret for her actions.

He was, after all, her beloved.

Eleven

He dismounted before he reached the house, then reached up and scooped her into his arms.

"You're tired, lass," he said gently, smiling down into her sleepy face. She'd nodded off during their trip home. He'd wanted to keep her at Glenlyon but had not wanted to cause dissention in his new family by doing so. Her parents would not understand, being English, that her Scots wedding was as legal as any obtained in England. Perhaps he could talk with her father and see if their wedding could be advanced. He disliked the idea of leaving her. Too, he realized that he didn't particularly want to wait many more days until they were wed in the English fashion.

He could imagine Coinneach's response to that admission.

She wound her arms around his neck and nuzzled her face into his neck. She murmured something, the feel of her lips against his skin too enticing. He had a long ride ahead of him, and she needed to be in her bed before the sun crept any higher in the sky.

"Lass," he said. " 'Tis true I've worn you out, but you'll

have to wake up now." His grin was quick as she mumbled something but made no move to open her eyes.

He set her on her feet and steadied her. For a long moment, she leaned against him. Then she sighed and stood upright, weaving only slightly.

"I should feel like a sinner, Lachlan. If nothing else, wicked. But I don't. Isn't that daft of me?"

He smiled. "We did nothing wrong," he said, his hands rubbing from her shoulders to her wrists. She tilted her head back and closed her eyes. This moment of parting was becoming more and more difficult. "We've done nothing the kirk would punish us for." He leaned down and brushed a kiss against her forehead. "I can't properly call you lass from now on, can I? But I've grown accustomed to calling you Ealasaid. Do you mind it to your first name? It's an ugly one, I'm thinking, and it bears no resemblance to you."

"Janet is not such a terrible name," she said and leaned against him, half asleep still.

"Janet?" He pulled back and looked into her face. Her eyes opened reluctantly. "Have you a bevy of names, then? I'm talking about Harriet; I've no liking for that one. You've not the look of a Harriet, you know."

She opened her eyes wider and shook her head slowly. "My name isn't Harriet."

He speared his hand through his hair, with the oddest feeling that he had not heard her words correctly. Or perhaps he was still asleep on the grass of Glenlyon, sated and pleased and more hopeful for his future than he'd been in a long time.

"My name isn't Harriet," she repeated. Her voice was soft, but he heard the words right enough.

He shook his head. "Aye, it is. Squire Hanson's daughter. My English bride."

It was as if the words he'd spoken had been carried on tiny bullets that embedded themselves in her heart. His English bride. Which meant, of course, that he could only be one person. Not simply a Scots reiver. Not a man from Glenlyon, but their laird.

She could see his face in the dawn light. His eyes seemed to scream at her.

"I am not Harriet," she whispered. She took one small step back from him. The distance might have been measured in miles for all the endless time it took. "My name is Janet."

She took one more step back from him. Then another.

"And you're the laird of the Sinclairs, aren't you?" Her voice trembled.

He nodded. Once. A short, sharp nod. "Didn't you know it, lass? That was my clan about me all night. They greeted you well enough as my future wife."

She shook her head over and over. But negating it didn't make this moment go away or wipe out the past few days. She'd fallen in love with him, with his smile and his laughter and his rueful admission of disliking reiving. He had loved her, and she'd held him when he'd shuddered against her, and he'd kissed her when she'd moaned. And now he stood looking at her as if she was a ghost.

"I'm not Harriet," she said once more.

"Then who are you?" The words sounded no louder than a whisper for all their harshness. Did he find this moment to be as odd and strange? As if nothing were right about it, as if it was a dream induced by too many comfits or too many spirits.

"I am Harriet's companion," she said dully. "I read to her when she's bored and straighten her threads and massage her forehead. That's all. I do not offer peace on the border nor a dowry for you."

Silence lay between them, a valley in which nothing grew. Not explanations nor apologies or regrets. What she thought was incapable of being translated into speech, and whatever he felt was trapped behind his silence.

The dawn sky lightened. The odd stillness between them was marred by the sound of a bird calling from a nearby tree. An alarm of nature. "You'd better go inside, then, before you're discovered."

She only nodded.

There were too many words they might say, and none they could. She lowered her gaze, turned, and walked away.

He told himself to stop watching her, to turn away as easily as she did. Both warnings were ignored as he stared after her. The hope that had so joyfully come to him the moment he'd met her and had only grown in her presence was gone. All his belief in the future was gone, too.

How many hours had it been? She'd tallied them so carefully. Ten hours—and then one magical night. That's all it had taken.

Twelve

"*Who is he, Janet?*"

The voice came from the yellow parlor. She stopped and turned her head. Jeremy stood facing her.

She looked at the chair that had been moved to the window. So, he had seen. *He is your sister's future husband. And my love.* Words she would never say. Should she not have felt more shame? Instead, she felt empty inside, as if part of her was missing. The most vital organ. A heart? Or perhaps only that place where such things mattered. It was not important if Jeremy labeled her a whore at this moment.

"You've been watching me all along, haven't you?" From the look on his face it was evident he had not expected the question. How unfair of her. But it made perfect sense. How else had she escaped detection? He had always been kind. Too solicitous, perhaps, even to abetting her wickedness. How had he turned Harriet's attention from her? By listening to his sister's complaints? By playing whist during those hours when Harriet would have checked on her?

"If you slip upstairs now, no one will know."

She stared at him. He was two years older than she, but she'd always thought of him as younger. A man barely out of youth, but there was something about him as he stood in the dawn light, something that had matured in the hours since she'd seen him last. Or perhaps it was only because she'd changed so drastically herself.

"Why not sound the alarm, Jeremy? Tell Harriet what you know."

"Would it make you feel better to be punished, Janet?" His voice was too kind, and she blinked back the tears that came too easily to her eyes.

"I suppose not," she said. "Thank you, Jeremy."

He followed her to the stairs, stood at their base, and looked up at her as she mounted them. It seemed as ponderous as scaling the highest mountain. When she stopped and looked back, he returned her look. His face was somber.

"If I can do anything for you, Janet, I will."

"Thank you, Jeremy."

"Will you let me know if I can aid you?"

"Yes, Jeremy, I will."

He was talking of scandal, of course. If anyone would discover her actions this night, or if she was with child, she'd be sent away in disgrace.

She opened the door to her room softly, closed it behind her, and sat on the edge of the bed, her arms wrapped around her waist. She rocked back and forth on the bed, the motion oddly soothing.

He was to be Harriet's husband.

She knew she would die of this.

"You'd be wise to stay away from me, old man." Lachlan glared at Coinneach, then turned away and handed the newly repaired pipe to James, who screwed it in place. Lachlan had been working feverishly since he'd returned to Glenlyon, but the occupations of his hands had done nothing to quiet his mind. "Or if you must be a prophet, tell me if this thing will ever work right."

Silence met his anger. Just as well, for he wasn't in the mood for a discussion. He was more likely to strangle the seer. Damn the Legend. Damn the penurious state of his clan.

He turned and faced Coinneach. The old man was smiling, if the twitch of his beard was any indication. He'd long thought the old man kept his facial hair in order to look more like a wizard. All he needed was a pointed hat to appear the part. That, and a genuine ability to see into the future.

"It doesn't matter, you know. You and your damn Legend. We'll find a way to survive without it."

The old man kept smiling.

"You never did believe in it. But your people do." Was there censure in Coinneach's eyes? Lachlan turned away again and bent to retrieve another piece of pipe.

"I'll talk them out of it. They'll never feel the lack."

"Aye, but you will."

"Don't be getting cryptic on me now, old man."

"Why are you here, and your wife in England? Ask yourself that, Lachlan. It is your own foolishness that makes you miserable and will continue to do so. Not any of my doings."

Lachlan narrowed his eyes and wondered exactly how old Coinneach was. Too old to fight, certainly. Too old to imprison in the castle cellar.

But the old man's words were true. He'd watched her walk away and had done nothing. Instead, he'd felt rooted to the spot, relegated to a private hell of his own making. He'd felt suddenly and oddly angry—at her, for not being who she was supposed to be; at himself, for endangering his clan. Or had he simply failed Janet? That thought had kept him awake during the long morning, and had made his perusal of his home one of stark and terrifying honesty.

The east wall needed to be shored up. The dark brick was shining white where the mortar crumbled. Glenlyon's better furnishings had long since been sacrificed to a greater cause—that of the '45—or simply survival since then. Their cattle were scrawny things; even their chickens had a gaunt look. Their only hope for prosperity had been for their laird to wed it, and he'd failed at that, hadn't he?

Because he'd gone and fallen in love with the wrong woman.

The prophecy didn't matter. He'd made his choice and made it for all the best reasons. She'd charmed and enchanted him and made him laugh. He wanted to know what she thought and the dreams she had. He wanted to touch her again, lie with her in a bed and spend hours loving her.

What power did a Legend have when measured against this feeling?

He threw the pipe down and strode from the cavern. To blazes with the Legend; he was going to get Janet.

The second explosion, however, delayed his plans.

She didn't bother to answer the knock on the door, merely curled up in the middle of the bed and kept her eyes closed.

"Janet?"

"Yes, Harriet." She wished there was a lock on the door. The very last person in the world she wished to see now was Harriet. Especially since Harriet had a way of discerning misery quickly and would easily see that she'd been crying. She'd made no sound, really; the tears had simply leaked from her eyes. A broken heart had not required any effort on her part.

There were some mornings when she'd stood at her window, watched the sun light the earth, turned north toward Scotland, and ached with longing. She would never be able to look homeward again, would never be able to bear the loss. Lachlan. Of course he was laird. She should have realized it. His speech marked his origin; the twinkle in his eyes, his daring. He had humor and wisdom, the body of a warrior and the face of an angel.

When she was a little girl, she'd dreamed of being so many things. She'd wanted first to be a princess, then to be a mother, then to work with her father in the distillery. When she was older, she'd wanted to fall in love, had imagined that she'd felt that way once or twice. When she was twelve, it had been Cameron Drummond. A year later, his brother Gordon. But none of the longing looks the two boys had exchanged with her had prepared her for this moment, or for Lachlan Sinclair.

Harriet's husband.

She clenched her eyes shut.

"Are you sickening again?" Harriet spoke from beside the bed, but she still did not open her eyes.

"I believe so, Harriet." *Please, go away and leave me alone.* It was a prayer said in the depths of her mind, but it had no effect on Harriet. She only drew closer.

"Have you slept in your clothes, then, Janet? How slovenly of you."

"Yes, Harriet." Perhaps agreeing with her would speed her from the room. But it was not to be.

"Or do you hide a greater sin, Janet?" A hand reached down and flicked at her skirt. "You're nothing but a whore, aren't you, Janet?" The words were said in such a pleasant tone that their meaning did not make sense at first. "All this time? Have you been a whore all this time?" The coldness of her contempt sliced through skin and nudged against bone. The horrible fact was that she had no defense for such words, nothing that would mitigate Harriet's scorn. There was, after all, nothing to say. She was guilty of all that Harriet thought. Worse, yet, she had sinned with the man soon to be Harriet's husband. She had ruined herself. A glorious night, true, but the voice of her long-dead mother echoed in her ear, all caution and propriety. Had it been her Scots nature after all? Or unbridled curiosity, or simple recklessness?

"Leave her alone, Harriet."

The sound of Jeremy's voice was an odd comfort. It was

surprisingly firm, even angry. Janet opened her eyes and sat up. Her gaze turned to Jeremy, who stood in the open doorway, sentinel against his sister's condemnation.

"It's all right, Jeremy." She swung her legs over the side of the bed and brushed her hair back from her cheek.

She had no time for mourning. Instead, she must be about the business of putting her future together. For the first time since Harriet had delivered the news to her, she was grateful she was not going to Scotland. It would be unbearable to see Lachlan day in and day out, all the while knowing that he belonged to someone else.

This moment, however, must be gotten through. Somehow.

Harriet looked from one to the other, like a terrier scenting a wounded rat. "What goes on here, brother?"

"Janet was with me, Harriet; more than that, you need not know."

At another time, perhaps, the look on Harriet's face might have been amusing. But not at this moment. Janet only wished herself far away from this place, from echoes of Lachlan, from the sight of his intended bride.

She stood and walked past Harriet until she came to Jeremy's side. She rose on tiptoe to brush a kiss against his cheek.

"Thank you," she murmured, "for your kindness. But it doesn't matter now."

"It does to me," he said, his eyes not veering from hers. "You need someone to protect you."

"What she needs, Jeremy, is to be banished from this house like the whore she is."

"No," Jeremy said, moving to stand between his sister and Janet. He looked at his sister, and his expression was cold. "You do not understand, Harriet." He turned to Janet and smiled. "I've asked Janet to be my wife, and she has agreed."

Thirteen

"What do you mean, she's not here?" Lachlan said.
"And where might she be?"

The man who answered the door was young and dressed in a uniform that evidently made him feel important. Perhaps that was the reason he looked down his nose at Lachlan. Or maybe it had something to do with the fact that Lachlan had a bit of the barley odor about him again. And a few scorch marks, too. The explosion had been all stuff and fury, yet the effluence from it had been as cloying as before. But rather than taking the time for a dip in the loch, he'd mounted a fresh horse and set out on his way to Janet.

Of all the miles he'd ridden, of all the times he'd come to England, all the border raids and nights he'd come to Janet, he dreaded this journey the most. It had nothing to do with the fact that he was tired, infused with a bone-deep weariness. It was that he felt like a blathering idiot. The minute she'd told him who she was, he should have swept Janet up in his arms and run with her for the border. But he had not, and that stupidity was going to cost him a bit of explanation. He had already thought of the words he might use, decided that it was time his pride bent a little. He'd thought that she might not make it easy on him, or might not understand that he'd only been flummoxed by her identity and the sudden thought that he would not be able to protect his clan. He'd imagined all manner of ways he might coax her to forgive him, but he'd never thought she might not be here.

The servant backed away, preparatory to shutting the door in his face, Lachlan was sure. Instead, the young man found himself being hauled up by the collar, his feet dangling a few inches from the ground. It was not so much the sudden blanched color of his face that pleased Lachlan, but the quick spark of absolute terror in eyes that had just a minute ago been filled with contempt.

Lachlan grinned broadly, showing all of his bright white teeth. "I know that your memory serves you better, now, doesn't it, lad? Now would you like to tell me where she's gone?"

The man sputtered, but a voice behind him spoke up readily enough.

"She left—that's all you need to know."

He turned his head. A woman stood there, dressed in blue, her hair braided and arranged at the top of her head like a crown. Not one tendril was out of place. Her hands were folded at her waist, and she watched him without expression as she lowered the footman to the ground. She dismissed the servant with a hand gesture.

Lachlan had seen pretty women all his life. This one was attractive, he supposed, but he thought first that she was too controlled. Not one emotion could be read in her soft blue eyes. Her smile was only a thin slash of full lips. He wondered if she disliked her prettiness, if she saw it as a curse where other women might have seen it as a blessing.

"She's left," she said again. "Isn't that enough?" Her voice was high-pitched and sounded as if she spoke through her nose. It grated on him.

"Where is she?"

She smiled again. He had no doubt who she was, any more than he doubted his very great good fortune at having avoided a union with her. Harriet. The name seemed to fit her.

"Where did she go? I've a thought you know perfectly well."

"She eloped. With my brother. Who is shortly to be disinherited. If you find them, you might tell him that. And tell him that I've sent word to my father as to his actions. She may change her mind about marrying a pauper."

His laughter seemed to surprise her, but no more than his parting words. "It's too late for that. She's already married to me."

Even as Janet left the house where she'd spent the last seven years of her life, she knew she was making a mistake.

What she had done the night before had not felt wrong, however the world might see it. Because of it, she could not quite see herself as ruined. Nor could she negate her feelings for Lachlan by entering into a marriage with another man, however much it might provide a future for her.

True, her prospects looked dim. She could never return to Harriet's employ, and she had few talents. Her schooling had been sporadic; her greatest skill had been that learned at her father's knee. She could, she supposed, get a job as a shop girl or a tavern maid. But where would she live, and how until she earned her first coins? No, not just dim. The future looked bleak.

"I cannot do it, you know." She looked across the carriage at Jeremy. He turned from his survey of the countryside and looked directly at her. "I'd ruin your life pining for another man."

"I'd thought to get halfway to Scotland before you'd object." His smile was rueful. "I'd even thought to get the marriage ceremony out of the way before you came to your senses."

When he leaned forward and clasped one of her gloved hands in his, she was even more bemused. "I'm a good sort, Janet. I would be a good husband to you."

She nodded.

"But it's not enough, is it?"

She shook her head. "No, Jeremy."

"Well, I had a stroke of luck. You were so miserable, you would have agreed to anything."

She nodded. She could feel the tears well up again. "You mustn't be nice, Jeremy. I'll drown us both if you are."

He dropped her hand and leaned back against the upholstery. "What shall you do, then, Janet? How will you live?"

"I don't know," she said, sighing. "Have you any friends who might need companions?"

"Your future would be solved if you would marry me. Are you very sure you won't?"

"I'm very sure. But I thank you very much for the offer, Jeremy."

"It was my first, you know. Perhaps I shall become adept at it, become quite a man-about-town, flitting from lady to lady, asking from each her hand."

"Someone wonderful will no doubt accept," she said, smiling wanly at him.

"Someone wonderful already has." His smile was soft and tender. "Unfortunately, her feelings are already engaged. Who is he, this idiotic man who hasn't the slightest idea of what he's missed?"

"Does it matter?"

"Do you think I'll challenge him?"

"You mustn't." Her feeling of horror was genuine.

"Thank you for that," Jeremy said, smiling. "I'll think myself a protector of a lady's honor, then. If not her husband."

"I do thank you, Jeremy. It was very sweet."

"Ladies, I have found, Janet, do not like *sweet*. They prefer dashing or exciting, but certainly not sweet."

At that moment, a shot rang out. The carriage lurched as the horses reared and then raced forward a few feet before they abruptly stopped. Janet was thrown forward and braced herself on the opposite seat.

A few shouts were heard, and then the carriage door opened. Lachlan, looking tired and dirty and extraordinarily surly, greeted her with a scowl.

"I hate to disturb you, Janet, but there's something that belongs to me in this carriage." She'd never heard his accent so thick, the deep rumble of his voice carrying not only the flavor of Scotland but the hint of danger.

"Another cow, Lachlan?"

If she hadn't been watching him so closely, she would have missed that twitch of his lips that measured his amusement. As it was, it was gone just as quickly.

"No, Janet," he said, and this time his voice was softer, overlaid with a hint of something she'd never heard from him. Tenderness?

He looked over at Jeremy and spent a scant moment seeming to take his measure. "She's my wife, lad. I'm sorry, but she's already taken."

"You said you'd not asked me to marry you, Lachlan."

"Silly woman, of course I hadn't. I had already wed you by that time." He reached in and pulled her easily to the ground. She sent one last look in the direction of the carriage. Jeremy leaned out the door.

"Is he the one, Janet?"

She nodded.

"He doesn't look at all sweet," Jeremy said, before pulling the door shut.

"Did the lad just insult me?" Lachlan scowled at the closed door.

She ignored his question. "What do you mean, we're married?"

She'd spent the last few hours grieving for him. That she could have been spared the misery with a few words from him made her wonder what she wished to do first—hit him or kiss him. When he swung up into the saddle and pulled her up to sit in front of him, she decided that it might be foolish to argue with a man so obviously determined. Therefore, she settled on kissing him. Long moments later, when she surfaced, he smiled down at her.

"You'll need to know a little about my country, lass. There's many a way to get married there. I made a promise to you, and then you lay with me. It's one of the time-honored traditions. But you'll learn to be a Scot in time."

"I am a Scot, Lachlan, although it's been many years since I've lived in Scotland. My name, which you've never bothered to ask, is MacPherson."

He stopped his horse and looked down into her face. His smile, when it came, was broad. "Truly, Janet? Well, that's a relief. Almost as much as not having to apologize. I'll not do it after I found you eloping with another man."

He leaned down and kissed her once more.

A few minutes later, she spoke again. "You didn't mean it."

"What?"

"You didn't mean it. You would never have married me if you hadn't thought I was Harriet."

He turned his horse and trotted back in the direction of the carriage. He didn't need another shot to stop the driver; the beleaguered man only turned and looked behind him, then held up both hands as if in surrender.

Lachlan dismounted and rapped on the carriage door.

Jeremy opened it and looked out at the sight of Janet still mounted and an irritated Scot standing before him.

"I've a favor to ask, Englishman."

Jeremy's eyebrows wagged upwards.

"All you have to do is witness this." Lachlan turned to Janet and gripped her hand tightly. "I'll have you for my wife, Janet. Will you have me for your husband?"

She blinked at him, bemused. There was a shadow of beard on his face, and he looked irritated and tired. There were several strange stains on his shirt and trousers, and he smelled like malted barely. But his eyes seemed to sparkle, and his grin was daring.

"Are you sure, Lachlan?"

"With all my heart, Janet. I'll welcome you to my heart and home as if you were the Bride of the Legend."

"What Legend?"

He frowned. "A bit of nonsense that has no place here and now. Are you not going to answer me, then?"

"Yes, Lachlan, I'll have you for my husband."

He turned to Jeremy. "Did you hear all that?"

"Indeed."

"Then, Janet, we're wed again. Is that enough for you?"

He only laughed when she punched him on the arm.

Fourteen

He had plans, wonderful plans that would somehow come to pass. He couldn't help but think that things had a way of working out, if you put your nose to the ground and kept believing in it.

His clan didn't have to know that Janet wasn't exactly the Glenlyon Bride. The fact that he'd been spared Harriet's presence in his life could be construed as a deep and heart-felt blessing. He wondered if she limped and added it to the list of questions he would ask Janet when she awoke.

He looked down at her. She'd collapsed against him again, her cheek resting against his shoulder. It was the very first time he'd seen her in the sunlight. Her hair was the auburn of a good Scots lass. He wished she was awake so that he could see her eyes, but he didn't jostle her. Perhaps now they'd be able to get a good night's sleep from time to time, since there was no need to stay awake at all hours of the night. But then, there were advantages to knowing that he could go for two or three nights without sleep. He grinned.

He had returned from a border raid with a true prize this time.

The sight of Glenlyon ahead filled him with pride and that ever-present feeling of homecoming. Mixed with it was the burden of its responsibility. Somehow, he'd find a way to keep the clan intact and his world together. Those who wanted could emigrate, but he'd provide a living for those who wanted to stay in their ancestral home.

"The beastie's going to blow again!" called a nearby voice.

Lachlan only sighed at the sound of another failure. As a greeting, it could have been better timed.

Janet roused, coming awake as easily as he did whenever he had a chance to sleep. She rubbed her eyes with the fingers of one hand and gripped his shirt with the other.

The cavern was being emptied of men as they raced for cover.

"What's the matter, Lachlan?"

They dismounted, and he pushed her back among the standing men. "It's a wee problem, Janet. Stay here where you'll be safer."

He walked into the cavern, expecting to see yet another oozing mess. Instead, the fire beneath the copper kettle was blazing brightly. But the hissing and bubbling that was coming from all the pipes did not augur well for the next few moments.

"The wort can't pass into the wash container, Lachlan."

He turned, and Janet was there at his side. But before he could ask her what she meant, she passed him, going unerringly to a series of pipes and curling vents. She turned one handle left and another right, and a pale-brown liquid flowed uneventfully into the huge copper kettle.

She turned and looked at the first of the men who peered cautiously into the cavern. "Is the yeast in the kettle?"

He nodded and came closer.

She looked over at Lachlan. "Sometimes the wort is too thick to flow freely, but when that happens, you have to dilute it with water. If you don't, you have a blockage, and the fermentation begins in the pipes instead of the kettle."

"Then it blows."

She nodded.

"And how would you know such things, Janet?"

She tapped the side of a smaller copper kettle gently, much like a proud mother would pat the cheek of a healthy babe. "You're wasting these mash tun solids. They're perfect for cattle feed."

Lachlan could only stare at her. It was as if she was speaking some odd language, and he could understand only every third word.

"Where's your germinating floor, Lachlan?" He turned to James, who looked at another of the men. He led her to the far side of the cavern where the barley had been spread out. "It's too damp here," she announced, and before Lachlan could blink, half a dozen or more men were moving the grain to another, sunnier, area.

"How do you know of such things?" he asked again.

She smiled over at him. "I learned from my father. I helped him from the time I was old enough to walk." She looked around her, the expression on her face one of deep pleasure. "Isn't it odd, Lachlan? I have forgotten most of my Gaelic, and my speech is too English, but I'll never forget a pot still and good malted whiskey. A legacy from Ronald MacPherson."

"Of Tarlogie?" James came forward, his face wreathed in a smile as bright as the morning sun.

She nodded.

James turned to Lachlan. " 'Tis said the excise men wanted him badly enough to put a price on his head. I've heard he could discharge a still sixty times in twenty-four hours."

"Ninety," Janet corrected, smiling. "He was a great one

for production. Nor did he have any great love for the malt tax. He always said that the demand from potential customers made the threat of fines worthwhile. But the excise men were a bit of a problem."

James continued to shake his head, his expression one of rapt joy.

"You've not installed the vent pipe," she said, bending and retrieving one extra bit of pipe they had left after the second explosion. She pointed to where it should be inserted at the top of the kettle.

Lachlan watched her in amazement. His Ealasaid had been replaced by a woman named Janet who was familiar with her surroundings, who tapped the copper pot occasionally as if to judge its contents. She twisted a pipe loose and replaced it right side up, then popped her head into a barrel and pronounced it too briny to use for aging the newly distilled whiskey. She wanted to see the container of yeast and tasted a bit of it; she seemed to study the steam that wafted to the ceiling of the cavern.

He thought his mouth was open, but he didn't bother to shut it. He turned, and the seer was there, his beard twitching over his lips. The old prophet was laughing; he was sure of it.

"She's the Glenlyon Bride, Lachlan. She knows the secret of *uisge beatha*, the water of life. You know yourself that she's claw-footed, and she'll scare all the dogs in the castle if she ever sings."

"But she'll save us."

"Aye, and you."

He slitted his eyes at the old man. "Are you sure there's no other clan that can benefit from your wisdom, Coinneach? Someone else you might bedevil? You could have made this a lot easier by simply telling me."

"But to truly fulfill the Legend, you first had to fall in love with her." His beard twitched again.

Coinneach turned, held out his hands, and raised them above his head. In a voice born to carry, he made his latest pronouncement.

"I see into the future," he declared, when he was certain he had attracted the attention of everyone in the cavern.

Lachlan shut his eyes and waited. Only a touch on his arm bid him open them, and he did, to see Janet smiling up at him. He enclosed her in his embrace and held her tight, steeling himself for what the old seer had to say next. But it didn't matter; he already knew the future. It stretched out before him in a long road. A dynasty perhaps, and happiness. Hardship balanced by laughter. Friendship and love. Perhaps even success. Maybe a name for themselves. Glenlyon Whiskey. He could almost see it now.

He bent down and placed a soft kiss upon Janet's forehead. Her hand reached to the back of his head and pulled him down for a true kiss—one that enticed him to think of trysting places in the daylight. After all, he was newly married.

Thus, the Sinclair laird and the Glenlyon Bride missed the words of the seer entirely. But it didn't matter, for the Legend had already been fulfilled.

KAREN RANNEY began writing when she was five. Her first published work was *The Maple Leaf*, read over the school intercom when she was in the first grade. In addition to wanting to be a violinist (her parents had a special violin crafted for her when she was seven), she wanted to be a lawyer, a teacher, and most of all, a writer. The violin was discarded early, she still admits to a fascination with the law, and she volunteers as a teacher whenever needed. Writing, however, has remained an overwhelming love of hers. She loves to hear from her readers—please e-mail her at *www.karenranney.com*.

Karen Ranney lives in San Antonio, Texas.

At Avon Books, we know your passion for romance—once you finish one of our novels, you find yourself wanting more.

May we tempt you with . . .

- **Excerpts** from our upcoming releases.

- Entertaining **extras**, including authors' personal photo albums and book lists.

- Behind-the-scenes **scoop** on your favorite characters and series.

- **Sweepstakes** for the chance to win free books, romantic getaways, and other fun prizes.

- Writing **tips** from our authors and editors.

- **Blog** with our authors and find out why they love to write romance.

- **Exclusive content** that's not contained within the pages of our novels.

Join us at
www.avonbooks.com

An Imprint of HarperCollins*Publishers*
www.avonromance.com